About the Author

... is an Indie author of romance and erotic romance. She lives in the rambling lush hills of Yorkshire, UK with her swoon-worthy husband and two children. She admits quite openly to being 'a hopeless romantic with a dirty mind' and when not writing, works as a Graphic Designer & Illustrator, something she's done for the past 20 years.

Other 'broom up the bottom' jobs include; mum's taxi, cooking and cleaning, cake baking, family therapist and complaints letter writer, for all and sundry - she's the one who won't take no for an answer! In between everyday life's tasks, she tries to lose herself with her secret lover 'monsieur kindle'- sssh... don't tell Mr. North.

Writing was always a hobby and took a back seat to University, work, parenthood and unfortunately later, chronic long-term illness. One day she woke and thought 'life's too short - I'm going to finish that blummin book!' She now devotes her time to writing love stories full of humour and naughtiness. When she isn't manically typing away or trying to be the model wife and mum, Alexandra can be found shoe shopping (shoes are her weakness), cosying up with back-to-back TV series and enjoying her very own Sebastian Silver.

Books by Alexandra North

The One Trilogy

Book 1 – The One Awakened
Book 2 – The One Addicted (February 2015)
Book 3 – The One Adored (coming soon)

THE ONE

Awakened

THE FIRST EROTIC NOVEL IN **THE ONE TRILOGY**

ALEXANDRA NORTH

Published by Alexandra North

Copyright © 2014 Alexandra North
All rights reserved.

ISBN – 13: 978-1500749576

Book Design & Cover Design by McCallum Creative
leighmccsug@gmail.com

Dedications

For my very own Sebastian - you know who you are.
My friend, my lover & my soulmate - I love you desperately.
You & me always and forever Baby!

For my 2 children, who put up with burnt food & un-ironed clothes for
months, whilst I slaved over this book. I love you both so much
& maybe when you're married & grown-up, you can read this - *maybe!*

For my parents who have supported me in everything I do,
through the good & many bad times; you are both such an inspiration,
both in your own achievements & your love of one another
- 44 years and counting. *Seriously though, Mum this book is for your eyes only -
thank you for your proof reading assistance – your positivity has kept me going x*

To my lovely in-laws - who've enabled me to write whilst
entertaining our youngest; from crafting, to school pick-ups and many
other fun activities, you're always there for all of us and so appreciated. x

To my Sister, who is Suzie in the flesh & your congratulation of your
own gorgeous new baby boy. Life deals us highs & blows but with shoes and
lippy, we can conquer the world. Love you.

For my family and friends -
Thank you for enriching my life & making it possible to draw
upon day-to-day experiences to create such wonderful characters full
of depth and naughtiness.

To all the Bloggers out there who work tirelessly to provide such an amazing service to lovers of reading and romance. Thank you so much for all your support in generating awareness for The One Awakened and The One Trilogy. You are super people who work exceedingly hard for authors and deserve 'mucho recognition'.

Quick mentions;
Francessca's Romance Reads (Francessca)
Reading The Sheets (Dawn Vickers)
Two Ordinary Girls & Their Books
Sizzling Pages
Amazeballs Book Addicts
The Book Enthusiast
2Bookaholics
Nice and NaughtyBook Club
Nancy's Romance Reads

and anyone else who has been kind enough to review and promote me
- a huge thank you x

❧

Sebastian & Lucia's journey has been so much more than I had ever dreamed - *The One* is out there for all of us.

❧

"What is a friend? A single soul in a two bodies."

Aristotle

Playlist

In no particular order for…THE ONE AWAKENED

❦

- Sarah McLachlan – Silence
- Fat Boy Slim – Right Here Right Now
- The Beloved – Deliver Me
- Coldplay – The Scientist
- Coldplay – Greeneyes
- Imagine Dragons - Demons
- James Blunt – Goodbye My Lover
- Ellie Goulding – Burn
- Chris Brown – Don't Wake Me Up
- Alex Clare – Too Close
- Rob D – Clubbed To Death
- David Guetta - Little Bad Girl (feat. Taio Cruz) –
- Portishead – Glorybox
- U2 – One
- U2 - With Or Without You
- Timberland /One Republic – Apologise
- Nelly Fertado – Try
- Snow Patrol – Chasing Cars
- Keane – Somewhere Only We Know
- Portishead – Roads
- Lana Del Rey – Young & Beautiful
- Sia – Breathe Me
- OutKast - Hey Ya
- Prince – I Would Die 4U
- Neon Trees – Sleeping With A Friend
- David Guetta – Titanium
- Eric Prydz – Pjanoo
- Sub Focus- Endorphins
- Faithless – Don't Leave
- Tinie Tempah – Heroes (feat. Laura Mvula)
- Adele – Set Fire To The Rain
- The Chemical Brothers – Hey Boy Hey girl
- Dr. Alban – It's My Life – (*She's my wife*)
- Groove Armada – My Friend
- Macklemore & Ryan Lewis – Can't Hold Us (feat. Ray Dalton)
- Roger Sanchez – I Never Knew
- The Source – You Got The Love
- A great big world – Say Something
- The Saturdays – Ego
- Rob Base, DJ E-Z - It Takes Two
- 2 Live Crew - Me So Horny
- Adele - Chasing Pavements
- Eddie (Oliver Nelson Remix) – Everywhere
- Sebastian Ingrosso – Calling (Lose My Mind)

Prolgue

Lucia

We enter the murky underground bar where pretty much every student at Lords Uni frequents, and smile at each other, anticipative of what tonight may bring. The Cave is a grotty, musty hole of a place, which housed crappy live bands, smelled damp and offered watered-down beer. None of that mattered though; the vibe was always great.

Abby and I had only been a couple of times since moving into Dorms, once to eat (never again!) and once, for Happy Hour. That night had been memorable and we'd definitely come away happy, or at least until we threw up the copious amounts of Malibu & pineapple consumed from dodgy plastic pint glasses! The Bar's aptly named and *the* place to go if you were single, with plenty of Neanderthal men - full of grunting, boozing and male bravado. However, tonight we were going to their Friday night blast. The theme is *Dance* and that's exactly, what we intend to do. We are 19, young, free and attractive. Life is good and we are open to new opportunities and exciting adventures!

"If one more waster, letches over me I'll lose it!"

Abby shudders at the thought and fluffs up her freshly dyed bright red hair. The picture on the box of dye had shown a vibrant girl with warm copper locks but somehow Abby's hair had over-developed into something more likened to scary clown than saucy chick; the results were *should we say*, extreme. I feel for her, but even the harsh, fiery red tones couldn't detract from her lovely face and big brown expressive eyes. She really could pull off anything and on a positive note; it certainly made her stand out in a busy crowd- I wouldn't lose

2

her!

"I thought you wanted to meet someone Abs? Behind every frog is a prince, or something like that!"

"Bollocks! You just made that up. More like behind every frog is a horny toad!" She whacks my arm and I burst out into floods of laughter. "Besides, I think I'll be lucky to attract Shrek tonight with this hair."

"True. But don't be so harsh yourself. Let's just have some fun. It's our first year at Uni. I, for one, am not interested in settling down or getting serious with *any* man - especially not one from *here*."

"Tell that to the guy with the cross eyes and spittle lips in the corner. He'd definitely be a grateful lover!"

Yuk! We both shudder and giggle in unison.

There's a huge scrabble at the bar, and feeling daring, I nudge in and order us two beers. I can feel pressure from jostling punters at my back and to both sides, but stand my ground. We'd quickly learned it was the only way and you had to be tough to brave the Cave Bar. As I turn to pass one plastic pint glass to Abs, impressed with my skill, I'm careful not to spill a drop; I groan as my elbow is knocked and the chance of saving both myself and my drink is negligible. In that split-second instant I become a walking-talking cliché – my nipples now perky and on show through my wet vest-top; the scent of weak 'eau de Tetley's' all over me. All we needed was a ton of wet mud and Abs and I would have every man in that bar at our beck and call; but purely for the wrong reasons. Tits and ass and female wrestling; the stuff of most young men's wet dreams.

"What the hell?" I'm sure the anger is evident on my face as I look down at my top. "Nice!"

Shaking my head incredulously, I spin around and am met by a solid male wall of heat. He was the culprit and the jostler at my back. Glancing up slowly, I lock eyes with the most intense blackened pools I've ever looked into, and review the drink spiller at my leisure. He is utterly devastating. Almost perfect apart from a slight bump in his otherwise straight nose, probably from a sports related injury - he certainly looked like he played a lot of sport. Yum!

Jutting cheekbones, a well-defined jaw and two-day stubble show off those amazing dark melted chocolate eyes, which are enhanced by short inky hair, worn slightly longer and messy on top; my fingers itch to delve into it. Even his clothes are effortlessly seductive - plain black slim-fit T, over black faded jeans. He is fit, and Drop. Dead.

Gorgeous. I know I'm staring, but I truly can't help it. He's the sexiest man I've ever laid eyes on - seriously heart-stoppingly, dry-mouth tasty. I watch as his brow furrows in question at my open gawking.

"Like what you see?" His magnetic eyes crinkle at the corners and his generous mouth smirks.

"Sorry."

My thoughts are interrupted and I feel myself flush, and flustered, shake my head to pull myself together. The air seems to have left my lungs and I'm struggling to breathe.

How full of himself was this guy? How annoyed are you at your obvious reaction to him? My disloyal inner voice sides with the drink spiller.

I find my tongue and moisten my lips before framing myself and grinding out.

"Actually no. I'm not bloody sorry. *You're* the clumsy oaf!"

There. That told him! "You should watch what you're doing in future."

My voice sounds weak and snooty and very unlike me. What I really want to say, as I watch his naughty bedroom eyes and sexy mouth twist is, *"for God's sake shut up and kiss me, you arrogant bastard!"*

Seriously Lu - you don't even know his name?

This annoyingly handsome male continues to smile at me, assessing my behaviour and openly staring at my now completely soaked chest. I fold my arms over my breasts in retaliation and lean back to put some space between us. I'm not sure why but he both annoys me and sends shivers over me all at once. There are definite sparks, something I'd not ever encountered before - and never on the first time encounter with a man. I am inextricably drawn to him.

"What are you studying?"

I hear the question but am too unnerved by his presence to answer.

"Studying?" he gently repeats.

And I stutter my response. "BA (Hons) in Design." *Chill the fuck out girl!*

"Really? That's *my* course – I'll no doubt be seeing much more of you." The emphasis is heavily put on *much more*, as he casually assesses my chest. *Oh crap - this guy was trouble. I should steer well clear!*

"Well, maybe not – there are several divisions of the degree."

He flashes lovely white teeth, grinning openly at my negative and harsh reply, his eyes darting back to my now *pointing to attention*, chest.

"I'm sure we'll bump into one another again but I won't make such a *boob* of it next time. I promise."

I give in at this and chuckle openly, despite my annoyance and his own laugh is genuine. The intimate moment and sexual tension are shattered as I hear my friend's voice behind us.

"Lulu where's the beer?"

Abby nuzzles her way into our circle of two and it's only then that I realise that clumsy sexy man has his arms loosely hung around my waist. As my brain reacts to their position, my skin sizzles beneath his fingertips and I shiver noticeably. I immediately grab those strong arms and push away, but not in time for Abs to raise her arched brow cheekily in surprise at my reaction.

"Let me get you both a drink; it's the least I can do." He smiles showing those pearly whites again, and his twinkly eyes are *still* focused on my ample charms. He is divine but *really*?

"No its fine, thanks." I'm being really rude and I don't know why. His model good looks put me on edge.

"Yeah Lu, it's the least he can do," Abby laughs, mimicking his sexy voice and puts out her hand to shake his.

"'Scuse my arsey friend. I'm Abby, and *this,* is Lucia. Nice to meet you." Her warmth is infectious and for the first time ever it irritates me as she is rewarded with a glowing white smile for her niceties.

"Sebastian. Sebastian Silver at your service," he pronounces clearly and with confidence. *Of course he'd have an alliterative name - like a bloody superhero!*

As I study his handsome face, I conclude that his name is perfect for him; magnetic, memorable, arrogant and manly - just like him; a silver-tongued devil. We're interrupted again, as a second male slaps him on his back. "Seb, my mate. Get the beers in. I'm dying of thirst here." He looks in our direction, his delight evident on his rather plain but friendly face.

"I was just about to when I bumped into the lovely Abby and Lucia." My name falls from his delicious lips with a provocative drawl and his bold eyes hold mine with every syllable.

I feel his mate's eyes rest upon my chest and cringe. I really need to get to the little girl's room and use the dryer, before I become the night's entertainment or get picked up for soliciting. Either way, I'm showcasing my trump card far too soon.

Sebastian continues. "Ladies, Niall. Niall, Ladies." He holds four fingers up to the rather sweaty barman struggling to meet the demands of thirsty, pissed up students and rests his elbows on the

4

bar, throwing over his shoulder, "Don't worry I won't touch you again."

I consider why I wish that that were not the case but I am not allowed the luxury for long, as Niall muscles in next to me, hiding me from Sebastian's view. He is Ok looking, with a definite, Indie-coolness about him, but is certainly not as arresting as his friend Sebastian. Realistically, he was probably more my type if I went by my previous dating history; his dress-sense is rock-star cool and makes him appear current, if a little eccentric. We chatter for a while, whilst Abby and Sebastian do the same. I keep one eye on them at all times.

"Don't worry about your mate," Niall informs me, leaning into my ear, his warm breath on my neck.

"Sebastian is all loved up - some Textile student or something like that. So he's not up for anything but a bit of a flirt – boy he *lurves* to flirt." He winks at me and I feel a moment of strange loss at his news of Sebastian's love of women.

What did I expect when the man looks that good?

And in that second, I decide to focus my charms on Niall for the night. He was safe, didn't scare the hell out of me and didn't send my emotions haywire and was a bit of a charmer, in a kind of cool, Oasis brother way - what would be the harm?

"Give me a few minutes to dry off and I'll be back Niall."

"I'm not going *anywhere* Lucia."

His face is intent and I smile to myself. It's always nice to feel like you have a man's full attention, even if it's not the attention of the man I can't seem to take my eyes off - my brain is telling me that but my heart is saying something else.

✦

After a few hours of getting to know him better, realising our mutual likes and dislikes of certain music genres and enjoying one too many tequila slammers, I consider Niall. He's actually pretty cool and has a dry sense of humour and is a rare commodity within the Cave Bar in that he does appear to have a brain; even though his hands are a little too knowing, I'm enjoying my time with him but cannot help being continuously drawn back to his mate Sebastian, who is now on the dance floor, with *the textile girl*. She is very pretty and he's looking sexier than ever.

I am at a loss as to why just the glimpse of him is enough to create a fizz of excitement in my belly. It's ridiculous. I've just met him and he's the epitome of a *player*. I'm pleased that I've decided to see past the movie star looks and muscled physique and listened to my gut instinct. *You keep telling yourself that love.*

Yes. Niall is much more my type I convince myself, and the moody artist character has always appealed to me. Plus, he was single, so why not have some flirtatious fun with a fellow classmate? It would never lead to more - I'm not ready or in the market for anything serious.

An hour or so later and Abby has already disappeared with a cute bloke from our dorm and given the choice between going back to hear her *getting off* in our minute, shared bedroom or getting-to-know Niall better, I choose the latter. This first year at University was looking like it could be interesting for each of us.

We wave our goodbyes to Sebastian and his *material girl*, as we get our coats to leave and clasping Niall's outstretched hand I follow him out the door. I look over my shoulder one last time for him and we lock eyes immediately, his penetrating mine, forest green boring into intense blackened brown. This man made me feel things I'd never felt before and it scared the hell out of me! We hold each other's gaze until the door swings shut on us, finalising any chance of taking it further that night.

✁

Over a decade earlier…

Sebastian

"Holy shit Mate! Well done you!" Niall slaps me on my shoulder and takes a gulp of his pint.

"What have I done?" I know exactly what he's talking about, but am irritated by his jubilation - she was *my* find.

"The girls! Bloody hot-as. And that Lucia is *something else!*"

I knew he had taken an interest in Lucia. For some reason I'm feeling very territorial about this girl. I'd never seen her before on campus, I'd have remembered if that were the case.

"It wasn't intentional we really did just meet at the bar."

I'd turned her into a Playboy-Bunny with one spill of a drink, like a complete arse!

My mind wanders from her face and the most striking dark lime green pools I'd ever encountered, to the shape of her fantastic breasts, their nipples darkening as the fabric of her top turns almost transparent. *I'm a sucker for green-eyes - more unique and revealing.*

I had never felt so sexually charged with one introduction. The second I touched her, I'd wanted more and found it hard to remove my hands from her curvaceous hips; my cock jumping to life in my jeans, like I'd been getting down and dirty for the past ten minutes. *Down Boy!* Yet my gut instinct wasn't to take her home and have the usual one-night stand.

"Well however you met, I owe you big time. This girl is special. She's soo hot and on our course too."

Niall appears incredibly pleased with himself and I sense his interest. In the short-time I've known Niall, I've come to the conclusion that like me, he is always up for a bit of fun with the ladies, but I haven't seen him this enamoured and know that his last long-term girlfriend was over a year ago.

I glance across to where the object of our conversation is animatedly chatting with her friend Abby. Her face is luminous and I don't think I've ever seen any one woman so beautiful. She was a feisty one though. Far too feisty for Niall and would bore easily unless both sexually and mentally challenged - I can tell after just five minutes in her company.

I lick my lips and peruse her further, travelling over her long, dark glossy hair and back to those eyes. Jesus! They brazenly oozed sex and the way they had looked right back at me, stripping me bare, feasting on my mouth. I could have had her then. I know it. *And her mouth!* Full, red and pouty - the things I could only imagine those lips doing…

Stupid dick! Why hadn't you just kissed her, right there? Because I wouldn't have been able to stop myself - I summarise inwardly.

I need to set my stake here before Niall drunkenly makes his own claim for the night. The reminder of Samantha, my on-off romantic interest, is not enough to dishearten me. Niall was right. This girl *is* special but I'm not ready for anything serious. God I'm only 22 and Lucia was not the type of girl to be trifled with - she was so much more than a fling. Maybe I should let this one slide for now and get to

7

know her better as a mate? Not sure that'll be possible though, as right now all I want to do is bury myself deep inside her and fuck the stubborn streak out of her; watch her eyes change colour from lime to wet moss when she climaxes around my cock, which clenches at the mere thought of touching her.

Where are these feelings coming from? I've only just met her!

I've never had a reaction like this to a female before and it disturbs me profoundly. *Get a fucking grip Seb!*

I'm enjoying Samantha's flirtations as we dance together to *OutKast's 'Hey Ya'* but I'm finding it hard not to keep glancing in the direction of Niall and Lucia. They are really hitting it off. He's certainly making her laugh and he's doing the intimate ear-whisper - *cheesy or what.* It pisses me off! It should be me touching her, inhaling that scent of hers - like cherries and vanilla; entirely lickable and edible.

Sam leans in to kiss me, her pretty blue eyes full of saucy promise and I respond half-heartedly. She feels good and looks great, no doubt about that. Fuck, she's fun in bed but something is missing - odd how I hadn't realised that until tonight? As I move to push away from her rather claustrophobic embrace, I notice Niall beckoning, to get my attention. Rooted to the spot, I watch as Lucia grabs her leather jacket, and slides it on, covering her now dry but none-the-less abundant assets. I sense a moment of sheer panic as I watch my friend grab her hand, moving towards the exit.

Shit — they're leaving… together. I should be the one taking her home and running my hands over her amazing little body; be the one whose name she screams out loud in the dark.

I don't blame Niall for trying and I couldn't hate him. I hadn't set my stake and I'm certainly not in the market for monogamy. *That's what you're going with?* I hear my inner demons retaliate.

My heart pounds ten to the dozen; body taut and I hear Sam call me. *Snap out of it man. She's gone.* I can't help but feel that I may have missed out on a chance at something *real.* Something that I *know* I am going to regret.

Turn around Baby; look back at me. Let me see those fabulous eyes of yours again. Let me know you feel it too.

I will her to stop and glance back in my direction — to show that this vibe is mutual. Holding my breath I watch and wait. Those seconds feel like a lifetime and then it happens. Lucia throws a brief look over her shoulder and I hear my sigh of relief. We lock eyes, heat glittering between us and I rub my head in thought; every part of me wants to go to her and kiss her thoroughly; pick her up and parade her out of that door like a true *man of the cave.*

But I don't.

My leaden feet don't move.

I stay, and let her go - go off with *Niall,* whose grin is making me want to smash his face into the nearest wall - smug prick.

Mates it is then, Lucia Myers.

Chapter 1

Present Day...

Lucia

My phone bleeps next to me for the umpteenth time in the past hour and glancing at it briefly, I screw my nose up and sigh. It was my ex, Niall - again! Well... he'd have to bloody wait.

"Right, I'm off!" I announce, pushing myself back from my desk. I begin to gather up my extensive paperwork, shutdown my computer and grab my mobile. "God, it's been a long week, and my feet are absolutely killing me."

I visualise someone giving me a lush foot rub or some long overdue reflexology; I can practically feel those stress crystals being massaged away. *My passion for fabulously high shoes is seriously not good for the soles.*

"Ok Lucia. Have a good one. See you on Monday and remember you have that meeting with The Ashton at 1pm," Jackie replies, in her cheery and infectious tone.

"How could I forget? I've slogged away on the concepts for the last few days – I really hope I'm on the right track with this one, as it could be just what we need to put Elysium Interiors on the map. *We really needed this job to bankroll the next few months but I wasn't about to tell my assistant that.*

"Colin is coming with me too, so mark him out of the office for Monday afternoon in the iCal please. He's on the phone at the mo, so say bye for me."

I make a quick mental note to text my rather flaky, but incredibly talented Associate Designer and remind him that Monday is a deal-breaker.

"Whatever happens, the designs speak for themselves and you've nailed this one so I can't see that they won't love them. You can set me on them, if they don't; I'll drill it into them," she grins cheekily and returns to her typing.

"Thanks Jack, I hope you're right, but tonight I'm switching off. I'm all designed-out and I honestly don't think I've got another creative bone left in my extremely weary body. I feel 89, not 29! At this moment in time, I can tell you that I never want to see another wallpaper swatch or carpet sample again!"

I grab my phone and shove it inside the interior zipper of my Gucci tote bag, slinging it over my shoulder. Right. All set to go.

"Have a great weekend and try and have some fun - it's long overdue!" Jackie comments, without looking up from her Mac. She really is a superstar assistant, and I mentally pat my back as I reaffirm my good sense in hiring her six months ago.

"Oh don't worry, I will, I have a hot date this weekend with my gorgeous toy boy; we may even have a play on the swings," I shrug my shoulder up in a naughty twitch.

"Ooh, lucky you, Josh and I considered having one of those installed in the ceiling of our bedroom but the joists wouldn't take the...," she suddenly stops and blushes uncontrollably, flicking both hands towards me in defeat. "Holy crap, you meant, with Finn... didn't you - in the park? Durr! How much of a perv do I sound?"

"Yep, I *did* mean Finn and you *do* sound like perv," I smirk at her. "But nice to know you and Josh have a healthy and experimental sex life. You can make up for the lack of it in my department." Still smiling to myself I wave over my shoulder. "Night love. Enjoy your weekend of drink and debauchery."

50 Shades sure has a lot to answer for I muse to myself and for the umpteenth time of late, sigh at my lack of action in the bedroom. It appeared everyone was not only having sex but hot, sweaty, dirty sex and I'm beginning to wish that I was one of them – not that I'd ever be that daring. Sex had not been high on my priority list for sometime, but maybe it was time for a little pleasure?

Smoothing down my pinstriped pencil skirt, I wait patiently in the lift, whilst it stops at what seems like every floor for staff to leave for the weekend; listening to their gossip and a small part of me is envious. The building housing my newest baby, Elysium Interior Design had four floors of immense square footage, all rented out and in hot demand due to its great parking, central position and sleek lines. It was slightly set back from the main drag of the shopping centre but near plenty of necessary amenities, Post Office, Bank and eateries. The rent was tough, but the way business had been, I'd been managing it comfortably so far and the location was unbeatable. I'd had to take the plunge or I'd be forever struggling to survive on a daily basis and I wanted more for my son than that. No, my motto had definitely been, *go big or go home*. It had been incredibly scary but the most sensible business decision I'd ever made.

My gaze returns to focus on the couple in front of me. They're so into one another that the sexual tension is palpable - obviously a forbidden work romance, with lots of arm brushing and finger linking. Lucky bastards. Oh how the other half live! I remember the days when Friday nights meant drinks after work, then drinks to forget about the drinks after work and then drinks in some dodgy sweaty club, where we could dance the stresses of the week away. You'd have no memory of what happened after the club, just incredibly sticky shoes in the morning from the copious amounts of alcohol slopped onto the dance floor.

Nice!

Now, my life was more about clock watching, than carefree abandonment and living in the moment. But although it was tough, I still wouldn't change it for anything, as this new life revolved around my best design creation of all - my little boy Finn. Even at the thought of him, I feel the familiar bubble of excitement begin in my belly that only a mother would understand; finally, it was time to collect him from Kiddie-Club and I can't wait. I've really missed him this week. My mum had had to assist with three of the pick-ups, as I'd worked late and I'd missed bath and story-time on each of those nights. That was *our* time, *our* routine and *our* opportunity, to catch-up on, the day's events. Tonight, I am determined to have some much needed one-on-one time with him. Then, tomorrow, I'd have some essential grown-up time at my Sister's birthday bash and let loose. Niall, my ex, had been harassing me with pitiful begging texts pretty much all afternoon since he'd found out that I was going on a second

12

date with my Banker friend and now all of a sudden, he thought it would be a good idea that he and I meet up to talk about *us*?

I shake my head just thinking about his weak little mind games. *What is it with men?* You break-up and the second they get a *whiff* that you're potentially attractive to another member of the male sex - they come running. As if Niall's ears are burning, my phone vibrates in my hand as I exit the lift.

Come on Mu Mu, meet me for a beer tomorrow?
Before you get together with the gang. I'll be in Lords too.

I cringe at his use of the nickname he'd insisted on teasing me with, for the 9 years we were a couple. Lulu was reserved for my best friends and special people in my life, but Mu Mu? I sound like a bloody cow! I choose to rise above and ignore his message but after a second text, where he blackmails me with the only thing that would ever sway me, I agree to meet him.

It's about Finny Boy

*

Ok. I'll text you where and when tomorrow

*

Good girl!

With a heavy heart at my own weakness, I unlock my car. *That man* was the reason I wasn't having sex right now - he'd put me off men for life.

Twenty minutes later, and I've been rewarded with a full-on, run and jump hug from Finn - a reminder that some males were still gorgeous. According to nursery, he'd told them that it was the weekend and Mummy was going to drink lots of *Jacob's Creep!* - luckily, I know the owner well and she is aware that I'm not a raving alcoholic but I must admit a glass of the *Creek* would go down swimmingly, after the week I'd had. Laughing at his funny little misquote, we head towards my two-seater Audi TT and I frown;

every time I carry my precious son to and from the sports car, I swear that I'll replace it soon for a more *suitable* vehicle - as my disapproving ex has suggested on numerous occasions. It's just that this is probably the only item in my life, which makes me feel like I'm still *me* and not just a single mum. *It really is a hot little motor though - goes like a whippet and I do like to drive fast, when I'm on my own.*

I strap him into his car seat and flick the CD on and the car is filled with our Play list of the moment and he wastes no time joining in. "You shoot me down and la la la!" the cute out of tune voice from the passenger seat shouts. Looking across my heart melts instantly, as I am struck at the sheer beauty of my adorable three year-old son, Finn. His blonde hair literally glows with health and so do his bright blue eyes - Frank Sinatra had nothing on Finn. They are so similar to my own, in every way, bar the shade; both having an unusual dark circle around the outside edge of our irises, his more navy and mine dark teal green. I'm pleased we have that in common, as our colouring couldn't be more different, Viking white *V* darkest brown - almost black. It never ceases to amaze me that *I made that!* Well with a little bit of help from my ex, with the emphasis on *little (he'd been a little short-changed in that department)*, I laugh to myself cattily. But *I* produced this fabulous bundle of exquisiteness. *I* had the war-wounds to prove it!

"You want me to play it again, sweetie?" I ask, hitting the repeat button for Finn's favourite song of the moment.

Nodding excitedly, he kicks his Cat boots manically on the glove box in front of him. I smile, as the familiar notes thump through the car as *David Guetta's, Titanium* starts its intro. Oh well, it's only the fifth time today; I'll manage and at least he's got good taste. We both lose ourselves, shouting out the words and laughing, as we sing in unison at the top of our lungs, both equally out of tune. As the music begins to end, I swing into our street.

"We timed that well didn't we Finnster?"

Pulling into the space outside our pretty four-storey Victorian mid terraced house on Rose Avenue, I smile with pride that I have managed to maintain this home, *our home* for my son and I. I'd worked hard to renovate the former psychedelic insult to interior design. I think the previous owner had decided that 'the-more-the-merrier' was the way to go when it came to patterns and had papered them to walls and laid them to floors, clashing catastrophically at every level. Plus, they'd had a fondness for the dreaded decorator's nightmare that was

14

wood-chip; it had been bloody everywhere! However, I'd been able to see past all that and visualise the end result and now four years later, we had a home to be proud of and it had padded and enhanced my portfolio - *had got me one of my first design jobs as a freelancer I remind myself.*

I just needed to get a few more contracts on my books; regular retainer work and then I'd relax and breathe at last or at least my bank balance would. *Plus you need a fantastic night of wild passion to uncoil the tension of the past few months.* I hear my best friend Abby's words in my ears and smile, shaking my head. She was right though. I decide to forget about work for tonight; no work and all play this weekend Lulu - it's time to let go and be bold - let's see what the weekend brings.

Chapter 2

Lucia

Folding my sleepy little man into his Spiderman-adorned bed, I bend over for a much-coveted sniff. It's true what they say, if the smell of a *just-bathed* child could be bottled, we'd make a fortune. I just can't get enough of it - oh and his soft chubby cheeks. It really is the little things that make it all worthwhile. For a split second I am sad, as I wonder why and how his father could have left this magnificent little bundle and walked away from these special moments. But I quickly remind myself that he does not think of Finn in the same way as I do; he saw him as a hindrance then and a volume which could not be turned down when he required it - which was usually for around twenty-three hours a day.

Snapping out of the gloomy direction of my thoughts, I gaze lovingly at my boy as he asks,

"Mummy?"

"Yes poppet?" I nod encouragingly.

"Why don't we live with Daddy?"

Oh God, not tonight, I inwardly groan – how is it that children always seem to ask the difficult questions when you least expect them and are totally unprepared? It was as though he'd been reading my mind.

I take a seat on his bed and discreetly inhale a deep breath.

"Hmmm, well Baby, Mummy & Daddy decided that we are much

16

happier living in different houses. Lots of families live like that Darling, like your friend Mason and Meg from next-door. Sometimes it's just better that way." I stroke his shining blonde hair off his forehead in the way that I know soothes him.

He takes on board what I've said; his small brow furrowed in concentration as he digests it.

"Mummy, does that mean that I am the man of the house now?"

I melt for the second time in the last hour. Oh my gorgeous little boy.

"Yes I suppose it does and you know what? You're doing a great job of it my Darling. Now off to sleep with you, you little monkey. Sweet dreams."

That seems to work as he continues to quietly ponder my answers, and snuggles down, relaxing into his pillow. I hope he's not worrying about the separation - too much. He seems to have handled things so well up until now; I had thought that he was settled. It has been nearly a year now, and the departure of his father had meant that we had bonded even more than I felt was possible. It was becoming increasingly more difficult, to make excuses for that bastard though; he was so bloody selfish. I just wish he would put Finn first, once in a while.

What I really wanted to tell Finn, was that his father was a spineless, dickless, brainless, tosser, who had been pretty average in bed, moody as hell, and left me in a world of financial shit! But obviously this was not possible; it was completely true, but not necessary to point out all of his bad points to a three year-old little boy, just to make myself feel better. No. It was all about Finn now and his feelings and well being, regardless of my own needs.

"Night Baby; best boy!"

"Best Mummy!" he responds, as expected.

It is our in-house *Walton's style* bedtime routine - very corny but something we had started since it was just the two of us. It maintained his routine and actually mine too. Seemingly pacified at that comment, Finn curls up in his usual ball and closes his eyes. He'd be asleep in a few minutes, meaning I could catch up on some much-needed Zzz's myself. Ha! Like that's going to happen. Who am I kidding? I have a mountain of ironing, at least two laundry loads to do, some layouts for Monday's new client and I could do with fake tanning for the weekend.

Smiling at my golden boy, I head down to the basement, where the kitchen rests. Right, now shall I cook something first or grab a quick shower and get my beloved PJ's on? I procrastinate briefly and then decide to go straight for the wine from the fridge and catch an episode of Holby City, my favourite British medical drama. Wine is the obvious choice for now and will help to dull the stress I can feel beginning to tap away at my temples; Holby City will make me feel like *my* life is better than the average person's and would allow me 60 uninterrupted minutes to get lost in someone else's drama. Sounded good to me.

Just as I am about to go into the kitchen, I hear a knock at the door.

"Come in!" I shout loudly, as I quickly nip down the last step to pour my wine. I am presuming it is one of my neighbours, as we all regularly pop into one another's homes on a *'Mi Casa Su Casa'* basis. It generally worked well between us if you didn't count the time I'd walked in on Gemma, a few doors down, whilst she was getting *down and dirty* with her latest conquest.

Wrinkling my nose at that uncomfortable memory, I climb the stairs back to the main living area and enter the room. I then stop dead in my tracks, dumbstruck and mouth gaping to the point of embarrassment; I'm surprised I don't drool. There, standing in the middle of the lounge, is one of my oldest and bestest friends and a real sight for sore eyes. Sebastian.

He's back already? I wasn't aware he was due home? What's it been – nine months this time? Maybe ten?

Composing myself, I swallow hard, lick my lips and close my suddenly very dry mouth, making my way towards him. It is *so* good to see him. He looks like Sebastian, but different somehow, better - yes much better, and very dishy and tanned in his black Ralph Lauren polo shirt and khaki combat trousers combination.

I hadn't realised until this moment, how much I'd missed him. I just want to envelope him in a big bear hug, but oddly something stops me, my feet are rooted to the spot, my arms tightly folded at my chest. I feel a little light-headed as I take him all in. *Did he always look this good? Shit, he looks good.*

His tall, well-muscled body fills the room; his presence everywhere - a fixed, considered gaze on my reaction. "Now then Chick, how's things?" he says in his deep husky voice, smiling at me, in the most appealing way.

His voice travels over me, and I gulp, literally. My brain won't function and I reach up to flick my hair away from my face - has the temperature risen several hundred degrees? His dark brown, almost black eyes follow me as I move towards the doorway. He seems as taken aback as me, at the strange vibe in the air; and also appears to be reluctant to hug me or kiss my cheek as he normally would - instead holding back.

Finding my voice on a croak, I usher him in. "Hi Love. Come in - sorry I thought you were Meg, from next-door. She was due to pop in at some point tonight. Come down to the kitchen, anyway and I'll find you a beer."

I am acutely aware that I'm rambling but I can't seem to get a grip. I blame it on the tension headache and the fact that I haven't eaten since breakfast.

Nothing to do with the fact that he looks soo hot, you're flushed from head to foot from the radiation kickback Lucia!

Following me into the hub of the home, I can smell him behind me; all clean, vanilla-musk and pure male, and instinctively quicken my pace to create more distance between us; mumbling incoherently over my shoulder.

"Have you eaten yet?"

We enter the kitchen and he positions himself in a corner, leaning casually against the entrance to the larder, where he usually posed during our many *kitchen gossips* over the years.

"Nope. I've not eaten yet, just got back this afternoon from Dubai; the build is *finally* over. Well, I've got to fly out for some promo work in the next month or so, but yeah, this one's been a long-one."

He removes his Ray-bans from the top of his head and places them on the counter top, rubbing the bridge of his nose lightly where the pads have been resting. "I thought I'd pop in and see my favourite person before I go face the mountains of unpacking. It's been a while."

Opening the fridge and glad of the welcome cool blast I feel on my face, I respond casually. "Oh, I've just put him to bed, literally ten minutes ago. You could check in on him though - he won't wake up. You know how he is when he's fast asleep."

"I'll do that now," he says pointedly staring right at me. "But whilst Finn is definitely up there in the top five on my favourite's list - I actually meant *you* Lulu."

Holy Crap! His words travel across my body and over every one of my nerve endings, zinging them into life. He hasn't called me Lulu in forever.

With my back to him, I compose myself, grab a Sol and gingerly close the door. He reaches out to clasp the beer I'm holding out for him, studying me intensely. Our fingers brush against each other in the switchover and the shockwaves that crackle on contact cause us both to look up in surprise. I drop my arm to hang at my side in a flash, and with hooded eyes watch him slant his head slightly to the left, then look me up and down appraisingly, for what feels like forever, but in reality is probably only a few seconds. He seems surprised at his own reaction, as he suddenly frowns, shaking his head a little and turns to climb the stairs, taking them two at a time.

I presume he's gone to see Finn. To be honest I'm glad to have a moment to compose myself. *What the fuck was all that about? Was it me or did there seem to be a whole lot of sexual tension floating around in the room?*

Oddly enough I'd never really allowed myself to think of Sebastian in that way. *Bollocks!* Well, only once, years ago, when we'd first met. I'd always told myself that he wasn't my type.

So why am I suddenly as nervous as I would be on a first date? He'd definitely never thought of me that way either?

Jesus, he's hot - Oh. My. God woman - you need to get laid!

There *had* been that one time at a mutual friend's wedding when we'd ended up very drunk, putting the world to rights in the gardens at the back of the venue. My ex had been inside, probably flirting with his latest crush. We'd downed too many Tequila Slammers to count and a cheeky cigarette out back had lead to a rather deep and meaningful conversation about life and love and commitment. Sebastian had commented that he'd missed his chance at love, when she had settled down with another. At the time, I'd been too inebriated to consider that *she* was possibly *me?* The moment passed, and we moved on, as we always had been – the best of friends. After all, I wasn't his type either - if his usual female company was anything to go by. Tall. Leggy. Blonde. The antithesis, of me; petite, not-so-leggy and brunette.

He'd always gone for the extra lithe, super ditzy women - usually picked up in each Country or City he was frequenting. Each relationship, if you could call it that, conveniently ended when his contract did, if not before. Sebastian had always said that he preferred it that way; a get out of jail free card - all the perks, without the pressure. He was known as a bit of a player with a girl in every port –

that kind of guy. Apparently his sexual prowess knew no bounds and for some reason, the reminder of that fact has me quivering.

Annoyed with myself, and my ridiculous thoughts, I quickly run to the fridge - the only mirror on that floor - to see my reflection and try to catch a glimpse between the many pieces of artwork by my talented son. Staring out between the green splodgey handprints and my favourite painting, showcasing a random blue slug, is a dark haired, green-eyed... Mum! Hardly the sex-goddess that would tempt a man, like Sebastian Silver.

My shoulders slump. *No. Stop! You are not just a mum - you're a twenty-nine year old, intelligent and attractive woman, remember that.* My inner voice chastises me.

Actually I didn't look that bad, considering I'd not refreshed my make-up since I'd returned home. My fitted black hook and eye corset shirt, showed enough cleavage to classily tempt and not turn tricks and my hair fell in heavy, glossy waves down my back, thanks to the last minute lunch cancellation at the hip new salon 'Gum', with my darling hairdresser, Sophie.

At least I'd gone for the wine option and not the fake-tan and PJ's decision, when I'd got back. A slightly relaxed woman with a large Spritzer was much more pleasant to look upon, than a St. Tropez smeared stranger with the eye-watering scent of 'eau de kebab'.
I shudder at that unattractive vision.

Why did I care though, it was Seb?

He'd seen me in considerably worse states. God, when I thought about the nights out we'd had over the years - namely in the student bar, when he'd held my hair whilst I threw up, got me home safely in a cab or let me doss down at his on the sofa. He'd even helped me get to the toilet after my Oophorectomy operation, when a burst ovarian cyst, warranted emergency surgery. I remember, him waiting patiently outside, - to carry me back to bed; such a gent. Niall had been busy with work - of course!

Yep - if a girl was in distress within a five-mile radius, Sebastian Silver was the man you called. He just made everything, well... better. Now I was beginning to understand why women swooned around him too.

Had I had blinkers on for the past decade? Nope Hun, you'd just been blinded by Niall's promises and deafened by his lies.

Sebastian hadn't laid eyes on me for the best part of a year, nor had he seen me much since Niall & I had parted ways, so shockingly.

The last time we'd spent time together, I was in the middle of a nasty break-up. I was still his best friend, but had also existed as part of a couple for nine years. I'd been two stone heavier and a blubbering, hormonal mess, trying to deal with the fact that I had just packed my partner off, and my future, as I knew it, had ended. I had probably appeared weak and lacking in my usual confidence and very un-Lulu-like. I shudder at the thought of the image I'd portrayed.

Whilst Sebastian visits my sleeping son, I take a moment to grab a pizza out of the fridge and switch the oven on. Then I prepare a small rocket and parmesan salad and mix up some french dressing. I suppose the one bonus of him arriving tonight, is that I might actually bother to eat. It is so much better cooking for two adults. I'd forgotten how nice it is to cook for a man, even if it is only to heat-up a ready meal. Most men are rarely on a diet and tend to eat so heartily, it relaxes you into doing the same.

I turn, just as I hear him bounding down the steps, his muscled body nimble, despite the three flights of stairs. It feels strange to have a man in the house again, or rather a man who is comfortable and knows his way around my home. Strange, but it's also calming; I'd missed that, without even realising it.

Thank goodness I have such a good male friend. My female friends have been amazing but you can't beat great male company. They just have a different type of energy about them and are great at helping around the house, with the crappy little jobs that most women don't have the required gene (or inclination) in them, to perform. Sorry, ladies if you're good with tools, big ups to girl-power, but unfortunately, I'm not one of those women - not that I won't give anything a go at least once; but I know my limitations, and plumbing, changing tyres and picture hanging are on that list - to name but a few.

"Hmm. Something smells good!"

I smile brightly at his tanned watchful face. "Hope pizza suits, it's all I have. Marks & Spencer's though, so it should be up to your high worldly - wise standards."

He swats me on the behind, and laughs as I squeeze past him to get the trays and cutlery, catching a gorgeous whiff of vanilla and spice and heat. My bottom buzzes literally and not from the soft smack and I stop a second to compose myself. He's only trying to lighten the mood.

What is wrong with me? Get a grip! This is your mate.

My phone springs to life on the counter between us; interrupting the tension but the second I hear the ringtone I freeze. Oh no I'm going to kill Colin. He's been at my bloody phone... again. Me so horny by 2 Live Crew bounces out, loud and bold in the kitchen. My cheeks blush as I watch Seb's eyebrows near his hairline...and his lips curl in a playful grin, as the words repeat over and over.

"*Oh* me so horny, *oh* me so horny, *oh* me so horny - me love you *long* time."

Seriously, could the timing be any worse?

"Nice ringtone Lu."

"I didn't set it - someone's been messing with my phone."

"Ok then - I believe you; many wouldn't. Either that or you're trying to tell me something."

I glance down at the screen and see Meg, my rather energetic and neighbour's name - I click the hold button, desperate for the song to end; I'll call her later and Colin was in deep doo-doo.

Ignoring his continuing smirk, I change the subject fast. "I think this calls for a TV dinner, don't you Mr. Silver?"

"Sounds good to me. Then you can tell me all about what's been going on and how it is that with everything you've been through, you look sexier than ever Lu!"

Oh My! Sebastian's always been a flirt but not really with me. Am I reading more into this? I really do need to have sex again... and soon. The dry spell is making me see things that aren't there. *Yes, don't be silly, it's you. He would never be interested in you that way and why are you openly considering him?*

We snuggle down on the sofa and just as I reach for my wine, my iPhone woofs at me, alerting me to an incoming text. It's Meg... again.

It reads...

Tried to call you - Just seen the hottest guy I've copped a look at in ages in the corner shop of all places. Then came home and saw him walking through your front door.
Fuck me, he's fit, you jammy bitch - Who is he? I demand to be introduced. Your gagging for it and very single mate.
Hint Hint ;)

I reply instantly, overcome by an unfamiliar and uncomfortable sensation, low in the pit of my stomach.

**It's my friend Sebastian, from University; I'm sure I've
mentioned him before.
Having a night in but will introduce you soon x**

Sitting back, I ignore Seb's sideways glances towards my phone, as
he piles rocket on top of his pizza. I am more concerned with the fact
that the saying about *green eyes* seems to be very apt, in my case, as I
realise that I am overcome with the undeniable and unwelcome
emotion, jealousy, at the sheer thought that my friend would appeal
to another.

Which is ridiculous, because why wouldn't he? He's single, as far
as I'm aware, extremely wealthy and gorgeous! Plus, that was his
thing; he had women literally falling at his feet.

He was *never* without a woman.

But he's Sebastian and Sebastian is a commitment-phobe and
because of that last pertinent point, I suppose I'd never considered
him relationship material. Meg would probably only want a one-night-
stand anyway though, I inwardly remind myself and am gutted that
I'm also stricken by that potential scenario. Seriously annoyed, I grab
my tray and dig into the food diligently, glad of something to do.
Sebastian considers me lazily as I nervously try to fill the quiet.

"So tell me, what's happening in your life? How was Dubai? Is it
really as hot as everyone says?"

Surely it's not as hot as you, I bet?

Waiting to finish chewing Seb nods. "All good; nice to be home.
Dubai is like Las Vegas, exciting and luxurious for a few days, then
after a while it just felt like a rich man's Blackpool."

His conservative response is disconcerting. He usually loves to
regale stories about the countries he frequents and entertain me with
tales of his wild nights out. I laugh, in spite of his lack of energy.

"Easy for you to say, when you've had the opportunity to
experience the world."

"Oh yeah, it's very exciting living out of a bag and dealing with
arrogant Emirati for nearly a year! I think it would have been easier to
have experienced pregnancy, complete with natural, drug-free
labour," he offers up casually, blissfully unaware of the ridiculousness
of his throwaway statement.

I practically choke on my food. "Oh OK, like you'd know all

about that Sebastian! Much easier to be pregnant for nine months then be split in half over a thirty-six hour labour, than handle a few difficult Arab princes with more money than sense!"

Chuckling, I settle back into my seat and I can feel him watching my every move. I begin to relax and feel that cocoon of safety that Seb always manages to create around me - something I haven't felt for a long time. He'd also always been able to put me at ease, but right now, I was both comfortable and on edge, if that was possible.

Confused much?

"Seriously though, you must be pleased it's all nearly over?" I ask, as he suddenly seems quiet for him. Dubai has intensified him, no doubt there.

"Yeah, yeah - I am. It's been great for the business, really great. We've got lots of rebound work from it. The Dubai Marina is amazing and what they are doing there is nothing short of futuristic. The Middle East definitely have vision.

"Does the hotel look fabulous?"

I refer to the spectacular Skyscraper *Jannah Hotel,* situated within Dubai Marina that Silver Construction has been contracted to assist in its completion. Sebastian had been overseeing the latter stages of the project at management level, negotiating, handling other contractor firms and assisting the architects and from what I'd heard, spent more time in a suit than his site-gear. He really was rolling with the big-guys now. He'd put into this one financially from both the personal and business coffers and now nearing completion and sale, the profits could be in the millions; so I understood the pressure to be immense.

"It's out of this world Lu - like something from a film set - pure polished steel, combined with glittering cut glass windows and the views! I'll show you the pics soon. You'd *die* for the interior."

The passion is there but he's not quite on the ball and I remind myself that the poor guy has just spent eight hours on a return flight from a different time zone.

"I'm just tired I guess. I was really ready for home soil," he sighs, running a hand over his newly cut hair.

My eyes are drawn to the familiar gesture, seeing it differently for the first time. I'm sensing that all is not as it seems with Dubai and that there is definitely more to tell, but recognising his reluctance to divulge at present, I leave well alone, for now.

Grateful to bypass any further questions he takes the opportunity

25

to revert back to me. "Enough about me. How's work?"

"It's great actually. Long hours and it's been tough trying to be there for Finn as much as I can and maintain his routine, but it's good. I've potentially a large hotel job on at the moment, which if successful, will be mean a *huge* bonus!" I smile in genuine excitement. "I feel like I'm finally doing what I was meant to do. Actually that reminds me, this may be a job for Silver Construction? Especially now you're back for a while. I've got my meeting on Monday but I'll get you to quote, if you're up for it - doesn't have to be you, Mr. Boss man - I know how busy you are, but maybe one of your many minions?

Seb relaxes back into the sofa and stretches his well-muscled arm out along the top. I can see that he's already inhaled his full pizza. It never ceased to amaze me the speed at which he ate. He pretty much did everything fast. *Or, maybe not? There I go again…*

I wonder if he'd fuck like that? Or if he'd be hard, yet slow? Stop Lucia!

"That's great Lu; you deserve it. Yeah, I'll take a look at the brief. Just send me the details," he nods, taking a swig of his cold beer. "I've always told you to believe in your skills. You should have set up on your own years ago - fuck, we should have hooked up." His eyes consider me seriously, watching my reaction.

Hooked up?

"Yeah, I can really tell that things are back on track. You are *you* again," he continues, oblivious to my confusion and pleased with his revelations.

"Me again? I didn't go anywhere," I respond, a bit annoyed actually and on the defensive.

"Yes you did Lu. Sitting in front of me, is the girl I met at University - happy, independent, strong and confident. Bossy. Stubborn. Funny. A girl who know what she wants," he laughs between swigging more beer, then keeps going. "… I haven't seen her for years - well maybe had a few glimpses of her now and then."

Correcting himself, he flicks a genuine smile in my direction, softening the blow, which allows me to calm my petulant childish thoughts and respond clearly.

"Well, redundancy, a break-up and becoming a single parent will do that to you," I joke, embarrassed at his compliments.

Had I really changed that much?

I already knew the answer to that. Unequivocally - yes!

"You either crumble, or frame yourself. I chose to survive. Life's good at the mo. In fact I'm dating… again."

I throw out this last bit in for retaliation really, although I'm not a hundred percent why but notice that he looks up in surprise and puts his fork down with a clatter.

"Really? Who?"

"Oh just someone I met via work. He's a banker, previously married, now recently divorced and likes Chinese."

I flash my eyes and raise my eyebrows in encouragement at that last snippet; Seb and I *lurve* Chinese and I hope that this will maybe sway him in Leo's favour.

"It's early days anyway. His name is Leo. He's the manager of the Osten Bank near Elysium, and he's taken control of my business accounts and loan management." Taking a bite of pizza I laugh, as I struggle to stop the mozzarella cheese dangling from my chin.

Very sexy!

"He's been a major asset to me in obtaining the funds I needed to boost the business."

"Clearly the best reason to date him then," his deep voice adds, sarcastically.

I look up at that droll comment and can clearly see that the information I've just provided him with has not gone down well.

He isn't laughing along with me. In fact his jaw is clenched in tension and he is staring at me intently, as if considering what to say next. He's probably just feeling protective of Finn and I, in the brotherly manner he has always portrayed. I can understand that he wouldn't want to see me rush into anything too soon. I decide to flip the switch.

"What about you? Anyone tempt Britain's most eligible bachelor?"

He watches me for an age, as though he's deciphering the words over and over and then with an upturned mouth barks, harshly. "Don't change the subject Lulu. So when do I get to meet this Leo?"

He practically orders it; struggling over Leo's name.

Hang on a minute, why does it seem like he's angry all of a sudden? He's not my father and who was changing the subject; me or him?

"Tomorrow night actually; if you want to? He's coming to meet up with us for drinks, for Suzie's birthday. You coming?" I add graciously, placing my drink back onto the side-table.

"Yeah, I'll see you there. Gino already invited me," he shrugs and makes to stand up. "Right I'd better be off, I'm shattered and I've got to go sort my shit out."

Why do men always use the term *'sorting their shit out'* as an excuse to escape you? This is just code for *'I need to be on my own now, crash on the sofa with a beer and kill someone on the playstation'*. I've got news for all you men - women have cracked the code!

"Yeah it'll be nice to be back in my own bed again. Think I've only slept in it a handful of times since I moved into the new-build." He refers to his relatively new, but gorgeous home, a perfect example for the Silver Construction portfolio.

Wait - hasn't he been luxuriating in a beautiful new build hotel, in Dubai of late? Life was *really* hard for some. Why has the mood changed so suddenly? It's rapidly become uncomfortable and I just want to get back to comfortable - just normal time with my mate.

"So you're off then? That was quick. Glad I could supply you with some home cooking, or at least a ready meal. It *really* is great to see you again Seb; I've missed you - rather a lot actually."

I smile up at him sheepishly, annoyed with myself for admitting my weakness. This would have been normal before - common practice between us, to admit our feelings and be open with one another.

Gazing down at me, his eyes scan my face thoughtfully. It appears as though he wants to say something.

"You look good Lu. Really good."

Hmmm - you do too!

"I missed that twitchy little snub nose of yours."

My fingers fly up to it, instinctively. What?

We lock eyes and his are narrowed and intense as he thrusts his hands into his cargo pockets. His body language is stiff, cool and appraising but finally he moves towards me, leaning in - I presume, to kiss my cheek - finally - normality between us at last! I can smell his scent - pure male, and feel the heat coming off his body. But I'm left hanging and feeling stupid, when he quickly changes his mind and gives me a fumbling shoulder slap instead.

"We'll catch up more tomorrow yeah?"

His eyes focus on my lips and I moisten them instinctively, only holding his attention further. Then with my mute nod he's gone. How strange? What was the *bro-pat* all about?

Men are so bloody weird.

I'd never understand them truly but what I do know is that something over the past hour and half has changed; no scrap that - everything has changed, between two best friends. I feel strange, sad, discombobulated, excited - all rolled into one, but have a strong sensation that something special is on the cards and God knows I am seriously long overdue a little *special* in my life.

❧

Sebastian

Sliding into the car, I click my phone into its holder, and ease my seatbelt around my torso, before placing both hands on the steering wheel in front of me. I grip until my knuckles go white.

OK then. What had that all been about?

I hadn't seen her in nine, no ten, months?

She looked good. Really good! Fuck - didn't just look good, she looked hot!

She was dating again - already? Why hadn't someone mentioned that to me?

I start the engine, and pulling away, flick a quick last glance at the terrace on Rose Avenue, home to my mate from Uni - my friend of ten years, Lucia Myers. I shake my head in annoyance. Time apart hadn't changed anything. No. I'm wrong; time apart *had* changed things - it had been like seeing her again for the first time. All I'd wanted to do was take her right there and then.

I still want her - now more than ever - and the chemistry between us had been clear today. Like someone had flicked a switch. I felt it, like electricity; knew she felt it too, just like that night all those years ago. A night both of us had buried and forgotten. Instead we'd forged an amazing friendship; with the obvious spark between us lying disconnected, all this time.

I visualise her face at the moment she'd seen me, her gorgeous green eyes, quickly sparking with lime, liquid gold and heat as she looked at me when I'd arrived. She'd definitely felt it too. I am sure of that. She was ready. It was time to take her before she was lost to me again. I'd given her the chance to heal after that prick had walked all over her and left her to pick up the pieces but she'd proven that she had the strength to pull through and be *my* Lulu again. And that little man - he was a corker, a real credit to her; yeah there was no doubt about it, my Godson is a total dude.

I run a hand over my newly cut hair, questions buzzing around my head, annoyingly. The problem is, I want her but do I want more than that?

Can I do the long haul? Ten-years ago? No. I hadn't been ready for it - but now? *Maybe*. Maybe now, I could do the pipe and slippers thing. Lucia is the only woman who had ever made me consider more than a quick fuck. The only woman I'd ever wanted to share my mind and body and life with.

Would it ruin our friendship?

Am I doing my usual 'chasing after the one thing I can't have'?

This time I have to try, or spend the next ten years living with regret. I can't miss out on this opportunity again.

Chapter 3

Lucia

Later, whilst I dutifully coat myself in St Tropez self-tanning mousse for tomorrow's night out, I ponder why I suddenly can't stop thinking about Sebastian, and not just as a friend. I hate the fact that for some reason, things between us aren't *OK*. In general, my life is pretty good. I feel great about myself for the first time in months. My social life is excellent, I have great single girlfriends (a must when you are in the single market) and my career is firing on all cylinders. And then there's Leo - I'd met him a few weeks earlier, and am due to have our second date tomorrow night. He is available and harmless - perfect to use as the *in-between rebound guy*, for a summer-fling.

Would he take me to wild sexual heights though? I'm not so sure.

Sebastian could (I'm sure of it) - argghh! Why am I now thinking about my best friend in that way?

I need to seriously get some bedroom action soon or I'm going to embarrass myself big-time! Thank goodness Meg was having her *'wild ride'* sex toy party in the near future.

Sebastian has always been a major part of my life and as Finn's Godfather; he had been an amazing role model for him in his early years. But deep down, I knew that it had been the break-up when he had shown his true support. He had been my rock then, truly incredible.

Niall had walked out only days before without warning, and without setting in place a plan of action for Finn or our finances. I'd been made redundant on the Friday from my part-time design and

31

marketing position, and to add insult to injury whilst serving up Sunday dinner two days later, Niall had informed me that he was *going*. It turned out he wasn't going to see his mate Mark, who lived a few streets away as I'd first thought, but in actual fact, was leaving me, and our two year old son, for pastures new, or 'vadge's new' as Abby crudely coined it. All, just as I was about to serve up a roast chicken dinner with gorgeous fluffy homemade *bloody* Yorkshire puddings!

At the time, that was what had annoyed me the most; the fact that I'd made my own batter from scratch; for him! Not a frigging frozen Aunt Bessie pudding in sight. Isn't it strange the things that go through your mind when your world, as you know it, suddenly stops and does a complete hundred and eighty degree rotation, leaving everything altered. Tilted. Shattered.

I had spent the next twenty-four hours in shock. After talking as rationally as I could manage, Niall agreed to visit the GP to see if it was depression, as I couldn't understand why he had suddenly decided that our partnership was over, even though looking back on it there were definite and huge holes in our relationship. Returning, he'd stated in no uncertain terms, "It is *not* depression, it is *you*. *You're* the problem."

Not the best thing to hear from your partner but little did I know that he was actually doing me a favour with those eleven life-changing words. They made me strong during an impossibly turbulent time and whilst he returned to work that day, I quickly withdrew into my protective armour, and packed his things into a case, one of the hideous old 'hearing aid beige' Antler numbers we'd inherited from my parents – I wasn't going to send the selfish prick off looking stylish! I'd spent the best part of ten years trying to turn him into a fashion icon and now that he looked passable, it was going to go to use on some other woman - pah!

The crime to luggage fashion was sitting heavily pregnant with its stuffing, at the foot of the stairs, awaiting his return that night, along with a pile of *man's crap* I'd been itching to throw out for years and had never dared. A post it note completed the rather blunt '*Fuck Off!*'

Go... now! ...

... Or by all means stay,

& I'll cut your little dick off,

with your weapon of choice

- the blunter the better!!!

For a while, I was still under the impression he was struggling with life in general and that it was all just getting on top of him. So I'd tried to be supportive and do the *right thing*, whatever that was, for Finn's sake more than mine.

The reality came at me, months later, like a car crash. No, sorry - that's belittling it somewhat - it could be more likened to a motorway pile up - complete with decapitation.

He was a lying, cheating, fucking asshole!

He'd had his faults but I'd *never* though he was a cheat. Apparently, he'd been having it away with some account manager at work for six months and she was more carefree than me and didn't have kids, so it was a win-win!

With hindsight - the glorious, unobtainable object that it is when you need it, I would have reviewed our situation differently - *well* before Niall had flipped out. Whilst we had been happy at definitive times throughout our on/off nine-year relationship, there had always been something missing; something lacking that was difficult to pinpoint. If I'm honest, I had always wondered if we'd ever make it to five-years, let alone nearly a decade. But, coming from a family where my parents had been happily married for thirty-five years, I felt that I owed it to Finn to *make do* and hoped that one day, the *much-coveted link* would be served up to me on a platter. The reality was that the aforesaid *missing link* had been there all along, right under my nose, in the form of Niall Wilson - cruel but so true.

Niall, as a fellow college student, had seemed pretty cool at the time; he was fun, unique, sensitive and arty and I suppose this made him appear moody and unobtainable. These attributes had appealed to me at 19, but had I just listened to my inner voice and ignored the *romantic in me* that thought I could *fix him*, I would have realised that he was in fact immature, temperamental and unavailable emotionally. I thought back to that night in the student bar, when circumstances had thrown us together and we'd kind of clicked. But he should never have been the one I'd gone home with that night.

His own parents' had divorced when he was nine, and although Niall had been raised by a wonderful stepmother and loving Dad, he found it hard to love unconditionally. It soon became apparent during the early days of our relationship that he was not the hopeless romantic I had originally hoped for, but was in fact just hopeless at romance. You'd think that after receiving an incessant bundle of hand made paper objects, recycled goods and mis-matched cotton underwear sets from Gap, for Birthdays and Christmas for the umpteenth time, I should have given up then and there. I was not and never would be a *hippy-chick*, or the type of girl to wear men's underwear - he liked that look - some women could carry it off. Personally I preferred to look like a *female*.

I'm all for caring for the environment, but occasionally, a girl wanted to receive a beautifully wrapped glitzy gift, full of tissue paper, bows and scented beads. Niall bought for *himself* - not for *me* - and inevitably *got it wrong* on every occasion.

There had been good times and when I fell pregnant with Finn, it seemed that the bad parts of *us* were worth putting up with, as the reward was so precious and worth waiting for. Unfortunately, Niall became even more introverted, with the arrival of his *competition*, as he complained, rather bitterly, about our son. It soon became apparent that he felt like he was constantly vying for my attention and he treated Finn as though he was the third person in our relationship, not an extension of it.

He started to become volatile, drink more and punish me both mentally and emotionally, to get a rise out of me. He hated the fact that I was still close-friends with Seb, so he made it his mission to separate us and become his ally instead. This happened for a while, as Sebastian, Niall and Gino, my sister's husband got together for boy's-nights-out. But I always knew that the reality was, I couldn't have it every-way. I couldn't have Seb as my best friend and Niall as my partner. It wasn't fair to him. So I distanced myself from Sebastian to help my relationship. It was an unspoken acknowledgement from Sebastian that this was occurring and he understandingly went with the flow.

Niall's behaviour towards me, however, worsened, and the belittling and nasty comments continued. Looking back I don't know how I stayed so long but I was deeply hurt that despite putting up with his crap for years for Finn's sake, he could make such a fool out of me.

Sebastian visited me, during the period after I'd thrown Niall out; it wasn't one of my shining moments. I'd looked ghastly; my eyes were so red from crying that I looked like I had a bad case of eczema, my hair hadn't been washed in days and I was visibly shattered; definitely not the Lulu he knew and respected. But that didn't seem to matter to him. He was the epitome of calmness and rationalism. He was just what I needed in my darkest hour.

He didn't come in and shout, like my Dad had. He didn't order me to *frame myself*, like my Sister had and he didn't say *I told you so* like my Mum did - although I'm sure he was desperate to do all three, at the same time. He just quietly listened to me, made copious amounts of tea, played with Finn - so I could shower and sleep - and then eventually he sat me down with my bills, helped me figure out a plan, and wrote me a considerable cheque to cover things for a while.

"That should get you through the next few months Chick. It'll help - at least so that you can focus on my Godson and getting yourself a job."

He really had been my hero, I thought, bringing myself back to the present to focus upon fixing the streaks that were annoyingly appearing on my legs. After pulling on an old faithful nightie I used purely for tanning purposes, I crawl into bed. The exhaustion of the week, and tonight's events, hit me like a freight train. Amazing how the ball of anger still fires up in my belly when I think about Niall and the way he treated me, and most importantly, his own son. Sebastian's visit had brought everything back to the fore. I was finding it hard not to compare the two men and Sebastian was winning hands down. At least Niall was attempting to make a go of being a Dad to Finn - finally. Let's hope it continued, because despite all his faults, I firmly believed that Finn needed to have Niall in his life; every child needs their father, no matter how flakey they were. It's the only reason I maintain any form of contact with him.

As I settle in bed continuing my trail of thoughts, the sudden and vivid image of Sebastian in that bed next to me, gives me an ache low down in the pit of my belly, reminiscent of a night years ago in the Cave bar. I certainly hadn't thought about that night in a long time -

the night that changed everything. Hell - I haven't thought about *anyone* like this in a long time - and certainly not my latest interest, Leo.

I am certain though that the direction in which my thoughts are heading has nothing to do with friendship and *everything* to do with pure unadulterated lust. I had just seen Sebastian in a totally different light and could still feel the tingles from the way he'd looked at me before leaving.

"Everything happens for a reason Hun," I tell myself quietly, looking up at the ceiling above, as I bite my lip and ponder on the idea forming in my naughty mind.

What if I asked Sebastian to be 'The One' - the one to break me in, so to speak, and spend the night with me?

It would be one night of amazing passion, with someone I trust. I know he wouldn't want more - he never did. His sexual reputation was well known by most so I could be guaranteed a fabulous night - something I'm *so* overdue. No, I'd definitely not have any fear of him wanting a relationship afterwards - he didn't do relationships and that suited me fine - I only had room for one little man in my life!

Maybe then, I could get on with work and being a mother without feeling so bloody horny all the time. I don't need a man! I just need a man for the night. I needed a rebound fuck.

Could I do it? Really? Put myself out there like that?

I'd rather the first time since my break-up be with someone who cares about me enough to take it slow. The more I think about it, the more I wonder why I hadn't considered this before. He was the perfect choice for one night of desperately required, unadulterated passion. Could I really proposition the one true male friend in my life; would he say yes?

What if he didn't want me?

I twist my hair loosely around my finger, considering all scenarios' and begin to elaborate upon my initial concept. The more I think about it, the more I think *to hell with it* - and just put it out there - the worst thing that could happen would be he said no.

You'll never find out unless you pose the question to him.

Chapter 4

Lucia

After several hours of supermarket shopping and a kid's birthday party, I'm ready for some *me* time. Finn had had his face-painted in full camouflage, and stealth-like in his approach, held his toy Uzi at me in pure delight before releasing a loud monotone barrage of machine pistol fire - pretty much all afternoon!

I'm now happy to bury myself in a deep luxurious bubble bath to sooth my aching body. Looking back, I agreed with the mum and host of the party, perhaps the guns hadn't been the best party bag gift. I grin to myself at the memory of my son's overzealous re-en-action of Rambo whilst moisturising my body to within an inch of its life, and settle down at my silver, shabby chic dressing table. He was now happily settled at my parents' for the night and I could selfishly enjoy getting ready for our big night out.

How nice to be able to spend more than five rushed minutes on my make-up. Usually, I prioritise Finn - whether it's bathing, dressing and feeding - leaving little time to concentrate fully on my own appearance. Lippy was often applied in the car, but *always* applied. Lipstick wouldn't save the world, but it certainly made it a better place and me feel human, the second I put it on.

I'd take full advantage of the extra time, and after half an hour, I could have given a Mac beautician a run for their money. Smokey lids made my eyes appear even bigger, and the dark green I've lined them with, brings out the same tone in my irises, accentuating the colour of wet moss, mixed with lime zest. I've gone for a dramatic look on the lips as well - red velveteen - *very Robert Palmer-esq*. The result is actually pretty hot and I'm pleased. My chosen dress is a black fitted little number, which falls to mid calf. I'd bought it from Suzie's boutique a few weeks before; I couldn't afford it, but she'd insisted that it would be the staple *little black dress* in my wardrobe which would never date - she was right and my credit card would just have to take the hit.

As I step into the crêpe de chine fabric and slide it over my hips, I sigh as it clings to my body in all the right places. My skin literally groans in delight. The neckline is low enough to suit my curvy bust and the smart little peplum cleverly covers up my C-section bump, and enhances my petite waist. The only problem is going to be zipping it up. *Where was a man, when you needed one?*

Struggling, I manage to drag it into place, but not without doing a complete contortionist act. I pair the dress with Kurt Geiger ruby red suede skyscraper stiletto's, which add at least five inches to my 5ft 2 frame - and add a black suede diamante skull clutch. My legs look almost…well lengthy - thanks to the shoes and my fake tan - a huge task in itself, when they were a mere 27 inches long, hip to toe (believe me I've measured them many times, in the hope that they may have stretched). Oh to be 5ft 7 barefoot!

Staring at myself in the mirror, I hardly recognised myself. My eyes are shining, my long dark hair, gleams and tumbles in sexy waves around my face and sleekly down my back. All I need now is jewellery. Selecting a large crystal cocktail ring, I add a pair of simple drop earrings with Swarovski crystal balls at the base. They swing softly as I move and always make me feel feminine when I wear them. I decide to leave my neck bare, as I spray myself liberally with Gucci perfume, my signature scent - which ensures that I smell divine too. Right - I'm ready. *Ready to offer my body to a certain male friend for the night.*

"Lu it's just me." I hear Meg coo up the stairs. She is early, but it's not a problem, as for once, things had gone to plan with my outfit.

"Hi Hun. I'll be down in a minute; I'm just about ready. Grab a glass of wine. There's an open bottle of Wolf Blass in the fridge and I'll ring a taxi."

Determined to remain calm, and focus on the matter at hand, I continue grabbing the necessities required for the night and shove them hurriedly into my clutch. I'm a bit jittery and spending much more time on my appearance than I normally would. Then again I don't usually have the luxury to do so.

Well that's what I'm telling myself is the reason. Deep down, I know it's for a certain familiar and delicious male friend and I'm apprehensive as to how I'll react in his vicinity.

38

Would tonight be the night, to pose my question to him?

My hands grow clammy at the prospect. Downstairs, I can hear Meg is watching Coronation Street, her fav soap, and as I carefully tackle the stairs in my heels, the theme tune rolls in. Entering the lounge, I notice her wineglass is already drained. She was on a mission.

"Hey Babe. Wow look at you! You look fab... u... lous!" she shouts, pronouncing every syllable. I smile, pleased with her reaction and do a little spin.

"Yes - we are two incredibly hot Mamas, ready to hit the town," I laugh at her.

She looks great. Her ash blonde, wavy hair has been freshly highlighted and sits like an angelic beacon against her white, sixties style tunic dress. She really does look good for thirty-seven. It seems that her extremely recent and relatively civil divorce from her ex-husband Bri, had really done wonders for her complexion.

We had clicked from the minute she moved into our street, the week before Niall walked, and then, subsequently been thrown out! Since then, our mutual circumstances and love of shoes and wine, combined with bitching about the ex's had resulted in a firm friendship, very different to my friendship with my best pal, Abby, and my closeness with my sister, Suzie. Meg understood what it was like to be a single-mother. She had two daughters, a fourteen-year-old, Lexie and a ten-year old Phoebe, both from her first marriage. She worked as a PA to a Director at the local Council but had also been a hairdresser in the past, hence the great hairdo. I really respected the fact that she managed to hold down a pretty demanding job three days a week, run a house and cope with two children. I honestly didn't know how she did it, as I struggled with just one child and didn't have the drama of a teenager to contend with.

We had sort of hung onto each other in our time of need and the fact that many of our friends were in relationships had meant us spending more time together. I genuinely liked her and felt bad for having a negative thought about her yesterday. Who am I to put a claim to Sebastian Silver, when really, all we had ever been was friends? Meg was a great girl and she deserved a good man like Sebastian. I just didn't want it to *be* him.

A loud beep coming from outside interrupts my thoughts, and grabbing my bag and keys, I turn off the TV and usher Meg out of the door.

39

"Come on Chickadee. Let's go do some damage."

We land at Lord's train station full of excitement and the buzz of what's to come, and head off in the direction of our gathering. It was now or never. Do I just keep going or do I tell Meg to head onto the Champagne Bar without me and that I'd see her there soon, once I've concluded some business?

Bloody Niall.

I choose the latter and after a lot of persuading, she manages to convince me that she will *not* let me climb into the jaws of the lion alone, and would be my second set of eyes. Looking at her own big blue orbs - the steely glint of stubbornness clear in them, I resign myself to her insistence and laughingly agree, and on teetering heels we make our way to the pub Niall was known to frequent, The Lazy Lounge.

The second we walk through the doors, he invades my space.

"Lucia - you came." Niall stands from his sofa'd, seating area.

I immediately assess the situation and count four other men watching over Meg and I with an interested gaze. Considering the bar was more of a *drop-in after work, early doors and watch the sport, over a pint,* kind of place, we had become the new blood. There were no other women in their group and it was Saturday so the bar was pretty empty for a City pub.

"What can I get you both - Meg is it?" Niall pipes up, charming in his comfort zone. He's dressed casually in a fitted t-shirt and chinos already sporting a beer flush and glaze to his eyes.

I rudely interrupt Meg, as she's about to place her order. We are not here to mingle or share a cocktail with my ex. Let's talk and get the hell out of there!

"No thanks Niall. We're on our way to the Champagne Bar. What did you want to talk to me about, face to face, that you couldn't do over the phone?" I use my hands outstretched to support the words, demonstrating the silliness of his over-the-top texting.

Annoyingly, he ignores my obvious desire to move things along quickly, and instead, steps aside courteously opening his arm in welcome, for Meg to take his seat. One-by-one, and excruciatingly slowly, he introduces her to his mates. She happily concedes, raising her brows at me in a *'I'll just go with the flow then, yeah?* kind of way - and recognising the three-men-to-one-woman ratio is utterly in her element. *So much for watching my back!*

Niall guides me over towards a darkened corner at the back of their seating space. I cross my arms over my chest in an attempt to hide my cleavage from his prying eyes but it only encourages his wandering leer. I feel stripped-bare.

I'd forgotten how seedy he could be.

"You look great, Lu. Smokin!"

He then turns to his mates - none of which I recognise - for their opinions.

"Doesn't she lads?" I should be flattered as they all give a resounding *Yes*, with beaming smiles and appreciative glances but I just feel grubby.

Especially when one of them says, "Miles hotter than Karen."

Niall muses this comment and considers me up and down, taking agonising time over my legs, hips, breasts, and back up to my face, by which time I've almost reached boiling point.

The fucking cheek of the man! I am the mother of his child. I deserve so much better than this.

He agrees with his mate, throwing a reply over his shoulder, whilst still assessing my every move.

"You're right there, Dave. Not sure *what* I was thinking."

Through clenched teeth, I remain outwardly calm and collected and accept the rather blurred compliment.

"Thanks. Now. What's this about Finn?"

"Come on Babe. Have that drink? I'm sure your banker boyfriend won't mind." His chuckle is malicious and I shake my head at his gall.

"You don't want to talk at all do you? You've used our son to get me here just to ruin my night?"

The manipulation techniques that he'd employed throughout our whole relationship were continuing to work on me, even after we'd split and I'm not sure who I'm more annoyed with *him* or *myself!*

"Don't be daft Lucia. I just wanted to see you - that's all. I miss you." The casual tone of his slightly slurred voice irritates me even further.

"Look, I don't have time for this. It's my Sister's birthday, Seb's home and the whole team's out tonight." His eyes squint at the mention of Sebastian's name.

"Sebastian's back is he?" his top lip curls unattractively. "Didn't know. Thought he'd gone onto pastures new and given up sniffing around where he isn't wanted." Leering possessively towards me, I push him off with the full force of both my palms.

What is he on about?

It's a shame Niall is such a dick - he and Sebastian used to be good friends.

"Get lost, Niall. You're already half cut. How long have you been out?"

"Few hours." His throw away comment is accompanied by a *so what* shrug.

"Right. Well I'm off. You'll see your son as planned next week. Have a good night."

"There's no need to be so bitter Babe - I know you still want me. You could have me too if you just chased a *li...ttle bit* harder."

He laughs at his comment and I bite down hard to stop myself from retaliating and ultimately giving him what he wants - the pleasure of seeing my night ruined - I clench my teeth with such strength that I nip my inner lip and flinch.

Jerk!

"Meg, we're leaving."

I ignore Niall's attempts to chatter away to me, and his suggestion that he and the lads accompany us to the Champagne Bar safely. Meg finally recognises my need to escape and is by my side in an instant.

"You alright, Hun?" she looks concerned and I refrain from hollering *where were your concerns just now?*

"I'm fine. Let's just go. We're already late."

I don't even say goodbye to Niall as I head out the front doors of the pub, but can hear him holler to us.

"Give your Sis a Happy Burp-day Kiss from me - might see you later Mu Mu."

I cringe at his babyish whine and the awful nickname he used to call me. *I don't bloody think so.*

Suzie, Gino, Abby and Jess are already at The Champagne Bar when we land and I'm pleased, as they've grabbed a corner of the hip bar in Lords City Centre.

"Yay! You're here, my gorgeous sis - Happy Birthday to me. Happy Birthday to me!" Suzie throws herself at me, a cloud of Thierry Mugler's *Angel* shrouding us, as she dances to her own tune. I smile in affection and envelope her in a proper cuddle.

"Happy Birthday Darling." Winking at Gino, I raise my brows and mouth-the-words, nodding in Suzie's direction, "How many has she had?"

"She is on the sauce as it is her birthday, in case no one else had realised." He laughs at this ridiculous remark, shrugging his shoulders, and lifting his arms up in a surrendering way. "You will need to buy plenty of tomato sauce to play catch-up, - you get it?"

Oh my word, Gino's jokes are renowned for being bad, but I giggle in spite of it. He really is so daft, especially with his Italian tinged Yorkshire accent.

"Meghaan," he purrs, "You look ravishing!"

Meg, who is usually unaffected by the smarm-charm and hates the use of her full name, blushes and slaps him playfully on his arm. "Suzie - you've got your hands full with this one."

Suzie tuts and waves the words away. "He knows he has the best Meg - and he'll never get better," she smiles smugly.

Gino just shrugs and adds, "I have my hands full yes, but tonight perhaps she will have her mouth full of Italian promise," he winks, and nods his head, happy with this thought, unable to see Suzie mouthing *in his dreams* behind him. But I watch them a little longer, and see her lean into her husband's body and seductively whisper something gently into his ear and know from the sexy smile that appears across his handsome face that the night *would be* full of promise for them.

Suzie's best friend, Jess, chooses that moment to launch herself at me, identifying herself, as my sister's partner in *lager and lime!* She's a fabulous ball of energy on any given day and is great fun. I haven't caught up with her in forever and have really missed her company of late, especially since she only lives around the corner from Finn & I.

"Lulu - how's things? I haven't seen you in fucking ages!" she grins genuinely, rubbing my arm in affection.

I laugh at her language. She reminded me of the lovely Irish - could swear like a trooper and didn't seem to offend, even though she was a Yorkshire lass, born and bred.

"I'm great Jess - how's the new job?"

"Fucking nightmare Babe, but I've got no responsibility and that suits me for now." She drains the last drop of her drink, like she has been stuck in the desert for a week. "You know me Lu, can't stay still for too long. I might get knocked-up and become domesticated; what a God- awful thought!"

I shake my head and snort. "You are naughty Miss Jessica. I adore my son and won't hear you *dis* domesticity. It'll come to you one of these days. It comes to us all."

"Oh Darling, Finn is a total superstar, but kids are not for me. You know that. I'm happy to be sexy Auntie Jess, but I'm too bloody selfish to be a full-time carer. How would I have the time to recover from my monstrous hangovers? Speaking of bottle-feeding…"

I take that as my cue and giggling further at her extreme bluntness I hold my hands up in submission. "OK. OK! Hint taken. My round, what does everyone want?"

"Ooh, I'll come with?" Abby's bubbly voice interrupts, "I need to talk to you!" Her eyes, burrow into my face with such intensity, I know not to refuse.

We head over to the fabulous Art Deco themed bar and squish as far to the front as is acceptable around the many thirsty customers. I smile at Abby as she practically bursts at the seams with her secret. She looks lovely tonight; very effervescent – I definitely sense something brewing.

"Oh. My. God Lubedoo, I'm in LOVE!" she explodes the information, her big brown cow eyes are bright and her brow furrows in what could be pain or maybe excitement? I'm not sure, but I laugh at her dramatic exclamation.

"Oh Darling, who is it this time?" Abby was well known for falling in love easily shall we say, and it was one of the things *I* loved about my best mate, that she never took life too seriously.

She rolls her carefully purple lined eyes as if I've completely lost the plot "Nathan of course. He's bloody gorgeous!"

"Nathan Silver?"

"Yes. Seb's brother - he's back and working with Sebastian now."

I let her words filter through and nod in understanding "I didn't know he was home, it's been a while since I saw him to be honest. He's a super nice guy though."

"He's soo dreamy! Suzie, Gino, Jess and I bumped into them at The Oracle just before we came here. You and Meg were late as per."

I ignore her late comment. I'm always late, but tonight I wish it had just been the old excuse *my hair wouldn't go* and not the fact that I'd been an idiot and met up with my ex. I choose not to inform her of my silly faux pas at that time and instead file it away to enjoy my night. That way Niall didn't win.

Looking brightly back at her I ask, "Them?"

"Nathan, Sebastian and his mate. Can't remember his name, sorry, I was too in awe of my Greek God at that stage. They're meeting us in here soon."

My tummy flips in expectant waves of the unknown and I swallow, giving the bar a quick recce - nope not here yet. *Why am I getting all nervy?* I try to hide my twitchiness from Abby and support her own crush. I've always had a feeling she and Nathan would hit it off if they met but they'd never been single at the same time. Maybe now was the right occasion?

"He is a lovely guy Abby. To be honest, I haven't caught up with him in a while. I think he's been in Australia?"

"Is he single? Shit, I hope he's single." She chews her lip in panic and I consider her pose. *She's not normally so on edge. Bless - she does really like him!*

"I honestly don't know. I know he had a long-term girlfriend a year or so ago, think her name was Penelope or Poppy but don't quote me on that - but not sure of late?" Shrugging my shoulders I shuffle between two male elbows on the black glossy bar, as a space frees up. It was packed and not a gentleman in sight at this bar – undoubtedly every man or woman for themselves, when it came to getting served here.

"I could ask around if you want?"

"Oh thanks Hun, but make it subtle won't you? I really need to work my charm here and not appear desperate. I honestly think if he asked me to *bob on* with him tonight - *I would!*" She looks disappointed at herself but at the same time resigned in the knowledge that she is powerless to it.

I giggle at one of her favourite nicknames for sex and drolly reply. "Wow! He must be *The One!*"

"Don't be like that. I'm serious he's…well he's really nice. I think he would be good to me. God knows I need someone to be good to me."

I grab her in a cuddle. "Babe, you don't need anyone to be good to you. I'm here!"

We embrace in a messy swaying hug and are interrupted by the barman. I promptly order two bottles of our favourite tipple, Laurent-Perrier Cuvée Rosé Champagne, not willing to lose the place in the queue and turn back to Abs.

"Just be yourself and he'll be putty in your hands."

Her vulnerable side appears safely tucked away again, and cheeky

Abby is back. "Don't bloody think so, nothing soft there, that one would be 100% solid Silver!"

I practically choke on my laugh, and shoulders shaking at her comment, we share out the glasses and ice bucket between us, manoeuvring our route between the hustle and bustle.

"Seriously though, how are you going to feel about seeing Sebastian tonight - now that you've taken the blinkers off?"

I barge her lightly with my shoulder to shut up. "Honestly? I'm shitting myself and I don't really know why?" I notice a few neck cricks from admirers, as we snake a path to our friends and I'm pleased I spent the extra time on myself earlier. It was paying off.

"You'll be fine Lu, you're hot right now — you won't need to do anything. It's like you're giving off some kind of vibe? Just go with it!" Her deep throaty laugh follows her as she leads the way. *Yeah desperation!*

We finally reach the table, arms aching and remarkably not a drop of the good stuff spilt when we see that our party has expanded and I can acknowledge a further three men are chatting amiably with Gino. One of them I can tell is Sebastian, even from behind. Oh and what a behind. I feel a little buzz of excitement fizz its way around my body. Since Abs had mentioned he was on his way, I'd had nothing but him on my dirty little mind.

Who am I kidding? I'd been watching the door for the past twenty minutes, trying to appear nonchalant in the hope that he'd make it - before confirmation that he was, in fact, already on his way.

I can see that Sebastian is talking to a good-looking guy, with a very cute smile and cool messy hair and as I near, I realise its Nathan his brother, whom I haven't seen in ages. Abby was right. He looked *good* and I send her a knowing smile, which she returns with a wink. The other male is standing, watching me as I walk towards them; his angular, stubbled face is difficult to read and I don't recognise him at all. He is good-looking in harsh kind of way- rather brooding.

Our arrival at the table is greeted with whoops and noisy cheers from Suzie for my choice of champers and I begin to dish out glasses to the many already out-stretched hands. I'm concentrating on the task, when Sebastian leans in and takes one of the bottles from the large mirrored ice bucket.

"Here, let me Lu. Hmm, the good stuff - you always have had impeccable taste," he approves, considering me from head to foot, his husky voice slicing through me. *Double-entendre already?*

46

"Thanks." My response is barely a whisper. That's all I can say. I sound reserved, although I don't mean to, and force a sparkling smile.

Why is the atmosphere so strained? I can't believe how much has changed in twenty-four hours. This is my mate, I just need to relax and enjoy my time with him and our combined friends; it's so infrequent these days that we are all out together. Either that or bloody ask him to fuck me and get it out the way. Lulu - you're losing it!

Sebastian hands out the *good stuff* to the many outstretched hands before saving the last glass for me and is about to release it into my fingers, when he's jostled from behind by an eager punter and the whole contents of the flute, are emptied over my chest. The moment is lightening-quick but feels like a slow motion replay; bubbles fizzing and trickling down my neck, across my décolletage and disappearing beneath the low v of my dress.

I'm transported back in time to a similar situation, ten years earlier - a walking talking cliché... again! At least I'm not wearing white on this occasion. My gasp of shock as the cold champagne hits my chest and soaks through to the skin, makes us both jump.

"So here we are again. Always thrusting those assets in my face Lulu."

My immediate anger dissipates immediately as shock gives way to memories. I smile back at him, and then giggle. Ten years! Where did that time go? How different things could have been?

"I seem to remember it being cheap watered-down beer. At least now its champagne."

"I seem to remember telling you I wouldn't touch you again. That won't be the case this time." His deep voice is full of promise.

I grab a serviette from the table and mop at my chest, remarkably, there is no stain and my cleavage has taken the majority of the hit and is now happily dry.

"I think I prefer you wet."

My eyes fly up at that comment. His dark eyes twinkle with mirth, and I swallow deeply to control the effect he is unknowingly having on me - his words sending signals of desire directly between my thighs.

Accepting the second chilled champagne flute he carefully hands over, I immediately take a large gulp to calm my nerves; the raspberry liquid fizzes in my mouth and the crisp vanilla tang of my favourite champagne slides coolly down my throat. It is delicious and I lick my lips to savour every last drop. I can feel the warm glow begin to emanate in my tummy.

I lurve champagne; it is one of the few alcoholic beverages that didn't make me feel ghastly the next day, providing I wasn't too silly with my quantities. I look at Sebastian and he is watching me intently, with particular focus on my mouth.

"Cheers."

He clinks his glass to mine and our fingers brush gently. It's as though we are in one of those Rosé bubbles, enclosed, away from everyone else. Whoa, this is heavy stuff! I can't believe how I am seeing my friend. I can hear Gino telling a dirty joke to the group in the background and lots of laughing and bawdiness but in our intimate party of two, we are secluded. Sebastian plonks himself down on the stool next to me. He looks so hot, wearing dark fitted Replay jeans, which fit his muscled thighs snugly (thank you Replay designers) and a grey silk-knit v-neck jumper. His shoes are expensive brown dealer boots, manufactured to look worn. The combination is so simple; he just looks … devastating; effortless - like an advert for GQ. I can smell his signature scent and I know it is by Dolce & Gabbana, as I had bought some for him for Christmas one year, after his mum had given me his wish list. I remember it being called *The One* and I laugh now at the irony of it all.

His face is stern, almost angry looking; his jaw strong, and arrogant. He'd cut his hair recently, probably for ease at work and now wore it shorter, not quite entirely shaved but cut short on the sides, and kept slightly longer on top, soldier style. It only adds to his raw sexuality. He has a *fuck off* nose, I'd always teased - it is slightly too long and angular but perfectly straight, despite having broken it on several occasions. It makes you want to run your finger along the edge of it, slowly, right to the tip. His colouring is so dark; he permanently has a shadow of stubble, which threatens to erupt at any moment and an olive tone to his fantastic skin. But it was his eyes that are now captivating me. They are slightly turned down in the outer corners and huge, almost black in shade, with sherry brown and hazel flecks if you caught them in a certain light, and eyelashes that any woman would die for, that fringed his bedroom gaze with full, sooty bluntness. The overall effect was one of power, arrogance, success and confidence, but ultimately, he commanded attention and women did not let him down. He was a great combination of Jason Statham, Ryan Gosling and Channing Tatum, all mixed into one delicious package - he quite literally oozed sex appeal and right at this moment I could eat him up with a cherry on top.

How have I not seen how hot he is until now? You did - you'd just forgotten, my inner voice reminds me annoyingly.

"Your brother's here. I haven't seen him since that party for your Nan's 70th at your Mum and Dad's last year." Finally, I stop drooling and find my tongue.

"Yeah, he got back from travelling in Oz recently and is now going to join me on site," he nods his head towards Nathan's direction. "It's really good to have him home - soft lad that he is." I can hear the affection in his voice.

I'm not really listening to him, as I can't stop ogling. I've spent years on and off with this man, hours sitting next to him in lecture theatres and cramming for exams. Why did I never see him in this way? My hand is itching to touch him. "Is he single?" I ask.

Nice one Lu. Didn't Abby ask you to be subtle?

Sebastian considers my question watching me inquisitively. "He's my brother Lu."

I'm confused by his disapproving response and my screwed up face and stutter probably show this, when he continues dryly.

"Yes he's single."

It suddenly dawns on me that he must realise that I am asking for myself and I laugh at his misconception. "Not for me, you ditz. I know a little bird who's enquiring that's all."

My information doesn't appear to have lessened his scowl. Grumpy bastard – where's fun-loving Sebastian gone? He's become very intense. Taking a swig of champagne he brings his brooding focus back to me but we remain silent. God, this is awkward. I have to get out of here. I'd hoped to maybe take the moment to discuss my favour with him.

"I'll be back in a bit - off to the Ladies."

"Off you go and powder that cute little snub nose of yours."

I know it's abrupt but I excuse myself and try to appear casual as I head in the direction of the toilets so that I can deep breathe in peace. I don't look back, but can feel the burn of his gaze on my retreating form and I ensure he gets the complete Lulu wiggle. All these comments about my appearance are wreaking havoc with my nether regions

Chapter 5

Lucia

I touch up my lipstick, blush and eye-makeup and spritz some more perfume over my neck and wrists. Not that I need to do any of this, I'm just desperate for something to occupy my shaky hands. *On edge* would be a total understatement for the mixed jumble of emotions that I am right now. Showcasing a prime example of it, I jump as I hear a voice shouting my name from one of the cubicle doors.

"Lu is that you? It's Meg-haann," she drunkenly giggles from her patch, mimicking Gino's Italian accent; she really can't drink champagne, if she's like this after only a couple.

"Hey, I didn't hear you come in, sorry love. Are you nearly done? I'm going to go back out now."

"Wait! Wait for me." She throws open her door dramatically, pulling her dress back down as she exits. "Do I need more?" She puckers her lips up at me like a little girl and sways as she squirts foam on her hands, rushing them under the automatic faucet.

"Maybe a bit more lippy," I comment. "You look fab still." I watch as she retouches and messes with her hair in the wall-to-wall mirrors. The manic finger combing is making her look like a wilder crazier version of Jane Fonda in Barbarella.

"Oooh goodie. I need to look my best tonight. We have some right fitties at our beck and call, don't we?" she grins impishly at me through the reflection.

"Whom have you got your beady eye on?" I enquire a little too harshly.

"W..e..ll we're spoilt for choice but I'm quite taken with Sebastian as you know, but his brother is hot too and the moody one; Chris is it? Anyway he is kind of smoking in a brooding Gerard Butler way."

She holds her feet up one at a time for loose toilet paper inspection. I shake my head and she nods her blonde head, pleased.

"Right. Come on Babe – let's go pester them."

I groan inwardly, Meg can be a little over the top sometimes and I definitely prefer the less desperate approach. I love her to bits but I'm starting to get really pissed about her liking Sebastian and I'm even more annoyed that I have no right to say that I don't want her to *go there*.

We tug open the door and are met with the sexy beat of *Ellie Goulding's* new track *Burn*; it picks me up immediately and I decide to go out, enjoy myself and try and ignore my strange feelings towards both of my friends. The night is young and I'm determined to have some fun.

The next hour or so is spent enjoying good times with great company. The champagne flows liberally and we celebrate Suzie's 27th in style. At all times I am aware of Sebastian watching me or it could be Meg as she and he, definitely appear to have clicked; she'd been mauling him for the past hour! However I consider whether this is just in my head as I'm pretty certain that when he thinks I am not looking, his focus is entirely on me – with a serious, rather unfriendly inspection. I'm definitely at a loss.

My thoughts are interrupted when my phone alerts me to a text. It's from Leo.

Sorry L but I'm not going to make it tonight after all. Work things! Can I take you to dinner next Saturday night? Let me make it up to you x

I'd completely forgotten I'd asked him to join us, so I am actually pleased that he's cancelled (although I'm slightly annoyed that I won't be allowed the opportunity to flaunt him in front of Sebastian).

I quickly reel off a response, the champagne making me ballsy.

House Party at my sister's Saturday night – be my + 1 - let me know if you accept?

I don't wait for his reply and just as I auto-lock my phone, a deep voice says casually, "I wouldn't have stood you up. He'd kick himself if he'd seen you in that dress."

I spin quickly to be met by Sebastian's mate. Suzie has already informed me he is definitely called Chris but I've yet to have a one-on-one with the guy. Meg was right - he did look like Gerard Butler, perhaps a little less sexy. I am a bit annoyed that he's nosied at my text, but choose to ignore the irritation and go with it. I'm not about to add to his obviously inflated opinion of himself and decide to act coy as to, who *he* is.

"Thanks, Chris is it?" I hold out my hand to shake his but am a bit taken aback when he ignores it and leans in towards me, planting a firm kiss on one side of my cheek and then the other; continental style. He lingers a little too long, our faces touching.

I could have sworn he just sniffed me?

"Sebastian said that you and he went to Uni together Lucia?" he continues, paying a considerable amount of attention to my breasts.

"Yes, we did three years together, for our sins – not behind bars but definitely propped up in front of them," I laugh back at him. He is Ok looking. Not as striking as Sebastian but has a similar dress-style, dark blonde short hair with a Beckham quiff and cool appraising icy-blue eyes.

"I'm working on a contract with our Mr. Silver for a few months and just moved in to his spare-room, so hopefully we'll be seeing much more of each other in the very near future." His voice is laden with confidence. I'm surprised, as I think he may be flirting, but I try not to show it.

"Definitely. We go out most Friday's to our favourite bar, Rehab, in Bodley so I'll have to introduce you to some of our friends."

I can see Meg manically trying to catch my eye behind Chris' back. I lean in closer to him and smile. "In fact I think you may already have an admirer in my neighbour Meg."

He turns to look over his shoulder, and Meg instantly pretends to have dropped something, disappearing under the table. I snigger to myself. God we are all so silly where men are concerned.

Chris returns to face me, his eyes sparking. "You do seem to have a good group of mates here. I travel so much with work, it's hard to catch up regularly with friends so you tend to drift apart. Sebastian and I go *way* back though and I'm pleased to be able to spend some quality time doing normal things in the same place for a while."

I smile at him and sip at my drink and I'm about to continue, when we are interrupted by the man, himself.

"Christopher – I see you've found Lulu." Seb slaps Chris on the back, looks between the two of us and takes a swig of his beer.

"I most certainly have. I'm pursuing her as we speak." Chris doesn't take his eyes off mine but I cannot hold his gaze. I'm left embarrassed, by his over-the-top statement.

"Are you now?" Sebastian's furrowed brow is apparent but Chris is oblivious to anyone but himself (a bad habit that I can tell he has developed over years of having his ego stroked!).

"Yeah. We were just discussing that now I'm going to be around more, we could link up? I need to be shown about town!"

Sebastian seems less chilled than his normal laid-back self. He looks like he has a distinct bad taste in his mouth and his jaw is tense. I watch the strength of his muscles, taut in their coiled position, under his grey v-neck and admire his body. My hands itch to reach out and touch him there. Slip my arm around his waist and feel his arms enclose around me.

"I'm back now Chris, and Lu and I have a lot of catching up to do but I'm sure you'll bump into one another. Besides you'll meet plenty of new people at my housewarming in a couple of weeks."

Wait! Did he just lay his claim? That's great but what right does he have to tell another man whether I can see him or not?

I don't even want to see Chris like that, but the attention is flattering and a little flirtation once in a while does wonders for the soul doesn't it, provided they don't get the wrong idea?

The whole scenario appears to have gone straight over Chris' head and he continues to flirt and chatter amiably. Sebastian is that wired, his strikingly tanned face and muscular physique is overwrought. I can't relax either. I need to say my peace and get the hell out of there or get over it and frame myself. With Chris there, I couldn't talk to Seb openly, even if I could maintain enough courage to actually say the words – something I'm still not sure I have in me.

I choose to leave them to their own devices. There is just too much testosterone in the air and I need a major girly overload. Looking around I can see that my sister is a lost cause and is deeply involved in what appears to be, some heavy going chatter with Gino and Jess. Meg is undulating in front of Nathan, stripper style, at another table and I can see the look of horror and jealousy on Ab's face. Poor thing – she has it real bad! Meg was harmless but I could see me having to calm a few frayed feelings after this episode. I head directly for Abs, practically drag her to her senses and we make a dive for the dance floor.

I can feel Sebastian assessing me as I let go to the infectious beat filling the bar. The small dance area is situated in a more segregated part of the bar and apart from the odd flickering light; the ambience is much moodier, enabling you to lose your inhibitions. Throwing cheeky glances in his direction as I relax and bump and grind jokily with Abby, I can see that Nathan, Chris and Sebastian are conversing, whilst staring at us intently. They make a handsome group but I am solely drawn to Sebastian as though he were the only person in the room. Our eyes connect, and smiling bashfully at him, I flick my hair forward, across one shoulder and revel in the freedom of the beat. At this distance I can let go and flirt confidently, face-to-face was a totally different story.

I shamelessly and purposely wiggle and slink in all the right places. I've enjoyed far too much of Monsieur Laurent Perrier. Abby giggles as she mimics my moves and I notice that Nathan appears as intent on her as his brother is on me - the Silver brothers seem bewitched. How sublime!

Several tunes later, thirsty but happy, we hug each other in our mutually tired but exuberant manner and head back to the group, who are now running on empty. Looking around I can see that the bar is beginning to empty as punters start to trickle out. I down the remnants of my glass and nip to the ladies to freshen up. Upon my return to the gang, I'm just contemplating making a move to go (I've got total head fuck where Seb is concerned) when I'm blindsided as I watch an extremely merry Meg, launch herself at him, full throttle, linking her arms around his neck and puckering up for a kiss. She really is thoroughly slaughtered.

"Why haven't you and I met before Seb…ashchun? I truly believe that our Lucy lady has been hiding you away. Naughty Lulu! Naughty girl!" Looking in my direction Meg wags her finger at me, in a wobbly fashion. She really is wrecked. I may be wishing it but I'm sure I see Seb push away a little from her cloying embrace. Didn't she just say something similar to Suzie about Chris?

"I don't know Meg but I'm glad we have now," he drawls.

Oh jeez don't encourage her!

This is all the motivation she needs. She grabs his hand and, as we all ready ourselves to leave, she hangs on to him for dear life and he doesn't appear to mind.

The night air is crisp as we walk to our cabs, even though it's probably still about twenty degrees. Lords City is lit up like a New York skyline; all full of promise and excitement but it isn't quite the city that never sleeps and the chaos is definitely at a much slower pace as we wander through the streets; it's rowdy drunkards having fun surround us, many of whom are actually from our party. My head feels a bit wobbly and I wish I'd eaten earlier. I link arms with my sister & Jess and we warble our way through several verses of *Ego* by *The Saturday's*, aiming it directly at the men ahead of us.

What a fabulous night – it had been just what I needed after a busy week but what I would do now to go home and jump Sebastian Silver's bones - shame I'd not plucked up the courage to ask him to take me home and fuck me sideways into the middle of next week!

"Bye guys!" I shout to Suzie and Gino, who are in the process of exploring one another's tonsils in the queue. They are very much in love and I'm lustfully envious.

"Get a room!"

Laughing to myself I join Meg and Jess in the back of the taxi. I presume Abby and Nathan are hitching a ride with my Sis and that Chris and Seb will do their own thing when that thought is thrown out the window as the front door is flung open and the man himself casually climbs into the empty front seat.

"Ladies - you're ok to drop me off at mine after, yeah?"

His sexy scent fills the small space, male pheromones bubbling around and turning all females within a five-mile radius wanton and pathetic - me included.

"No problemo Mr. Gorgeous!" Meg lunges forward from her central perch and drunkenly strokes his shoulder.

I sit back and tight-lipped, stare at the back of Seb's head, boring holes into it with narrowed emerald eyes, determined not to succumb to jealousy - I'm not sure how much longer I can watch though - Meg has spent most of the night pawing him and thrusting her own ample breasts into his face.

If it had been any other man I'd have been pleased for her, but

Sebastian was *different*. He was…*what?* What was he to me? Not my boyfriend or even a potential boyfriend. I couldn't describe my territorial right to him, he was just… *more mine than hers.* The problem is, I couldn't tell her to back off, as it wasn't like we had anything going on. Not yet anyway. Plus she didn't know about my proposed proposition yet so it wasn't like she was making a play for what was mine.

But that's exactly what's she's doing and I fucking hate it.

I had no right to tell either of them who they could and couldn't flirt with. I squinted my now glowing green eyes in annoyance. It was all *his* fault; he looked and smelt *too good* and was obviously doing it on purpose to mess with my head.

As the cab pulls into our street, I have already determined that Seb and Meg are in fact about to ravish one another back at her house and do the dirty. I feel nauseous just at the thought of it and really pissed off. Odd, as I'd spent years attempting to set Sebastian up with friends of mine, whilst I was with Niall. *How could I have been so unaffected by the thought of him with someone else?*

Pulling up at our first destination, we begin to pile out and Seb, the gentleman that he is, offers to pay the driver.

"Night Sebastian. Thanks," I throw out, desperate to get away from him and my mate and their obvious building sexual tension.

"Night girls, see you in the morning."

Smiling, I wave, as I notice that they make their way to their own respective doors, Meg at Number 45 and Jess around the corner on Horton Street.

I don't look back and presume that Sebastian has followed his next conquest or set off home in the cab. God that man was a disgrace; It appeared he'd bobbed-on with anyone and everyone… but me – I'm not sure which annoyed me more, the fact he was a man-whore, or that I wasn't one of his conquests. *Unfortunately I fear it's the latter.*

My inner reasoning annoyingly reminds me that as he is single, Sebastian was well within his rights to fuck whomever he pleased. *And unless you can find a backbone, some seriously big hairy bollocks and proposition him Darling, he is going to continue to fuck whomever he pleases!*

Angrily rummaging around, I finally find my keys, in the bottom of my metallic sequined handbag - covered in make-up. Fumbling I manage to open the door, muttering to myself, when I suddenly sense I'm not alone and cast in shadow.

"I'll come in for a drink if that's ok Chick; it's far too early to go home yet."

Surprised, I jump and literally fall through the door, as my brain and body wrestle to work together. The rubbing the tummy, whilst patting the head manoeuvre comes to mind, as I try to propel myself forward and extract the keys from the door at the same time. I can't even muster a response as I kick my shoes off and flick the light on, swaying slightly and instantly regretting the *big light* syndrome. I hastily twist the dimmer, adjusting it to a softer, more forgiving radiance and relax a little.

"Yeah. Sure. Help yourself, I'll just go change into something more casual."

What the fuck? For God's sake, get a grip girl he is just doing what he's done a million times, over the years. Stop acting like this is any different.

I am annoyed with myself that I'm smug in the knowledge that at least, if Seb is at my house, that means he is not doing the dirty with my neighbour. Heading upstairs, I take my make-up off quickly and cleanse and tone my already rapidly dehydrating skin. I was under no illusions that Sebastian saw me any differently than normal but without my war paint, it meant I wouldn't hope or try. I am suddenly very tired.

Slipping out of my *killer outfit* and into my nightie and pink fluffy marabou slippers I assess my appearance - maybe I should have left my dress on but I'm shattered and the gown is still sexy; after all, I still had my womanly pride, even if she is rather tipsy right now. Scrunching my hair up and giving it a good shake, I check myself in the mirror. Good - just got out of bed look, tick; sexy - but not too desperate look, tick. Hopefully the fact that I'm already dressed for bed will make Seb leave for home sooner. I had actually hoped that I could come home, order a disgustingly guilt-free pizza - to soak up the booze, drown my sorrows and put my favourite PJ's on; then indulge without anyone watching.

"Lu, you're ok if I just crash here aren't you tonight?"

Seb peers around the bedroom door and leans against the oak doorframe, his gorgeous face crumpling in an adorable plea. I hadn't heard him come up the stairs? I thought he wanted another drink? Shit I hope he hadn't been there long.

"Er, yeah, yeah, I suppose so." I stutter and suddenly feel rather naked. Why hadn't I put my dressing gown on?

"I'm just knackered and can't be bothered ordering another Joe

Baxi," he continues and moves towards me and I step back until I hit the wardrobe. Feeling stupid, as I realise he was just heading towards the bed, I watch, silently, as he removes one boot, then the other and begins to take his top off. I cannot seem to look elsewhere. I am immobilised, as I sneak a peak at the hair, which lightly covers his chest. I think I may actually be blushing; either that, or the heating had kicked in big time. *Why is he undressing in here?* I think his close proximity is affecting my body temperature - something that surprises me, as I have seen him shirtless before and managed not to become a dry-mouthed, goggling moron. *That was before you woke up and smelt the companion from heaven!*

"I noticed you've not got a guest bed, anymore, the other night, when I looked in on Finn. If it's OK with you, I'd rather not wake up to the Toy Story montage tomorrow? I'll just share with you. Or the sofa's fine too if you prefer?"

He is so casual that I conclude that in his mind there is nothing weird about sharing a bed with a mate. As he stares at me intently, awaiting my approval, I feel like I'm being pushed into a corner, yet at the same time, he seems so relaxed and unperturbed, I realise that this *moment* doesn't seem to be affecting him in the same way as me. I feel a little foolish to be honest.

I hear myself reply more calmly than I feel. "The bed's fine, you daft thing, it's a king size. We probably won't even know the other is there."

Ha like that is bloody likely!

I leave him throwing the many cushions onto the floor muttering to himself, under his breath.

"Women and cushions - I'll never get it!"

As I clean my teeth in the bathroom, I can hear him moving around in the bedroom. My scalp prickles with a mixture of expectation and fear. I decide to harden myself to it all and just try to treat it, as any other time Seb had stayed. The problem was we'd only ever stayed under the same roof a few times and each one had been in separate rooms and separate beds. Even at University we'd never shared a bed, maybe some floor space in our student accommodation but never a mattress. I really need to get a grip and ignoring my heavily beating heart, and clammy palms I enter my room. The only glow emanating from it is from the fairy lights strewn across the headboard. The effect is very cosy and I instantly rue the day I hung them.

"Right I only have three rules. I get the left side. No socks in bed and no duvet hogging."

I climb into bed and automatically pull the cover up to cocoon my body. Any extra layers will hopefully stop me feeling so vulnerable.

"Alright Boss," Seb smiles sexily and slides, under the bedding. I'm so glad I changed the bed this morning. The sheets are fresh and plumpfy and feel luxurious under my touch.

I'd only managed a brief glimpse of his amazingly buff body in black fitted boxers, as he'd climbed into the bed, and sprawled on his stomach. Now my eyes are drawn to the large bold black scripted font that curls across his back, between his shoulder blades. It spells out *Nuno est tempus* and adds a rakish edge to his classic good looks. *Nuno est tempus* - I think that means *now is the time?* My Latin was seriously rusty from Grammar School, so I might be way of the mark here but we'd done a huge project on the design course using Latin wording in our second year and I'm pretty sure this motto, rang a bell. It made me want to reach out and trace the letters, raised in their darkened ink - feel his skin under my fingertips. I clench my fingers into a fist to stop myself. He has another tattoo of rose, with a cherub on his arm and more script wording. His tattooist was seriously good. It looked very romantic and a true work of art in black and grays, with fabulous shading; my mouth waters.

Could he get any more delicious?

I lean over to turn off the light, desperate to stop the torture and the darkness enfolds us. Instantly I'm cushioned in security. *At least now he won't see me drooling. When did Sebastian become such an Adonis? It must be all that construction work.*

"Night Seb." I snuggle down chewing thoughtfully on my lip.

I can feel him shuffling around and getting comfortable. The break in silence is a welcome relief and I begin to relax and close my eyes, when his deep voice shatters me.

"I'm not tired… yet."

WTF?

Why the hell had he come to bed then?

"You'll drift off soon. I'm shattered," I lie.

The reality was I'd probably not get a wink of sleep, as I'm surrounded, by his masculine scent, body heat and the copious amounts of testosterone now filling my bedroom. The usually cavernous bed, most definitely feels smaller with him in it. He is so broad and long. *I wonder if that is the case down below?*

Silence.

Then I feel his finger at my back, barely there. His hand increases its pressures, sliding slowly and softly down the centre of my spine, tracing each vertebrae sensually. My skin instantly blazes under his touch and my heart begins to pound incessantly in my chest. I can hear the blood bubbling in my ears, the silence around us is deafening. Surely he can hear my heartbeat? I try to stay still and swallow deeply to wet my already drying mouth. I'm struggling to breathe.

Breathe you silly woman. Breathe!

The air is taut with thick sexual tension.

What is he doing? Please don't stop.

He continues his trail along my back, tracing a fingertip lightly over my nape on the way up and drops his palm, cupping my shoulder firmly. Tingles of excitement shoot up my neck and up across my scalp and I roll my head in towards his hand. It stills. *What am I doing? This is my friend and we're both fuelled by alcohol.*

Feeling a little uncomfortable with what is happening, I gently lift his big hand and turn to push it back towards his chest.

"Go to sleep Sebastian, you're pissed. I think you're forgetting who you're in bed with. It's *me* Lu."

I catch a glimpse of him briefly, over my shoulder; his slow sexy smile says it all.

"I've had a few, yes, but I'm not inebriated Lulu. I know exactly whose body I'm enjoying - *or trying to at least*!"

I can feel him grinning against my neck. His breath grazes the soft baby hair there and sends sharp electric currents coursing underneath my skin and to all my most sensitive areas. He continues on this path, dropping his mouth to trail soft languid kisses along my shoulder, reaching the top of my collarbone with a slow feathery lick.

"What are you doing Seb?"

God it felt good. My body burns like it is awakening from a deep and delicious sleep.

"Something I should have done a long time ago," he murmurs gruffly into my hair. "You smell so good. You are most definitely an edible little one."

I am most definitely turned on but also incredibly confused. My body and my brain seemed to be fighting a war against one another.

"Don't be silly, you're not with it. Let's just go to sleep."

Although part of me, thinks - *really? Does he really want me? I don't want this to stop and isn't this what you ached for, deep down - what you wanted to ask him to do?*

"I don't want to sleep Lu. The one thing that has got me through the last months away from home and my family and friends was the fact that you were here, in the centre of it all."

I spin around to face him, in shock, pulling the cover away from us both. My eyes have adjusted to the dark and I can see him albeit vaguely. My heart is pounding so fast I can feel it in my throat.

"I don't understand Seb. I thought you liked Meg."

He tilts his head to one side and slowly slips his hand around the back of my neck, drawing me leisurely in towards him and commands in a deep sexy voice, "Stop thinking, you stubborn woman and just go with it."

As I'm about to reply, his warm mouth covers mine, creating a seal, which I can tell he is smug about. I am trapped and can't speak. His low groan of success is a complete turn on, as I give myself up to the first intimate kiss we have ever shared. His tongue licks mine tentatively, inquisitively, stirring me and with my moan of rapturous approval, he moves in to deepen the arrangement. His hands are at my back and I can feel myself becoming breathless with anticipation.

Who would have known that Seb, could kiss like this?

Who would have known that he could make me quiver like this?

Why had we not done this before?

"I can still hear the cogs turning Lu. Relax and let me do this... please."

He pulls away for a moment to slide me under him, so that he is gazing down upon me. He is completely in control and I can tell he likes it that way. In an instant he swoops down and his mouth is on mine again, teasing, smiling whilst he plants small feathery kisses on my face, nose, ears and down onto my neck.

"It's time we tested our chemistry. After a decade, *its time*," he states with absolute certainty.

The playful mood quickly changes as he comes back to my mouth and looking into his eyes I can see the raw passion, he has for me. It is the same passion I saw in his dark blackened eyes, whilst he watched me dance in the bar earlier that night. They're like dark glossy chocolate, with hazel flecks and glittering with need.

I still can't quite believe it but I am enjoying this too much to stop. Instead I decide to deepen the invasion and encourage him to continue his investigations. The only thing I know is that for this

61

moment, I do not want these igniting sparks between us to fizzle out. I need to see if we would be as good together as I felt we could; even if it was for one mere night. I am undeniably certain it would be worth it - worth the tarnish, of being another one-night-stand conquest. We could offer each other something. He could enjoy the challenge of bedding his long-term friend, and I could be awakened sexually, my body brought alive by a man's touch again.

"OK." I succumb weakly as my breath catches and give myself up to months, no years of pent up frustration.

Chapter 6

Lucia

For what seems like hours, but in reality is probably only a few minutes, we glory in the sensation of our touches; mouth-on mouth, breath on breath, hearts beating hard and fast against one another. Seb moves downwards. His wet lips move along the line of my black lace nightgown and hooking his finger loosely inside the strap of one arm, he slowly flicks it down, freeing my straining right breast, as the silk falls to bare me to him. His gaze is greedy but his temperament is calm and I arch my back, instinctively, pushing against him in desperation, as he bends his head and takes my already swollen nipple into his mouth. The moist, hot sensation as he draws deeply on it, almost undoes me, as he slowly, teasingly traces my nipple with his tongue and suckles. Then cupping my breast almost roughly, he pulls on my peak until it screams to attention, before moving to the other already erect breast to repeat the mouth-watering process, over and over again. Oh. My. Fucking. God, this is exquisite - all slow and sensual with an air of frenzy at the same moment.

"God you turn me on!" he practically growls the words and pulls me closer, grinding his pelvis into mine, his freshly brushed breath on my face. "I've wanted to do this all night."

I arch my body, pressing myself into him, his words a complete turn-on. There is no mistaking his reaction to me. He seems to be revelling in my body and worshipping it in a way I have not experienced before. I'd forgotten how good it was to be touched and my body is responding to every stroke, every lick, and each sensation. I'm shattering slowly from within.

Niall had been much more about *getting on with the matter at hand* -

'shove it in and off we go'. There was nothing quick about Sebastian's leisurely appreciation of my quivering body. He was all about the foreplay.

"Such beautiful breasts Lu, I've always wanted to see if they were as amazing to touch as they looked. The days at Uni I daydreamed about them," he grins wickedly in the shadows.

I moan and push them up into his hands and slide my now trembling fingers down his sides, lightly grazing them with my nails, towards his hips. He shivers under my touch and his cock juts, pressing into my thigh. This is not the reaction of a friend and he does not seem drunk. I feel dizzy with arousal, confusion and am trying to just enjoy the moment, but there are so many unanswered questions. Oh God, he is doing things to me that I didn't know I was capable of feeling.

"Take this off," he demands almost desperately. "I need to feel skin on skin."

I remove my nightie and toss it to the floor at his command and hear his hiss of approval. Our mouths meet, teeth clashing, tongues duelling, his hands cradling my face before relinquishing his grip and dropping a roughened palm to cup my heavy aching breast. My low moan of acceptance makes him growl.

"Beautiful. Sexy. Tonight you're mine." His words roll over me, like teasing fingertips and I feel myself grow wetter. He moves lower and trails soft kisses down my torso and onto the top of my pelvis, lightly licking my hipbone. *Don't leave. Stay up this end. Please.*

I flinch almost immediately as he nears my c-section scar. *Oh shit.*

Automatically, Seb senses my tension and looks up at me. "Too much Baby?"

I nod mutely and he comes back to kiss me intensely, deeply. I can feel myself hot and wet and ready for him and my sensitive nub aches for some hard attention. It really has been too long! I am just about to trace my hand down the front of his Calvin's, when he unexpectedly pulls away.

"I wonder if we are taking this too soon?" he whispers into my neck, whilst stroking my face with his knuckle in a repetitive motion.

What? No. Don't stop!

All of a sudden the room is completely silent, deafeningly so. It's like a cold slap, to an already highly tempestuous situation. Like the spindle on a record player has been crudely scraped across a vinyl. I instantly recoil, the defence shutters come down with alarming ferocity and I move away from underneath him. The only sounds are our laboured panting.

Sebastian tries to stop me retracting but I continue to push against him. I feel claustrophobic, panicky and yes… fucking stupid. Suddenly I need some serious space. *Does he regret it? Maybe he saw my scars and decided he no longer found me attractive? Maybe he was actually just pissed and was sobering up to this being a bad idea?*

I can feel my throat getting raw and suffocatingly tight with emotion; I sense that given half a chance, I could breakdown and sob uncontrollably and I'm not a pretty crier. I feel totally humiliated and need to be alone, yet every part of my freshly awakened body is crying out to be satisfied. Maybe I should just pounce on him? But then he may not respond, which would be another devastating blow to my confidence. He has just ruined a truly special moment by being a gentleman or I have with my sensitive body issues? I don't know what just happened but… *fuck!*

I gaze across at the alarm clock on the bedside table. It glows 4am. I've got to get up in a few hours to collect Finn from Mum and Dad's. Rolling over, I take a deep shaky breath, followed by a gulp to stop the impending tears and quietly say, "I think maybe you're right." And for the second time that night I repeat, "Let's try to get some sleep."

I roll onto my side, pulling the duvet like a cling film vacuum around my body. I can't bear to have him near me; I'd explode. This way he can't see my desolation and the fat teardrop that rolls down my cheek and plops onto my arm.

He is silent. We lie in bed, back to back. The air is thick with emotions, unsaid feelings and unfinished business.

⧽⧼

I get no sleep, as I procrastinate over the last few hours' events and chastise myself over and over again, for potentially ruining the best friendship I've ever had with a man, with my bloody horniness!

I quietly turn to sneak a glance at him, whilst he sleeps, careful not to disturb anything that might wake him. I sigh. I'm dreading seeing him this morning. Oh my God! *How did things go so wrong?*

This is why you don't mix sex with friendship. Someone always got hurt. My bloody gut needs to shout its instinct much louder in future. I'd forgotten about my war wounds, probably because he'd sprung things on me and I'd been relaxed by champagne; no man had seen it since Niall and he had hated it with a passion and made me very aware of that fact. A constant reminder of Finn's arrival and my body changing, he'd never *gone down on me* again - *"It's repulsive"* - had been his words and I had to agree. The scar angrily worked its way across my body in a zig-zag fashion, from hip to hip, red and angry and a total mess.

Finn's birth had been traumatic to say the least, 36hours of labour, barely 4cm dilation and his heartbeat had slowed, resulting in an emergency section, where the only available surgeon at midnight had been a 4ft 11 junior, who needed to stand on a box to perform the cut. It had been barbaric.

My *not so* little boy had been far too large for my petite frame, causing huge internal bleeding, a cracked rib and many necessary blood transfusions, just to get him out - weighing a healthy 9lbs at only 36weeks. Heaven knows what he'd have weighed had he gone full-term or worse over - perhaps I would have delivered a fully grown man - I'd certainly felt like that was the case at the time.

Many had thought Niall's coldness after Finn's birth was a direct result of post-traumatic stress but he denied it and in the end I gave up trying. I'd nearly died giving birth to his son; our son - the most beautiful baby boy and my joy, and now I was to be punished.

To me my scar is evidence that I had worked hard to bring Finn into the world but I am also aware that it is brutal looking and now my fears and hang-ups, may have fucked up my chances at continuing to moving forward. Learn from your mistakes Lu - I can hear my parent's voices in my head - they were right. This wasn't going to define me. It was a hurdle I had to get over and Niall wasn't my lover anymore. Niall didn't own me anymore. It was his hang-up, inflicted upon me and he would never have the privilege of having sex with me again. Now Seb on the other hand…

Chapter 7

Lucia

I wander into the kitchen and flick the red metallic Dualit kettle on. I'd managed three hours sleep and I seriously ache like I have done ten rounds with Tyson. Sebastian is still in bed and I can't hear anything overhead so he must be out like a light.

Oh my word – what the hell was last night all about?

I actually feel physically sick. I sense that we've stepped into some kind of alternate universe, and that he will walk in any moment and act as though nothing had ever happened and it was my saucy over-sexed mind working into overload. I'm dragged from my thoughts when I hear a rustle behind me.

"Morning Lulu." He cheekily slaps me on my jean-clad bum. "Ahh! Cup-of-Tea."

He grabs the cup and snatches a triangle of my toast and marmite. Screwing his face up when he starts to chew. Then slowly he starts to shake his head from side to side, weighing it up and jutting out his bottom lip, a la De Niro he mumbles, "Not bad. Always thought I'd be a hater."

I do nothing but stare at him, frozen to the spot. *What the fuck?* Why was he acting like nothing had happened? I *am* in that dreaded alternate universe.

"Any chance of a lift home Lu? God what did we drink last night? I'm not sure I'll be hitting the gym today." He rubs his forehead, wincing at the slightest touch.

"Champagne. Beer. Wine. Oh and those slippery nipple shots that Jess made us all do." I instantly regret mentioning the word nipple, as my obvious blush prickles up over my face and across my scalp. He

67

either doesn't notice how uncomfortable I am or decides to ignore it and continues.

"Oh God yeah. Good night though - your mate Meg's fun. Oh I borrowed your spare toothbrush. Hope you're OK with that?" he frowns at me inquisitively, lifting my favourite red and white striped mug to his mouth - *my* cup of tea.

"Urgghh!" he sputters after a big gulp, handing me back the mug. "I forgot you have sugar in yours." His face wrinkles in disgust. It served him right.

"Maybe you should get your own, next time," I mutter, going to the sink to pour the offending tea away.

Is he kidding me? What an arse-hole. I can't believe he even mentioned Meg. Well two can play at that game. "Chris seems nice too? I'll need to get to know him better, now that he's staying at yours."

One look at Seb's face and I know that I've touched a nerve, and it's had the reaction I'd hoped it would - even if he isn't sure of it yet and the knowledge comforts me. If he were jealous about that then he wouldn't want Chris to be my first since Niall - or Leo; or worse yet, Niall again. *He doesn't need to know it probably wouldn't be any of them. Chris and Niall, not a chance. Leo highly unlikely, but the jury's still out.*

I can't be around him any longer though, not with this stagnant uncomfortable banter and I need to get out of his vicinity right now, before I jump him - no sex for nearly a year and lets face it nearly a decade of crap sex, meant that a quick fumble without release, with someone who knows what they're doing is like putting new batteries in the vibby and sticking it on full-blast, then - responsive much?

Grabbing my car keys and not waiting for a reaction from him I huff rudely. "Right, come on then, as I've got to pick up Finn. I haven't got all day."

I don't wait to see if he is following, I know he is. I can feel his sheer presence at my back; it's palpable. Everything is totally fucked up. As I lock the front door and we climb into the car together, I realise that he doesn't appear to remember anything that happened between us last night, and I'm not sure whether what I am feeling is huge relief or massive disappointment.

The drive to his house is shall we say - difficult. We both remain resolutely silent. I concentrate on the winding road ahead and he seems to have found the view out of the passenger window, particularly interesting all of a sudden. Luckily, he only lives ten minutes away from mine but those ten minutes feel like a lifetime though enable me the quiet time I need to put my plan in action.

I've barely pulled to a stop outside his house when he unclips his seatbelt, jumps out the car, slamming the door in his desperation to exit. It's been a while since I'd been to his new home and hunching down I look out of the passenger window up at the imposing structure. Its huge glass windows wink at us, like watchful eyes, hooded by the immense dormers that house them. The finished article was a masterpiece - a real piece of architectural design.

As I watch him fumbling with his keys outside the car, I grab my phone and hurriedly locate his contact info, to create a new message.

It was now or never.

Last night had been a total disaster but it hadn't been planned and what it had shown me, was…

A) He was interested in me sexually!

B) We were compatible; boy, were we compatible!

C) I had issues about my body that I just needed to get over - with someone I trusted.

I'm bloody sure he could manage one night of passion with an old friend. He was willing to tumble almost anything in a skirt, surely he could help a girl out in need and be my fuck buddy?

I type the words I'd been forming in my head all morning. The letters blur in front of me in my hurried fumbles. I'm keen to send the text quickly and see that he actually receives it. A quick glance up to see his whereabouts, tells me that Sebastian must have pressed a button on his keys, as the huge gates lurch into motion and they seamlessly open inwards into the curved driveway. He strolls through them and they begin to close. Quickly running my eyes over my typed message, and licking my lips in both determination and apprehension I hit send, before I can back out.

I have a proposition for you.

Consider this - one night of sex between friends.

No ties, no commitment. I'm open to anything.

I need to get back in the saddle and I trust you in every way.

Think about it. L x

Oh Shit - what have I done?

Wincing, I peek to see his reaction. *Surely he's got it by now?* My hands are literally trembling and I span them firmly on the steering wheel in front of me, my knuckles whitening as I take a deep breath. I glance one last time in his direction and in that moment Sebastian turns towards me, having the decency to bend and mouth, "Cheers!" but obviously in a hurry to escape. I see him extend his thumb and little finger and put them up to his ear, waggling them in the *call* sign.

Cheers?

Then I watch him locate his phone from his pocket, presumably peruse my message and stop dead in his tracks, his back to me, obviously deep in thought.

Bet you never thought I'd be this daring Mr. Silver?

I wait a few seconds longer, watching to see his next move before losing all bottle and flooring it to escape any potential embarrassment. He could message me his answer, that way it felt more official somehow and if he said no, he wouldn't see my utter devastation.

"Mum… meeeee!" Finn throws himself at me like a launched missile, as I walk into my Mum and Dad's house. I wrap his chubby little legs around my waist and bury my nose in his freshly washed hair, spinning him around until he squeals in delight.

"Hey gorgeous. How's my favourite boy?" He giggles and plants a wet kiss on the end of my nose.

"I'm your only boy Mummy, silly billy."

Yes you are! I think to myself. He doesn't realise how true that statement is and until now it hadn't really mattered. I carry him into the kitchen, where my mum is dutifully cooking Sunday lunch for us all.

"Hey Hunny."

She glances up and then goes straight back to stirring the gravy. The smells evaporating from the enormous black Aga are divine and envelope me in much-needed home comforts. Trust your mum to always make things better.

"Hey you, yourself. Thanks for having Finn Mum. You're an absolute star." She smiles in adoration at our little man. "It's my pleasure Darling. You know how much we love to have him. He was as good as gold, as he always is for his Ninni," she stresses in the goo-goo-ga-ga baby voice she reserves only for him.

70

He preens under her gaze. *God we really don't help women do we?* From the minute these men are born, they are pandered to, pampered and generally made to feel as though they are Gods in our eyes. I have to admit this little guy was to me but I was going to have to watch it, as he grows and ensure I don't turn him into a total chauvinist - his future partner will thank me in years to come!

My mum continues chattering. "He slept through until 7am and then came into our bed and bounced on your Dad, until he finally caved and took Finn to the wreck with Madame Tina, to burn off some energy."

She is of course talking about the family Shih tzu, so named due to her uncanny likeness to one of Mrs. Turner's infamous stage wigs. I laugh at the thought of my Dad juggling the two of them at *sparrow fart* o'clock. Poor thing, he is good.

Kissing Finn's soft hair again I put him down onto the oak floor and pat his squishy bum. "Off you go and find Gramps, whilst mummy helps Ninni with the food."

I give my mum a big hug and kiss her Chanel No.5 scented skin. Nina Myers still looks fabulous with a figure and velvety skin that any woman half her age would be proud of. Unfortunately I haven't inherited her size 8 genes - Suzie got those, the lucky bitch - but I did get my green eyes from Mum, and as there are apparently only 2%, of the population with green eyes, I am grateful for their uniqueness, at least.

"Love you mum. You're so good to me."

She puts down the tea towel she's been drying her hands with and places one hand on the sink to balance herself.

"Everything OK Lulu?"

Bless, she was so intuitive. No everything was not Ok I inwardly screamed, I am desperate to talk to someone but my Mum was not the person… yet anyway. She adored Sebastian and had spent years trying to encourage (in her non-gentle patter), a romantic relationship between us but if she was given even a glimmer of hope that this was on the cards, God help us all. She'd have her wedding fascinator all picked out by the end of the day.

"I'm fine, just very tired that's all. I didn't get much sleep." Due to the fact that I had a beautifully buff man lying beside me all night, who had started something monumental, thought better of it and seemingly not remembered anything in the morning.

"Did you and Suzie have a good night most importantly?"

Hmm, what could I say to that? "Great night actually."

Which was partially true. "We went to the Champagne Bar in Lords, and boy am I paying for it today. Serious hangover."

She wrinkles her nose in disapproval. A devout non-drinker, she didn't like it when her daughters went on the lash. It wasn't feminine or necessary to indulge in alcohol, which blurred the lines of reality.

I hold my hands up in a defensive pose. "I know. I know, but it was Suzie's birthday and I needed to blow off some steam. They made me do it." I pouted and followed it with a chuckle, as memories of chanting *down in one, down in one* came back to haunt me.

Mum continues peeling the vegetables that are neatly arranged in front of her. "Gino told your Dad that Sebastian is back from Dubai. Is that true?"

God you can't keep anything quiet from our lot. Through gritted teeth I shrug, "Yeah, he joined us last night. It was good to see him again."

Stop there! Don't – say – anything - else. My Mum has a natty way of getting information out of people that they neither wanted to provide, nor often realized that they had. She could have sidelined as an interrogator for MI5.

Admitting defeat my mum patted my arm. "Go call your Dad Honey to wash up, we'll be eating in about 20 minutes. Get Finn to show you the new bike we bought him, he's getting really good with the stabilisers on. God that little boy is cute. We're all thoroughly obsessed!"

She is right of course, we are all devoted to Finn and I immediately feel guilty again that I've been acting more like a floozy than a faithful mother.

"Are you sure I can't do anything to help?"

"No off you go. Your Dad needs some time with his little girl."

Smiling to myself I head out to the garden - I'm hardly his little girl anymore but she's right I do need to spend some time with my Dad. He seemed quiet these days, since he'd retired from the legal circuit. It really was beautiful here; a hidden dip, nestled in the Yorkshire Dales, which relaxed my inner turmoil's the minute I arrived - it was a stress heads paradise - the ideal mix of tranquility and opulence. My dad had found the land, whilst out jogging thirty years earlier - an old mill site desperate to be developed. And that's what they did - built, dug and renovated to achieve their dream home, complete with granny flat and huge lake. My stay-at-home mum had utilised her naturally born design skills on the interiors and I'd been, bitten by the bug, watching her develop and choose colours and fabrics. It had been wonderful growing up there.

Snapping out of my thoughts I hear squeals of delight ricochet in ripples across the lake, echoing alongside Madam Tina's incessant barking at Ken the swan. Finn is obviously finding it hilarious. My Dad, as calm as ever, is going into the extreme details of the lesser-spotted woodpecker, happily tweeting away in the tree above them. The smallest and most rare of the woodpecker family, so unusual to find in our vicinity, Finn's far more bothered with removing Gramps flat cap and launching it into the water beneath them. Simple things!

"Finland - don't do that to Gramps' hat." I try to sound cross, and fish it out of the pond, twisting hard to drain the excess water.

"Soz Dad."

"No worries Lulu. It's Finn's new game. Thanks for rescuing it. Wasn't so lucky with my reading glasses, this mornings paper and one of my slippers."

I wince - maybe we should find a fishing net?

"Mum said lunch is nearly ready so we should wash up but I just wanted to watch the Finnster on his new bike."

"Yay!" Finn wriggles his body to a point where my Dad has to release him, before he drops him from a great height. "Watch me Mummy." I grin as he puffs his chest out with pride and disappears into the garage to clamber onto his shiny new toy.

"Thanks for treating him Dad - you've spoiled him… again!"

"Gramps' prerogative my chucks." Drawing me in for a cuddle, I relax into his familiar strength, squeezing back when he drops a kiss onto the top of my head. "We enjoy it. Brings back lovely memories of you and Suzie. Just wish I'd been around more to enjoy you two."

I look up at him then - his eyes wistful. Mac Myers had just retired after 20 years as a Crown Court Judge, and 22 years previously as a criminal Barrister in Lords. His reputation was second to none - a demon in the courtroom, and a gentleman on the golf course. He really had made it in his chosen career but at the sacrifice of his family time with us when we were young, and now that I have Finn, I understand how hard it must have been for him.

Trying to lighten the mood, I chatter about Suzie's birthday, work and The Ashton as we marvel at Finn's capabilities on the new bike. I'm surprised when he changes the subject. "Bob Silver and I played 9 holes the other day. He's got a wicked slice. He said Sebastian is back in town?"

Here we go. "Yeah. I saw him last night actually. He was out with us all."

"Really? Bob said that Silver Con is booming - something about a Dubai Hotel, Juna something or other...?"

"Jannah Hotel," I correct him.

"Jannah... well, anyway if the sale goes through, at the expected price, Sebastian is set to make a cool 10 million from his investment. That lad is going places; real drive and ambition. Always knew he had it in him. 10 million!"

This is just like Dad - trying to sell Sebastian with his achievements and financial stability. I understand it - after Niall I need to feel safe - but this is probably why I'd never looked in Sebastian's direction seriously before. Everyone wanted us to be together - the pressure was immense and I'm not sure we could ever live up to it. God I hope The Silver's weren't pushing me on Sebastian - how embarrassing.

"Yes Seb is doing really well Dad. He's never home but goes with the job I suppose."

"I like him - good solid upbringing and family values. Bob & Bitzi Silver are lovely people. Is he seeing anyone?"

Really? "I'm not sure." *Please let's not go into this.* "Finn come on pet, time for lunch."

We turn to head back towards the house, and I link arms with Dad, as Finn zooms past at breakneck speed. "Ha ha beat you!" We both laugh at his silliness.

"Hasn't Seb got a brother too?"

Oh come on?

"Nathan. Dad I'm fine you know."

"I know you are Darling. I just want you to be happy and it'd be nice for Finn to have a male role model, under 50 to look up to on a daily basis." *I can't disagree there.*

I lean in to kiss his cheek. "Not all men are as fabulous as you Dad. Thanks for caring though."

"A father never stops worrying Lulu. Us parents know a good thing when we see it - it's our duty to point it out to you and Sebastian is a *good thing*."

Admitting defeat here I smile up at him and we head into the dining room to eat. He's right Seb *is* a good thing. He's also *very very* bad...

74

As I leave my parents' house, stuffed to the gills and the car brimming with cling-film covered tupper-wares that would feed Finn and I for the next week, I smile with fondness. I do the usual six-beep salute, 1-2-1-1-1, as we cruise up the winding, Christmas tree littered drive and laugh, as I see the full-family send-off in my rear-view mirror. They never disappoint. The minute I reach the top of the drive, my phone woofs at me. The reception must have finally kicked in and glancing at my iPhone I can see that there are two missed calls, and a text. They are all from Sebastian. I want to punish him by ignoring the text for at least 24hours but curiosity gets the better of me - I've butterflies in my tummy as I open it.

What if he says, "no thanks?"

Thanks for last night Lu. Must do it again soon. x

Eh? What does that mean?

No mention of my offer? Does he now remember what happened or is he just being a mate about our night out? Talk about cryptic. I decide not to reply and to sleep on it, something I hope he's also considering. I desperately need some serious shuteye and my head is in fucking bits.

Why did I put myself out there like that?

Turning round to squeeze Finn's foot, I focus on him and join him in the *Bob the Builder* theme song. Can we fix it…yes we can! How apt.

I'm not sure that is the case this time.

As I settle down for the night I decide to reach out to Abby. We've not spoken since last night and she had no idea about what had happened between Sebastian and I or my proposal of a night of passion to him. I type the words and as I do they sting. The fact that Seb didn't want me enough is soul-destroying in itself but I'm annoyed that I'd put myself out there only to be left feeling vulnerable and weak and more importantly really *stupid*.

**Lu: Seb & I got down & dirty but didn't finish the deed!
He chickened out - now I feel like crap!**

Left in limbo. Got stupid text from him saying THANKS! WTF?

*

Abby: What a Seb...ASS...tian!
Play him at his own game Babe. His interest is peeked; now peek at other male interests. Maybe you & Seb are BEST as BEST FRIENDS without the complication of sex? X

Abs always gave great advice but the last sentence of her text is something I'm not ready to hear. She may be right but seeing it glaringly illuminated, is way too real.

Lu: Should have probably consulted you before I offered him 'me on a platter for one night only', no ties; no commitments just hot sex x

*

Abby: You did WHAT? Wow Lulu found her balls at last. Proud of you girl! It's about time you got laid and may as well be with an expert. Too many years being fucked by an amateur, now its time to get down and dirty ;)

*

Lu: I know - that's what I thought! Ha ha you make me laugh. What about you - anything happen with Nathan?

*

Abby: Just a peck - Was hoping for his PECKER!
He's asked me to S & G's on Sat night. Yay!
I like him Lu Bu - really f**king like him.
Crap! Better go I'm knackered. Love U. Mwah!

It's only as I'm about to connect my phone up to my charger I realise that I've another text come through, whilst I've been messaging Abs. It's from Niall.

I messed up Saturday. Let me come over Mu Mu?

I slam the phone down and turn the light off. Total douche-bag! It

76

is Sunday night, Finn's in bed and I've work in the morning. I'm annoyed with myself that deep down, I know that if the text had been from Seb, I'd have unlocked the door and forgone my beauty sleep - especially if he was there to give me an answer to my proposition.

Sebastian

Popping the top off a small Belgian beer, I pad through to the living room. Chris was out for the night leaving me alone with my thoughts. I'm glad of the silence. After Lu had dropped me off, I'd headed straight for bed and slept for five hours straight. Yet I still felt drained; my mind filled at every moment with *her text*.

One night with Lucia Myers - the girl I'd lusted after, for over a decade.

I have to admit she had nerve, to put herself out there like that. Especially after I'd fucked things up so badly last night. *What was wrong with me?*

I had wanted to kiss her all night, thought about nothing else really, since I left her Friday. I'd watched her bumping and grinding with Abby on the dance floor; couldn't take my eyes off her and neither could Chris! That had been an unexpected annoyance. At least that new boyfriend of hers hadn't shown up!

I'd managed to cleverly manipulate the situation so that I was in their cab, ended up back at hers and even sharing her bed and yet she still couldn't see how much I desired her. Finally, connecting with her after all these years had been everything I could have hoped for and more - she was receptive and hot and we'd gone much further than I'd ever intended to, our first time - I'd probably pushed her too hard. I think back to the moment I neared her scar - she'd flinched. There was definitely more to that issue - Niall had been an odd ball about it, I know that much. Gino had told me in the past but I'd never discussed it with Lu before. We were close as mates but some things you didn't talk about with the opposite sex unless you were bedding them!

I didn't give a flying fuck about her scar. She'd had a horrific time when Finn was born - scared the hell out of me at the time but I want her to be uninhibited when we finally have sex. I've waited too long for it not to be right.

This morning had been shit. I'd waffled on about marmite and booze and knew she was desperate to get rid of me; I was desperate to escape and if it had been any other woman, I would have sneaked out whilst she slept. But I couldn't do that to Lu. My cheeks still ached from the fake bright smile I'd plastered across them. And that drive to mine - it was the most uncomfortable experience of my life. I wracked my brain, considering what, if anything could be said that would make this whole situation any better. *I should never have forced the situation so soon. I should never have tried it on with her.*

Dropping down onto the sofa, I switch the TV on with a flick of the wrist; scrolling through the planner and shaking my head at my stupidity. I groan aloud.

Cheers? What the fuck was I thinking?

I'd forced her into a compromising position, felt her come alive and let go in my arms and then left her hanging. Then I'd asked her for a bloody lift home!

Dick!

I can still see her face, her response, as I waggle the phone signal at her - utter contempt didn't cut it. It was at that second my mobile had buzzed and everything had changed. I'd been bowled over by her proposition - never seen it coming and pretty much everything else had gone out of the window from thereon. I found it hard to breathe, dry mouth, sweaty palms - there was no way I could think on my feet. How could I control this situation and get things back on my terms?

Fucking Cheers!

She'd left before I could respond, driving like a lunatic as per usual, to go collect Finn. Now, as I glance at my phone, my mind working overtime, I make the positive decision to send out an olive branch to her and punch out a reply - I'm still not sure how to play this? Yeah, best keep it safe! I've got to send something, have some connection with her - no connection would be like sticking two fingers up at her!

I need to sleep on things before going all in or keeping things friendly. I want to take her to bed badly but I'm still not sure if I want long-term and am I just being a selfish git? Is this just about the challenge again - as it had been with so many other women? If I go all in, *this is it*. Keeping it friendly - I'm not sure I can do that either? Problem is, she's all I can think about - her lime green eyes, those kissable lips, those amazing breasts and having her naked beneath me, open to everything, with no ties, no commitment, just friends becoming fuck buddies - Jesus, she was making it easy for me - I'd be a fool *not* to accept!

Tomorrow I'll make it clear to her what my ultimate decision is. The chance is there to take, without ties, so what is stopping you?

Chapter 8

Lucia

I'd been manic at work all morning and finally pushing my chair back, I stretch and head for a much needed cuppa. Mondays were always hectic but today more than usual.

"Oooh are you brewing up?" Jackie begs pouting in desperation, as she glues a pantone colour swatch onto the mood board for our latest client.

We've both been busily putting the finishing touches to the portfolio of ideas for our Holdgate Hotel *The Ashton*. I am so excited about my concepts for this current job - they are rocking – all baroque, damask and flock. I'm literally salivating at the thought of it all coming together. One word *sumptuous*; that's the theme I'm going for. The dramatic vision I have created for their new honeymoon suite is something I've had in my head for months, but not had the right project to apply the creative juices to. If this goes well, we are guaranteed to get each and every other room in the hotel, which is being re-vamped by the new owner, James Marcell. Plus he knew everyone, so the word-of-mouth marketing would be fabulous. Colin will flip if we get this coup.

"Quick cuppa and a bite to eat and then I must go face the client."

I wander into the little kitchenette at the back of our studio and ready our drinks. I still haven't replied to Seb's text and wonder where he is at the moment. My thoughts are interrupted when Colin comes hurtling through the door.

"Oh. My. God." His hands are held up in front of him and move dramatically, pausing with each dragged out word. "What a weekend.

Did you go out Babe?"

He looks at me for the first time properly. "What the hell's up with your face? I know I'm late and I know we have The Ashton thingie but I had to get my hair blow-dried for it. Please don't be mad!"

He whines and despite my gloomy mood, I smile and relax a little. Pouring out the teas, I add another bag to a china cup for him. "Your hair looks fab Hun. I'm not pissed at all, just glad that you're here and ready to blow this one out of the park."

"I'll be happy to blow James Marcell, *in* the park, if it will help us get more work; the man is blu...ddy gorgeous," he comments seriously in his camp Yorkshire drawl.

I chuckle. "Er no, that's not necessary Darling, not until this job is done." Reprimanding him lightly. "Colin Duttine, you are a raging hormonal, proud, gay man, but we need this job and there will be no extra curricular activities with it."

He had history in this department. Bless, he was fucked if he ever got kidnapped. Stockholm syndrome seemed to take effect with every difficult male client we took on. The more pernickety the boss, the deeper he fell... well until the next contract anyway.

Col pouts prettily but grabs his and Jackie's cups and wiggles his way out towards his desk throwing out, "Someone didn't get any... again, this weekend!" in a petulant snide.

"Hey, no fair, actually I kind of did but I'm not sure what to do with it now."

"Stop the bus. You dirty bitch, tell me everything."

I suddenly remember the embarrassing ringtone. "You need to leave my phone alone you naughty boy."

"Ah you liked this one did you? Very appropriate me thinks..."

"Col - leave my phone be - Finn could have heard it!" I give him my best schoolteacher face but his fluttering eyelashes undo me.

"Soz Babe - tickled me pink - I nearly set your text to 'me *fucky sucky*' but was actually thinking about the boy then, so played it safe."

"No more."

"Yes Boss. Who heard it?"

"Sebastian."

Col clasps his hands together at this tidbit and hollows his cheeks dramatically. "Well... my lovelies, my work here is done. About fucking time you two got it on - you did didn't you?"

God, Colin was funny. He really was a tonic on a crappy Monday morning but I am not about to divulge my inner most thoughts to such an opinionated gossip, even if his opinions were probably correct. I'm just not ready yet, but maybe a little teaser... "No. I'm not divulging." I say firmly. "There is a time and a place and now is not it! Needless to say, I never would have thought that Sebastian Silver, my best friend of years, would be such... a good... kisser."

Bullshit - you always knew he'd be amazing!

I shrug off the comment and bite my lip in memory, instinctively rubbing my thumbnail along my bottom lip with the concentration. I'm overwhelmed by short film snippets of the live sex show that was my life on Saturday night, replaying in my mind. I feel myself growing warm with the memories and at the same time remind myself that I'm acting like a giddy teenager!

"Party pooper!" Colin shakes his head and tuts but thankfully lets it go – he obviously hasn't noticed the heat generating from my vicinity.

"Oh Lucia before you go, I forgot to mention there's a delivery arrived for you from Fresh Water Couture!" Jackie yells across to me, with an excited raise of her eyebrows.

"Lucky Bitch – someone's flashing the cash." Colin's mouth is reduced to a small bum hole in annoyance.

I giggle at his pretend spitefulness and head over to Jackie who disappears underneath the reception desk and hands me a long narrow black velvet box, tied with a red satin ribbon. Like an excited little girl on Christmas morning I make fast work of untying the elegant fastening. Fresh Water Couture or FWC as the beautiful, monogrammed crest is branded, is a luxury boutique florist in the centre of Lords and my favourite of all time!

I ease the velvet lid off and peer inside. Sitting on silver branded tissue paper, is a deep red, almost black velvet rose, its stem continually supplied with water for its transit by a small glass vial at the base of the box. I marvel at the beauty and simplicity of the bud. Its blood red and plum petals are nestled softly against the lush fabric and a diamante Swarovski crystal is pinned in the centre of the stigma, where the rose is a pure ruby.

I take a moment to take the lovely gesture in.

It's completely interrupted by Colin's petulant sulky voice. "Well? Who's it from Lady Boss? Do tell? We're waiting here on bloody baited breath!"

Underneath the silver tissue, I reveal a minute envelope, which houses a thick cream note card with a printed message, in a beautiful scripted font.

It reads…

FWC

I accept your offer

x

I hear my breath hitch as I gasp, and quickly remembering where I am, then smile and hold the note up to rest on my lips in thought. *How lovely & romantic and so unlike Sebastian – or maybe not? I'd never been privy to this sexier side of him.*

"Well? Don't keep us hanging?" Colin practically screams at me.

I return to Jackie and Colin's desperate stares. "I'm not sure. There's no message."

My reply is tinged with guilt as I tap the side of my nose coyly. This is met by a resounding noise of boos and hisses but I laugh them off, and grab my bag, placing the card safely and secretly inside and the rose back into the display box. I pat the note through the fabric of my Gucci and slap Colin's behind.

"Chop Chop, my lovely. Time to go woo Mr. Marcell."

Colin is alert and ready within seconds, making woo-ing sounds, similar to the coo of a pigeon; he's completely off his rocker! I burst out laughing again. I knew the mention of our male client would put a firecracker up his tight little behind and change the subject - swiftly diverting attention from me to him – his favourite subject matter!

Cruising along the long sweeping gravelled path up to The Ashton, Colin whistles loudly next to me in appreciation. I grin knowingly, as I'd forgotten that he hasn't been to the hotel yet. He's worked on the project for a few weeks now, but only from photographic evidence in the studio, as I had taken the initial briefing last month.

"It's fabulous isn't it?"

I still couldn't believe we had the chance to add this place to our portfolio. I really couldn't mess this one up. Our overdrawn business account was counting upon it.

"It's the bloody bomb!" he yells giddily. "Ooh, am I going to have to have a wild passionate night here!" He rubs his dancing hands together excitedly and wiggles his shoulders; first left then right then pretends to wipe away a fake tear. "I'm totally e… mosh!"

I glance from him back to the hideaway haven, which sits majestically in front of us; its Regency Style design appears both traditional and contemporary, due to the recently sandblasted stonework. The result is clean and fresh and showcased the four huge Tuscan columns, which supported the Portico central front porch, to perfection. There are two huge, semi-circled turrets and dozens of beautiful floor to ceiling picture sash windows, which wrap around the Pride and Prejudice style architecture. The effect is breathtaking. All it needed was Mr. Darcy to walk in, dripping from the nearby tranquil lake, in white shirt and breeches and I'd be completely in heaven. Colin would have to fight me for him.

"This really is out of this world!" Colin comments again dreamily, as I swing my Audi into what I hope is an allocated space. We head up to the huge twelve foot double doors, which are painted a glossy black and flanked by two pretty bay trees in black and chrome steel planters, each tied with a white ribbon. The door is instantly opened, allowing entry to one of the grandest hallways I've ever seen and our names promptly taken; the efficiency from start to finish is exemplary. Colin has noticed it too, as he pulls his Kenneth Williams face at me and I disguise my unprofessional, escaping giggle.

The Reception continues the monochrome theme, with regency busts, pillars and glossy marble black and white tiles. In the centre of the room, a huge glass circular table sits with the largest black & white striped rococo urn I've come across. It reminds me of a huge humbug and is filled with all kinds of fresh flowers - lilies, roses and hydrangeas - all pure white and neatly packed around cascading ivy, which spills out of the vase and onto the tabletop.

Pure elegant chic – *I am decidedly buzzing with creative inspiration.*

Directly above the table, is a magnificent smoked crystal chandelier and similar lighting adorns the walls. The chandelier is more modern than would be expected and a teardrop design; at a guess it would be about ten feet high and is truly a focal piece; its hundreds of bulbs winking above, each like individual high carat diamonds. The main lighting is cleverly hidden behind shelving and with littered glass hurricane lamps giving what could be a cool interior, the warmth required to relax its clientele. I look upwards to the domed ceiling, where the light seeps down through a turret of glass and then lower my focus with an immediate reactive gasp at the beautiful long staircase. Separating into two further mini staircases on the landing, both left and right, it then flows out at the bottom, like a regal bride's veil. The central part of the stairs is protected by a ream of black and white striped thick pile carpet, which rolls over the marble steps, secured by chrome and crystal stair rods. The effect is exquisite. It would make a fabulous wedding venue.

"I wonder who worked on this place before us?" Col thinks out loud, echoing my own thoughts, whilst ogling his surroundings.

"I'm not sure Hun but they did a fabulous job – although I think a lot of the inherent parts of the building should be grateful to the original regency designers; this floor for example – it ain't new! It might have been re-vamped, but the fundamentals were definitely already here."

Colin hmm's his agreement and we continue to explore. We are happily surveying each nook and cranny and soaking up the inspiration, when we're collected and taken into another room, branded on its plaque as The Library; a complete contrast to the hallway, where its clever use of colours and textures have created a hip boutique feel. It was all sultry and decadent, rather like its Owner, speak of the devil. There, relaxing on a plush purple crushed velvet settee studded with crystal buttons and oodles of fur and silk cushions, sat a cross-legged James Marcell. He looked like he was posing for a Sunday Times' photo shoot. I feel Colin melt next to me. God help us.

After a delicious and unexpected afternoon tea with fluffy scones, thick strawberry-jam and clotted cream, accompanied by a steaming pot of Yorkshire Tea, I sigh in sheer delight. Then, reminding myself that we are not there as guests but to in fact work, I gently push my rather relaxed potential client to review our design mood boards. I'm starting to wonder if this may have been more of a *tricky tea* for James, as his ruddy cheeks flush deeper.

85

"So James, what do you think?" I ask apprehensively, hoping that my keenness to obtain this project isn't too apparent to the client.

I watch his over-collagen enhanced face for any positive sign. It was hard to tell, as his obvious love of Botox has meant that his tanned but very smooth face only really offered one expression. The presentation has been delivered really well, if I say so myself. The rich velvets, pewters, reds and greys appear to be a huge hit, going by the many *Oooh's* and *Ahh's* throughout the spiel. My suggestion to add a large open fire in the sitting room to the suite have been welcomed with enthusiasm and the only thing now we had to agree upon was the Designer's Guild fabric for the furniture - oh and the budget, of course.

Finally the boss speaks. "Simply put Lucia, it is wonderful and just what we are after here at *The Ashton*. You really have done a fabulous job." He places a well-manicured hand on a thick swatch of scarlet velvet and flicks his eyes back over the sample of £100 a roll, black-flocked wallpaper.

"Perfect," he mutters to himself, deep in thought.

I glance at Colin who is now mouthing to me, "In the bag. In *THE* bag!" as though he's suddenly working as a speech therapist. God he doesn't do subtle! I nervously fiddle with a stray piece of hair that's worked its way loose from my up-do and raise my eyes to focus on the beautiful ornate cornicing around the room. When at last, I hear him clear his throat and removing his red thick-framed designer glasses, he looks directly at me, and nods, straightening his back on the sofa.

"When can we start?"

I exhale the breath I've been unknowingly holding and stand up, smoothing out my navy Roland Mouret *moon* dress. Yes! We did it. In my head, I hi-five, someone, *anyone,* in utter triumph. Where was Finn when I needed to do a victory dance? He always joined me in a mutual admiration boogey.

"I can have the builders in to knock things about within the next 2 days. I'll finalise some building quotes for you this afternoon and re-check their company schedules, then e-mail them across. Providing everything goes to plan, and what's behind those walls is what we think is behind those walls, we could be finished in the best part of four - six weeks."

James bobs his rather narrow head up and down, in all the right places. "Wonderful Lucia. You really are as good as Malcolm told me."

I make a mental note to thank Mal, for the referral. I'd recently completed refurbishing his small Bed and Breakfast, *Rooks Hill* and the three individually themed en-suite bedrooms are going down a storm with his customers. They are fully booked for the next six months. My own personal favourite is *The Garden Room,* with thousands of tiny twinkling lights installed into the hand painted ceiling to replicate a starry-night. The effect is breath- taking and exceedingly romantic. I return my attention to James who then nods at Colin, who is literally standing in a puddle of drool at James' feet.

"Right - now the tough part...budget. I love what you've planned but I'll need to shave a bit off here and there to ensure there is enough in the kitty to enhance the other rooms in need of a facelift," he muses, placing his glasses back on to peruse the mood boards once again. "If we call it £80K for the Honeymoon Suite budget? Does that work?"

I am so relieved that he is being realistic and I move to shake his outstretched hand immediately to seal the deal. "That is a healthy budget James and fair for the luxury that you expect that the room and hotel deserves. You've already had my quote for Elysium's fee...Yes? That would be in addition to this budget, however." I need to get this part in, as I'd been stung in the past.

James agrees. "I'll have my PA send you a completed, signed purchase order by the end of the day."

I mentally relax. Uncomfortable part is over. Now the hard work, but also the best bit begins. I can put my designs into motion and create!

"Colin, do you want to *come*... and help me *stretch my tape measure* around some of the other bedrooms? After the success of this meeting, I am going to *place the balls*... in your more-than *capable hands.*" James clears his throat and stands to leave.

OMG the innuendos are endless. I do wish heterosexuals were as obvious. It would definitely make life easier all round. Sensing there is no need for me to stay I shake hands with James again and begin to gather up my work, as he and Colin disappear; Colin sending me the OK sign over his shoulder in glee. I'm not sure I'll see him again this afternoon.

Chapter 9

Lucia

I'm about to leave the library when I hear my name called. It is James' PA, Debbie.

"Ms. Myers, there is someone waiting for you in the drawing room. He says he is here to quote for the honeymoon suite's building work?"

I frown at this but smiling I thank her, and turn to follow her willowy figure, our heels clicking simultaneously upon the striking black and white checkerboard tiled floor, as we enter the reception area. She ushers me to a corner hidden from the doorway. There, sitting on a chaise longue, one leg resting casually upon the other knee is Sebastian. He is reading the paper and looking entirely at ease in these luxury surroundings.

As soon as he hears my shoes on the marble flooring, he looks up, locks eyes and stands to welcome me. If it isn't enough shock that he is here unexpectedly, he is wearing a fitted, grey pinstriped suit with crisp white shirt open at the neck and a sexy smile. My mouth waters! I am in real trouble here. Deep breaths… Lucia!

"Lucia, you look lovely," he drawls appraisingly, his eyes sliding up and down my hourglass figure. I feel like I'm stripped bare in front of him and I twitch uncomfortably in my nude heels. It's worse now that he's seen what is under my dress but also that I've laid myself open to him with my proposal. *Talk about vulnerable. Stop fidgeting Lu!*

I'm distinctly aware that Debbie is long gone and remind myself that I'm blatantly gawking. We haven't spoken since yesterday morning and I am acutely aware that I hadn't replied to his crappy 'thanks' text. But he *had* responded to mine. The Rose had been stunning.

Suddenly, I'm exceedingly aware that everything between us has changed and it's making me really nervous.

"Thanks. What are you doing here?" I respond a little too rudely.

"Nice to see you too," he laughs taking my elbow and manoeuvring me towards the ornate staircase. "You and I have a date in the honeymoon suite love and if you don't hurry up, I'm going to carry you over the threshold to follow with tradition."

He arches a dark brow at me and I'm not sure if he's kidding. Either way I practically glide up the immense steps and head full-throttle for our destination, leaving Seb to jog alongside me to catch up. I can feel his eyes assessing me, boring into me - the skin at my neck burns from it, creating a buzz of friction all over my reactive body.

"How did you know I was here Seb?" I question, continuing along the long corridor towards the back of the building.

"I called your office and *Jillie* is it? She said you'd be here and I thought I'd meet you to measure up for this building quote you wanted doing."

I decide that I'm going to throttle Jackie when I return to the office. Then instantly berate myself - it wasn't her fault.

"*Jackie* not Jillie. I forgot how crap you are with names." I can hear the annoyance in my voice and I'm disgusted at my shrewish attitude. The new seductive jovial Sebastian combo is certainly bringing out the worst in me.

I try a calmer tactic. "You should have called me. I might not need you after all." *I refer to both contracts; work and play.*

"Hey no probs, but whilst I'm here, I may as well take a look."

"Well if you're sure - I thought now Silver Con had hit the big time, you would have employed a site manager to come survey these smaller jobs?"

"I have. Several in fact, but this quote needed my... touch."

I quiver under his words and sigh in relief as we reach the end of the *Alice in Wonderland* style corridor, and with a deft flick of his wrists, the double doors fling open.

"Wow!"

Glancing across at his gut reaction I can't stop the simmering smile playing over my mouth. Genuine excitement pours out of him and I *get it*; it's exactly how I'd felt the first time I'd witnessed the room. Peering inside the en-suite space brings on more purrs of contentment.

"This is a great space - all that natural light from the sash's, and original moldings. What a project Lu! Yeah, this will definitely give you something to sink your teeth into – take a big bite of the creative pie." I swear he purposely nips his lip for definition. "Get the juices flowing…" He has the decency to smirk at his sexual innuendos but I'm a mess and take a deep, slow releasing breath.

Sebastian takes a notebook and pencil from his inside pocket and the laser measure he'd carried up with him, and begins to get serious; his face intent on renovation. I need immediate space and utilise this distraction to my advantage, pretending to do my own scribbles. It is as I lean against one of the floor to ceiling windows, my forehead touching a cool pane of glass as I enjoy the beauty of the Italian garden beneath me, that I sense him at my back.

"Right - I'm done – all measured up. You want a fireplace putting in here, yeah? The re-fit of the bathroom, flooring, decorating, re-plastering - the Works?" he enquires, his head tilted in business mode. God, this Sebastian was even more lethal than relaxed Sebastian.

Speak woman, he's asking you a question, I inwardly remind myself.

"Yes. I have a copy of the plans and our requirements in the reception. If I give you that, you can review my notes and get me a quote? Soon-as though." I cringe at the short notice, knowing it would be a tough call for anyone to achieve and part of me hopes that he won't be able to accommodate me.

"No probs Lu. For you, anything," he says seriously, his genial mood and persona has changed in a flash. I sense we are bringing it back to the text I sent him.

"No more business though…" The look in his eyes is devilish as he moves towards me, forcefully pushing my body backwards against the window again. "Now… its all about pleasure."

Cupping his hand roughly around my neck, he draws me to his mouth, planting his lips firmly and fiercely onto mine. The electric shock ignites and zaps through my body once again. Head to toe. I feel myself in his embrace, deepening the hungry kiss myself. I am so aroused, I feel like I could explode right there and then. I am not prepared to appear easy… yet again, but this is all I've wanted since yesterday. A low moan escapes from my lips, as we crush our mouths together. Hot and wet. The sound triggers something within me and I am brought back to reality, and sense myself fighting against his chest.

We separate, chests heaving, both heavily panting. He looks as surprised as I am - at the effect we have on one another. I feel a small victory at his less than calm veneer but am adamant that he can't just kiss me like this, at the drop of a hat… here! It needed to be planned and I needed to feel in control. Here and now I was neither.

"We can't do this here Sebastian." I remind myself as much as him.

"Like bloody hell we can't." His voice is husky.

He isn't as composed as he usually is and takes a minute to think, his hand rubbing his shaven head in thought. My own, still trembling hand is clasped in his warm male palm. I feel the tug, as I'm dragged firmly towards the doorway.

"Fuck it. Let's go and book a room and we'll finish whatever…*this* is between us!" He lifts his free arm up and down in a dramatic demonstration of *this*.

My blood begins to boil and I honestly don't know if I could seriously clock the man over the head. I had asked him for one night of sex between friends, but that meant one amazing night, not some half-cocked tumble. *What cave had he crawled out of today? Me Sebastian, you Lucia! I don't think so!*

Besides, we hadn't even discussed it… yet. He is obviously used to getting his own way with women but he should know with me that I am more than a match for his stubbornness. I am not his typical subject and I would not just rollover and perform at his command. This had to be on *my* terms. I am furious with him and struggle to pull my hand out of his tight grasp, as it dawns on me that I am still connected to him. The minute that he succumbs, my hand falls loosely by my waist and I instantly regret the loss of contact.

"Apart from the obvious point that I can't just go and book a room in the hotel owned by my most affluent and important client to date – so that you can scratch a fucking sexual itch - I don't *want* to go to bed with you now… I've changed my mind." I fold my arms across my chest primly to stress my decision is final; nothing could be further from the truth so I hope I'm convincing. "After the other night I would have thought it obvious that we just aren't a match and I don't know what I was thinking sending you that stupid text yesterday. It was a ridiculous idea?"

My mouth struggles to voice the words, as I hate telling lies and blush. Annoyingly, this only assists in encouraging the chase for him. I can see the fire in his beautiful eyes and know that the same embers burn hotly in his belly. His demeanour has become almost aggressive.

"You're a shit liar Lu. Besides I've already set the wheels in motion. I accept your proposition, challenge, whatever you want to call it. There's no going back now. You are right - Saturday night did not end well but it did prove we are compatible and if you need a man to get you over that *prick,* I'd rather it was me." His slow sensual smile is my undoing and I swallow as his dimple twitches. "You're going to get the night of your life - but *I'll* be the one in control and *I'll* determine the time and place."

At my shocked furrowed expression he continues. "It's a deal breaker. Agreed?"

I stare open mouthed at his audacity, desperate to tell him to go fuck himself. He was so sure of himself; so overly confident. So fucking sexy. *Oh God, what am I doing? There's no point backing out now. I really want this; need this.*

Instead I just nod. "Agreed."

"Good. Because when we fuck, and I mean *when* Lucia, we'll do it properly, willingly, honestly and openly, with no holds barred!" His voice is seductively promising in its arrogance. Hypnotic almost, and with these last words he raises his hazel flecked ebony pools to my deep green ones, and smugly shrugs. "Be honest with yourself. You and I *were always* going to happen one day. It's been in the post for over a decade. You knew it and I knew it; the only questions to consider now are, *when, where,* and how many times will you come?"

Licking his tongue along his full bottom lip sensually, he is back to his cool and collected manner – obviously incredibly impressed with his boldness. Self-indulgently, he nods at his statement as if agreeing with himself and bending to kiss me lightly on my cheek, his bristles creating havoc with my soft skin, he whispers in my ear.

"I'm going to show you how sex should really be. No ties, no commitments just pure unadulterated pleasure. I'll be in touch with the FBR's."

I withdraw from him and frowning mutter, "FBR's?" in confusion.

His sexy grin is back in flash. "Fuck Buddy Rules - a must, with this type of agreement *Love.* I've already given you FBR number 1: I decide where and when. You'll know the rest in time." Then he is gone. Leaving me standing in a mirage of lust and fury.

My cheek tingles where his lips left their mark, and I touch the spot myself to capture it. The frustration rushing through my veins is bordering on violent; my mind is so numb, I couldn't manage to respond with a sharp retaliation to his shocking questions and my body is so alive, that I don't even know if I want to retaliate.

That fucking man! He is infinitely different to any Sebastian I have ever known. This is a completely new side to him. Illicit. Dangerous. Controlling. This is the side that all his previous conquests have been party to. Now I understand why he's had so many.

He is magnetic - worryingly so. The combination of this extreme magnetism and sexual prowess with the friendly, funny, sensitive, loyal Sebastian that I'm already familiar with is deadly. I sense that I am in *big* trouble but as a sensual smile plays across my lips, I also think I might be in for some delectable fun - if I could just let go and start thinking more with my bits than my brain!

Chapter 10

Lucia

Back in the car, I slide my phone from silent to accessible and I notice a missed call from my sister Suzie. I click her number, sending my phone automatically into dial mode and crunch the car into gear - I needed to head back to work. Within seconds her bubbly voice echoes through the hands-free system.

"Hey Lulu. Where you at?"

"I've just left The Ashton and guess what? We got it. Yay!" I do the drum roll noise our Dad always did when we were kids and continue with my mini tune. "We did it, we did, we won it, we won it! Who's the mama, who's the mama?" Attempting to complete a little victory dance in my seat, I move my shoulders up and down as best as I can without crashing the car. I can hear her laughing at the thought of how I must appear to the other drivers in my near vicinity.

"Ha ha. I can't breathe! You're off the wall. Well done chickadee - Didn't expect anything less from our very own Kelly Hoppen."

"Thanks Suze. Seriously though, I was pretty confident with this one but the pressure was on. It's a *lot* of money and will really boost the Elysium name and coffers. Anyway, enough about me - how's things at your end?"

"I'm ringing to see if you'll work your creative magic over the house for Saturday night? I'm thinking 80's theme – what do you think?" Her voice becomes more babyish the more she goes on with her begging.

I roll my eyes and grin to myself; she knows I can't resist the *baby* voice. "So what you're saying is I've got four days to pull a fabulously

94

80's - themed decor out of my arse – on a budget I presume?"

"You got it," she responds tentatively. I can practically see her pretty pout down the phone.

"OK, but only because it's you. Do you have any decorations already we can work with?"

"Well I've got some bits but I'll get you some cash for the rest. Just let me know."

"Ok. I'll have a look into it. I might have some props left over we can adapt to suit."

"Why don't we just go with the neon 80's colour palette and then it doesn't have to be too literal? That way we have current music and NO fancy dress! I mean it Suze!"

I say the last few words, very firmly as Suzie is a dress-up kinda of girl, even if the rest of us aren't. I'd made the mistake of looking for something in their guest room wardrobe once and the clothes stashed in there would put a sex shop to shame. Nurse, Police, Fireman - pretty much all the emergency services actually, with the odd quirky character thrown-in. Maybe a Smurf, if I remember rightly? Say no more. I'm scarred for life.

"I can nip to the wholesalers on Thursday night to grab some napkins, cups, etc. and if we keep it simple, the *short-notice* of it all will not be glaringly obvious."

"Sounds fabby. I knew you'd know what to do. Anyway I've gotta go – Gino is demanding that I accompany him to some dull-as Sales drinks do! Gotta go wear my shortest dress for him to attain this new potential investor. Lucky me. Love ya!"

"Bye Hun." I chuckle and shake my head disconcertingly at the seedy thoughts in my head from her scene setting. Gino's usual dress code for women was *dress slutty* but I loved him none-the-less. He loved my sister unconditionally and wholeheartedly, placed her on a diamond-encrusted pedestal everyday and that was good enough for me. His good looks and charm worked on most of the female population but he only had eyes for Suzie. I would love to have half of what they had together.

No sooner have I ended the call, the *House of pain* ringtone starts to *jump* again but taking a quick glance, I don't recognise the landline number flashing up on the screen.

"Elysium Interiors. How may I help you?" I answer trying to sound proficient, switching from laughter to businesslike in a nanosecond.

95

"Is that Lucia Myers?" a rather snooty female voice enquires.

"Yes that's correct. To whom am I speaking?" I do try not to sound waspish in return but fail miserably. I can't do with snooty callers; they irritate the hell out of me. Let's hope it isn't an Ambulance chaser or Payment Protection mis-selling call.

It's none of the above.

"This is Sebastian Silver's PA and I've been asked to call you with a quotation for The Ashton Hotel."

"Oh hi. Wow, that was quick." *He must have sorted things the minute he left me. It's been 15 minutes at the most.*

"Well, Sebastian – I mean Mr. Silver, does like to work effectively. I have already e-mailed you the quotation and a purchase order to sign, however he wanted me to call you with the numbers- apparently this job is *very last minute*."

I pick up on her disapproval. It's obvious that's she is inferring that *I* am disorganised, not Sebastian. I immediately get a full on visual of him, he really is considerate and despite my annoyance at him, I cannot help but respect his own efficiency. She continues on in her rather patronising voice, and feeds me some figures, which sound OK, whilst I do my own sums. I am very aware that I'm more annoyed that Sebastian has a female PA who seems to act like she knows him more than I do. I thought Sebastian had said his PA was called Tony anyway?

Putting my professional *butter wouldn't melt* voice back on, deliberately killing her with kindness, I respond.

"Ok, thanks for that. I'll be sure to forward these on to my client to confirm and if you could inform Sebastian that I'll be in touch with my decision." I revel in that last snippet, knowing that this woman will probably be annoyed by it.

"I would much rather you contact *me* with the purchase order so that *I* can inform Mr. Silver. We have a very close relationship!" Her voice is sharp and official. I dislike her even more. Should that not be *working relationship*? I choose to rise above it.

"No problems, I'll do both." Ha, silly mare. I can play you at your own game.

"Right. Good. Well thank you Ms. Myers. Just ask for Toni, with an *i*, when you call."

She doesn't wait for my response. The line goes dead.

Of course she would be a chick, with an '*i*' at the end of her name; I wouldn't expect anything less from Sebastian. So *this* is the infamous

Tony - sorry Toni with an *i*. I'm surprised how annoyingly niggled I am by the fact that *he* is in fact a *she* — she definitely had obvious designs on Sebastian. Women's intuition was an amazing superhero power; it even worked down a phone line!

Later that night I'm cuddling up watching the fabulous animated movie, *Despicable Me* for what feels like the hundredth time; Steve Carell's accent is really amazing throughout. Finn's boneless body is sprawled all over me and relaxing; I take a moment to re-live the day's events. I've not really had the opportunity to relive today's events at The Ashton. I am aware that given 1% less stubbornness, Seb would have had his wicked way with me, then and there, on the dusty wooden floorboards - the only worries filtering through my mind would have been splinter extraction.

Yes, just a smidgen more courage and we'd have spent the afternoon tousled in luxury Egyptian cotton hotel sheets, blissfully scratching this impossible sexual itch. I tingle at the thought but immediately that 1% rears its head and I'm thrown into *protection mode* again. Our *relationship* whatever that is, is extremely messed up at present. I'm not really sure what I actually want anymore from Sebastian. Is it really wise to mix friendship with sex?

We'd always just been Seb and Lu. Best mates, unequivocally. Now the main basis of our relationship was stilted and had been replaced with some serious sexual attraction, which threatened the friendship that meant so much to me. Sebastian *and* Lucia was a completely new concept to me. The reality is that deep down, if I am honest with myself, I want both - friendship *and* hot sex and I'm not sure that's possible.

Fumbling around on the floor for my iPhone, which alerts me that I've reached a new level on temple run, (bless my little lad, he is so good with technology but my phone is continually dying as the battery is eaten with crappy apps) - I notice that I've received a text from the man himself. I purse my lips in thought. I haven't heard from him since earlier at The Ashton and I'd been phone watching all night (loathe though I am to admit it). I'd wanted to thank him for the flowers but didn't want to spoil the secretive illusion. Annoyed with myself at such indecisive behaviour, I bite my lip and read his message.

If I haven't made myself clear I'd be happy to show you how sex should be done Lulu but be warned, I'm no Niall.
FBR Number 2: One night will not be enough for me to take you to new sexual heights - believe me you'll want more.
One proposition = one month of pleasure.
This is non-negotiable x

My cheeks are on fire. I can feel bits awakening just at his words. Wow, he is good, and incredibly full of himself. This is already getting out of hand, it was only ever supposed to be one night - do I want more? A month? *Who are you trying to kid?*

I punch out a quick message, hesitate briefly over pressing send, shake my head and just do it anyway and snuggle back down to watch Gru and his minions capture the moon.

Your wish is my command x

His reply flies through in seconds

I like the sound of that x

Chapter 11

Lucia

I kick the door shut behind me as I juggle my files and the overly packed three shopping bags from Sainsbury's or *Snobsbury's*, as Abby & I liked to call it. Quick unpack and then I'd get tea on. I am cooking Finn's favourite homemade Spaghetti Carbonara and really need to crack-on before my ex brings him home, after an impromptu crèche collection, which pissed me off but I went with it for Finn's sake. I'm in the throws of multi-tasking; boiling pasta, stirring sauce on the hob and setting the table when I hear a knock at the back door.

"Lucia."

Niall drawls as he enters without my permission, carrying Finn's backpack. I'm surprised how little I feel towards this man whom I spent so many years of my life with. The *just punched* sexual feeling I get when I see Sebastian now, after only one night together - and an unfinished one at that - combined with shockwaves of tingles that filter along every nerve ending, their end goal met at my apex is so unique; I'm not sure I *ever* had that with Niall?

I cared about him deeply - of course I did - we'd made a child together - but it wasn't a gut-wrenching *need* - it had been more a companionship of sorts. The type of relationship I thought Sebastian and I had until recently.

"Where's Finn?" I snap out of my daydream and attempt to peer behind Niall's lean designer-clad body. His hand stops me, grabbing my wrist and anchoring me in front of him.

"He's just playing in the yard in his Shed. Fab is that! Did your

Dad put it together for him?" He stares at me inquisitively and walks into the kitchen, helping himself to a piece of crozalled-crispy bacon.

Annoyed at his entrance and familiarity, I pull my arm away from his grip and rush forward to the hob, where the spaghetti is now beginning to boil over.

"Er, my Dad built it for him, yes and they painted it together a few months ago. Dad says every man needs a shed!"

"Too true." Niall nods chuckling. "Something smells good?"

My back is to him and my skin prickles in annoyance at his obvious hint. "Yeah, its Finn's preferred tea, this month, Basgetti Carbon rar rar – last month was meatballs, or brains, as he likes to call them."

"Spag Cab – he's got good taste. I'd forgotten what a good cook you were Lucia." He says my name as though I'm being reprimanded and he is my teacher. How had I not remembered that disdainful habit of his?

"I've only made enough for two I'm afraid."

I'm aware that I sound brusque but I continue setting places at the granite island in the centre of the huge basement Kitchen, fully aware that Niall's eyes are on me at all times. I wonder why, after ten months, he is now throwing out compliments and spending more than a second in my company? Something was up!

I brush my hair away from my face with the back of my hand, as I'm holding a pan in one and a wooden spoon in the other. I flinch as Niall raises his finger to assist me and tucks a stray wavy strand behind my ear. I do not feel comfortable at all and the atmosphere is quickly becoming stifled.

We both spin in shock when a deep voice from the corner of the room drawls, "Getting a bit steamy in here isn't it?"

Sebastian.

His timing is a Godsend and his question laced with double connotations. He must have made his way down the steps and into the kitchen from the front entrance and is standing, looking seriously gorgeous and unimpressed in a fitted black t-shirt and ripped jeans.

I go to put the pan and dirty spoon in the sink. "Seb! What are you doing here?" Following it up with a babbling, "Oh it's the pasta boiling. I forgot to put the extractor on."

Why had I explained that? Now it appeared that there had been a moment between Niall and I. Now it looked like I was trying, rather unsuccessfully, to cover it up.

"I knocked but there was no answer. I tried the door anyway – yet again unlocked Ms. Myers!" His tut is condescending but rather than piss me off, it warms me that he cares enough to mention it.

"Thought I'd pop in to see what your thoughts were on our quote for The Ashton. But I can come back though if you're busy?" Sebastian arches his brow looking from me, to Niall and back to me again, searchingly. He has no intention of going anywhere, with that glint in his eye. Competition was like honey was to bees, where Seb was concerned - he needed it to survive.

"No. No don't be daft. Come in," I pacify him. "I'm just about to serve up some food for Finn. Just give me a second."

Why has he come now? When I'm a sweltering hot mess from the stove, already in a foul mood from Niall's presence and all over the place emotionally, after yesterday's Ashton episode and his acceptance of my offer?

I can feel the two men at war with one another behind my back and cringe. They used to be friends but Sebastian hasn't seen or heard from Niall since he'd left and not become reacquainted since Niall had recently come back into Finn's life; I think more out of loyalty to me but I know he's severely pissed at him. When he'd walked, he walked out of everybody's lives.

"Niall," Sebastian offers up, seething.

"Sebastian," Niall nods back sulkily.

Bugger! This was going nowhere.

The testosterone in the room was so thick I could see me walking out of here with a full-grown beard at the end of it and that would not be pretty! One of them needed to leave now and I didn't want it to be Seb.

Sebastian goes to the shiny Red SMEG fridge and grabs a beer, making it exceedingly obvious to Niall that he is at home in my house. He doesn't offer Niall one. He may as well have pissed on the floor, to mark his territory. I smirk to myself despite the awkwardness. I can tell that Niall is trying to weigh up the situation and thinks that there is something going on here. There isn't of course, but then I correct myself and think well, actually maybe there is?

Sebastian takes this opportunity to place a hand firmly on my behind and squeeze it possessively, as I walk past to call Finn inside. I jump at the overly intimate gesture and turning to question, see the humour and control in his eyes. It was just for show; to wind Niall up and it seemed to be doing the trick. Niall is practically puce by this point, his face straining against his top buttoned shirt, unsure what to do but aware that he has rapidly lost command of the situation. He strokes his imaginary beard, in that God-awful affected way he used to, and evidently ruffled, quips,

"Lucia, we *need* to talk, preferably without being overheard by uninvited-passers-by. I'll call you."

He leans in to ruffle Finn's hair, as my boy launches himself through the door, at breakneck speed, obviously now bored with playing with the shed. "See ya lad."

"Submarine!" Finn is completely oblivious to Niall and screams in delight, at the sight of his pal, running to grab hold of Sebastian. "You came back!" He squeezes his jeans clad leg.

"Hiya Mate!" Seb returns the squish but turns Finn to face Niall. "Your Dad is on his way out, so why don't you go say goodbye?"

"Bye Lion." My lovely little boy responds with a wave and a quick leg hold – it's the name he uses for Niall, as he couldn't say it when he was two. We're not sure why he suddenly stopped called him Daddy to his face but my parents thought it might have been a psychological knock-on effect of the break-up.

"It's Daddy Finn. Daddy," Niall reprimands in a unreasonably firm voice, obviously irritated and I giggle behind my hand, when Finn continues to ignore him and instead bares his teeth and claws the air with his pudgy fingers, shouting, "Basgetti carbon rah raahh!" just like a lion.

Seriously exasperated Niall rolls his eyes, showing the impatience of someone who is not used to handling small children. "See you next week Finn. I'll call you Lucia. Like I said - we need to talk. Things have adjusted, shall we say and I'd like to run through a few theories with you. We didn't get the chance the other night as you ran off!"

He pointedly stares in Sebastian's direction and then back to me - his blue eyes cold and full of annoyance. "You look good Lucia. Real good." He spitefully smiles at Seb and leans in towards me to plant an unexpected and unwanted kiss on me. I move with lightening quick reaction, just in time for him to connect with the side of my mouth.

He whispers in my ear before leaving, purposely lingering against me, his body pressed into mine. "I miss you in my bed. You're still my Mrs. you know."

Oh. My. God. No way is this man on our planet. Sebastian had pissed on the floor territorially - Niall had curled one out and left it steaming there! What

102

are men like? - Utterly pathetic!

My mind is racing through different options of what *adjusted* and *theories* would relate to and what the bloody hell that seedy comment was all about, but frowning in complete confusion I just wave him away. I'm totally drained and too tired to crack Niall's secret code or play his mind games.

I close the door on his back and ignore the disgusted looks I can feel burning into my back from Seb's brooding dark pools and return to serve up Finn's tea, placing him at the granite island on a high backed red leather stool. I'm suddenly not hungry and glancing across to where Sebastian is discussing the differences between Hulk and Spiderman and their pros and cons, I hold up a spare bowl in question – he catches my eye and giving me a thumb's up returns to superhero world.

Finn and Seb, tuck into their pasta, as though they haven't eaten in weeks, whilst I tidy away the mess and load the dishwasher. The atmosphere is calm and casual, as I listen to Finn's chatter about his day and Sebastian's banter.

"Sophie kissed me today Yuk – she said she wants to marry me!" he scrunches his horrified face up and makes monster noises. I look at Sebastian and we both share a smile.

"Hey Mate, you didn't say you had a girlfriend. Is she a looker?"

"She's ok I s'pose, but she's not my girlfwend – I like Holly," Finn shrugs his small shoulders without apology. God they start young.

"Ahh Holly!" Sebastian nods his understanding and laughs. "Come on, eat up Romeo!"

"Romeo? I'm not called Romeo - My name's Finn!"

"That it is Mate, that it is."

They eat their food in congenial silence, boys enjoying their carbohydrates with uninhibited gusto, whilst I inwardly melt at how wonderful Sebastian is with my son. He's the ideal mix of fun and firm and watching my son chat happily, I know that he adores Seb and always has. *I know the feeling.*

"If you're Ok down here with Finn I'll go run a bath for him."

At Seb's silent perusing nod, I disappear upstairs.

⚬⚬⚬

As I enter our recently re-modelled grey and white bathroom, it hits me that the last time he was here, upstairs, things had not ended

103

so well - or rather not ended the way I'd wanted them to. I just hoped that he'd leave before I ready Finn for bed.

I swish the bubbles about in the warm water and stop the tap, nipping up to the top floor to Finn's room to collect his PJ's. Arriving back down on the landing, I find a naked little man, dancing about shouting, "It's naked time!" over and over, whilst Sebastian desperately tries and fails miserably to grab his giggling body and dunk him in the roll-topped bath. The sight is adorable. This strong gorgeous male and the soft innocent little boy are having a whale of a time. So much for him leaving before bath time!

With lots of coercion and some serious doorway blocking we jokingly hi-five at our achievement to corner Finn. Making a dive for him I clutch at his wriggling waist and lift him into the air, blowing raspberries loudly on his puffed out healthy belly. Two seconds later and he's happily snuggled deep in bubble bath, playing with his magic frog. Sebastian is positioned in the corner of the bathroom, leaning casually against the laundry cupboard watching me keenly as I kneel at the bath side, and pour water onto Finn's body with a small jug.

"So Lu – how's things?" he shrugs, managing to look completely relaxed when inside, I'm a bag of nerves. How does he do that?

Why is he asking me how's things? Yesterday he'd talked dirty to me in The Ashton and then left me with serious head-fuck, sent saucy texts and rules. I turn to look at his face unsure how to answer - things used to be so much simpler between us. The big white elephant that floated around us was my fault and I knew it - I was the one who'd asked him for uncomplicated sex.

"I'm fine." The blunt answer creates an uncomfortable silence between us.

"Did you get the quote I put together?" he smiles, his lovely mouth softening and I relax a little.

"Mmm hmmm - I spoke to your PA yesterday - She's a law unto herself."

He chuckles. "Ahh Miss Toni. Toni is hard on the outside but she means well. She's been instrumental in assisting me with the Dubai project, from the U.K. base. But she can get a bit territorial I agree."

I raise my brows at his rather blasé description of her. A *bit* territorial?; talk about understatement.

His phone buzzes and I watch his behaviour in the mirror behind the bath. He seems annoyed and punching out a quick reply, slips the phone back into his pocket.

"Everything alright?" I throw over my shoulder.

"Just Chris - he and some of the lads are heading out to the pub."

"Well don't let me keep you." *God woman you sound like a nag!*

""I'm not going anywhere... yet. I need to talk to you Lu. I'm going away on business until the weekend."

The feeling of loss is an unfamiliar sensation, low in the pit of my belly. He was always away - I need to get a grip.

"Oh?" I mutter, whilst trying to lather Finn's hair into the regular Mohican hairdo we replicate at bath times.

"Yeah. Don't worry about The Ashton. I've brought Nathan up to date on things and he's promised he'll be around if needed. I'd ask Chris as he seems pretty keen to work on this project - matter-of-fact seems pretty keen on you Lu... but..."

"Is he? I wouldn't know; he seems a bit full of himself but I'm sure he'll look after me." I interrupt and am aware I'm deliberately goading him.

"Yes, Toni said she thought you two would be well-suited."
There's an unasked question in the depths of that statement but I choose to ignore it. Of course Toni would have encouraged a relationship between Chris and I - it paved the way, free and clear for her to land Sebastian.

"Toni is rather keen on you too, me-thinks."

"She's harmless. Like I said, means well."

Bollocks!

"Anyway, Chris can't be around *to look after you*, as he's accompanying me on this job."

"No worries - Nathan is great." I'm inwardly relieved but still pissed off about Toni.

He hooks his thumbs inside his denims, one leg propped against the tiled wall. Effortlessly casual and looks so good I could eat him up with a spoon. I've gone from seriously pissed-off to actively turned-on in a matter of seconds.

I choose to ignore his passing comment about Toni. She is *not* harmless but if I disagree with his viewpoint, I'm the one who'll come across as bitchy. Men can never see a manipulative woman coming. Instead I chuckle as Finn blows bubbles in my face.

"Right you, let's get you out of the tub and all cosied up in your PJ's."

Lifting Finn out into a pre-warmed towel taken from the heated radiator, I enfold his now shivering little body and pat him gently dry.

"Now's not the time Lu so I'll go put the kettle on and you get The Finnster to bed. Then we'll talk. Little ears and all that."

Join the queue - who doesn't want to talk to me at the mo? I want to shout but I nod without answering him, knowing from the tone of his voice that it would be futile to disagree and watch as he bends to kiss Finn's damp hair, inhaling his Johnson's baby shampoo scent.

"Off you go big lad. Be good for your ma and snuggle up."

"Night Sub. I'll be good." Finn blows a cheeky raspberry at him, showing the antithesis of good.

"Night, you little monkey." With a deep chuckle he heads downstairs.

I return to the basement kitchen and pad along the oak floor. The boards are soft and comforting beneath my feet. Sebastian is indifferently leaning against the sink, hands gripping the worktop, his back to the huge picture window, legs loosely crossed in front of him. The only light comes from the glass extractor hood and his appearance is shrouded seductively. The effect is beguiling.

Black pools virtually undress me as I enter. "Did he go down OK?"

I lick my dry lips responding quickly. "Yeah no probs – sorry for the delay. I had to read all of his favourite Spiderman book… again!" Combing my hand through my hair I make my way towards him.

"He's a great kid Lu – fantastic little man." He shakes his head in wonder and I understand and smile back, knowingly. He is mine, but I totally agree, whole-heartedly; Finn is a superstar.

I take the mug that Seb offers me, with appreciation; I'm glad to finally *stop,* as a wall of tiredness hits me. It's been a long day - hell of a long couple of days. Taking a seat on a high stool at the island in the centre of the room I decide to make the first move. Perhaps it's craziness or just weariness boosting my confidence but I am keen to begin. Good or bad.

I take a look at his handsome face, so well-known to me yet now I'm noticing other details, such as the slight dimple in his cheek and his high cheekbones and the way his eyes crinkle at the corners when he smiles - he is the total package.

"What did you want to talk about Seb?" I ask blowing gently on my tea to cool it, as the steam encases me and I frame myself with a deep breath.

I can see he is staring at my mouth, has been since I licked my lips and it instantly makes my disloyal nipples react; they could cut diamonds! My loose white chiffon blouse feeling suddenly tight over their sensitive tips.

He takes his eyes from my chest for a second. "I wonder what the prick wants to talk to you about?"

I presume he means Niall.

"God knows – Niall still thinks he can click his fingers and I'll drop everything for him." I sigh as the gulp of sweet tea, slides silkily down my throat and warms my belly.

"But you won't?" Seb raises his brows in question.

"Hell no! That man is a law unto himself but that ship has sailed, sunk and been robbed by gold diggers."

"Good." He appears pleased by my answer but continues. "I don't think he was too happy to see me here."

"Why? You're Finn's Godfather, my friend and it's *my* home," I defend him immediately but smile haughtily. "Not sure the pat on my bum helped though."

His deep laugh fills the kitchen and I enjoy the fleeting moment seeing him so relaxed, his straight white teeth and dimple in his right cheek flash briefly. My own giggles join his laughter and we share a smile. For a fleeting second its Seb & Lu, mates again.

"You're probably right but I couldn't help myself. He's lucky I didn't punch his lights out."

I nod, savouring my mug between my hands. I know how protective Seb is towards me, regardless of the new changes between us – he would always be my friend.

"I can manage Niall Seb, he's harmless; a complete twat, but harmless, but thanks for caring."

I can feel him watching me, quietly absorbing my words. "It appears you are popular at the moment Lulu. Leo, Niall, anyone else I need to meet at midnight for a duel?"

"Seriously though Lu *we* also need to talk, about the other night. Don't we. About your proposition too." Anyone else would have posed it as a question but not Sebastian. It was most definitely a command.

I shake my head, my eyes huge and focused on his black ones. I can't do this. I thought I could but I know if we cross over into unknown territory, there was no going back. It was fine when it was harmless texting but face to face?

But I'm not given the chance.

"Saturday night… it was great Lu. Really great." I feel an overwhelming relief but also sense a *but* is on the cards. "But you know how things are with me? I'm never here - I think that's why I slowed things… I was pushing too hard."

My shoulders dip a tad, hopefully not enough for him to see my sadness and I desperately try to remain centered, as though his words are not cutting right through me. Be strong - he's just changed his mind that's all!

"Hey Seb, its *you* and *me* – you don't need to do this. We had fun and you just decided that you weren't into me that way. I get it. Let's call it that."

I shrug off the fact that I think I might cry at any minute and that my body is almost in pain, like I'm breaking into tiny little pieces. In that instant he is at my side. Here we go again, this bereft, feeling. I'm never so desperate or dramatic. I'm disgusted with myself.

Perhaps it's the fact that I'm shattered from the long working days or that I haven't fully recovered from the sexual interruption to our friendship. His scent surrounds me, all clean and musky with that twist of vanilla.

"I should never have propositioned you. I don't know what I was thinking?" I run my hands through my hair, exacerbated at my own behaviour. "When you tried it on with me I figured, hell, it shouldn't be too hard for him - he must think I'm alright for a shag." I lower my head in annoyance at the wobble of fear in my voice. "All the girls are saying I need to get back in the saddle and I do, but it's been a long time and I've not slept with anyone besides Niall since I was 19. You came home from Dubai and were standing in my kitchen all-gorgeous and male and I thought, why not? You're my friend and I trust you. I would rather it be with someone who won't think badly of me and expect too much - you know?"

His black eyes watch me spill my emotion out into a puddle at his feet. To give him his due, he just listens, and then nods in understanding before rubbing his head.

"The thing is, I'm not sure what to do here? All I want to do right now, have wanted to do since I left you at The Ashton is … this."

He leans forward, tilting my face up to his own stubbled one, moving a stray piece of hair and gently stroking a finger down my cheek. I hold my breath in wait as the nervous frizzes run around my body at the simplest of touches from him.

Why is he giving me such mixed signals?

He bends in further kissing me tenderly on the tip of my nose. "I've missed your cute little snub nose," he smiles, knowing he is repeating this comment, every time we get together and continues his trail across one cheek and then the other, lightly rubbing our noses together, so that I scrunch mine up.

"That's what I like – the little Elizabeth twitch!

I scrunch my nose up higher in utter confusion. "Elizabeth twitch?"

"You know - Elizabeth Montgomery from Bewitched? My mum loved that show and Na & I always had a bit of a thing for her – definitely now have a thing for noses." I nod my acknowledgement and smile lightly at his boyhood crush. "And boobs and ass. That's a given." His eyes twinkle devilishly at me.

Bending, he kisses my forehead and finally reaches my already puckered lips. His big comforting hands are on either side of my face, holding me prisoner, as he looks right into my eyes.

"You have the sexiest green eyes. You know that they give your innermost thoughts away don't you Lady Lu? I can read you so easily; always have been able to." His own, black pools hypnotise me with their depth. I look down, long eyelashes fanning my face, to hide my responsiveness from his x-ray vision.

I am dizzy with arousal and realise that I have unconsciously already opened my legs to accommodate his body, allowing him to slip into the 'V' I've created. "You mean something to me. You've always meant something to me - will always," he corrects himself, his voice breaking with emotion.

I can actually see real anguish in his expression. I've never seen Sebastian like this, so out of control. Control he puts above anything and everyone. The man with the cool calm and collected exterior has developed a slight crack in his armour.

"I want you to continue blossoming into Lulu again, getting YOU back and as my message said earlier, I'm all in. But… there are those FBR's."

We watch each other, weighing up the charged air between us and, reading my mind, he bends forwards reaching for me; our lips meet eagerly. He slides both hands along my outer thighs, grabs them underneath the backs of my knees and pulls them upwards, his palms massaging my calves, anchoring them in place. The position is so carnal that I rue my earlier decision to wear jeans - the barrier an annoying interference with our craving for spontaneous lusty sex.

We explore one another's mouths leisurely, his finger travelling lightly from my neck to the base of my spine, stroking through the sheer fabric in small delicious trails. I shiver at the delicious sensations and my breasts strain against my top, desperate for some of the attention. I push them into his warm solid chest, tired of holding back; tired of letting my fears get the better of me. Sebastian grabs hold of my hair in his fist, winding it tightly around his hand until I'm held, immobilised. Our tongues mate angrily and in that moment something inside me clicks.

What am I waiting for? I stop in my tracks, chewing my lip, desperate to feel him against me.

Oh fuck it. My hands seem to have a life of their own. They work their way up towards his neck. My palms push against the steely muscled warmth emanating from under his cotton t-shirt. Our eyes lock and I continue on my path, dipping down the hem before slowly lifting it. I tense, as my small hands are immediately enclosed in his hard rough male ones and stilled. He holds them there for a moment and then lets them drop. Our panting slows, as we lean into one another, forehead to forehead.

What had just happened?

"Why?" My voice is hollow and broken.

His groan, low in his throat shows frustration and annoyed I break free from his grasp.

Again? Really?

"I want you Lu; God I want you." The huskiness in his voice is unmistakable. "But not here. Not now. I want this to be special for you. Rule number one; I decide when and where."

Oh crap I'd forgotten the rules.

I chew my lip, anger swimming inside me, ready to erupt volcanically. This guy just isn't worth the hassle. *The problem was that that was utter bollocks - He was totally worth it and I knew it!*

"Rule number two; like I said I will need more than one night together. To satisfy you completely, I'll need several nights… or days … or afternoons." His sensual smile is seductive with its promise but irritates me.

"I don't know whether I like this. Maybe I want to decide *if, when, where, how* - or just keep us as friends. Why are you the one who gets to choose when?"

"I know you're having a hard time with this, believe me - so am I -

rock-hard!"

His eyes drop to his evident erection, straining through his jeans and it warms me that I did that.

"You know Rule number 2. Rule number 3; you mentioned that you're open to anything. If I ask you do something you must trust me to try." His dark chocolate eyes search mine for a reaction and satisfied with my outwardly undisturbed manner, he smiles. *I'm starting to regret saying I was open to anything. Shit, what would he want me to do? I'm not a backdoor action kind of girl.*

"Like I mentioned, I'm going away on business for a few days. Think about *my* offer and say yes to all my rules when I return. I'll forward the remaining FBR's whilst I'm away."

It isn't a question and his voice is remarkably calm, annoyingly so. His handsome face studies me, willing me to retaliate and then he makes a move towards the backdoor. I'm completely silent.

"Right. Well I'll be off then. I'll see you at Suzie & Gino's do. Saturday night?" he asks, stroking his head in thought. I nod, desperate for him to leave me to my embarrassment.

"Lu…when it happens, the first time, its not going to be some quick fumble on the kitchen floor. You deserve better than that… than me really. But I promise you; I'll drive you wild. After the first time, we can get down and dirty wherever you please." His voice lowers with the latter statement, causing me to look up at him with wide green eyes. I watch him head out through the backyard, stopping only to wave casually over his shoulder. If I hadn't seen the huge bulge in his jeans, I'd think that this whole bizarre situation wasn't affecting him at all?

Like I concluded yesterday, I'm in seriously big trouble. How had this started out feeling like I was the one controlling the terms and now Sebastian was at the helm of our agreement?

Chapter 12

Lucia

The next few days in my Elysium diary are booked out solely for The Ashton. It deserved my full, undivided attention and as I juggle quotes and source materials with relish on Wednesday, I'm grateful for the distraction from my sex life. It only left every other waking moment to consider my discussions with Mr. Silver on Tuesday night. The man in question was in Manchester until the weekend, bidding for work on a large chain-project there, which was a major coup for Silver Construction - or so Nathan had mentioned the few times we chatted about Ashton work, this morning.

He was never bloody home! To be fair to him, wasn't that one of the excuses he'd used last night for us not taking it further?

I suppose if I'm honest I am glad of the time to breathe and think clearly. I've pretty much made up my mind to forget anything ever happened between us, forget the bloody rules and offers, of amazing sex at all hours, and move on. *Like it was as easy, as that.* The man was total head fuck; I want you, I don't want you. I want you, just not now. I'm going to drive you wild...

Arrgghh!!! I'm thoroughly disappointed that since my stupid proposition, we don't seem to be able to connect verbally. Before all this palaver, Seb would have told me about this Manchester gig. We'd have spent hours hashing out the tender together, be it on the phone or e-mail. We always asked one another for advice, in both our businesses. Now it appeared we'd stopped the small-talk altogether, stopped the banter, stopped anything... well with regard to everyday life. I missed it and I missed him as my *friend.*

I'm glad I'd managed to fit in my yoga class this morning after dropping Finn off at Crèche - I'd never have had the energy after work. Plus it had given me some serious time to focus my thoughts and channel all this nervous energy.

I'm about to sit down at my desk, when Jackie excitedly shouts across the room from her own office area, headset securely in place - very Madonna circa 1990. "New potential client alert!" Pointing her well-manicured finger at the handset close to her ear. "I'll punch it through to you?"

I nod acceptance and clear my throat. "Hello Lucia Myers speaking - how may I help?"

A polite woman with an infectious laugh and real verve for her small boutique public house, named Carolyn Walters is keen for Elysium to work our magic over her five bedrooms, with a potential to extend that number to ten, budget dependent. Twenty minutes of Mrs. Walter's positivity and the day feels better already. I had a good gut instinct for people and I knew from one phone-call that we'd work well together. By the end of the call I have an appointment to visit a Country Inn in desperate need of refurbishment, all courtesy of James Marcell. Already it appeared that The Ashton was looking profitable and I hadn't even waved my magic decorating wand over the rooms yet. I make a mental note to thank him for the referral and scribble down a few notes.

Chewing the end of my pen, I mull the potential brief over. *The Gilded Fox* - What a fabulous name for a hotel. I'm already brimming with creative inspiration for themes, fabrics and colour schemes and couldn't wait to go and site survey the venue.

My phone buzzes next to me and I quickly take my eyes away from my work for a second to check the text. It's from Leo. I try to ignore the slump of my shoulders in disappointment of it not being from a certain other male.

Really looking forward to our night out Lucia.
Couldn't remember if I'd text you but I'm happy to accept x

Poor guy. I'm really not that interested, especially now that I'm considering sexually exploring another man - even for a brief period. I'm a one-man kind of girl - always. I can't even get excited by a text from him that shows he is really keen or be bothered to reply. I remind myself to reply to it later and settle down to catch up on the mountains of work scattered across my desk. However, after several minutes of unproductive paper pushing and post-it organisation, I sigh deeply and throw myself back in my chair dramatically. I need a serious pep talk and grabbing my phone I text Abs, hoping to grab her for lunch.

**Fancy lunch at The Velvet Cupcake;
Man trouble x**

Abby is a text maniac and the response flies through faster than it usually takes to push through the ethos.

Sounds good. B there in 15 ☺

"Right - I'm nipping out for lunch. Won't be long, I holler to no-one in particular." Locating my purse, sunglasses and bag.

"Slacker!" Colin shouts slyly from his desk in the corner of the studio and minces his way towards me. "Where's your head at Lu? Certainly not here! Maybe giving a little too much head away elsewhere?"

My attempt at disproval at his racy comment is hollow and instead I reply evenly. "I'm fine - just a little preoccupied. How are you getting on with sourcing the flooring for The Ashton?"

I try to remind him of our working relationship. Not necessary really as Colin was a star and usually his little risqué quips lifted me but I needed one of us to be on the ball with work.

"Keep your sexy panties knot-free - s'all good. I'm now on with the lighting. It's bloody lush!" His eyes telescope dramatically upon the last word, causing me to giggle. "There you go. That's what we like. Now bugger off you crotchety bitch and eat cake or something - anything to chill out. You're seriously wired tighter than a nun's crotch!"

I smirk at his silly analogy, only a gay man would feel comfortable talking about a woman's vagina, with other women, but I nod in agreement and give him a pair of cheeky *victory v's* in retaliation, stroked slowly up and down my face. His belly laugh makes me smile further.

Patting Jackie's shoulder tacitly in acknowledgement of my impending absence, so as not to disturb her current telephone conversation, I jump as she plants a firm grasp over mine. With her serious secretary face on she holds one slim finger up in front of me, mouthing the words silently but expressively. "It's Mr. Silver for you."

Oh Shit, I'm not ready to speak to him yet - its been two days but the longer we leave it the bigger the divide is becoming. I'm waiting for amazing sex, with this amazing man but at every turn I feel like he's doing me a favour.

I shake my head and hands frantically, "No - no I'm out!" and wait silently until she's managed to get rid of him.

"Soz Jackie. I'm on my way out. I'll ring Sebastian back when I'm at lunch."

"He is rather persuasive." Jackie eyes widen with her comment.

Oh if only you knew Jackie.

"I think this is from him as well? She reaches under the desk and hands me another FWC box.

My eyes light up in excitement. "I've waited for years to get anything from this florist and now twice in one week."

"Fuck me!" Colin crudely shouts from across the room. "That's two of these spectacular boxes now – Ms. Myers must be allowing her very own *spectacular box* to be de-flowered by the right man to warrant this type of attention! Monsieur is serving it up on a Silver platter me-thinks?" The Kenneth Williams' drawl is back.

I swat his comment away in embarrassment. I still haven't fully determined who sent the first rose, last week; I'd just presumed it was Sebastian but he'd never mentioned it and I hadn't thanked him in return. Somehow, it seemed to add to the mystery of our relationship and I admit that I like it.

"Er that's not *all* Lucia. There's also *these*." She wanders over to the small kitchenette area, whilst taking to me over her shoulder and disappears inside, promptly reappearing, carrying the largest bouquet I've ever seen. She peeks her head around the side of the greenery and smiles cheekily.

"I Know. I mean. WOW! I think these are from him as well. Here's the envelope but they *were* delivered from Silver Construction so no prizes for guessing who sent them."

I smile at the delicate pink peonies, white and pink lilies, and lime anthurium's all wrapped in pearls and tied with a huge pink bow. They showed he'd really thought about the arrangement, *and therefore moi.*

"Would you put them back in the sink Jack and I'll grab them tonight."

"Of course I will. Don't forget to open the box too," she shakes her head and returns to her desk. "I'd be happy with one flower delivery. You really need to tell me your secret Lu. Josh is getting rather complacent."

The ringing bells of the work phone save me having to respond to her ascertaining gaze, as she switches back to receptionist mode and I turn to cast my eyes over the black velvet box next to me and lift the lid. The rose inside is practically exactly the same colour and position as its predecessor, with the same diamante pin added to its centre. It was beautiful - if a little gothic in comparison to the stunning peony bouquet I'd also received. They couldn't be more different but I suppose they showed both of Sebastian's sides.

I check my watch and grabbing the accompanying envelope and the one from the peonies, practically run out of the office. I was going to be late for Abby. It's only as I check my phone in the lift that I realise I've had four missed calls and two texts from Sebastian. How had I not seen or heard them? It must have been whilst I was on with Carolyn Walters.

His text reads.

I can see that Elizabeth twitch from here – it's making me hard!

Licking my lips I quickly check behind me. *Was he here? No stupid you're in a lift!* I quickly check the second text.

Ahhh I made you look. Call me Lu! Stop ignoring me! Don't back out now!

In that instant I'm rendered useless! I was weak where sexy Sebastian was concerned but even weaker when he made me laugh. He knows me far too well. I remember the cards in my hand as the lift nears the ground level and roughly tear the flap open from the one that came with the rose, first. The bold printed script font spells a simple message that speaks volumes.

FWC

Missing You!

Touched by the simple message, I turn to the other envelope and slide it out, unfolding the handwritten note. It couldn't be more different.

FBR NO.41

WE KNOW EACH OTHER AS FRIENDS
BUT WE ARE STRANGERS AS LOVERS.
FORGET OUR HISTORY TO ENJOY
YOUR SEXUAL EXPERIENCE.
I KNOW YOU LU, STOP THINKING
& JUST LET GO!
SEBASTIAN X

His raw sexuality is apparent even in his block capital scrawl; he'd always written in capitals and I smile at the sentimentality before shaking my head. He was right. For this to work, I had to forget our history to enjoy the ride and just the thought of the possibility of such a ride made my sex clench in anticipation. So much for forgetting the whole proposition and moving on - try telling my bloody responsive body that!

I quickly punch out a reply to his text and press send.

I'm not ignoring you. I'm busy at work.
I'll see you when you get back. I like FBR 4 x

❦

Twenty minutes later and I'm watching Abby enjoying her bagel with gusto and I'm envious. I've found it difficult to concentrate on food since Sebastian has thrown me this curve ball of emotions. We're cosied up in the corner of our favourite little cafe, famous for its cupcakes and quaint lunchtime treats. Cucumber sandwiches, smoked salmon and cream cheese fillings and delicious crab and mango salads. There was always something to tempt us. Usually anyhow. My appetite is non-existent but I order a pastry to fend off future dizziness and allow Abby to revel in her hmming moans, enjoying each morsel greedily.

117

"Soz babe. If I don't eat it now, I won't later. I've got a feeling your news will put me off - am I right?"

I shrug complacently.

"So spill. Let me be the judge and jury." Placing her scrunched napkin down, she chews her last bite slowly, focusing her full attention on me at all times. Bless her - I knew she was madly busy with an Ad Campaign for a national telecoms company and it touched me she'd take time out of her chaotic schedule to lend an ear.

"Oh Abs I'm a mess. Its all such a wanton mess." I add sweeteners to my tea and take a slurp, pathetically.

"What's happened?" she asks concerned, also taking a sip of her cappuccino. "Has he been in touch since the crappy *'Thanks Pal'* text?"

I close my eyes fleetingly in memory of a pair of hypnotic hazel flecked ebony pools and smile back at my lovely friend. She looked great -very trendy in black cigarette pants, green silk shirt and large turquoise statement necklace. Her signature sleek bob scraped back off her elfin face, Sharon Stone- esque.

"Things have changed dramatically since then - you look *hot* by the way."

She wiggles her shoulders wickedly. "I'm meeting Nathan after work for drinks - but enough about him, stop changing the subject. We're here for Senior Silver."

I laugh at her nickname for Sebastian. He was the older brother yes, but he was hardly ready for meals-on-wheels.

"Well... I took the bull by the horns and propositioned him by text, but you know all that - basically after he'd tried it on with me I knew there was something there. I really need to move on sexually Abs, as you keep reminding me..." I pause and look up at her sly smirk. "...Anyway, I thought why not and asked him for *'one amazing night without ties!'* The next day he turned up at The Ashton, to quote for the building works looking bloody gorgeous in a designer suit, wearing a sexy smile; I was totally unprepared."

"Oh my word - how did it go? Did you get the project?" she side bars, back to work.

"Yes. Yes - loads of work; going to be manic. Amazing project. James Marcell is fab... u... lous. But back to Seb."

She laughs at my bossiness and mutters *'Sorry'* sarcastically, under her breath. I'm on a roll now and need to get the *chaos* that the past few days had been off my chest.

"After the weekend, I just thought that he didn't like me that way. We'd finally kissed; had a fumble in bed. Well actually it was soo hot, so much more than a quick fumble and I would have bobbed on then and there, slutty I know, but he'd changed his mind. I thought it was me - I completely froze when he went near my scar."

"Oh Lu - nasty Niall has a lot to bloody answer for."

"He does, I agree, but it was the first time another man had been near it and I just... well, froze. Turns out it was the perfect excuse for Seb to back out."

"I've told you before, the fact that you've got a zip, means your vajayjay is still in tact. Women pay a fortune to have it all tucked back up and trimmed."

We both shudder together at the thought.

"Well - I decided the next day that if I didn't sleep with someone soon, I'd always feel inferior, thanks to Niall and after Seb came home last week, I knew I wanted him to be the one to ease me back into it. Seems to work for all the other bloody women out there - why not me?"

I blow on my tea and taking a large gulp, shiver as the hot liquid slides down my throat. "Anyway on Monday, I received a rose from Fresh Water Couture with a message that said *'I Accept Your Offer!'* You should see this rose Hun, its stunning, all velvet box and diamante pin, really lovely.

"Sounds amazing; so you're on then?" I smile at my friend's rapt attention, her elbows on the table, hands cupping her face.

"Well yeah - he turned up at The Ashton, and told me we *were going to happen* and *it had been on the cards forever!"*

"Bloody hell! But he does have a point." she wrinkles her brow softly in agreement.

"I know, but seriously, the best is yet to come. He said the only things I should consider were when, where and how many times I'd come! I mean come on - the man doesn't play fair!" I rub my hand frustratedly across my forehead. Just repeating it had brought home how shocking the moment had been.

She nearly chokes on her coffee. "Sexy mother fucker!"

"I. Know!" Sniggering at her crude language, I repeat my earlier comment more forcefully and relaxing take a nibble of my cinnamon whirl, the sweet pastry melts in my mouth. "Then, after driving me to the edge of wantonness...he...he just left me there!" I stammer the words annoyed at my own weakness and my friend's, knowing smile.

119

"Don't look at me like that Abs. I'm seriously pathetic around the man."

Patting my hand in a motherly fashion, Abby reapplies her lipstick and, smoothing back her hair, settles back into her tub chair. "I've never seen you like this Lu. Have you seen him since?"

Through a mouthful of icing I nod. "Yesterday! I was cooking tea. Niall brought Finn back…"

Abs interrupts my spiel by screwing up her pretty face at the mention of my ex's name again and I flick her disapproval away with my hand.

"Yeah I know, the knob himself. Anyway Niall brought Finn back from Crèche and ended up stopping a while. We were chatting when Seb turned up." I can see from Abby's raised eyebrows and dramatic 'o' shaped mouth, how much she gets me and how much she realises that that kind of confrontation would be nasty.

"It wasn't pretty. They haven't seen each other since Niall walked. Niall kept saying he wanted to talk about something - he was really touchy-feely actually, when I think about it. I wonder if he and Karen aren't getting on?"

"Poor Niall - That would be awful for him if things didn't go his way."

We giggle together cattily as only best girlfriends can when discussing their ex's. Niall was nothing if not spoiled.

"After Niall had gone Seb & I bathed Finn." I continued but Abs interrupts me again, clicking her fingers.

"Ooh very domesticated. That's my girl."

I laugh at her. "Stop it naughty. He wanted to talk but I needed to get Finn to bed, so two birds, one stone blah blah."

"Two balls, one rock and drag him to bed, Flintstone style and just get on with it." She mutters saucily and I belly laugh. This is why I needed to be with her today. She was a star and much more spontaneous than I've ever been.

"Get your mind out of the gutter… I finally got Finn to sleep and we started to talk. Something we've always had no problem doing. One thing lead to another and we were bloody kissing… again!"

"Did he make the first move or you?"

I look at her face, intently focused on me and ponder her question, remembering back to last night, his hands on my body, electric currents fizzing along every nerve.

"He did." *I didn't put up much resistance though, I think inwardly.*

120

She just nods and encourages me to continue.

"There were loads of mixed signals. He said it was *me* and *him,* and that he was never here, made lots of excuses for the *fuck-up* that had been last weekend but at the same time kissed the socks off me. I was so turned on I made a move to take his t-shirt off, thinking *sod it,* we're grown-ups, we've agreed to *service one-another* and he stopped me... *again!*"

Her big liquid brown eyes mirrored my own confused expression and I wince.

"I know, right? All the men in my life want to do is *talk* to me... and all I want to do with him is *touch.* Now I'm getting flowers like it's my birthday and *Missing You* messages and the latest in a long line of fuck buddy rules... look!"

I thrust the handwritten note in front of her face and calmly she retracts it from my clutch and thoroughly examines the evidence.

"Woah! - Rule number 4 - how many will there be?" she hands it back to me before adding. "All very illicit though - I like his train of thought. This should be done properly or not at all and you definitely need to go with the flow, if you go down this route; he's the expert after all!" Her wink makes me grin and I chew my lip in thought.

"Do you want my honest opinion though?"

"Of course."

"Sebastian and you have unfinished business. There's obviously something there; we know that, probably always has been. But... and I know you don't want to hear this - you've been out of the game a while, he *is* and always has been, a player and I don't want you to get hurt. I'm proud of you for putting yourself out there and moving on from that dick Niall but I'm worried that you won't be able to stop at *a brief affair?*"

I nod mutely, it's my one niggling fear too but I can't just *'not do something'* for fear of getting hurt, and I repeat this to Abby, who agrees wholeheartedly.

"OK. So you're decided you *are* going to do this, go into it with *open eyes* and *open legs* Missy." Her deep sexy laugh is contagious and I join in before she holds a hand up and adds,

"Hey, what about Leo? Aren't you supposed to be taking him on Saturday night?"

Crap I'd forgotten all about him. "Yep."

"Well give him a chance, as date experience and worst case scenario you can use him to make Sebastian jealous. You'll only be following rule number 4: Forget your history and act like strangers, to enhance the plea…suurreee."

Giggling as she puts on her sexy voice, I consider her words. "You're a wise old bird Hun but what about all these FBR's? No.1: He decides where and when, No.2: Not just one night but more, No.3: I need to trust him and be open to anything… blah blah blah." I catch the glint of humour in her eyes.

"What?"

"You just don't like the fact that he's more in control than you are babe. Don't drop everything for another man though. Your thong maybe but don't let him have it *all* his way… unless you're up for a bit of submission?"

I shake my head at her excessively. *I'd never really got all that Yes Sir. No Sir. Three bags full sir, bollocks.*

"Don't quaff at it unless you tried it Hun; not so bad," she raises her brows saucily at me.

"Seriously too much information. What about you and Na?"

"Oh God I've so much on with work, I didn't think I had time for anything remotely related to a love life, then Nathan came along and boom - I'm a goner!" Her face shines with radiant excitement. "… and enough with the old!"

"Talk about delayed-reaction!"

We laugh together and start to gather up our things. It was unfortunately time to get back to our respective offices.

"You know me Lu, caution is not my strong suit. He sent me a text asking me to go to S & G's with him and I literally danced Gangnam style around my computer, I was so ecstatic. Hardly playing it cool - hey? Behind every frog…" she smiles coyly at our favourite analogy of finding a good man, amongst the many crappy ones and we shout in unison, "… is a horny toad!" and collapse, giggling like silly teenagers.

"Seriously though, Nathan is most definitely *not* a frog. If it runs in the family I don't think there'll be anything cold-blooded about him. Rather so hot you'll sizzle!"

I correct her teasingly and feel for my best friend. She had it as bad as I did. These brothers had cast a spell over us both and within a week we were bobbing around in a wave of quick silver, clawing at any scrap they threw our way - disgustingly desperate and it worried the hell out of me.

"I'm seriously going to have to be careful with this guy Lu." Her face crumples at the inevitability of what is undoubtedly to come. "One kiss and I'm ready to let him delve in and fondle my fortune cookie!"

It's my turn to cough up the last remnants of my drink in shock but she continues,

"Honestly! – It's desperate to have its path crossed with silver." Her dirty laugh fills the room. Eyes twinkling, aware of her bluntness and open mouthed with innocence she shrugs. "I can't help it Chick. My cookie has turned into a monster!"

We collapse in laughter until putting our jackets on, Abs stops in her tracks, a familiar look upon her face. I knew that face; she was forming a plan.

"Forget the bloody men - you and me Friday night - drinks at Rehab. I won't take no for an answer."

Her perfectly threaded arches dare me to decline and I sigh.

"It *is* Niall's weekend. Although he's bringing Finn back Saturday morning and then taking him again in the afternoon, complete pain for Finn and I."

"God that man's rubbish - I swear he does it on purpose! You know, so its impossible for you to have a man stay overnight?" I think she's hit the nail on the head with her opinion; I've often thought the same thing myself.

"But... I was going to chill, as we're out for Suzie's party the night after. Maybe give myself a mani-pedi." *Get myself prepared for seeing Seb tomorrow night.*

I feel her swat me on the arm. "You need to get out there babe - forget Mr. Silver and have some fun Abby-style." Her wiggle tips me over the edge and I grin.

As we make our way to the till, arguing over whose shout it is, I reluctantly concede and allow Abby to pay our tab. "Thanks for being there Abs. Not sure I'm any further forward but certainly feel better for getting things off my chest."

"Well a problem shared and halved and all that." She drops a tip in the bowl for the drippy little waitress we'd scared off with our sex talk.

"Or in our case - brothers - at least they're not twins, that would be way too weird!"

Laughing cheerfully we hug each other goodbye and set off in opposite directions to settle back to the business of design. I head off feeling much lighter and brighter, turning back as I near the end of the cobbled street to wave happily at my Bezzi. Life was unsettled at present but I could always count on this best friend to boost me.

⚜

Sebastian

I run like I'm being chased by a serial killer. My feet pounding on the ground, sweat pouring from my body, pushing my muscles to their limits. Continuing on the path, up past the local pub 'The Babes in Arms', through the snicket that takes me over the local farmer's field and up a hill for another half a mile until I reach the reservoir. My music pumps from my earphones, Right here, right now by Fatboy Slim blasts out - fantastic tune! Each bloody song brings me back to Lu.

It had taken every ounce of willpower I had to walk away the other night and only two things were keeping me sane right now - relentless exercise and cold showers! I wince as I'm haunted by memories of her beautiful hot body pressed up against mine, her tongue darting in and out temptingly, eyes shining with lust. I could have taken her right there on that God damned kitchen top but *oh no* - I had to be the knight in fucking shining Silver armour, all decent and respectable. I'm seriously regretting my offer of a special night of pleasure rather than just getting our freak on, on the floor - puts far too much pressure on us both now.

I stop at the sty, to catch my breath and readjust my ever awakening cock - my stonking hard-on was making things rather uncomfortable - then head off to finish the final leg of my run.

God she was stubborn!

I thought I was stubborn but she was beyond the mule - I liked that she was independent and knew her own mind but together we were a pair of recalcitrant teenagers. Our arguments will not be pretty - I've already had a taste of that. At least she'd been agreeable to my offer of when and where and more than one night. If we were to venture down this untravelled path, we had to have some time to explore and now that we would be working on The Ashton together, I'd be able to fix things, so that was *plentiful!* One month of enjoying Lucia's temptingly curvaceous form - my smile widens at the notion.

As I reach the top of the hill, cows gently mooing at my right, greenery abundant I take a deep breath and enjoy the Yorkshire Dales rolling in the distance, transferring my view over the resplendent reservoir; tranquility at its best. Here things were simple.

My thoughts drift back to Niall. *What was his game?* Lu's so bloody innocent she can't see how men look at her but I did; I saw his eyes and the territorial gleam there, when I grabbed her arse. He'd been seriously pissed that I was fucking things up for him. *Well tough - you had your chance mate, now sling your hook!*

It'd been odd seeing him after all this time and sad really that I still held such contempt for him. Finn was such a little star, I'd winced as he'd launched himself at me, rather than his Dad, but then again you get back what you put into relationships. Niall had, and always would do the bare minimum with any relationship. I feel myself chuckling as I'm reminded of Finn calling Niall *'Lion'* and growling expressively and then the memory of the look of disdain on his father's face stops my smile in its tracks. *Arse!*

I take one last look at the lake; the sky mirrored within it and ripples mesmerising as they form across the surface. I'd have to bring Lu up here with me for a run and maybe a picnic.

The woods were dark and secretive and there'd be no chance of being seen within them - just the thought of ramming into her, outside, amongst nature - naked! *Jesus Seb you're not helping yourself here mate*, an inner voice reminds me as I readjust my cock again.

A quick stretch against an old tree trunk and I head back in the direction I'd come. My music switches to Roger Sanchez, I never knew and again I'm reminded of Lulu; the words are seriously spooky.

I wouldn't press you wouldn't want to stress you, cause we're friends and I don't want that to change but last night when you kissed me goodbye, don't know but I was feeling strange, like I didn't want to leave you, wanted to protect you, want to see you smile all night. I thought maybe I was crazy baby... but when you touched me it felt so right!

I need to get my head out of the clouds and back in the game - not like me to be so sentimental. I'd loved the domesticity at hers the other night, it had felt like coming home after a long day at work, to a home-cooked meal, a freshly bathed kid and sexy woman I couldn't take my eyes off. I'd never craved that before, always enjoyed coming home to quiet after work, sport on the TV and a cold beer in the fridge, but I could get used to it. I roll my lips in frustration at myself; I know me, something deep within is stopping me from letting go.

Tomorrow night we are S and G's for their annual summer bash and Saturday is going to be the night - if I can hold out that long. Thank God I'd been away on business or I'd have had hell on keeping away. I'd sent her flowers on Wednesday; to accompany the latest FBR but to be honest I'd just wanted to be close to her. It was taking everything not to drive over to hers and seal the deal.

FBR No.4 was spot on though; we definitely needed to be strangers to become lovers. We needed a second chance to meet for the first time, which was impossible so this was the next best thing.

I'm nearly home as my phone snaps me out of my daydreaming and I answer. Gino.

"Big G!" I answer pleased to hear from him.

"Mate. How you doin? You 'ome?" His Italian accent is much stronger on the phone and I smile at the familiarity of it.

"Yep just landed now. Why what's up?"

"Na and I are going to Rehab tonight for a couple of beers - you up for it. Si?"

I consider the question. Maybe a night out with the boys is just what I need to take my mind of her.

"Sounds great. Text me when you're on your way down in the cab, you can slide by mine."

"Great. See you bout 7.30."

I click the red button, end the call and jog up the drive to the house, heading off upstairs to shower. Yeah - a night out is just what I need, one without an annoying fuck buddy to invade my mind at every turn.

Chapter 13

Lucia

The sweet sounds of Chris Brown's latest hit *'Don't wake me up'* thrum through the doors as I walk inside our bar of choice *Rehab*. A trendy little bar, built from what was left of the old Bastian fire station. It's main pull was the fact that only 25's were allowed entry and two sturdy bouncers watched the doors at all times, one of which we had nick-named Jerry-curl due to his uncanny resemblance to Daryl from the film Coming to America. This type of security kept it stylish and allowed a consistently high dress code.

Its modern decor was designed in a hotel boutique theme, with plenty of dark segregated areas for good conversation and a dance floor, which appeased the more energetic punters. The best part was it was only five minutes from my house by taxi and although local, definitely competed with the inner city bars, which charged £10 more for a fancy cocktail. I'd been trying to meet with the manager for a few months now, to get in, before they began work on converting the space above the Bar, into a restaurant - mental reminder to e-mail him again next week.

I feel positive. The rest of the week has gone well. Colin & I had grafted on The Ashton and things were in place for next week's construction to begin and I'd managed to get to the wholesalers last minute on the way home from work last night. I'd even managed to make a Paper Mâché alien mask for Finn to take to *Futuristic Day* at Crèche. Complete with googly eyes, tentacles and flared nostrils. Finn had promptly named him Cuthbert and declared me the best mummy ever! I felt like the model mother and I'd found it hard to let him go to Niall's tonight and would have been happy to cuddle up in front of the TV with pizza and a movie.

I'm glad I'd stuck to my plans though as although shattered, the music is boosting me - I'm obsessed with this song, so it's a good start to the night. It makes me feel free and is one of my favourite driving songs on my ipod - on permanent repeat whilst I sing along.

Everything has gone, as I've wanted it to with my appearance. My hair, is gleaming, my make-up sharp; I'd even put some false eyelashes on and my green-eyes now stand out piercingly from two dramatic black brushes. My clothes make me feel sexy and my new pony-skin stilettos, from Dune, (which are kindly assisting me in the height or lack-of-height department) and skinny ripped jeans-blazer combo work perfectly. The naughty no top under the blazer has added a great feminine touch to a relatively safe, boyish outfit and my cleavage is doing what it does best - peeking out, all bronzed and pert.

I feel confident and confidence stands for sexiness, right? All is good and I'm glad I've come out at Abby's insistence. She was right we needed to shake it all off and have some fun. As I reach the bar and ask Abby what tipple she fancies, I glance over my right shoulder. That's when I see him.

Shit!

He is hidden by the central pillar, so is not entirely visible but it *is* him and God he looks hot, dressed in a dark fitted t-shirt, jeans, and black thin skin leather jacket. He is with Nathan, and Gino.

Oh crap! He sees me too.

Our eyes meet for a long second and I immediately feel flustered and turn to put all of my energy, into the guy behind the bar.

What was he doing here? Tonight was supposed to be Seb free?

My heart is pounding as the music throbs around me. There's no denying my disloyal emotions; I'm bloody excited! He's home again.

What did Abby say she wanted? My mouth is totally dry.

"Hi. I'll have 2 large penis' please... oh and soda." I add cheekily smiling at the good-looking young man. He knows I mean Pinot Grigio and I'm sure he's fed up the in-house joke we all use regularly, but like a good sport he chuckles anyway. I flirt outrageously with him, as I feel Sebastian's eyes burning down on me.

Has he noticed? Why would he be bothered anyway, who I chat up? That wasn't against the rules.

Feeling more in control of my emotions we move over to the farthest corner of the room, so I don't appear desperate but still have a good enough view of his nibs.

"Are you alright Lu? I didn't know they'd be here - honest." Abby looks really worried and I immediately give her a quick hug. "So much for having a girly night to wash away the Silver stress."

"I'll be fine. It was just a shock that's all. Just a shame he looks so hot." I bite my lip, considering him again. It was obscene to look *that* good.

"Well so do you; let him see what he can't have on tap – it's time to flaunt what you've got and flirt with the lot of them. You deserve some fun," she offers generously. "Remember what we spoke about the other day."

I laugh at my best friend's cockiness. But I agree with what she has said and as if they have heard my thoughts, someone softly taps me on the shoulder. I spin around into an unexpected face.

"Hey Leo."

His friend Simon is with him and smiles approvingly at Abs, who seems to open up like a flower under his ascertaining gaze.

God Abby, could you look any more desperate?

"Now then Ladies. How are we tonight?" He smiles slowly at us. "Can I get you a drink?"

Holding up my full glass I smile warmly. "We're fine thanks Leo, we've just been served, although good luck getting yours, it's a busy one."

"Lucia, I need to talk to you at some point tonight. Can I get you alone for a while?"

Really? Talking. Again!

He smiles at me with his straight and definitely cosmetically enhanced, very white teeth. I do like a man with nice teeth but why am I always reminded of the scene from friends, when Ross' teeth glow in the dark, whenever I look at Leo's?

Trying to refocus I quickly reply, "Yeah sure. What's up?"

"Nothing's up. Just wanted to make my intentions clear to you again. I'm not sure that I did that properly, when I missed drinks last weekend."

I inwardly groan. I wish Leo were… well a bit less obvious about his interest. Maybe then I'd find him more attractive? Knowing that Seb could be watching us, I ignore the nagging feeling in the pit of my stomach and give Leo my full attention leaning in to talk closer.

"It was fine you missed our date. I understood - I said that on the night." To be honest I was glad that he hadn't turned-up, as I would never have had the chance to experience my flustered fumbles with Sebastian.

"I know you did, and its great we're going to your sister's on Saturday night - I just wondered... you are still interested aren't you?" He takes a long drink of his pint of lager, giving me a moment to quickly find an answer that won't offend but before I can respond he continues. "You just need to say; I really like you Lucia but I can take a hint and my fragile male ego is becoming more and more delicate by the day," he laughs a little nervously but it breaks the ice, none-the-less.

I laugh too. He is funny, in a kind of cheery boyish way, totally different to my moody ex and the overly confident and super sexy Sebastian. He was respectful, had a great job, (cheap mortgages as Abby always reminded me) and seemed to be really into me but something was stopping me from carrying on with our *early days* friendship. I definitely hadn't felt the initial buzz yet, that you get with a new interest. Maybe that was *it*?

Who am I kidding? I know deep down *what* it is or rather *who* it is... and he really needed to just *do one*!

God why are men like buses? They come all at once, or not at all. Three weeks ago, I would have jumped at this opportunity to date a fairly good-looking, stable man who didn't seem deterred by the fact that I was a single mum and came with lots of baggage; the majority of which came from Toysrus.

I look across to where the object of my thoughts is chatting animatedly and notice that he doesn't seem the slightest bit interested in my own activities. Chris has joined them and is laughing at something Seb is saying. Sebastian is so different to Leo, he commands attention and gets it, easily. I watch as a girl I'd known years ago from the pub I'd used to waitress in, whilst at University, muscles her way closer to the group of attractive men; her eyes transfixed on her prize... Sebastian. My stomach juts with that unfamiliar sensation, jealousy. Thoroughly annoyed at my reaction, I place my hand teasingly onto Leo's arm and look at him as intently as I can muster.

"I like you too Leo; I haven't been ignoring you. I've just been really busy with work the last week or so and Finn of course."

I can see Abby mentally encouraging me as she works her own female magic with Simon – I now realise that she too is probably using him to make Nathan jealous. She really does want me to try dating Leo, even if it's whilst experimenting with Seb.

I take her very obvious head-nodding in Leo's direction hint and remember that I should be using this fabulous opportunity that has landed in my lap, even if just to see if Sebastian is actually bothered. I glance up at Leo, through my eyelashes, giving him my undivided attention and thank the heavens for Eyelure falsies and whilst drawing my spritzer, slowly through my straw I smile at him encouragingly. He smiles back and seems to be transfixed with what my mouth is doing to my straw.

"Oh OK. Good. I think you and I could be a good fit."

"Yeah? I mean I'm new to this dating game and I'm not promising anything but let's see... OK?" I place my hand comfortingly on his arm and smile up into his grayish blue eyes, hidden behind dark Bakelite trendy spectacles.

His hand covers mine and squeezes. It's warm and comforting but there are no electric currents; no instant fizz along my skin.

"I've watched you from afar for a while and now I'm helping you with Elysium, I'm hoping to see much more of you Lucia." His eyes are hooded as he watches me for a response and I'm about to respond when I'm roughly knocked to my left and then grabbed in a big bear hug. The remnants of my drink, held in my free hand, are launched all over Leo in the commotion.

"Alright Sis. Lookin gorgeous as ever," a handsome Italian face grins genuinely at me.

"Well maybe before I was all messed up by you G. What are you like?" I reprimand him and lean in to give my sister's hubby a kiss on his designer stubbled cheek.

I notice that Leo seems to have been shuffled out of my near vicinity with the chaos and looks none too pleased and not as dry as he had only moments earlier. I wince for him. I'm also sharply aware of a protective shield, which seems to have wrapped itself around me.

I know it's him. I can sense him. The immediate tension cloaking us is thick and claustrophobic and entirely evocative.

"Look's like he's a bit of a drip, your Theo," he drawls, leaning in towards me, his voice smooth and vaguely sly.

"Don't be awful and it's *Leo* not *Theo*!" I frown at him but find it hard not to smirk, looking past Sebastian at Leo's current appearance. "Leo is great when you get to know him." My voice sounds overly bright and enthusiastic.

"And have you?" His face is deadpan.

"Have I what?" I know exactly what he's asking but I'm not going to make it easy for him.

"Got to know him… properly yet?"

"It's none of your business Mr. Silver, if I have - but actually no, not in *that* way." I say begrudgingly.

Why did I just play my trump card so soon?

"Good, because I'd be seriously pissed off," he snarls.

Recognising my chance to use my last ace, I stare at his deep brown darkening orbs. "I hadn't finished actually, I was going to say, no not in that way… *yet.*" Feeling extremely smug I spin to give my full attention back to Leo; the present company was starting to thoroughly piss me off.

I gasp as I'm grabbed forcefully at the elbow and twisted almost painfully to face my supposed *friend*. "Lu, don't play games with me." He looks furious his face is stern and tense.

"Excuse me? *You* are the one who made the first move, taking us from friends to whatever… *this* is." I lift my hands in frustration and continue now on a roll. "Then when I'd considered all the pros and cons and offered myself on a bloody silver platter to you with my text you agree, before rejecting me… again!"

I take a breath and go to take a sip of my drink, immediately screwing my nose up at the empty slurp as my straw hits ice. I need another one and fast. Looking up at him, we lock eyes and watch each other intensely. To give him his due he looks chastised and I can tell he is thinking about his next move, running his tongue languidly along his bottom lip.

"You're right. Everything has changed between us and I've made a total mess of it until now - its just every time I see you all I want to do is…"

His voice sounds sexier, more husky, and I watch his beautiful mouth as he slowly forms the words unhurriedly.

"… take you."

Oh. My. God!

Desire curls around my body, heating my very core. Arousal is evident in his own eyes but I'm tired of the games. I kick myself for getting sucked in again.

What I would do for ten minutes with my old friend Seb; hormone free. The need, the pure ache I have for him is not enough to risk our friendship. *Is it?*

"Look, maybe this isn't such a good idea Seb. I'm your mate." I look up at him with heavy eyelashes, protecting my true feelings, before adding, "Just leave me alone. Please." I bite my lip; aware that I'm asking him to do something I do not truly believe *is* the best option for us.

"I can't. You're right, I started this but we've entered into an agreement now and I most certainly am not backing out. I can't leave you alone."

He shrugs nonchalantly and leans into the doorpost, managing to look annoyingly sexy and cool all at once. His handsome face makes me want to cup the side of his jaw and lean into him - to smell his Sebastian Scent.

His voice halts my thoughts. "Believe me, I've tried. You're frighteningly hard to shake off."

Nice - like some stray annoying dog!

I try to compose myself and aware of my lack of drink, grab his pint from his clasped hand, take a huge unladylike gulp and smart as it burns my raw throat on its travels down to my belly. I ignore his deep frown at my rather rude behaviour.

"Don't worry, let me make this very simple for you. Maybe I wasn't clear the other night."

I can feel the emotion in my voice, my throat fills and my eyes begin to burn with expectant tears. I can sense that during our discussion, our friends seem to have moved away. Annoyed, I try to switch it down a notch, so my voice becomes much colder and more detached.

"We are supposed friends and that's all we are, all we've ever been, I get it. Recent kind of fuck buddies I suppose you could say!"

Raising his brows, his head furrows and lips purse in obvious anger. "Fuck buddies obtain pleasure from their mutually beneficial arrangements. *We* haven't... yet."

I bite my lip at his crudeness but choose to ignore him. It would annoy him more than any quick retaliation.

"Look Lulu..." Seb moves forward, as if to try and pull me towards him but I deliberately step backwards and placing my arm out, I take a deep breath. It's now or never. I need to get a grip on this situation and take back some control over my life.

"Right OK. Well now that that's all cleared up. I also need to say, don't ever, ever tell me whom I *can* and *can't* see again." On a roll I take a deep breath. "If I want to sleep with Leo, or make my way through the entire Lords' Rugby Team, all at once, I bloody well will.

It's my body and I'll bloody well fuck who I want to!"

Taking a deep breath I throw in my parting blow, hoping it might make a small, well maybe minute, dent in his humongous ego. "Maybe tonight should be the night!"

I glance over temptingly in Leo's direction, with no intention of ever following through with my statement.

Ha, that should do it.

With that I pivot on my beautiful but already crippling new stilettos and flounce, and I mean flounce, it isn't delicate, probably more like Miss Piggy than Miss World, but I think I get my point across, as I head towards the Ladies' toilets. God that man makes me soo angry-my blood is literally boiling. How didn't I see this before and why am I seriously hoping that he's still there when I return to Abby? Talk about self-harming - a bloody self-harming schizophrenic.

It's only as I'm nearly at the turning for the ladies corridor that I give into the temptation and turn to see if he's still watching me.

He is.

He's staring right back at me, his eyes now black, his mouth grim and he looks completely confused. There's definitely a storm brewing of turbulent anger and perhaps, could that be possessiveness? I don't fucking know anymore.

The night pretty much goes downhill from there. I should have left after our altercation. I can't focus on anything but Sebastian and Leo is *far* too keen. An unimpressed Abs calls in the big guns and lines up a row of Jager- bombs, figuring that the Red Bull and Jagermeister shots will boost my abysmal mood! It kind of works and after several dribbly attempts, I'm relaxed into having a good giggle. Even with Sebastian and Nathan hanging around in the background, looking hot as, it isn't enough to stop me finally beginning to loosen up. Niall has Finn tonight and again tomorrow night but as he is working tomorrow, I have him in the daytime. I can't be too hung-over. My responsibilities as a mum are so important to me but surely there's no harm in me letting go a little, guilt free?

"Stop thinking about men and chill out," Abby reads my mind, squishing me to her comfortingly.

"I know. Ignore me Babe I'm just not in the mood. I'm shagged," I sigh dramatically.

"Or not... being the problem!" Abs chuckles to herself and raises her wineglass to mine in celebration of her wittiness.

"What about Nathan? Have you and he spoken tonight?" I pipe up, hoping to change the subject.

"Kind of. Lots of sexual heat and chemistry - that man is *so* going to get it," she winks at me, her pretty brown eyes full of promise and I smile at her confident body clad in skinny jeans and blingy vest top.

"I'm going to make a move Hun. Don't be mad. Are you ready to come with? We'll go to Aldo's and get a disgustingly fattening veggie combo Pizza."

I'm pretty sure that this will sell it to her, when she is grabbed from behind by the tall and handsome, Mr. Silver.

"Sorry Lulu - Abs is indisposed tonight - she's going to be dining a la Silver service," Nathan winks saucily at me and I grin back at him.

Abby beams,, before turning to face Nathan; her face now poker straight. "I'm not particularly hungry."

Nathan laughs at her bored approach; another man who loved the chase. "Neither am I... not for food anyhow."

Oh my! Sizzle. Lucky bastards. I literally shove Abby in her destiny's direction. "Go! I'll walk out with you and you can drop me at the taxi rank."

Abby raises her brows and shrugs her shoulders in an excited *what's a girl to do* way and we grab our coats. I look back to see if Sebastian and Gino are leaving too but its way too busy to see them in the fast filling crowd and as Abs clamps a hand on my wrist I'm dragged through the crowds at break neck speed. *Nothing like playing it cool Abigail!*

As I clamber into the taxi, my phone bleeps. I click my seatbelt on and check the screen.

Make sure you lock your door and bolt your drawers
from unwanted wanderers!
Only one person allowed entry Ms Myers
& I have the Silver key.
I'll be there in 10 minutes x

My heart begins to race and skin flushes in expectation, as I will the driver to put his foot down and get me home ASAP. Jesus, I'm all over the place. After how he's just made me feel, how can I be excited that he's coming back to mine?

Within minutes I'm inside, and am about to lock the door when I hear his sexy drawl, through the glass pane. He pushes his way through, eyes on me at all times.

"Keys." I nod in the direction of the console, standing mute as he locks up, and places them back down where they'd been, and moisten my lips. Even in the dark he looked gorgeous. I realise I'm panting.

"Are we alone?"

"Yes."

"No Leo or Lords' bloody Rugby Team?" His sarcasm is obvious.

"No." It's a whisper of a reply.

I watch as he steps towards me, predatory in his stance, until he stops, cups both palms on my face and draws me in to meet his lips. "Rule Number 5: Whilst you and I have sex, you are mine and mine alone."

Our mouths crash over one another, warm and wet and searching, desperate to unite and with each flicker of his tongue my sex clenches and my nipples buzz. God the man had moves. I press my body into his heat, molding our bodies together and wrap my arms around his waist, drawing his pelvis to mine. I feel the evidence of his arousal digging into my stomach and groan in pleasure; his desire for me was clear now. I feel him move from my mouth to my cheek, the tip of my nose, and trailing to my ear, sending shivers and electric currents throughout my skin and into my veins. I literally buzz allover.

Then he suckles my earlobe, around my drop earrings, licking gently, making my mind go completely blank and filled with nothing but ecstasy, as his hand travels to the single button on my jacket, popping it open, deftly. I push my nipples out to be released but he teases me, running a finger lightly from my breastbone, down my cleavage and over my front fastening bra - continuing down my abdomen, circling my belly button and resting at my jeans waistband. I hear the swallow, as I clear my drying mouth and try to regain some control, shivering in the dusk of the lounge and melt as I feel his mouth lick a path from collarbone to collarbone. I moan and move under his caress, desperate to appease the throb between my legs and the heat burning all over my body. As I throw my head back, his lips on my neck, I feel his fingers at my buttons and the bite of cool air hits my skin; his teeth lightly nipping at the soft skin there.

"What are you doing Seb?"

"Giving you a taster of what's to come in the post Baby."

His fingers graze my now soaked panties, and push the lace aside, before I sigh as his finger plunges within me, lifting me with its force. I arch my back and moan as he mixes circles of pressure with his thumb over my clit and dips inside my scorching heat to fuck me with his fingers. I rotate my hips in rhythm, desperate to come, desperate to continue down this winding road of aching desire; desire that has needed to be fulfilled, by him since last weekend; perhaps always.

I'm nearly there. Nearly peaking when I hear him growl. "No other man will be here. Not Leo. Not Niall. No other man but *me.*"

Then he forcefully fucks me with two fingers, pumping in and out of me with such speed and expertise, each sensitive nerve ending accommodated and zinged into life. Rubbing my wetness upwards, slowly with splayed fingertips and onto my clit, he returns those delicious fingers inside me and with his thumb in tandem; he applies full pressure on my nub, in circular motions. I come with spasming technicolor, immediately clenching around him, trapping him within me. The moment is carnal and violent and fucking amazing.

As our breathing slows to normal I feel him draw me into his warmth and I allow him to hold me there - my jeans undone, pussy throbbing, and the scent of my sex in the air. His cock is hard against me. I want him now.

"You have to be the most frustrating woman I have ever met Lu. We are in this together now. The next time we are together will be FBR No.1".

He kisses my nose. "Such a sexy nose. Soon we'll come together Baby. The when and the where to be decided."

I nod, our heads propped against one another.

"I'll see you tomorrow Lady. Think of me whilst you go to sleep. I'll be thinking about you."

I bite my lip as I watch him unlock the door, close it behind him and post the keys. It's only after he's gone, I realise I didn't thank him. I can't believe that Sebastian, my best friend of over a decade has just had his hands all over me and in me and given me the best orgasm of my entire life. He was right. One night would *not* be enough. I'm all in for one month of pleasure, if this is just a *taster* of what I've to expect.

⁂

Just as I'm about to drift off to sleep my phone flashes next to me.

FBR No.5: Its just sex. No strings. No emotional relationship. I'm not boyfriend material Lu & afterwards we go back to being best friends.

FBR No.6: Finn cannot be around when we connect - a given I wld have thought but just checking. You'll want to be able to scream out loud without restrictions! Sleep tight. Don't let anything but me bite x

Chapter 14

Lucia

Niall drops Finn off at 9am and I flinch as the sun filters through the lounge window, blinding me with its happy rays. My head hurts and tummy rumbles; I never did share that 16inch pizza treat last night - then again, the toe-curling orgasm had been enough to send me off to sleep like a baby. My muscles ache slightly in that department in remembrance and I squeeze my thighs together savouring the thought.

"Lucia - I've been meaning to call you."

Ugghh I can't be arsed with this now. "Really? What can I do for you Niall?"

Encouraging Finn to go sit in front of the TV, I pull the door to; Niall liked the sound of his own voice.

"Have you thought about what I said the other night?"

"The other night?"

That shocks him. *Hmm, maybe its finally clicking that you are not my be all and end all anymore, you narcissistic prick.*

"Oh, I remember now - no I've not." I hide my smirk at his odd expression.

"What's got into you lately Lu? You used to be so…"

I interject, filling in for him. "… easily manipulated."

"I was going to say forgiving." I ignore his unimpressed frown.

"People change Niall."

"Well, better go - I'll be back for Finn tonight about 5pm - I'll feed him."

"Ok. He loves this time with you, you know. I'm glad you're

spending it with him Niall." He nods brusquely before letting himself out and I release the tension from my shoulders in one big whoosh.

After closing the door on my ex, I cover my boy with suffocating kisses all over his head and face, to giggles and protests of *No-More-Mummy*. Then off we go, down to the kitchen to cook up a breakfast feast of pancakes with Nutella, blueberries and whipped cream - his favourite.

"Did you have fun at your Dad's baby?" I ask Finn as he tucks into his first warm fluffy pancake, dollops of chocolate sauce dribbling down his chin.

Through garbled chewing he nods. "Hmm, we watched a movie and I went to bed but I'm not keen on Karen."

Karen is Niall's rather athletic, overbearing and extremely non-maternal girlfriend.

The one he cheated on me with; the one who is entirely welcome to him now.

"Why Poppet?" I wipe his chin and put my plate down. I sense all is not well. His little shoulders seem over burdened and stooped with worry.

"She said that you were a stupid beach."

Oh she did, did she? Deep breaths; keep calm here Lucia. Consider how you handle this.

"Don't worry Finnster - I'm sure Karen didn't mean anything by it." *Yeah right.*

She's probably just pmt'ing and jealous that Niall is onto his next conquest. The man has a massive difficulty with monogamy.

Finn pouts up at me, his mouth full of blueberries and swallows before professing passionately. "Beaches aren't stupid; I like beaches and I like you Mummy!"

I look at his beautiful little face and cuddle him to my chest. God I could eat him up. Why couldn't Karen care about him - I understand she wouldn't love him like her own but she could try surely, if she loved Niall enough?

"Poppet, what matters is you and I and your relationship with Daddy. I'll chat with Dad and sort things out, OK?" He nods quietly, his huge cornflower blue eyes watching and trusting but still not quite convinced. "I Love you sweetie."

"Love you too Mama."

In that instant food becomes the most important thing in the world to him again. My work is done, as I watch him delve into his breakfast with stress-free relish. Bless him, defending my honour. That woman needs putting in her place big-time! I wish I'd had the opportunity to discuss it with Niall this morning but I hadn't known then and I'd found it hard to say *Hello,* let alone have an in depth conversation. It would have to wait until tonight. I can't help but get the feeling that this is all down to Niall though. All was not smooth in his new love life.

"Right. Eat up cherub. We have a date at Auntie Suzie's to decorate for the party and I'm not going to achieve anything in my PJ's. Give me twenty minutes and we'll go and visit the park on the way. Sound good?"

I laugh at his happy squeals of delight and head upstairs, Finn in tow, to make myself presentable for the day ahead.

❦

"Where do you want me to put these Hun?" I ask my sister Suzie, who is in the process of trying to hose down her black rattan patio furniture in her back garden. She spins and wiggles the hose, threatening to dowse me and shrieking, I leap out of the way.

"Ahh. Nearly gotcha," She cheekily moans and greedily reviewing the dishes I've brought and the pack of beers, gestures with her pink, marabou cuffed marigold finger towards the backdoor. "Just put it all in the kitchen Lubedoo – that'll be fine. Thanks for bringing them. Give me two minutes and I'll stop for a break," she smiles happily back at me.

Even dressed in denim cut offs, and a plain white vest and flops, she looks gorgeous. Her silky blonde hair is pulled up in a loose bun and her favourite MAC lip-gloss adorns her ever-pouty lips. The effect is effortless but knowing Suzie, probably took her some planning. Her life was consistently about fashion; she lived, ate and breathed it and had recently made her dreams come true and opened her own shop in the centre of our hometown, Bodley. It was a bijoux Ladieswear boutique, which had gone down a storm from the day she'd made it her goal. I was really proud of what she'd achieved and now *Dolly's* was thriving!

I decide to check out what is happening inside the kitchen and from the main window, which rests over the sink, the view is interesting to say the least. The garden looks like a hurricane disaster zone, with tables and chairs strewn everywhere, giant Jenga puzzles and twister mats and in the centre of it all, a *Bucking Bronco*! I laugh to myself. Only Suzie.

Tonight was going to be fun, if not a little surreal.

Suzie and Gino always threw great parties; they were epic! Last year had been a toga party, and put it this way, the lawn the next morning, looked like a Chinese laundry. How the guests got home with their pride in tact is anyone's guess but they were predominantly in the buff.

My eyes are drawn to the garden again. In the middle of the chaos is an enormous black canvas, which appears to be moving across the lawn. Looking closer I realise that it houses two huddled men, struggling and failing miserably to resurrect the huge gazebo which Suzie has insisted is *a must* in case of rain. Gazing up at the bright blue sky above, I feel sorry for Gino, but the Yorkshire weather could be as temperamental as a hormonal woman, so it was probably for the best.

Upon closer inspection I can see that it is my brother-in-law and Sebastian, who are battling with the pegs and ties now. I instantly find it hard to breathe and my gut instinct is to exit and do it fast. Last night had been amazing but in the cold harsh light of day did I want to see him face-to-face?

With that definitive thought I make the decision to escape and return later before he realises my attendance. That idea immediately goes up in smoke, as my darling son, who has been chattering to his Auntie Suzie runs full pelt at Gino and Sebastian.

Oh crap!

He's immediately scooped up and plopped on Sebastian's shoulder in fits of giggles. They run in zigzags around the garden; Finn using Seb's head like a drum. I smile in spite of my dour thoughts and decide to get a grip and put myself to work, laying the long kitchen buffet table and blowing up balloons and displaying them around the house. I may as well crack-on and put my frustrations to good use. At least Finn would be entertained with *the men* for a while and he was in his element. A little family male company would do him some good.

Half an hour later and the effect of my creative input is pretty much immediate, and the cool 80's neon theme looks fantastic. Suzie would love it. I am so pleased I'd gone the extra mile at the wholesaler's and got the zillions of glass tea-lights in bright neon colours to distribute around the garden - they would look amazing when lit later that night.

Many, many balloons later and I am slightly light-headed from lack of oxygen. I jump, as a cheeky voice hollers up to me at the back door.

"Always knew you'd be good at blowing Lulu!" Gino winks.

God he could be crass sometimes, but I humour him anyway. It was also his main charm, say it as it is and it was hard not to smile around him, albeit often slightly embarrassing. I regularly cringe on Suzie's behalf.

"Oh I am, G boy, but the trick is, one little prick and they explode, it doesn't take much mouth action."

I retaliate smugly. Ha, stick that in your pipe and smoke it.

Gino practically chokes at my response, laughing uncontrollably.

"Ah, but not all men have small pricks, some are large and inflatable and can stay up *all* night," a deep voice comments dryly behind me.

I spin around jumping out of my skin. *Where the bloody hell did he come from?*

I can't think of a witty reply. I am too shocked at Sebastian's crudeness and the realisation that it was meant to be a sexual innuendo and directed entirely at me, in front of witnesses.

I am gladly saved from any form of comeback, as Finn walks in through the backdoor, swinging his arms, shoulders hunched.

"Mummy – Auntie Suzie sent me inside. I'm a tired chicken." His bottom lip is out and he looks weary and very cute. Our time at the park and all the playtime with the guys must have worn him out.

"Right Finny Finn, let's get you home for a do-do's before you go to your Dad's tonight."

Picking his cherubic body up and snuggling him against my hip I wave over my shoulder to Sebastian and quickly make to exit.

"See ya Finnster mate," I hear Sebastian call out behind my retreating back.

"Bye Sub," my little one replies with a sleepy murmur, resting his head in the crook of my neck.

"Later's Lulu. See you tonight FB. You're looking great, definitely got a glow about you - done something different - maybe with your hair, or skin?"

His teasing smile makes me blush from head to toe but I compose myself and ensuring Finn is safely half way out the door, I flippantly lower my voice, replying, "Yeah - it's that new face-cream by L'Oreal; Orgasmic - because I'm soo worth it."

I close the door on his deep sexy chuckles and shiver at the way his voice has managed to send a direct signal to my awakened sex.

Would tonight be the night?

Well I hadn't cancelled with Leo, and whilst I wasn't overly bothered about a date with him, I was adhering to Abby's advice and not just bending over backwards for Sebastian. I had to maintain some control in this arrangement. He hadn't said I couldn't date, just that no man other than him could get in my pants and Leo most certainly would not be going anywhere near them.

Later that night as we drive up into the hills, in the direction of the party I fuss with the hem of my dress and question for the umpteenth time that night why I hadn't just cancelled my date with Leo.

I look across at him, flickering over his short brown hair, and down over his profile. He had good skin. Check. High cheekbones. Check. Ears were a little big and he could do with being a inch or two taller. His dress sense was presentable but that could be bettered, with a credit card and several hours of shopping - the shoe department being our first port of call. Men had to have good shoes. Crap shoes meant that they were crap in bed. Glancing down into the foot well, I spot his sex-offender, matt black specials and wince; going by those, Leo would be abysmal.

Finally, I drop my gaze to his hands. Long lean artistic fingers grasp the gear stick, normally hands do it for me but whilst elegant, his have seen nothing but a keyboard in their time. They'd feel soft and smooth on my skin, unlike a certain friend's roughened touch. I couldn't picture him pinning me against a wall and ravishing me; he would definitely be more of a missionary man, probably with his socks on. *Stop Lu - don't be cruel.* But I know I'm right.

I couldn't see him sending me Fuck Buddy Rules and talking about sex so candidly. I couldn't see those fingers getting me off the way Sebastian's had so expertly last night.

"Do I have something on my face?" his teasing glimpse is warm and I smile back, embarrassed at being caught out at my obvious perusal of him. Thank goodness he couldn't hear the mental pros and cons list going on in my head.

"Not at all. I was just thinking about work and a new potential client I may be taking on." I fluster my way through a blag of an excuse and it gives us something to chatter about the last few miles up to Suzie's. Leo was great when we spoke about business and actually really interesting but I am fast learning that it seems to stop there. He's as dull as the dark burgundy metallic Mondeo he'd picked me up in. Bring on the alcohol!

"The place looks fabulous Lulu, thanks so much for all your creative grafting. You're so clever." Suzie squeezes me to her in a rushed, excited embrace.

"You're welcome. It was fun," I smile back at her stunningly made up face and to-die-for figure.

"You look great Lu. Are you ok? You seem a little nervous?" she suddenly stops arranging glasses and looks at me quizzically.

"Thanks love." I'm touched that she's noticed I'm a bit off my game. I hadn't had the opportunity to discuss *The Proposition* with her yet but now was not the time.

"I'm fine, just a little tired, that's all." Then annoyingly I give in and ask the one thing I wanted to be casual about. The one thing I'd spent the whole afternoon procrastinating over.

"Is Seb bringing anyone do you know?" *Because I have.*

"I'm not sure. I think Gino said he was coming solo, but you never know with Sebastian, there's always a lady in tow. Why?" she grins across at me, whilst now placing crudités on a large white dip platter. "Have you finally started to see that Seb is a living breathing, delicious single man, who has been right under your nose all these years? I thought you two were going to eat each other up in the Champagne Bar!"

I wrinkle my snub nose, ignoring her latter comment and stress unconvincingly, "I've always known that Suze, but we *are* just friends. Sebastian and I, we'd drive each other crazy in a week and ruin what friendship we already have." I mutter it more to myself than to anyone else. I'm reluctant to divulge our agreement as yet to Suzie - I didn't want Gino knowing.

"*I* think you'd be perfect together. But what do I know? Besides isn't that the point to drive each other wild with craziness? Better

145

that, than dull and safe – like bloody Niall?" Suzie blurts out with her own unique bluntness.

I hold my hand up in a stop sign. "Enough. I'm not even his type. I'm not even sure I'm ready for another relationship yet."

I'm not ready to tell her about our proposition.

"Rubbish, the sooner you get back in the saddle the better Lu. You've been the model single mother, worked your butt off and devoted your life to your little man. It's high time to introduce a *big* man into your life again, or at least your knickers. The bigger the better," she chuckles cheekily. "There's nothing wrong with raw, lusty, sweaty, dirty, great sex with a hot man sweetie. It won't make you a bad mother, just a less uptight one."

Kissing me on the cheek, I'm surrounded by a cloud of expensive scents and I smile fondly as I watch her carry the now heaving platters out towards the patio, weaving between the throng of early guests, her amazing legs watched all the way by male admirers. I loved her to bits!

I'm left pondering what she has astutely perceived about Sebastian but I'm also very aware that I have arrived with another man and with that reminder I go in search of Leo. I'd left him with Nathan and Abby who'd arrived at the same time as us, whilst I checked some final details for the party. Last night must have gone well for them as Abby was lit up like a Christmas tree.

Dumping my handbag, under the sink so I can locate it later with ease, I grab a chilled glass of Sancerre and headed out to where the cool dance tune, *Little Bad Girl*, blasts out from what seems to be every corner of the garden. The men have worked their magic again with the PA system and lighting, calling in a favour from a Sound Engineer mate. Suzie had even got a well-known Lords DJ mate of hers from her clubbing days to do a stint for us and he was busy setting up, huge ear defenders at the ready. The vibe was already hot.

I take a moment to look around and people watch. The beat of the music is summer in a bottle, intense and exciting - the night full of promise. The majority of S and G's friends I know, as they are mutual - ditzy Jess being one of them, grinning naughtily at me. However I can see several new faces in the mix. Perhaps they are G's colleagues from work? Either way it is a great turnout and I am pleased for them.

I laugh as I see Gino, mouthing the words of the song to Suzie, as she boogies on the spot. They are such exhibitionists but just fab together. Gino steps towards her and begins to throw some shapes, continuing to mime.

"They tell me I'm a bad boy - all the ladies look at me and act coy. I just like to put my hands up in the uuurr…" He dances around her, his arms waving madly in the air, encouraged by her mirrored dancing and continues, "…I want that girl dancing over thuuurr."

He points at her, undulates his hips and grabs her close to him for a rewarding smooch. They're an inspiration and from the raucous applause many of the guests agree.

I look away smiling, and focus my attention on the garden, which has been cleverly segregated, *if I say so myself*, into zones. The *raging bull* has pride of place in the centre of the manicured lawn. To the left of it is a chill-out area with huge cream floor cushions, which are joined to create one giant mattress. Low rattan tables, housing hurricane lamps, separate sections every so often to create several intimate compartments. Further along, the immense water feature has been completely made over into an exotic fairy woodland, with pinks, blue and greens diluting the water, to form a rainbow fountain, which tinkles elegantly, and continues the neon theme.

Along the large fences, which wrap around the garden, I'd hung bright coloured paper lanterns and every so often staked long sticks with mosquito repellent candles, in the same pinks, yellows, blue and limes. The food area is housed under the offending gazebo, which now stands proud and secure. I want to say *erect* but it instantly makes me think of Sebastian and his hard-on last night.

Get your dirty mind out of the gutter Lulu. My inner voice conflicts with reality; that desire had been for you - you did that to him.

Blushing, I guiltily turn in search of Leo and see him chatting amiably with Nathan, Abby and a few others near the Drinks table.

"Hey you." Abby wraps her arms around me, hugging me happily. "All sorted?"

"Yeah all good Hun." She is such a good friend and I can tell that she's totally into Nathan. "You look lovely Babe." I rub her arm affectionately and wink back.

"What this old thing?" batting her eyelashes brazenly at me. "Courtesy of the catalogue and will probably cost me three times its value, over the next year but it really is worth it, isn't it?" She does a little spin with her hands jutting out at the sides, and struts her stuff proudly. Her bright pink dress will definitely get admired tonight, even if it's only when screwed up in a pile, on Nathan's bedroom floor.

"Anyway snap!" she exclaims standing back and looking me up and down, with a nod of approval.

I look down at my short white figure hugging bandage dress and have to agree, it's one of my favourites and looks great with my olive skin and turquoise suede peep-toes and the large acid torque collar necklace completes the look. It is a perfect choice for the neon theme.

We are chattering contentedly about Finn, shoes, catching up on EastEnders soap gossip, work and as quietly as we can about men, but with Nathan and Leo in deep conversation about shares, next to us, it is difficult to talk freely. Then I hear Abby, "Ahem" loudly, and with her hand over her mouth she grunts *"Sebastian,"* mid cough, to camouflage the warning. The hairs on my arms go up and I shiver. I'm itching to disappear back inside and hide.

"Stop fiddling," Abby hisses into my ear as she moves on to top up her drink.

I drop the strand of hair I've unknowingly been toying with and glance sideways.

Don't look to your right. Don't look to your right. You are not here with Sebastian.

I glance up at Leo and recognising my interest in him, he places a palm in the dip of my lower back, drawing me into his body, his attention still entirely focused on solving Nathan's ISA issues. As I watch him talking animatedly, my shoulders relax and feeling sorry for him, I realise he's trying really hard to fit in. I need to cut him some slack, forget Mr. Silver and try something new for tonight's date. I just wish I could manufacture some attraction to him.

I place my hand teasingly onto Leo's arm and look at him as intently as I can, whispering, "Sorry I left you to just fend for yourself. Party all sorted." I smile coyly up at him, flirting openly, to boost my mood and show willing. It works and I take the opportunity to sneak a look over my shoulder. The coast is clear. My shoulders drop and I step away from Leo's fold. If he notices, he doesn't flinch but I don't need to play the doting date at all times.

I'm about to go mingle when I halt at the sound of my name on *his* lips. I'd know his voice anywhere but now it's rippling over every sensitive nerve ending, doing silly things to my skin.

"Lucia."

The seductive tone is enough to make me take a deep breath

before turning to face him.

"You look beautiful."

Black pools appraise me from my long GHD blown wavy hair, sensuously over my breasts, hips, and legs and down to my painted coral toenails, peeking through my heels. "Nice shoes." He knew I had a shoe fetish.

God he oozed sex appeal.

"Thanks Seb. You don't scrub up bad yourself."

The comment couldn't be less underplayed ... he looked hot! Sizzling in fact! Trademark roughed up jeans, bright pink and pale blue striped Ralph Lauren shirt, sleeves rolled up and worn dealer boots. My eyes are drawn to his hands, his fingers - not that long since they were working their magic on my bits with such immense skill.

After a few seconds of silence, I tear my eyes away from his intense gaze. He didn't look mischievous or playful tonight. He was agitated. I rub my hands over my arms to fend off the goosebumps rising there but I'm not cold. His eyes are focused on my mouth, where I'm chewing hard on my bottom lip.

"What are you doing Lu?"

"What do you mean?" I can't meet his eyes. I know exactly what he's inferring.

All calm demeanours go out of the window as Seb grabs me at the elbow tightly, twisting me to face him and look up at him. My skin burns at his touch.

"Oh *come on*. You know exactly what I mean," thrusting his head in the direction of Leo and rolling his eyes. "*Mr. Interesting* in the corner." He looks furious; his face is stern and tense, the muscle in his jaw twitching as he tries to maintain control.

"Excuse me?" I'm suddenly exceedingly irritated. I came here with the full intention of making tonight's date with Leo a success and he is fucking ruining it. *You keep telling yourself that love.*

"I'm on a date Seb. I told you I was dating again; last week. You just didn't get the chance to meet him in Lords." I step backwards a little and pull my arm free, taking a large gulp of my wine.

He looks shocked at his own behaviour. "I know. I know. I just didn't know you were bringing him here tonight. I told you last night. Rule no.5!" Raking his hand over his head, I can see that he is anguished but at the same time annoyed with himself for giving a damn.

"Sebastian *I realise* that I should deem myself exceedingly fortunate that you have agreed that *I* should be the latest in a long line of lucky ladies, waiting with baited breath to be tumbled by the almighty Mr. Silver." My sarcastic tone does not go unnoticed by him and fuelled I continue. "But - it doesn't mean I should just roll over and spread my legs at the click of your fingers. Although last night was pleasant enough you may remember you manoeuvred me into that position last weekend and then couldn't even finish the deed." I practically spit the last word out, vehement in my statement.

My eyes are bright and glassy; my body so fraught with unspoken feelings, tension and in need of immediate release. I look up slowly at him - everything I feel is reflected there – in his deep pools. The music thrums around us and guests laugh and roar at the latest victim of *the bull*. It's as though the world is going on around us and we are invisible from them all. Leo included. I've definitely pushed him too far, his chest is heaving and his beautiful mouth is tight with frustration.

He looks drop dead gorgeous and all I want to do is reach out and place my palm on his chest - to tell him it wasn't just pleasant - that was the understatement of the year - it had been earth shatteringly, mind-blowingly good.

To give him his due, he replies with such steely calm I'm impressed at his control.

"I'm not even going to justify that with an answer Lucia. You and I both know that you are bull-shitting to stop yourself from truly feeling and getting hurt. With regards to not finishing the deed, we have already discussed this, but believe me I *can* perform. I can cross the fucking finish line so many times that that line becomes blurred after a while. You'll be so wet and wanton, you'll be begging me to fuck you then and there, again and again until I'm buried so deep inside you, we won't know where you begin and I end."

With a slow, arrogant smile on his lips, he rubs his chin roughly with his hand, smug with his parting comment. Then turning at the last minute he throws over his shoulder. "Close your mouth Lu or I'll be tempted to put something in it!"

The gall of the arrogant... *sexy, mother fucking bastard!*

Chapter 15

Lucia

I clamp my gawping mouth shut immediately and nervously disappear inside to freshen up and refill my drink. I cannot get my head around the different side to my friend Sebastian. There was nothing friendly about his suggestions.

Rule No.3: We must become strangers to become lovers and I have to say he's definitely a stranger to me right now. I'm not sure which one I prefer but I do know I miss the funny Sebastian who makes me laugh uncontrollably and is easy to be around. I'd only fleetingly seen that side of him, since the night he'd returned from Dubai. I'm mulling over my thoughts and thinking that I better go and find Leo, when I spin at the sound of my name.

"Lucia. There you are – I've been searching for you." It's Chris Booth and his self-assured smile, which makes me feel like I deserve his attention. It's extremely irritating. God I wish they'd all just piss off and leave me to have some fun.

I politely nod. "Chris - how's things?"

"All good at my end. Great news about that Ashton job! That place is *very* swish."

"Yeah I'm really happy to be working on it and have Silver Con involved. Sebastian said that you were going to be project managing the lads with the *knocking about*?" I politely enquire.

"I begged him to work on this one, to be honest," he says leaning in close, as though to tell me a secret. "I think you and I could work really well together." His voice is laced with promise, "Besides, it's small fish for Sebastian – he likes the travelling – the *big* projects! His feet are too itchy to stay in one place for too long. That's why he and thing-ummy-jiggy worked well together."

Thing-ummy-jiggy who?

I choose to ignore both this and his flirting, although I have to say he looks very smooth tonight. His lightly tanned skin and pale blue shirt show his icy eyes off strikingly and his dimpled cheeks soften what is a relatively harsh face. He was attractive but did nothing for me. I could see why Meg was keen. Shame she'd not been able to come tonight. Something about her eldest having a dance show.

I grab my glass and refill it with the nearest bottle of white wine and decide to try and make more of an effort with Sebastian's best mate, for nothing other than the fact that it looked like we were going to be working together a considerable amount.

"I'm looking forward to it Chris – but I warn you I'm a hard task master!"

"I do like a strong woman who knows what she wants." Oh dear he really does like to *sex* it up. "Plus, Seb is pretty busy with work and the *ladies* of course," he adds winking at me cheekily. "So it'd be nice to meet some new people."

I'm instantly irritated by his topic of conversation and it isn't really his fault. It was the truth. But unknowingly Chris continues oblivious.

"He's such a lucky bastard. You know it was only this week just gone, we'd driven to Manchester to quote for some Restaurant Chain remodel and all the way through the pitch, some bird had made her intentions pretty clear to Seb."

My ears prick up at this tit-bit of gossip and I feel the unwelcome growl of jealousy low in my belly. "Oh yes?"

Enjoying the sound of his own voice, Chris continues on a roll. "Oh yeah, we stayed the night. This blonde was gagging for it and Sebastian took full advantage. Never one to refuse a lady or a piece of the action," he says seedily and I cringe.

"We went out that night for drinks to seal the deal and she was all over him like a rash. Stacey, I think it was?" he stops to think.

The more I get to know Chris, the more I wonder about the level of his intelligence. He's definitely a bit of a jack-the-lad.

"Yeah, Stacey that was her name! Anyway he left us lot early with the hottie and I didn't see him again until breakfast. Like I say - he's a lucky bastard."

He swigs his beer and shakes his head. "He'll never settle down

152

that one. Thought he might for a mo with his latest in Dubai, bout as serious as I've seen him but nahh!" He raises his bottle again and chuckles openly, "Anyway it gives us thirsty lads some rather amusing tales of his adventures - more than enough to wet our sexual appetites."

Oh my God, I can feel the ball of nausea rising up my oesophagus, burning a track inside me. I'm pretty sure that soon I'm going to disgrace myself. I take a deep breath and exhale. I smile through the conversation not willing to show Chris my true disappointment at Seb's indiscretion and faking a laugh to encourage Chris' loose tongue I ask.

"When was this then? Last week you say?"

"Hmm, it was Wednesday. Was a good night," he nods, smiling to himself, inwardly reliving the memories. Suddenly, as though he's remembered some snippet he quizzes, "Hey, didn't you and he recently have a dabble? He's been on about trying to take it to the next level since you were at University and we never thought he'd have the balls or the opportunity - what with you being with...?" He clicks his fingers continuously, grasping for a name.

"Niall." I fill in for him weakly. Oh my, I really do feel sick.

Chris is still oblivious to my discomfort. "Niall, that's it. Bit of a dick from what Seb has told me? Anyway, obviously now you're single the chance was there, and Sebastian must have grabbed it. Said you had an amazing pair of...," he uses his hands to cup imaginary breasts on his chest.

What the fuck? Did I just hear him correctly?

I have no right to be so completely devastated and feel such disloyalty. We are not together. Made no promises to one another. Why do I feel like he's cheated on me with this bloody *Stacey*? I really need to go home and cry this one out.

"Do excuse me Chris, I need to go find my date." I smile overly brightly at him, not willing to show him any weakness or suggestion of my turmoil.

He seems surprised at my quick exit but just shrugs and says smoothly, flickering his eyes over my body appreciatively.

"No probs Lucia. I'm looking forward to getting to know you better. I think we have a lot in common and Sebastian and I have very similar taste in women."

He rubs his fingers up the outside of my arm, sending a shiver of distaste around my body. I literally want to go and jump into the fountain to wash the feelings I've had in his vicinity away; I shake it off, turn and not responding, disappear outside.

"There you are Babe. I was ready to send out a search party." Abby grabs my arm and leads me towards the food table. "Are you OK? You look like you've seen a ghost?" She disappears into her clutch, fumbles around and locating her Clinique compact, shoves it at me. "Blush and lippy - now!"

I shrug at her bossiness and holding my hands up in resignation I complete her instructions.

Suzie joins us, nibbling on a cheese and cracker. "You alright Sis?"

"Oh I'm fine. Chris just took great pleasure in telling me that Sebastian had given him the lo-down on mine and his shenanigans last week," I declare, blotting my lips on a tissue. "Oh and that's not the best of it - Chris happily regaled how apparently according to Seb I had a nice pair of boobs!"

"What?" Suzie and Abby say in unison, their faces horrified.

"I know. He wouldn't do that would he?"

"I don't know love. Men can be pricks, especially if the booze is flowing," Abby acknowledges sympathetically. Giving me a cuddle, which Suzie mirrors, leaving me squished, laughing between them.

"Lulu Sandwich!" the girls cry out giggling and Abs adds, "To be fair you have got fantastic tits Babe - I'd brag about them if I'd had a go in the ball pool."

We laugh consecutively again - she always cracks me up.

"It doesn't sound like Sebastian though," Suzie ponders, calming herself down and smoothing down her dress.

"That's not the worst of it! Apparently Sebastian pulled a client last week, only a few nights, after *our* night together. I know we didn't complete the act but *still?*"

I look at my two dearest people for support, my desolation marking my open-book face.

"OOHHH!" Abby cringes, pulling a severe Wallace and Gromit mouth and spins around to grab another nibble. Mouth full, she mumbles, shaking her head, "That's not good. I don't know; you and Seb have always had unfinished business but you're both too bloody stubborn to see it."

Suzie hmmm's her total agreement. "But maybe you two are just meant to be friends?"

"To be fair to Seb, you're not a couple!" Abby rubs my shoulder in affection, wincing a little at her own bluntness. "Besides you're dating again too. *You* came tonight with Leo?" she reminds me gently, "Even though he is soo not your type - at least you tried!" she giggles, more than a little pissed.

I glance towards Leo, who's still deep in conversation with the others, Sebastian included and concur with her last comment. She was right but she'd encouraged me to go for it. She was also right about Seb; I had double standards.

I was just annoyed that Sebastian wanted to *do* anyone else, after *we* had connected in that way. I suppose I had narcissistically thought that if we ever did get it on, *I* would be enough to change his philandering ways; that *I* would be special enough. Not looking likely.

God he was turning me into a needy, desperate mess. How had that happened?

A night of messed up, strung out emotional disaster and one amazing orgasm and I was talking about a relationship with him. Well he could go and jump. That would never happen!

I look across to where he laughs happily with Nathan and my eyes are drawn to a pretty blonde at his side, draping her amazing body over him at every opportunity. He must have brought someone with him after all? Talk about double standards? At that moment the blonde locks eyes with me, and smiles smugly like a cat - reaching to whisper something intimately into Sebastian's ear. I watch him lean in and smile, at her words.

What had she said to make that smile reach his eyes?

It had been enough for him to return the favour and draw her towards him, before they clinked glasses. In that moment I realise that I don't see him as just a friend anymore - I'm too disturbed by his contact with another woman. I can practically feel my eyes glow kryptonite green and I realise that he was right, if we were to ever act upon my proposition properly, we'd have to act as lovers before friends.

I spend the next few hours taking full advantage of the great company and the copious amounts of alcohol flowing freely. I am determined to find strong fun Lulu and ignore the irritating blonde permanently glued to Seb's side.

Gino is singing to Suzie... again! She looks utterly exasperated with him. Funny! *Dr. Alban's, It's my life* is playing and I love this retro song but he's altered the words to *'She's my wife'* and is happily regaling it in front of her at every turn of the repetitive lyrics. He's certainly no shy retiring wallflower.

I then double over in laughter as we watch Jess attempt the bull, ungainly climbing aboard, dress and all. She lasts less than a minute and flashes a brief menu of what she'd had for tea earlier, before being thrown like a rag doll onto the mattress below and sparking up a fag. She's such a laugh but such a lad!

Then Stu, one of Gino's work mates loses a bet and the good sport that he is, submits to his dare; riding the bucking bronco, full throttle, sliding around uncontrollably at every jerk and thrust, whilst wearing only a sock on his knob! *Classic.* Not surprisingly, others are reluctant to sit on the bull after his stint there!

It's as I'm watching Stu wander around, swinging his sock at anyone within a 5mile radius, I sense I'm not alone. To my left stands the clingy blonde, sipping her punch daintily, head tilted in my direction, eyes perusing. Her artistically highlighted hair is worn similarly to my own, and falls in waves around her shoulders, with caramels and honey lowlights woven in and amongst the more platinum shades – I want the name of her hairdresser; he or she, was an artiste.

She has large, heavily made up deep blue doe eyes and a tall, lithe figure with a small waist and a good bust. Yes, definitely Sebastian's type – I sulk to myself. I want to be a better person and try to warm to her but it's unlikely to happen and I can tell she feels the same.

You can't get on with everyone, especially when a certain gorgeous male contractor was the common denominator and the ultimate goal – for her of course; I remind myself!

"Lucia isn't it? At last we meet. Sebastian and I have talked *all* about you."

How is it that someone can make such a simple sentence sound so bitchy? How do I play this?

"I'm sorry I'm on the back foot I'm afraid?" My nonchalant tone hopefully knocks her down a peg or two but it was true I didn't have a clue who this woman was, other than the latest in a long line of Sebastian's scores.

"Really? I find that hard to believe but I'll go with your play. I'm Toni. Sebastian's…well his everything," she ends her statement with a forced tinkly giggle.

Ahhh of course– the cogs turn, and the heavy click of realisation kicks in – this must be the illusive Toni with an *i*!

Upon closer inspection, her face isn't quite as pretty as I'd first thought, in fact was more angular and now spiteful in its glee of her branding of Seb. She's very attractive though, in a Cameron Diaz kind of way. I consider her carefully, smiling back at her, never taking my eyes off her face, well maybe once to look her up and down condescendingly - *I just can't resist.*

Finally I speak. "And?"

That floors her. I can tell by her narrowed glossy pout and the way she's shaking her hair about ridiculously that she's annoyed at my lack of emotion and attention.

"Sebastian said you had a strange sense of humour. I just thought I'd introduce myself as we'll be working together on The Ashton project."

Ugghh I'd forgotten about that.

She continues snootily. "We spoke on the phone?"

You mean when you spoke to me like a piece of crap?

"Yeah I remember now; Toni with an 'i'. You and Seb are *very close.*" Her eyes narrow, probably weighing up if I'm being genuine or sarcastic. "Sebastian said that you and I would get on famously but I'm not so sure. I don't believe that men and women can be friends without sex and Sebastian does like sex." She nods at her own assessment. "He doesn't need a friend, when he has me. So maybe keep it professional, hey?"

What was this chick on? Maybe it was the fact that I'd suddenly seen Sebastian as a sexual object, rather than a mate but Toni with a bloody 'i' was seriously pissing me off.

"Look Toni, Seb and I have history, both professionally and as best friends. I don't like to be told who I can and can't see, by anyone - let alone someone whom I've never met." I add rather cattily, smug at her apparent irritation at my comeback.

Why am I being so off?

I can see Abby snapping her fingers in appreciation, rapper style behind Toni's form and I smirk and return to my opponent's steely gaze.

"Well there's no need to get your knickers in a twist about it, I just

157

think that it's best that you leave this project to me to sort. Sebastian really doesn't have the time for these menial decorating jobs of yours and there won't be any mates' rates you know!"

WTF? Menial decorating jobs?

This woman was about to go down. I can't stick her after only a few minutes in her cloying perfumed company. I'm thankfully saved as Abby rescues me, introducing herself politely and asking the one thing I'd actually wanted to hear fall from the PA's lips.

"So Toni, who did you come with?"

"Sebastian of course - oh and Chris."

"Nice - a kind of works outing?"

"Well no but we all work together obviously." Her nervous laugh is enough for me to see that she wasn't truly with Sebastian tonight.

"Right Lu it's time for you and I to strut our stuff and throw some shapes. Nice to meet you Tory."

I smirk at the deliberate mistake and it doesn't go unnoticed by Toni, if her narrowed blue eyes are anything to go by. We escape unscathed this time and I lick my finger and hold it up to Abby, stroking it through the air with a sizzle noise - definitely 1-0 to moi.

Chapter 16

Lucia

It is during those next few hours as I begin to relax, keeping a close eye on the PA from hell and Seb, and flirting outrageously with my date, that I conclude that lovely though he is, Leo is just not for me and never would be. We just don't connect in anyway; we have no history, no spark and he's dull as dishwater. It was time to end things before it went any further.

If I'm honest I'd always known it but I had wanted to take the chance and test the theory that not all relationships were built on initial fireworks! The problem with Leo was his rocket had never left the soil. Whilst I'm powered with Dutch courage - courtesy of the lethal Pimm's punch Suzie had concocted this afternoon, I take the opportunity to grab Leo for a one-on-one. I feel very guilty. He had come to this party at my request, mixed with everyone, most of whom he didn't know, and whilst he certainly hadn't been the life and soul of the party, he'd at least tried.

"Lucia. A moment alone at last," he smiles genuinely at me.

Oh bugger this was going to be harder than I thought.

"Have you had a good time Leo?" I try to ease into my end game, soothingly. *He even makes me sound dull.*

"Hell yes. I've had a real laugh. My mates are less — shall we say — expressive?" he laughs at me and I join him. I can imagine the banking world full of uptight, stressed out tech-geeks and sympathise with him.

"I'm glad you had fun. I'm really sorry my head's just not been in it tonight. I am glad you came though." I look up at him, wishing that

159

I felt something more for this rather simple undemanding man.

"Wouldn't have missed it but I'm enjoying every last part as I know it'll probably be the last time that we do anything together again, as a couple. Am I right?" his voice softens and lifts in the hope that his assumption is incorrect.

God I feel awful. I hated letting people down.

No be firm Hun. Now's your chance and he's making it easy for you.

I nod, scrunching my shoulders in and my head down, as though I'm about to duck for cover. "I'm so sorry Leo. Its not you…"

"…it's me," he interrupts. "Thought you were more original Ms. Myers." His comment is heavily laced with sarcasm but I can tell his feelings are hurt.

"No it's Ok really. I really like you but I can tell if a girl is into someone else and I'd rather be Numero Uno. Pretty much a deal breaker for me." He shrugs amiably, "And I don't mean your son."

I look up at that, screwing my nose up. "Someone else?"

He smiles at me. "Your builder mate, Sebastian. I knew it the first minute I met him tonight. I've spent most of my time trying to avoid being visually hung, drawn and quartered."

I snigger at his last comment. "Sebastian and I are just friends. We have been for years."

"You may have been friends initially but I'm telling you now, from a male perspective, that man is *in to you* big time!" He says sadly but firmly.

"Sebastian is a law unto himself, always likes a challenge – don't let him make you uncomfortable. But I'm glad you understand that you and I are not meant to be. I'd like to remain friends." *I'm not about to tell him I've propositioned my best friend for sex. I've a feeling Leo would have gladly taken me up on the offer, had I posed it to him.*

"I'd like that too - when I'm around you, you relax me, I'd definitely like to see you more. Besides you and I have some serious hours to spend together over the next quarter to ready your books and balance your sheets, so we need to get along."

Shit.

I'd forgotten all about my tie with him and Elysium but business was business and he was taking this really well so I'm sure things would be fine. I'm suddenly grabbed in a cuddle and squeezing me slightly, he leans me back and kisses me softly on the mouth, perhaps lingering a little more than I would have preferred. I feel his hot breath against me; he tastes of beer and antiseptic. There is no tingle,

160

no buzz that heads straight for my greedy bits, its just rather… blah. The moment is entirely awkward but I'm reluctant to make him feel any worse than I have already, so just go with the flow and statuesque, wait from him to release me. As we part I look straight into the eyes of Sebastian, who's watched the whole scene from afar. He doesn't look impressed - his liquorice blacks narrowing in discontent.

"Thanks Lu for your honesty. You've definitely got me back into the game. After my divorce I've found it hard to trust again but you've helped me. You're special. Anyway, I'm going to make a move before the bull's-eye on my back is hit by an angry jealous *mate's* dart."

So even Leo had felt Seb's disdain. We laugh together, at his correct assumption and he quickly hugs me to him again. This time I immediately withdraw. I didn't want to hug him; didn't want to give him false hope.

"You're OK to get home?" he checks, ever the gent.

"Don't be daft, I'll get a taxi, later on but thanks for asking. You're a true gentleman Leo Peterson. You'll make someone a very happy lady one of these days."

He smiles, waves off my comment and weaves his way to the gate at the bottom of the garden, car keys jangling, thanking G and Suzie en route. I'd forgotten he was driving. No wonder he'd found us all a little overbearing. Poor thing!

⸎

After Leo has left I throw myself into having the fun I'd promised myself I'd have that night. Abby and I dance away, to the cool music beating around us. She is flushed and happy and I can tell that Nathan's interest is having a good effect on her. They are really good together. It seems like they'd been a couple for some time, - all very natural.

My friend's brown eyes glint mischievously, her dark bob sleek, as she holds her nose and with her arms wiggling in wavy lines, she dips in a Sixties' dance pose, similar to Mia Wallace in Pulp fiction. I copy her rhythm and before long Suzie, Jess and others have joined us, jiving like Travolta. We must look ridiculous but we don't care, we just enjoy our carefree abandon. I feel relaxed and happy and at that moment I sense someone is watching me.

I look over towards the fountain, where guests congregate around the seating area. Several are enjoying the games, twister in particular, some the music and many each other. My eyes are drawn to one couple in particular and I recognise the female, as one of Suzie's friends. She and her husband are devouring one another with mouths, hands, everything, and taking full advantage of the huge bed of floor cushions. I am incredibly envious of them at their desperation to be together, never mind the voyeurs. Out of the corner of my eye, I see a movement and turn to focus more clearly.

It is then that I see *him.*

The object of my own confused state of mind and my need to be close to him overwhelms me. I have never felt such a driven desire to be with another man.

He's the one watching me.

Smiling and enjoying my dance, as though it is just for him. I sheepishly shrug, slightly embarrassed but fuelled by wanton confidence. I seem to be providing him with a non-stop parade of exotic dancing recently, all free of monetary charge – the cost is to be determined later and I am concerned that it will be great but I don't care; the courage of my lack of inhibitions, gently pushing me towards this infuriating but mesmerising man.

I'm not sure whether it was the feisty argument we'd had earlier, the build-up since last Friday night, the fact that Leo was a definite no-no and on his way, or the sexy couple giving a live porn-show in the garden – whichever, I am consumed with such immense sexual need and drawn to Sebastian with a pull which is too irresistible to resist. All I want him to do is kiss me and we could figure out the rest.

The small fizz of excitement forming low in my belly is enough to boost me but my mind is saying he should be pursuing you, not vice versa so I stay rooted to the spot. The music switches up to something more current and as it starts Abby points to her ears and yells.

"OMG listen!"

As I hear the first words begin, I recognise the latest track by Neon Trees, blasting throughout the garden and I laugh at the huge coincidence. What were the chances? Actually slim to none, as the wand of reality sprinkles over me and I clock my cheeky mate's wink. She shrugs her shoulders in time to the beat, while mouthing dramatically, 'Cos this is trouble, yeah this is trouble... *sleeping with a friend,*" and in that moment I know she'd requested the song.

I smile coyly at her to assure her *I'm fine with it* and let go, getting lost in the throng of fellow movers, smiling every so often at Abby, as we energetically throw ourselves into enjoying the DJ's expert mixing. The beat of the dance music is loud in my ears and hums under my feet and for a short while, I forget everything and just move, swaying rhythmically. It feels good. I feel sexy and know from the many admiring glances I'd received from other men, I looked good. I could feel my confidence growing, with the added boost of alcohol infused buoyancy.

I suddenly jump when a firm hand grips my hip and I know instantly it's Seb. I hadn't seen him make his way over to us but I'd been oblivious to anything but the music ebbing around me. I continue to move, my arms in the air, as I looked at Abby and she winks at me, moving off in Nathan's direction. Her work here was done.

"It seems they're playing our song Babe," he grins at me, moving sexily to the beat. *He'd picked up on the words then, recognised their relevance to our situation.*

"I've been watching you wiggle your sexy curvaceous butt for the past five minutes. In fact, several other admiring voyeurs accompanied me. Was that your intention?" he drawls, grabbing both hips in his hands. "Either way, I am here to save you from one of them. Lean back into me."

It was a demand, a compliment and an insult all in one; I couldn't decipher which annoyed me more or what his intention was. However, I do as I'm told and lean back into him and we continue to dance together. He moved like he kissed. He had a modern sway to him, which was both sexy and forceful and the position we were in, cried out *erotic*. It was so nice when a man could actually dance. No silly moves, just great timing and pure confidence, mouthing the words of the track, directly to me… 'Ooh Ooh, you got me in the mood… Oooh we're in danger, sleeping with a friend.'

I'm totally turned on, my belly tightening in excitement. Something about the music, the beat, the words, our bodies grinding, just makes me feel naughty.

I twist my neck to look up at him and he leans in towards me and moans into my neck. "You have no idea what you do to me."

I tremble. God I'm already damp with expectation. If I'm honest, I had been all night. *Why is he constantly giving me such mixed signals?*

He moves to twist a strand of my hair around his finger and I back away, reluctant to lose myself in a moment, which is so unexpected and probably would not end well.

I decide instead to tease him and move away further into the makeshift dance area to escape, as my mood is not one that wants to submit too soon. Suddenly, another guy leaps at the chance to join me and moves in close, trying to gyrate against me. I do my best to disentangle myself from him but he is incredibly persistent and *very* pushy. Abby's gone and I can't see Seb. I think I recognize the gyrator as one of Suzie & Gino's neighbours. Working my way backwards towards the edge of the floor, the guy is leaning in and trying to lunge at me, whilst suggestively forming the *hourglass* shape with his hands. *Yuk!* He really needs to get new material. Abruptly the man is shoved aside, as Seb places himself between us, with a triumphant but annoyed expression.

"I think you should dance elsewhere *mate.*"

At the word *mate,* the thruster looks a little surprised but doesn't give up, obviously infused with beer courage. "What the fuck Pal? Who are you?"

I laugh to myself, at the irony of the question.

Yes who is Seb? Who is he to me? What am I to him?

"I'm the guy she's with. She's mine. Ok... *mate?*" He laces that last word with serious contempt.

The guy gives a light shrug and skulks off in answer, with a nod of understanding that only men would appreciate. I'm not sure what to say or if I can speak. I'm both relieved that Seb has pushed away a potential problem and yet annoyed that he feels he has the right to do so on my behalf. I can also feel the telltale thrum of excitement weaving its way around my body, as I recognise this to be a monumental turning point in my life.

The music thumps around us forming a kind of invisible bubble, away from everyone else, as I turn to stare at Seb. His eyes bore right back into mine, with particular focus on my mouth and I lean in to speak to him, to be heard over the music.

"Thank you." That's all I can think of to say.

He looks angry and slightly annoyed and seems to be struggling for control himself.

"Told you that arse would get you into trouble Lucia. Let's go get a drink. We need to talk."

Feeling completely reprimanded I dutifully take the hand he offers me and follow him to a quieter part of the garden. He is looking at me in such a territorial way – there is definite passion there, even if I question what is happening to us, I don't question my eyesight.

"I think about you all the time. Not as a friend."

He looks pained and nervously rubs his hand over his head. "I think about your mouth, the way I know other men do and imagine what you could do with it. What you could do with it on me." He sighs exasperated, "Now I can't get it out of my head."

He steps back onto his foot, allowing us both some breathing space but immediately thinks better of it and shifting balance he clasps the fence post that stands behind me. It was odd seeing him so unnerved but I didn't want to interrupt. This had to come from him. I continue to chew my lip, intent on his face. Amazingly calm and quiet for me. His eyes seemed to bore holes into my face, as he searches every part of it, seemingly looking for answers to his own confusion.

"Since you sent me that request all I've wanted to do is take you home and fuck you until you can't walk. I want to make love to you slowly, passionately, until you shatter around me. I want you - no, I *need* you Lu." He brushes his thumb over my lip and rests his forehead against mine. "I didn't see this coming but to be completely honest I've wanted it forever."

Nervous bubbles of excitement began to build up inside my tummy, sending an electric fizz along every part of my skin. He slips both hands underneath my hair to cup the back of my neck, easing me closer to him.

"I'm coming home with you tonight Lu. Tonight is the *when and where*." he demands assertively.

The cocky arrogant bastard; he never asks he just demands. Rule No.1, I presume. "What about your date?" I raise a brow in question.

"Who?"

"Toni."

"Toni isn't my date tonight. We came together in a cab, with Chris but that's all."

I nod my understanding and glance across to where Chris and Toni are currently attempting twister, then look up into deep black pools, willing him to kiss me.

"What about Mr. Interesting?"

"Leo left ages ago - it was never going to work between us."

With the gentlest of touches, he plays his mouth over mine, increasing the pressure and connection between us, as he feels me relax. This quickly turns into a devastating slide of lips, which whispers untold promises and I weaken. As he deepens the kiss, a hot sensation pools low down in my belly, and washes over my entire body; exploring every part of my mouth thoroughly and slowly. I can feel the passion building to a craving so desperate, that I become weak and yet completely addicted. I don't want it to end. I wrap my arms around his neck, drawing him into me and sigh as his chest grazes mine where my nipples scream to be touched and swollen breasts ache to be enclosed in his large palms. Wanting more, I grab his shoulders and feel his hand lightly graze the side of one breast, before continuing on to cup my bottom possessively, his finger pushing gently at the inner part of my perineum, through the fabric. Shivers rock over me indecently as his tongue flicks over mine playfully and I melt as the spark ignites and fizzes. If he lifted my skirt right here and now I'd go with it.

I'm not given the chance, as he pushes me away from him and moistens his mouth. "Stop chewing your lip Lu - you've no idea what it does to me. Time to go."

Duly reprimanded I immediately do that and gazing into his blackened eyes, I tremble and take a breath. The severe throb between my legs is controlling every thought, beating in time to the music ebbing around us. Frustratingly at that moment, we are interrupted and Sebastian turns at the sound of his name.

"Oi Seb; Beer?" Chris hollers in his pissed-up state, waggling his own empty bottle in reference.

I cringe and am gutted at his timing - just as it is getting good and I'm thinking with my body rather than my brain for once.

"Not for me Chris – Ta – I'm good." He salutes him across the garden.

This unfortunately doesn't deter Chris and he hurdles over one of the rattan chairs, nearly breaking a leg in the process and launches himself at Seb.

"Ah come on mate – have a nuvva, the night is young!" he whines in a put-on southern accent. "We haven't let loose in a while, besides that girl Mel is it? - Suzie knows her anyway? She is really into you – fink you're on a promise with that un and Toni. Take your pick!"

I know he's drunk but I'm finding it harder and harder to like this guy. He always seems to be...well... there - in the way. And appears determined to stop us becoming, an us!

"Lucia, tell him!" he wraps an arm around my waist, far too close

166

for comfort for my liking and looking at Seb's face - his too.

I untangle myself from Chris' hold. "Sebastian's his own man Chris. He knows what he wants and knows how to get it." I say the words directly to Seb, as though Chris isn't even present and turn to head back up to the house. I'm suddenly very weary of the games and decide that it's now or never.

"Yeah, Yeah. Anyway Seb, come on! I've got her lined up. Come show us how it's done."

I hear Chris brag and look back to see him arching his brow and nodding in the direction of two blonde women. I follow his path. Both ladies, if you can call them that are in the process of trying to dip their now bare feet into the fountain, whilst showing everyone who cares to look, what they had for tea; the neon lights glowing through and up their now transparent minuscule dresses. Time to make a move, with or without him. I couldn't be arsed with this anymore and couldn't compete with a wet t-shirt competition, been there, done that, a long-time ago and it hadn't got me into his bed then.

Chapter 17

Lucia

Fifteen minutes later, I'm mulling over how much had changed in one week. We're now in practically the exact same predicament we had been last Saturday and are sharing a taxi, after Seb has surprised Jess & I, as we clambered into the cab and hijacked our ride home. In my mind, I'm clear about being dropped off at Rose Avenue, first; he could do whatever he likes. The man frustrates me too much to share anything other than a lift - I'm too annoyed at his constant *player* tendencies.

The air is fraught, as I nervously fiddle with my bag, desperate to have something to do with my hands. He had to be the one sitting next to me in the back – Jess is in the front, chattering away to the poor overworked driver and is clueless to the tension exuding from us.

"Have you been busy?" she rabbits away mouthing the usual *Groundhog Day* patter that I'm sure every cab owner hates.

I am wound so tight that my back aches from holding myself so rigid. How come he'd left Chris I wonder and *The Promise* in the minuscule dress? At the same time, I'm honest with myself and I don't really care about the why's and why not's – I'm just grateful he's going home… alone.

We pull up outside my house and I scrabble out, frantic to get away, so that he can't see how much I want him and how weak I am at that moment. One look at my face and Sebastian will know how devastated I am - that he isn't standing by his earlier decision to stay at mine.

Jess isn't letting me escape in a hurry though and flinging her arms around Seb and I, she pulls us all into an uncomfortable threesome; a clumsy huddle of banged heads and squished bodies.

"Night Bitches!' she shouts at the top of her voice, walking backwards barefoot towards her street, which adjoins mine at the junction, her wedges swinging from her waving hand. She salutes us - à la Simon Cowell, and disappears around the corner, giggling tipsily, evidently amused at herself.

It's only as I cheerfully wave her off in amusement and turn, I realise that Seb is now perched on my top step, his arms resting lightly on his knees and his black brooding eyes focused completely and directly on me. The Taxi is dust.

"Give me your keys you silly woman," he commands obviously irritated and staring blankly back at him, I just hand them over, without argument. Clearly the lack of comeback is due to the extreme shock I'm experiencing. The audacity of this man is un...fucking...believable!

He opens the door, waits for me to enter ahead of him and then does the same, locking it behind him. I glance up, admiring his ability to look so fucking hot at 2am in the morning. God only knows what I look like. He walks towards me, forcing me to move backwards until I meet the lounge wall, which backs onto the hallway stairs, hitting it with a clap. I've a serious moment of déjà vu, with flickers of last night's knee trembling orgasm running over me.

"You and I have unfinished business lady. I agreed to a night of sex... that will make you melt."

He stands in front of me, his arm propping him up against the wall. He smells divine, all fresh and musky and male. My instinct is to buckle under the extreme glare of his now sparkling black orbs but my legs are too wobbly to move.

"You've paraded yourself in front of me all night, in that tight little number." He looks me up and down and his eyes stop at my mouth, which I unknowingly moisten, rubbing my lips together.

I stutter dryly. "But Chris...?"

"Chris can be a dick... and his timing is shite. I told you tonight was FBR No.1!"

I'm racking my brain to form words into a sentence. I'm fresh and antsy and so bloody horny I'm on fire. My inner voice is berating me and reminds me that this is exactly what I want - have wanted since last Friday night - perhaps since we met? Our body language has altered hugely and we've been dancing around the tension all night, literally. What a hussy I am! I went to the bloody party with another man and now here I am, about to go to bed with Sebastian.

I look up at him, aching to feel his lips on mine, at last.

"I'm going to fuck you Lucia; long and slow and hard," his deep voice emphasises the last words, drawing them out, exquisitely unhurried, to enhance my reaction. I swallow and take a deep breath inwards. It worked as I feel my panties soak and core clench, in expectation.

Oh. My. Word.

"We are going to do what we should have done years ago. It's time now; our time."

His mouth twitches at the corner, smug and sexy in its pose and reaching down to clasp my hand, he draws it up to rest on his teeth, grazing my knuckles lightly with them. Sharp tingles of desire shoot through my body and I shiver at the simplicity of the gesture.

"The only question is, am I going to carry you up the stairs or do you think your legs are steady enough to walk?"

I'm open-mouthed at his pompousness and annoyed that his interpretation of my inability to move is correct. God this man loved himself but boy did I want him and unfortunately I know that he is totally aware of the effect he is having on me.

I retract myself from his grip, slowly and calmly and smooth down my dress. Just a few steps and I'm in the hallway, where I casually kick my bright turquoise suede heels off, at the bottom of the stairs. Looking over my shoulder back at his handsome face, where he's focused on my every move - eyes intent on my legs, I tremble. He is expectant but still so sure of himself. For a second I want to tell him where to go - just a second.

"Give me a couple of minutes then come show me what you're made of!"

❧⨯❧

I thank God that my bedroom has not been left as it usually is after getting ready for a night out - as though I've been burgled, with clothes and make-up strewn all over. Nodding at my quick perusal of the tidy bedding and scene setting, I quickly nip to the loo to freshen up. I clean my teeth and jush my hair in the mirror and double-check that...yes, I have my amazing bra & knickers set on, the one with the black and lime satin lace combo.

It is then that I see him leaning against the doorway. He has removed his shirt, and his well-developed arms, from years of construction work are perfectly showcased against a more than perfectly ripped torso and chest. My eyes continue to enjoy the scenery, leisurely traveling over his battered blue-wash ripped jeans and stopping as long as I dare at the large evidence of his arousal at his crotch. A glance at the floor tells me he's also removed his shoes and socks and is now dominantly barefoot; he really is a walking-talking Athena poster.

My mouth is watering as I allow myself this moment to unapologetically absorb his male perfection. He smiles confidently at my obvious approval and stares right back at me, branding me with a look so hot, I sizzle. I'm undone already and he hasn't even touched me physically.

My mind is battling big time. Part of me wants to just grab him and connect. The other side of me is screaming out, "This is Sebastian, your friend. *What* are you doing?"

Do I really want to destroy our friendship just to appease the throbbing ache I have in between my legs?

I think Sebastian senses that I'm wavering and he decides to make the first move. With his eyes fixed on me at all times he lowers his fingers to unbutton his jeans.

Oh my fucking word.

I bite my lip in anticipation and watch as he begins to slide the denims over his lean hips, looping his fingers inside the elastic of his boxers and dragging those down in unison. I can feel myself panting too quickly and draw a steady breath just as he has finished his strip, the remnants of his clothing kicked to one side. I hear myself gasp. Our eyes remain locked – jet-black v brilliant emerald.

He determinedly stands there in all his glory, allowing me the time to take it ALL in. His beautiful body; on show just for me, and my very own pleasure. I can feel the heat coming off him, smell his masculine scent and I've never been more turned on.

There was no going back now.

His confidence is apparent and why shouldn't he be with a body that could probably get you off without touching you? My greedy eyes are again drawn directly to his groin, where his immense cock, which bounces as he walks over to me, stands upright, straining, veins engorged, the head slightly moist already with his arousal. When erect it nearly meets his navel and his heavy sac swings tight and full, ready to be emptied …into me. I cannot seem to tear my eyes away from it and guiltily blush as his husky voice interrupts my thorough inspection.

"Like what you see?"

I nod and lick my lips in appreciation and anticipation. I know he is assessing me too. I can feel my nipples harden and my other set of lips dampen at the very thought of connecting so intimately with this male perfection.

"Come here. Don't think!" he again orders me to comply and on wobbly legs I move to meet him midway.

He is the only man who has ever looked at me the way he does now, with such need. His hunger and raw passion for me is evident in his brooding chocolate eyes and clenched, clearly defined jaw. This softens slightly allowing two hollows to emerge below his cheekbones, as he sucks in his breath sharply, at my increasing proximity to him. I smile realising that he is not as unaffected by the moment or as calm, as he would like me to think. It makes me feel powerful and more in control.

We meet somewhere in the centre of the room, our lips crashing together in their desperation to join. His eyes go hooded, smouldering in the darkness as he leans in to kiss me gently - placing a hand lightly on my jaw to cup it and bring me to meet his mouth. He smells of his signature scent Dolce & Gabbana The One - my favourite and I savour it for a second, allowing myself the time to catch my breath, whilst he kisses me softly once, twice. His piercing stare is intense and intimate - the moment so profound, that when he speaks, his deep sexy murmur, rolling over me, I melt into him further.

"You and me. Finally."

We unintentionally bang into the bed as we satisfy our frantic need to be *skin on skin*; tongues swooping in and out of one another, exploring, sucking, circling, in and out, in and out, our mouths fucking. The sensation is so erotic that I am out of breath within minutes.

Becoming impatient at the barrier that is my dress, between us, I turn around for him to unzip me. The lightest touch of his index finger, grazing the back of my neck, nearly undoes me and I wiggle to assist him in pushing the fabric down my body - desperate to be free and open for him. It lands in a pool at my feet and he spins me around into his arms, allowing me the leverage to step out of the offending article.

"You're perfect Lu. Absolutely stunning."

I sigh and preen under the sound of his words, and wish I'd left my high-heels on now as I stand in front of him, the chartreuse green underwear glowing in the duskily lit room, whilst the black lace sexily clings to my smooth tanned body. His eyes never leave me, and travel leisurely up and down in waves, assessing every curve before pressing me into his body.

The last time we'd been in this position, it had been in bed, we'd both been horizontal and I'd definitely been less self-assured. I'm not sure why but even though everything is screaming that this is probably not a good idea, my body has not quite caught up with my mind and it is crying out that this is sooo right.

He envelopes my waist with warm, muscled arms, the hairs on them tickling me, as he lifts me off my feet slightly to move me towards the bed. Sliding his palm down my bare arm, he expertly slips it out of one strap then repeats the performance on the other arm. I lift my arms to wrap them around his neck, pressing my breasts to his warm, lightly haired chest and sigh with the overwhelming sensation that our bodies create together. I still can't believe we are doing this, Seb and I.

I lean into him for support, and sensing this he places both hands loosely onto either side of my neck to steady me, sliding them up to cradle my face. Our assault on our mouths deepens, as this strong yet sensitive man shows me that he knows exactly how experienced he is. But as his tongue skims my bottom lip, he growls deeply.

"Let's slow this down. I want to savour you."

Gently stroking a roughly callused thumb against my right earlobe, sending shockwaves of lust straight to my already aching breasts, his sexual whispers continue.

"God Lucia, you turn me on." His breath only adds to the shivers of excitement, making waves all over my goose-bumped speckled skin, causing a slickness to form between my thighs.

He continues a wet trail of licks down my neck, along my collarbone and reaching behind my back, as I arch my breasts upwards, he skillfully unhooks my bra; it drops to the carpet soundlessly, glowing brightly in the dark. The freeing sensation is so erotic and sensual and he immediately takes advantage of the situation, taking both breasts in his palms and lovingly kneading them. His hands are roughened as he slides them up the outside curve of each of them, lightly grazing the delicate skin there and I am pleased - his manly touch is delicious and I am reminded that although I never thought I'd looked at Sebastian in a sexual light, I had spent many a minute regarding his hands at University. Now I knew what they felt like on my body and the reality is even better than I'd hoped.

Sebastian groans in appreciation, as he bends and takes my already hardened nipple into his mouth. He must feel me watching him at work, as he lifts his lids sexily to show black pools full of desire. He stares right back at me, holding my gaze, willing me not to look away, whilst he suckles, then blows gently; the moment is so intense, I find it hard to breathe and after only a few seconds let my head hang backwards and I close my eyes in defeat.

"I haven't been able to get your luscious tits out of my mind since last weekend."

The pressure increases with his rhythmic motions and I thrust them into his palms, mouth; the cool air - anything that will graze the sensitive nerve endings there and cause contact.

I sigh as I relax and allow myself the luxury of concentrating on the immense jolts of pleasure rippling through my taut peaks; my hands now clasped around his waist. I hear him grunt his satisfied content. He knows he has the power; he obviously likes to be in control but suddenly that annoys me and I pull at his head, to draw him back up towards my mouth.

Clashing our lips together, I put one arm around his back, pushing him against me forcefully as his cock juts against my stomach and in that instant I realise he is not in as much control as he'd like to think.

With this powerful insight I am energised and use my other hand to slide my fingers down his smooth rib cage, feeling him jerk sensitively with the contact. Continuing across the hard slab of muscle that is his stomach I smile in appreciation - holy crap he's ripped! Using the tip of my index finger, I gently trace one side of the sexy *v*-shaped dent that runs from his abdomen to his groin, in bliss. I do love a man with a *moneymaker*. He really is a magnificent specimen.

I had seriously not focused enough time on ogling his body over the years.

I can feel the anticipation growing between my thighs, my bits are swollen and ready and I try to close my thighs to ease the building pressure and can feel the damp heat desperate to escape. This exploration was supposed to be affecting him more than me. I begin to stroke my finger lower and lower, desperate to reach my desired end goal. His breath hitches but I continue on my path, drawing tantalisingly down the side of his shaft, amazed at the steely rock hard strength there, encased in luxurious hot velvet.

I'm enjoying my exploration when somewhere to the right of me, the room lights up and I flinch, as we are lit in an ultraviolet glow and my phone vibrates and bursts full blast into *House of Pain's, Jump Around*. I instinctively diminish my sexual immersion of Sebastian and turn to switch it off but my hand is firmly grabbed and clasped tightly behind my back, forcing both aching breasts outwards, demanding attention.

He leans in and against my lips demands me to, "Leave it!"

I happily do just that and weaken under his grasp. Sensing my loss of concentration Sebastian takes his opportunity to seize charge again, cupping both hands over my behind and tracing a finger naughtily down the lace strip that creates the thong, before pulling hard. My panties slide down and with his hands he pushes them further to drop to my ankles before tapping my bottom, encouraging me to step out of them.

We are standing entirely naked, in the dusk of the room, my scars on show and imperfections for him to witness and I don't care. I feel free. Drawing me into his divine physique, cradling me like a porcelain doll, I hear his growl of approval.

"You and I are always going to struggle with control, but we'll be fine as long as you know that I like things my way," he groans into my mouth and kisses me softly.

"Oh - and that I'm *always* right." *Arrogant…Sexy…Bastard!*

He guides me back towards the bed, placing a strong arm beneath my back to support me, as I flop down onto the mattress. With his weight on his knee, he climbs onto the cover and carefully lies down on top of me; I immediately feel the difference between our skin as we connect - his all hard and full of muscle, against mine, soft and velveteen.

The coarse hair on his legs and chest tickle the heightened sensitive parts of my body, which at the moment seem to be everywhere. I am on fire and alive as he cradles me to his body with a definite need so great that I am happy to go with it, as I feel it too. I sense his cock, positioned at my inflamed entrance and lift my hips to angle myself so that he will easily slide into me. I've never wanted a man so much, so soon - never needed to be filled so badly.

"Soon Lady. Soon - I'm not finished with you yet," he commands and breaks free from my grasp, lowering his head to devour my chest. "All in good time."

He licks a long wet trail in swirls around each quivering mound, each areola and suckles on both crests, one after the other; before blowing over each damp path, caressing my body with an icy breeze. The effect is so sensual I shiver in delight.

"You like that Lu? I knew you would be this receptive."

Watching his crooked smug smile, his tongue flicking out to lick my nipple again, I moan in answer as I'm just too turned on to speak. No words could convey the pleasure I am experiencing.

He reaches a finger and holding me in his vice-like grip, slips it inside my open mouth and instinctively I suck it; swirling my tongue around the tip, drawing it deeply within my warmth and teasing him as though it were his cock. He watches me, his eyes sparkling like black diamonds, and withdraws his finger, before rubbing the wetness over a nipple, between my cleavage and over the curve of my stomach. It feels so damned sexy.

I cry out in pleasure, and roll my head back in abandonment, giving in to the immense luxury of a man worshipping my body and then I sense what is about to happen and instinctively try to close my thighs, in sheer panic.

"Easy Baby. Let me taste you. Let me be here."

I'd never had a man ask me before in such a way that felt both gentlemanly and utterly filthy. Relaxing my hips, I ease myself open to his eyes, mouth and tongue; spread open for him to feast on me - the latter of which now flicks teasingly at the top of my folds. Licking upwards with one long wet trail, he reaches my clit, circling, then washing over it, sending shockwaves all over, pushing side to side and back and forth, applying firmer pressure with each lave. This man knew his way around a pussy.

"Oh God Seb…astian…"

I hear my ecstatic reaction ease out of my mouth as I push my hips upwards. I'm still holding a part of me back, as it's the first time we've had sex, let alone oral sex, but as his tongue plunges deep inside me, curling against my inner wall and replicating what his cock would be doing soon, I hoped, I relax and go with it. The amazing sensations were blurring my mind and vision.

It's as though Sebastian recognises he's won and rewards me by thrusting a finger inside me, once, twice, in a pumping motion. *Fuck*. My bottom makes small rocking swivels back and forth to meet his thrusts. He continues this pumping invasion, and with his tongue rocks round and round, across my most sensitive nub. I'm so close.

"Tell me what you need?"

My mind is blank "You."

"Tell me exactly what you want me to do to get you off Lu?"

God I'm turned on and his words are bringing me even closer. "Say it Lu or I'll stop."

"Lick my clit."

"More!"

"Then suck me... fuck me with your fingers."

Where had these word come from - I'd never been so vocal but it felt good to be in control and I hear his triumphant groan as he starts to replicate my words.

"Play with your nipples Baby - let me watch you."

I raise both hands and cup them, fondling them before rolling my nipples leisurely. It felt amazing, knowing he was turned on viewing my enjoyment of my own touch.

The hollow bubbles of pleasure begin throbbing and aching deep down in my body, and start to loosen and float upwards, ready to pop in their travels to my release.

I lick my lips in anticipation; one hand reaching down to cup his head in an almost primal act, whilst his free hand moves from stroking my inner thigh to lie flat along my lower abdomen. I feel it trace over my scar, flinch automatically and take a breath, the night's alcohol, numbing the pain of previous memories - and as I lift my throbbing pussy to his mouth to finish me off, he growls in victory at my acceptance.

The waves begin to wash over me, slowly, deep from within, but building with quick succession. Sebastian continues to reward my pulsing core by lapping and suckling me. The wetness of me as he flicks, creates a repetitive slapping sound and I am set alight as the embers begin to leap and burn. The primitive sound only urges me on, until at last the waves of fire become one fireball and I explode, with exquisite juddering peaks of pleasure shattering and popping around me, my heart pumping so fast I can almost hear it, my skin glowing, body on fire. I thrash about, and moan aloud.

"Oh Baby."

As my orgasm slows, a sensation of complete relaxation engulfs me in the dark and I collapse. Seb allows me a moment to revel in the ecstasy of my climax before I hear him shuffle.

"I need to be inside you Lu. Now."

It is said in almost desperation and I comply by opening for him and hooking my legs around his waist. I am weakened with desire but the twitching ache at the apex of my thighs is still there and I feel desire like nothing I've experienced before, to feel his cock inside me.

I raise my hips to meet him and am so wet his tip enters me immediately. The sensation is delicious. Rocking backwards slightly he enters me fully with such a force, my inner muscles contract instantaneously and he cries out rasping,

"Fuck Lu, you're so tight."

Our mouths meet passionately, lips bruising each other in their intense invasion. I can taste myself on him and it turns me on. Something I've never experienced with another man. The need to experience everything with this man and lay myself bare is a desire I'm not familiar with. He grabs my hands and raises them high above us, entwining our fingers into a tight clamp that he uses to brace himself. Thrusting hard into me with such a force my head bangs against the headboard behind us. I don't care.

He slows the moment down and I shout out breathlessly "Please Seb...as...ti...an - don't stop!"

I am lost to the powerful strokes of pleasure created by our mating and the pressure building between my legs yet again. I have never come with penetrative sex, in and out, in and out - slow and deep, then faster and faster. The immense connection between us is all consuming.

"Oh God Baby," I hear Seb cry out, his broken, husky voice completely undoing me. "I'm going to come."

Turned on by my own ability to wrench this climatic release from him, I grab his sexy tight behind and push him deeper into me. Feeling his muscles there, start to clench for longer and his thrusting become even deeper, I arch my back in acceptance. I can sense the moment he caves; then elated at the moment I'm filled by hot gushes of the evidence of his orgasm. He continues to grind against me, as his orgasm comes to an end and I know that at any second I will shatter around him. With one more thrust, I do exactly that and he crushes me to him, our chests heaving and our bodies ebbing in satisfying sync with one another.

He smoothes my hair from my face and leans into me, delivering a long and deeply moving kiss. I revel in the weight of him, the warmth of him. He'd certainly delivered me one night of pure pleasure. I'd never experienced anything like it before. It had been life changing. Romantic. Sexy. Dirty. Horny. Filthy. Desperate. Wanton - one of the most momentous nights of my life.

"You undo me Baby," he states, looking deep into my eyes. He appears as surprised as I am at his declaration.

"Me too," I agree, whispering the words whilst staring intently into his blackened pools.

"I told you once wouldn't be enough though. You're truly addictive." Sebastian tells me, grinning into my neck and kissing me there.

Oh my God this is Seb, my friend and he has just completely rocked my world. We hold each other tightly and slip into a cocooned bliss. My best friend had now become my lover and we were strangers, starting out again.

Chapter 18

Lucia

I awake to a feeling of uncertainty; I'd fallen asleep the most relaxed and contented I'd felt in a long-time but now reality has dawned on what an incredible and monumental night we had shared. I stretch in delight but immediately am burdened with painful aches appearing – I've pulled muscles in places I didn't even know I had!

With a sneaky glance over to where Sebastian is hogging the duvet, I see he is still deep in a state of slumber. His face is softened in sleep and appears almost beautiful in its perfection. He looks young and stress free and vulnerable; a side that many didn't often see, underneath the hard, controlled exterior. I feel very privileged to glimpse this moment and itch to stroke my hand down his face - his straight *fuck off* nose, but I don't, as I need to freshen up in peace, without his presence. I need to think…alone… and in private!

My mind is completely clogged with the possibility of *us* after what was undoubtedly the best sex I have ever had, but at the same time, it is managing to cloud my happiness with a big dose of reality. *Maybe we should keep this as the one-nighter I'd originally requested? After all he is predominantly more of a one-night stand kind of guy.*

I'm amazed at how bereft I feel at the possibility I would never experience a night like last night again. Maybe never have Sebastian inside me again, although protection needed to be discussed - we'd definitely been careless last night.

We'd also never got around to talking about *Stacey from Manchester* or *Boobgate, or really discussed Toni* I remind myself; I suppose we'd been otherwise occupied. I smile secretly to myself. Perhaps the arrangement that we have, means that discussions like that are out of bounds?

Who had dared to ring me, during such hot foreplay?

I check my phone and see the missed call, from 1.18am. *Chris?* Why would he have been calling me?

It's already 9am now - I really need to get a wriggle on, if I'm to pick Finn up in a few hours. Deciding to ignore all my negative thoughts and stop over-thinking things, I slip off to the bathroom before he stirs. I flick the shower on to warm up and scrub my teeth, wincing as the jiggling movement alerts me to the gentle thump in my head - definitely a combo of booze and lack of sleep - not to mention banging against the headboard.

Sooo worth it though - the lack of sleep bit anyway!

Stepping into the shower, I gently pull the double doors to a close and stand statuesque under the watering can head, letting the hot comforting water cascade over every part of my rather well worshipped body. Smiling at the warm glow building, as memories of how worshipped I'd been by Sebastian begin to fill my fuzzy head; I ponder on how amazing we were together. Not that I'd had oodles of sexual partners to compare it to, actually, only four, including Sebastian, but I am positive that what we shared together last night was incredibly unique. I'd certainly never connected so powerfully with Niall. Sebastian and I had been better together than I could ever have hoped for in my wildest imaginings! It had been instinctive and life changing.

Isn't it strange how two people who have never had any physical connection, other than friendly pecks and the odd hug here and there, could unite sexually and it be so mind-blowingly raw, passionate and... well, desperate? It could very easily have gone the other way and that could have ruined our past, present and future friendship.

It is whilst I wash my body, wiping away any scent of sex, that I open my dreamy eyes to the clatter of the shower door being yanked open behind me, and before I have had the chance to turn, I am immediately enveloped in a warm, exceedingly male and attentive embrace and pulled backwards against his solid form. The doors shut behind us, enclosing us in total privacy. The temperature of the cubicle goes up several degrees and I hurriedly switch the tap to a cooler level.

"Morning Beautiful!" his voice is gravelly with sleep as he wraps his arms loosely around my waist, bending to plant a barrage of soft, wet kisses on my shoulder. I melt again and lean back into his firm body. I'm immediately met by his straining *morning glory*, as it rests its jutting, searching head against my lower back. The reaction I have to this is almost primal; this is much better than the last morning he stayed, I remember to myself. The walk of shame had been cataclysmic.

"You didn't think you could escape a repeat of last night did you Lady?" I feel his satisfied grin, as his new-growth bristles prickle against my sensitive jaw and cheek.

The humidity rises further, steam cloaking our bodies, secluding us from the outside world. There is no longer a need for words. Sebastian continues kissing my neck, sending shivers and a heightened sexual buzz along my lightly goose-bumped skin. My nipples pebble instantly at his touch – I'm so responsive to him, it scares the hell out of me. I groan aloud and quickly close my mouth in annoyance. I didn't expect this so soon - if ever, but I need him, like it's the first time all over again.

Once is definitely not enough!

The water streams over and trickles down our joined bodies, soaking them, and creating a suction effect between us. The silky, satiny smooth feeling of the water filtering over our skin is so sensual I shudder with the sensation. Taking the shower foam I'm holding in my hand, Sebastian squirts some onto his palms, instantly creating a foaming lather, which he transfers to my breasts, delicately smoothing it over them in repetitive circles, kneading them, in unison. The foam expands and pretty soon my breasts are being lovingly massaged with masses of bubbling soap. They feel slightly tender, with an almost bruised sensation, from last night's exploits but this only adds to their heightened receptiveness and I am surprised at his gentleness. I lean in to him further to allow him better access. His balls are sitting against my bottom; they feel huge and tight. How is that possible after what we did last night?

He is hard and lean everywhere and craving to touch him I lift my palms and place them over his, keeping the pressure there, where I need it. His big hands fit my more than ample cups perfectly and I run my hands up his arms, the water and soap softening the hair on them. He is solid in every way!

He whispers words of encouragement into my ear, pulling simultaneously on both nipples, teasing the sensitive tips and continuing the process over and over again. It's as if there is a direct link to my core. If he doesn't do something soon, I'd disgrace myself and come at the mere caress of my breasts.

My cervix aches and I clench to alleviate the throb now beginning between my legs. He acknowledges my need and slides one arm down my waist, across my stomach, trailing along my scar gently and towards the apex of my thighs. I do not flinch this time and open myself to him freely.

As he parts my folds and leans forward into me, to slide one finger inside, he sucks on an earlobe. Then licks down my neck, his finger slowly sliding in and out, his thumb circling my jewel, whilst his tongue travels my skin; the combined actions are so erotic I can feel my womb contract in delight. I feel myself growing wetter by the second as his finger delves in and upwards towards my g-spot - flicking back and forth, pressing the now swollen fleshy mound there. He washes me intimately with more shower gel, using his free hand to part my lips further, so he can continue his *thorough exploration* with the other. The result pushes my clit out further, and provides much better access underneath the small strip of soft hair there. I blush at the carnal act.

I move my arm to hook around his butt, grabbing his taut buttocks in need. He removes his finger and flicks it upwards towards my now pulsing clit, working around it rhythmically in small dipping circles. The whole time we haven't kissed and I crave his lips, his tongue - to be more connected to him. I lick my own lips in desperation, as I near my desired end goal.

"Come on Baby let yourself go!" he encouragingly coaxes me, breathing in my ear. "Now!"

That last order undoes me and I try to respond, gulping as I find my mouth dry and voice broken. I can't speak or focus on anything but the spiralling waves, building within me.

"I need your mout... ahhh," I groan out the words but can't finish, as the crest of pleasure begin to build and ache. Moving my hips to assist him in getting me off; his magic fingers plunge into me again and again and with one excruciatingly deliberate move he eases a slippery finger, back and forth over my *screaming for attention clit* and the fourth orgasm in 24hrs, tears into me.

I explode into a zillion splintering pieces. My release is so violent that I jerk uncontrollably, spasming and twitching as I fall down the tunnel of glitter. I throw my head back and cry out with pure emotion and the complete abandonment of all my inhibitions.

"That's it baby, *come hard* for me," his voice is guttural and demanding.

I am struggling to stand as my knees begin to buckle, my body boneless and the blissful ebbs surround me, as he decreases the pressure there and then stops, just before it becomes too much.

The man was a master of sex.

In the next second, he spins me around to meet him and his beautiful, rock-hard and ready cock. Sebastian gently places a finger beneath my chin, lifting my face up to his penetrating piercing gaze. With the other hand he delicately moves a wet strand of hair from my eyes, behind my ear; his gaze connecting with mine at all times.

God this is intense!

This gentler, lazier side to Sebastian is as sexy as his raw and rampant one and I watch in awe, as droplets of water bounce off his head, chin and then down onto my eagerly awaiting breasts. The simple movement is undeniably erotic.

I reach out to catch a glittering drop with my tongue and in one fell-swoop; his tongue is inside me, duelling with mine. He crushes his palms either side of my now soaking head and the kiss amplifies. It is beautiful, intense and all consuming. We are demanding, and infinitely hungry for one another; it is as though we can't get enough from mere touch and taste alone. I feel him reach around me and his firm touch as he grabs both cheeks of my bottom and instinctively, I know he wants to lift me, wants my legs wrapped around his waist. I want that too.

Letting go, I allow him to support me and as I bounce back down I'm pushed hard against the travertine tiles on the wall of the shower. The shock of the coolness of them, makes my nipples stand proud and more erect. He lifts me higher and bends to suckle on one of them his eyes are fascinated with their bobbing movement as he fits my areola into his sexy mouth perfectly. I watch him flicking his tongue back and forth over my ruched peaks and at that exact moment he looks up at me, and smiles, like he has a dirty little secret.

"You like to watch me lavish your body?" I nod shyly and close my eyes in retaliation to his control over me. I hear him laugh huskily.

Oh Sebastian, what are you doing to me?

I can feel his eager cock is patiently waiting at my entrance, the feeling is so *right*. He is meant to be there. I need to have him inside me. This overwhelming drive to have him buried deep within me at that moment is *urgent*. I need him now!

His hands lightly massage my rear cheeks, still cradling me and with one slight pullback, he thrusts into me. I'm impaled on the full length of Silver charm and flinch at the depth and the soft tissues of my oversensitive pussy wince slightly as it stretches in pain. This quickly subsides to a pleasure-pain as I take a moment to adapt to the fullness.

At my pause, he questions, "Are you Ok Baby? I'm going to fuck you hard. NOW!" His voice slides over me like thick velvet but I can hear the control that he has to maintain from pushing into me, to the root.

"Just fuck me!" I don't recognise my voice but I stare right back and wriggle alluringly in circles of encouragement.

Taking his cue, he does just that, pumping so deep I wonder if I can take anymore. The crudeness and raw passion there is such a turn on as I bob up and down on his glorious cock, I do not want it to end. I watch his straining face, as he throws back his head, his neck taut and yells out, *"Fuck! That's it, Baby!"*

He climaxes hard and powerfully, pouring himself into me as we come together, my inner muscles clenching around him, his scorching semen a welcome warmth on my now cooling body. I feel him twitch with the last remnants of his orgasm, our breaths ragged and lips parted, gasping, as his buttocks clench one last time.

He eases me backwards towards the wall and he carefully lowers me to the floor. I know tomorrow, will be an interesting day in the *aching department*, as I flinch at the stiffness of my hips and thigh muscles. They really aren't used to this type of exercise.

Hell… if a gym workout was like this I'd be there every second of everyday.

He protectively holds me to him, assisting my balance, and we lean against one another, under the water, now warm again, at his sweep of the switch. The quiet is our haven, the only sounds are our heavily panting breaths, and he whispers into my wet hair.

"Thank you Baby, you were incredible. Good Morning!" I shiver at his breath on my neck.

It is only at that moment as I surround myself with his maleness, which dominates my thoughts, my body and my shower that it abruptly dawns on me, that we didn't use any protection… again!

Oh Shit! How could I be so irresponsible?

~✦~

185

Chapter 19

Lucia

What a way to begin the morning I smile to myself happily. There is nothing like a huge amount of toe-curling sex to enhance the glow of your skin — better than any expensive face serum in my opinion. It's knocked years off my complexion.

Must be that new L'Oreal Orgasmic Face Cream? I smile inwardly to myself at our in-house joke.

Sebastian has already left to go back home and change, whilst I ready myself in private. I am glad for the hour of clarity. I'm meeting him soon for breakfast with Abby and Nathan, who have both already text us consecutively with an invite and I'm looking forward to it. I'm also pleased to be arriving separately to our chosen meeting place, *The Brew Up*. A trendy modern take on the greasy-spoon Café, which had taken to opening on Sundays, due to customer demand a few months earlier.

I remind myself that we haven't really focused on anything other than our own sexual appetites and fulfilling them, for the past 24hours! I am not expecting that our escapades now guarantee a ring on my left finger; I'm just relieved to have moved forward sexually and feel very fortunate to have been taken to bed by a man who *knows* women.

Jesus does Sebastian Silver know how to please a woman! He had moves. I'll give him that.

The thought disturbs me; already I fear the time when it will not be me underneath him. When his sexy hands will be playing over another woman's breast, his magnificent cock buried deep inside her. My body had never reacted to a man the way it had last night and

186

then again this morning. It still felt electrified and hummed pleasantly in all the right places - entirely awakened from the deepest sleep. It had probably never fully reached its potential, since losing my virginity. He'd managed to give me a orgasm far superior to anything I could ever have given myself and that was the true test, for who knew a woman's body better than herself?

My mind is drawn to the one thing I didn't want to focus on, but know that I must.

What had I been thinking? Stupid question Myers. You know what you were thinking with and it wasn't your head!

He definitely didn't use a condom. I'd have known and we were in the shower, for God's sake. How could I be so careless? I know it was Sebastian and I suppose that there is an element of casualness over protection, because he is my best friend but he's got a very sexual past and after having Finn, I know that I'm fertile at least.

I'm a single Mum and should have been more responsible. Hell *he* should have been more responsible! I just can't seem to think straight where he is concerned.

I'm going to have to pay a visit to the chemist on Monday, and collect the morning after pill. Walk the walk of shame. Great, I've got the week from hell work wise and now I'd be spending the first few days of it throwing up!

I finish my hair and make-up, on that upsetting thought, and tuck it away to consider later. Selecting a jersey maxi dress in a muted khaki shade from the wardrobe, I pair it with a tan plaited belt, dull gold flops and a faded denim jacket, collar up. I grab my bag and lock-up. Finn isn't due back from Niall's until 3pm, so the day is mine to do as I please. It's nice to feel so free. If I hadn't been preoccupied so long in the shower, I might have had time for a run on the treadmill. Maybe later - I really do need to get back into my exercise routine but am reminded that the thorough workout I'd experienced this morning was probably better for burning off the calories of last night's alcohol, than any 5mile run could ever achieve - blissfully more appealing.

I literally spring down the steps, towards my car; sunglasses propped upon my head. I really need to calm the *re-energised* Lulu down, or everyone will know what has caused my new radiance. Just as I reach my door, I see something out of the corner of my eye.

Sitting on my bonnet in the dip where the wipers are situated, is a black velvet box like the one I'd had delivered to work last Monday and Wednesday. I grab it excitedly and jump into the car to open it more comfortably. This time the box is sealed with a purple satin ribbon and untying it, I find a third black velvet rose with the now familiar sparkly diamante crystal in its centre. I look underneath for the expected note card and see the baroque-style, scripted font.

It reads…

FWC

When I'm with you I want More!

My core clenches in agreement. I feel exactly the same.

With my good mood only increasing I turn the key, starting the engine. *Moloko's The Time is Now,* immediately fires up through the radio, full blast - the only volume option when I drive. As I swing out of our road, I consider how very apt the song is for the morning after I have stepped over into the unknown in relation to Sebastian and I.

His words replay in my mind. *"We are going to do what we should have done years ago. It's time now; our time."*

Where we go from here is anyone's guess but in the bedroom, we weren't strangers anymore but lovers. As friends, I'm not sure what we are.

⬿⬿

Entering *The Brew Up,* I immediately spot Abby waving manically at me from a table, towards the back of the café. It is not our usual corner so they must be busy. I can see Nathan in talks with Sebastian, who has his back to me. My mouth dries and I take a deep breath, smile and exchange niceties with the owner, Rory and make my way over to them; bubbles of nervous excitement carrying me along for courage.

"Quick - the waitress has just taken our order Babe," Abby shrugs apologetically, "I'm bloody starving; couldn't wait another second."

"Sorry everyone. Parking was shocking." I take a seat at the already extracted chair – Sebastian's tanned muscular arm rests lightly

188

along the back of it.

"Lubeedoo - looking good!" Nathan whistles and I flick his gesture away with my hand, secretly delighted; I could kiss him for showing that I appeal to other men, on this morning of all occasions.

"What?" he puts his hands in the air in mock-surprise "You do. How is that - after the amount we supped at Suzie & the Gstar's?" He pats his flattened midriff. "That's two weekends on the trot now! At our age we need to start pacing ourselves."

Abby swats him playfully in response. "Speak for yourself!"

I relax and smile at my friends but am aware that the man himself is unusually quiet.

"What do you want Lu?" Sebastian's deep sexy voice interrupts our general banter, caressing every nerve ending. *Seriously can that man read my mind?*

Fuck woman, he's only asking for your breakfast order not your life plan – answer him! Hmm you served up on a plate please!

Annoying myself at my neediness I blush; it doesn't go unnoticed by his blackened orbs and it dawns on me that he'd posed the question in that way to get this exact reaction from me. *The bastard!*

I'm tempted to call his bluff and retaliate with "*I'll have the Full English with a side order of Cumberland sausage,*" but instead I refrain.

"Scrambled eggs on toast please and a mug of tea." I thank him calmly and place my bag on the floor next to my chair. When I've straightened up I see he's already left to place my order at the countertop. I remind myself that this is something he would have naturally done, prior to last night, before we'd ravished our bodies and had seen each other naked – but I am touched all the same!

"So, good night last night Babe wasn't it?" Abby props her lovely smiley face on beautifully and brightly coloured manicured hands; resting her elbows on the table.

I recognise the same satisfied sensual demeanour in her that I saw this morning reflected in my dressing table mirror and I'm so happy for her. Nathan is a lovely bloke and mouth-wateringly hot! Bob and Bitzi Silver have created sons that could compete with Greek-Gods in the hunk department - they must both be so proud of them.

"Awesome night. Shame about the head though," Nathan dramatically strokes his brow. "Felt like a bugger this morning didn't I, Abs?"

Abby raises her shoulder to her ear (a gesture I know she does when she's been found out) and acts evasive. "I wouldn't know Nay."

They snigger together privately.

Bloody hell. This was really moving fast. *Abs and Nay!* Nicknames already? Stolen looks?

I really hope that it continues smoothly, for both their sakes. Long-term they'd make a cool couple - *Abnay or Nayabs - very Brangelina!*

I change the subject, to take the onus off them. "Great idea to come here. I could eat a horse!"

"Must have worked up an appetite?" Sebastian rejoins us and winks at me, sliding his lean 6ft frame back into the leather chair. I can feel his presence pulsating around me, via our legs, which are millimetres away from connecting, thigh to thigh underneath the table. The heat emitting from our combined proximity is enough to boil me another pot of tea and I wish I could rest my leg into his, just a bit more; then we would touch. The need to have some form of physical contact is all consuming.

I'm aware that the three of them are chattering away and discussing the events of last night but it is all a blur as I take in the male body radiating cool, unadulterated sexual prowess next to me. He's changed into a fitted white t-shirt and Diesel Jeans and looks fresh and clean and.... my mind is taken to the gutter again, as I recollect the way in which he got clean. I lick my lips and blinking to jerk myself out of my idolising, I try to return to the conversation. Luckily Abby has picked up on my discomfort and discreetly asks if I want to nip to the toilet before the food arrives.

We pop upstairs in silence but as soon as the door secludes us in the Ladies, she pounces on me. "You did it didn't you? You did the dirty with Sebastian?" Spinning round in squealing shock, exceedingly pleased with her private investigator talents. "Well thank *fuck* for that!"

In that split-second I want to lie and say no, to savour the secret to myself for a little longer but looking at her expectant eyes I realise she is too good a friend, not to see what is pretty much tattooed on my forehead and I can't do it to her. I cave.

"Yep. Seb and I had sex after the party. FBR No.1 when & where turned out to be last night; at my house." My shoulders slump almost defeated and I sigh. Sensing this Abby grabs me in a big bear hug to her Chanel perfumed chest.

"Oh Honey, that's great news isn't it? Especially after the mess up the week before?" she pushes me back to thoroughly view my reaction, rubbing my arm gently.

"It is... yeah. I'm pissed though as we never spoke about that hook-up from Manchester, Stacey? You know that girl Chris said Sebastian conquered only a few nights after he took *me* to bed? Not that he really has to explain himself - we're fuck buddies that's all." I look up at her confused, scrunched up face and finish. "We didn't do much talking anyway."

"Oh yeah. I remember now. Well she obviously isn't *that* important to him, is she?" she suggests comfortingly but even I can see her argument is flawed.

"Was it worth it? The ten year wait I mean?"

I nod again quietly and crumple. "It was fucking amazing Abs!" I admit quietly and resolutely.

"Oh you poor baby. He's gone and bloody ruined it for other men hasn't he, the bastard. I knew he was hot but I didn't think he'd be *that* good!"

I nod mutely pouting pathetically and we giggle together. "Well... it must run in the family," she continues in a know-it-all voice, "... cos Nathan blew me away last night too! Well actually I blew him away first and then he did me but who cares, the *long* and the *not at all* short of it..." She breaks with a contented look of pure cat that got the cream, on her face and purrs, throwing her arms in the air excitedly, "... it was fucking amazing!"

We both take a second to mull over our respective experiences and at the exact same time pull a fake silent scream at each other; thinking what the crap have we begun?

"I like Nath, Abby. He's one of the good ones." Rubbing her shoulder I open the door for us to head back. "We need to talk in depth about this, you and I, very soon. But I'm not telling anyone else yet, apart from you and probably Suzie. OK?"

"My lips are closed," she pretend zips her own and with a naughty voice mock drawls. "I promise! Well... these ones anyway!"

Dirty mare!

Back at the table the lads are buttering toast and dunking teabags. The smell of coffee and bacon fills my nose and my stomach greedily gurgles in expectation.

"Come on girlies - the food's getting cold!" Nathan states and hands me a steaming mug of perfectly brewed tea. "Ooh just how I like it Nath. Cheers!"

He smiles back, his brown eyes, the same shape but slighter lighter than Seb's crinkling in the corners. "Only the best for you Lulu."

Sebastian has almost finished his full fry up, as I begin to enjoy my scrambled eggs. At first I'm not that into them, too high on pleasure for food, but pretty soon I'm scraping my plate clean and feel so much better for it as my seriously shrunken stomach adapts to a full meal. My body soaks up the sustenance and practically sighs in *thanks*. I sense that I'm being watched again but choose to remain fixated upon Abby – it is the safest available option. If I cave and look at Sebastian I'm done for… again.

"What you up to today Abs?" I prompt her, encouraging her assistance with my exaggerated wide eyes.

"Not much to be honest," she grins at Nathan and I presume that whatever they are doing… will be with each other; either that or they'll be *doing each other!*

Rolling my eyes and smirking at her vagueness I take a gulp of hot sweet tea. "I've got washing and ironing coming out of the woodwork; it's got to be tackled soon, so nothing particularly sexy at my end either."

I swear I hear Seb say, "I beg to differ," but it's almost a whisper and he continues to watch Nathan, so I continue - I must just be hearing things.

"Maybe a visit to the supermarket if I can be arsed? Very boring but it'll be nice to chill out. I can't take the hangovers anymore."

"I hear ya girl!" Abby agrees and I giggle at her *girlfriend* swagger.

"Finn is back at 3pm but I wondered about maybe taking him to see a late afternoon movie?"

Abby nods in all the right places, her mouth still full of her bacon & egg sandwich.

Normally she would have offered to come with me at that point; she loved watching kids films and used Finn as a reason to not appear sad at nearly thirty, going to catch anything Pixar and Disney related. This time however she doesn't bite anything other than her butty.

I study her face. She really does look glowing and I wonder if people can tell just by looking at me, that I was seriously fucked the night before? *Surely not?*

I do hope that isn't the case considering Niall was dropping Finn off this afternoon. The last thing I needed was his accusing mind prying into my love life. Although he still appeared to think it was his God-given right.

We comfortably chatter about Nathan joining Sebastian at Silver Construction and I'm pleased they confirm he'll definitely be working with me at The Ashton on and off in between other jobs. His joinery skills were second-to-none and he was creating the most amazing bed frame and headboard plus window seats for the immense floor to ceiling bedroom sashes in the suite. I couldn't wait to see them finished.

Before long, we are all happily replete and as we start to rise from the table, Nathan bluntly points out. "Bloody true what they say about the best cure for a hangover. Morning nookie followed by a large fry-up! I feel almost human again. Wouldn't you agree Seb?"

He is immediately dug in the ribs with a flying elbow from a slightly flushed Abby. I feel for her but when Nathan throws his arm around her, drawing her close to him, I realise that they are in the very early stages of a serious romance and not just a fling, even if they were still unsure of it themselves.

I am so happy for them. *Who cares if everyone knows?*

The only problem is that the divide between Sebastian and I has grown in the short time we'd been there and their closeness is only showcasing our own stilted atmosphere. Maybe that isn't the case to all and sundry but it is to me and I hate it. I can feel my mood going south rapidly. Sebastian only adds to the chilliness when he answers Nathan's question gruffly.

"I wouldn't know mate!" I am pleased that he hasn't bragged about what went on between us but I am also crestfallen that he is acting as if nothing ever happened, especially after sending me that beautiful rose!

We head to the counter, to settle our bills and Sebastian waves our money away, insistent, instead handing over his card and treating us. It is a nice gesture, but after the coldness that is apparent between us, I am irritated by his controlling ways…again. I recognise that this would not have upset me before last night and that now everything had altered. Our friendship had tilted already.

In the car park, to the rear of the café, I hug Abby and promise to call her next week for a girlie catch-up; we are long overdue. I make a mental note to talk in depth with her about my contraception debacle.

Nathan kisses me on the cheek and does some convoluted handshake with Seb that they fail miserably to complete and chuckle over and then the two new lovers wander over towards his truck. They'd shared one car to come meet us I begrudgingly acknowledge.

Why had I thought arriving separately would be a good idea again?

"Right, well thanks for the breakie Sebastian."

I can hear the frost slicing through my voice. I think that Nathan and Abby's familiarity has made our own lack of it too clear and I'm gutted. This wasn't how I thought today would go, not after *the shower* episode.

"Woah, Woah, Woah! Where do you think you're going Lady?" He grabs my wrist as I spin away from him; hurt welling inside and getting more confused by the second. I feel emotionally hung-over.

"Are you OK?" he seems genuinely concerned

"I'm fine!" I put on my best *happy* voice, "Just a little tired that's all."

Act like nothing is wrong Lucia, don't be a drama queen.

He rubs his hand over his head, drawing me to focus on his handsome face. "Me too. I need some serious shut-eye. Didn't get much last night."

I think that's his attempt to lighten the mood but he fails miserably and the moment is still awkward and clunky. We don't know whether to hug, peck or kiss.

We both choose to do neither. It's all a complete disaster.

"Anyway thanks again. I'll see you soon," I offer smiling tightly whilst I begin to walk backwards, my insides crumpling at the emptiness I feel.

Why do I feel as though I'm about to cry? Bloody turn around and go before you do!

"No probs Lu – I'll call you," he nods, staring at my face as if he wants to say more; do more. He doesn't act upon it but to be honest I don't give him the chance; I just want to get out of there.

We turn and head to our respective vehicles. Everything is up in the air; too much is unsaid but both of us are too wary to push it. It's as though we have finally figured out how to be together physically but now we couldn't be friends. He'd gone from hero to Zero in the space of eating breakfast.

WTF?

Sebastian

What the hell just happened? How did things go to shit between her screaming my name for the neighbours to hear and buying her breakfast?

We've just had the most amazing sex I've ever experienced - connecting in a way I've never achieved or thought possible. It had been hot, dirty; sexual, uniting and gut wrenchingly toe curling, all in one. Our bodies fitting together like they were made for each other. Her touch making me come so easily - I'd feared I'd not be able to give her the momentous night I'd promised.

And this morning - God! I'd never needed to be buried inside a woman again so badly, so fast, that I couldn't think straight. I'd been so caught up in the moment I'd forgotten all about protection - I'm pretty sure she's on the pill? Isn't she? She'd have said if that weren't the case surely?

How could I be so irresponsible?

My mind is brimming with questions, as I pull up outside the office. A few hours sorting through my mounting emails would help me focus. I should have stayed with her this morning. We should have driven down to The Brew-UP *together*, like Na and Abby. *Why didn't I think of that?* My brother was playing it well - he seemed to be falling hard for Lu's friend. I hadn't seen him quite so enamoured before. Good on him, but he was making me look like a fucking amateur.

I shake my head; laughing to myself as I unlock the main doors, hit the alarm and head through the empty office space. I loved coming in to Silver Con on a weekend - it was quiet with no phones ringing to interrupt my progression. Heading straight over to the cappuccino maker, I set up a frothy coffee with full fat milk and add two sugars. Sweet coffee yeah, but not in tea - don't know how Lu does that!

Settling at my desk, I buzz the iMac into life and set up my stall for business. She'd said she was going to take Finn to the movies this aft hadn't she? Maybe I should join them? I quite fancy a bit more of that *domesticity* lark. *I can't leave things the way we just had.*

Sipping my coffee I click on a few emails, adding one immediately to the trash. *Be honest with yourself - you need to be near her again.*

It's true - only an hour apart and I'm itching to have full skin-on-

195

skin contact; place my palm in the dip of her back and smell her luscious hair; stroke the back of my hand down her soft cheek. I might just be following my baby bro's footsteps here and it scares the be- Jesus out of me.

I need to taste her again!

She was like a drug and now I've had my first hit, I crave more.

So much for playing it cool!

Odd how in the past if I'd had an issue with a woman, I would have rung Lu for her amazing therapist advise. That wasn't an option now. Let's face it I'd never really cared enough to spend the next morning driving myself insane with the thought of a woman. I'd certainly never put a woman before work.

Stretching back into my chair I look up, as something catches my eye, on the CCTV monitor to my right. I squint, looking closer, and see a car. The camera image is black and white and the cars windows are tinted, so I can't see the driver. Maybe it was a delivery? I watch and wait, as the car waits a while. It's a dark saloon, *VW* or maybe a *Vauxhall*, I can't really tell from this angle. Then as quickly as it arrived, the vehicle is exiting the driveway to our office, careful to manoeuvre wide, around my own Range Rover, cleverly avoiding the camera. *Now until that moment, I'd just thought if you weren't here with a delivery mate, you'd made a wrong turn - now I'm not so sure.*

I'd parked in a shitty place. *Crap!*

If I hadn't been lazy Sunday driving, I'd have been able to see his plate. Don't want people casing the place for a burglary; we had a lot of technical equipment in here, plus some serious tools and vehicles, in the workshops. I run off a message to Toni, asking her to keep an eye out for any other suspicious ongoings, then finish the last dregs of my coffee. After firing off a couple more emails, one to Paul, a major shareholder, about the Jannah Hotel project in Dubai and another to the architect firm involved. Within an hour I'm done. It's futile to deny things any longer. I was no good to anyone here.

Grabbing my black leather jacket, I slip it on, check for my phone and keys and switch off. I'm already decided that my next stop is Lucia's. I'm going to swing by hers and see if I can manipulate a little boy into letting me take him and his yummy mummy out for popcorn; anything to be in her company, a little longer.

Chapter 20

Lucia

After a chilled few hours on Sunday afternoon, catching up on my soaps and impressing myself at my skilful ironing achievements (I hate ironing!), I am feeling a little more me. I've even tackled the ironing in *The Basket*, which I save for *angry days* - full of impossible to press duvet covers and linen clothing I wish I'd never purchased and would never get wrinkle-free. I smile, secretly satisfied at my efficient laundry duties. Now all I needed was Finn back in my arms and I would be able to forget Sebastian for a while. I should have been tackling some of the mountains of work I need to address for the ensuing week but I can't focus properly.

I am fortunate that I do not have to see my ex, as Finn is delivered back by Niall's Dad, Pete, a tall lean man, who adores Finn and has great family values. He asks after me and appears to want to linger but I don't ask him in, and instead chatter briefly on the steps up to the terrace. He really is a pleasant man, if a little blinded by his son's inadequacies and I am touched that Pete has often mentioned that I'm doing a great job but never seems to forget to slip in the remark, *'How nice it would be if you and Niall gave it another go - Maybe make it legal this time?'* and I cringe. He means well but doesn't know the full story of our split, or what a shit his son had been and fully aware that he's Finn's Grandpa, I'm reluctant to shout, *'When hell freezes over!'* in front of little ears. Instead I politely choose to ignore his rather insidious comment and encourage Finn to make a fuss over him with a goodbye cuddle.

Waving Pete off, I close the door and we settle down to reflect on

Finn's time with that side of the family before I tell him my surprise. It's not long before I can hear him *Brumming and zooming* with his favourite toys in his room and I smile at the comforting sounds, I hadn't realised I'd missed them until now.

"Finnster – would you pop into mummy's room for a minute?" I call up to his bedroom on the top floor of our home.

I begin to put the freshly pressed clothes away as I wait for him to join me. He lands on my bed and at least half of the hanger-free items tumble into a pile on the rug. He screws his face up and winces in apology. Smiling at his worry I shake my head to say it's fine as I collect the fallen items and place them back onto the bed. "Poppet - how do you feel about mummy taking you to the cinema to see Despicable Me 2?"

I ask him, already knowing what his reaction will be. I'm excited for him, as his giddiness is contagious. His little face lights up automatically in wonder.

"Yaaay!" he bounces up and down all over the now rather crumpled laundry.

"Whoa! Calm down tiger." I enfold him in a huge cuddle and lift him off the bed to save what is left of my hard work.

"Can we have popcorn?" his cute helium filled voice begs.

"*Of course* - it wouldn't be movie night without a bucket of popcorn my Darling boy!

Just give me a minute and we'll go and then maybe grab something to eat on the way home? Sound good to you?"

He nods his lovely cropped & quiffed head gleefully and grabbing his latest favourite *hot wheel* car, starts to make 'brumm brumm' car noises, driving the garishly coloured lime and purple flamed toy up and down my bedroom door. I wince at the grooves left in the wood. Oh well… this isn't a show home; I remind myself!

I'm so happy to have this time with him, the one true man in my life who never judges me. We are just about to leave when there's a knock at the door. Finn, sneaks a peek out of the lounge window and shouts, "It's Sub, its Sub," thrilled at the sight of his Godfather.

He practically dangles from the door handle, tugging it open and eventually Sebastian does indeed step inside. I'm rooted to the spot, unsure how to react with the combination of both Finn and Sebastian.

"Hey little man." Sebastian does the same complicated handshake that he'd done that morning with his brother – the amazing thing is that Finn achieves it. I laugh out loud as when they finish, Finn brushes away invisible dust, off one shoulder and then repeats the action on the other shoulder – *how funny is my boy?*

Sebastian and I laugh together and at that moment he raises his eyes to mine and I get that goose bump feeling that he seems to create whenever I'm now near him.

"A *little bird* told me that you were going to the movies Finnster?" Seb winks at me. *Cheeky bastard!*

Finn nods smiling. "We're going to see Depict..abull ME,'" he struggles over the words but pleased with himself rocks back on his feet, hands behind his back and points a finger at his chest, when he pronounces *me*.

Seb ruffles his head in affection. "Do you think I could come with?"

"Oh please, Mummy, please can Sub come - Pullleeese?" he yanks on my dress, leaving me in an impossible position – staring between the two pairs of pleading expectant eyes, Seb pouts like a child and I give in and chuckle.

"OK sure – but we must go now, as it starts in 40 minutes."

"I'll drive," Seb drawls control stepping in again and then I realize he'd have to anyway, as I only have a two-seater.

Its only as we climb into his new gunmetal Range Rover Sport that I notice that he's already got a car seat in the back and he's taken charge and plugged Finn in safely. *That was so thoughtful. He just keeps continuing to surprise me.*

"Nice car!" I appraise, as the sharp scent of new leather fills my nostrils. It's deep red interior is pure luxury. Trust Sebastian to always have the best.

"She is isn't she!" he is unapologetic for the 3litre drain on the environment "She's my new company car – and belongs to Silver Construction but I had to have her!" His words are animalistic. "She called to me, to *drive her home*." The statement is wicked and I catch a glimpse of his knowing smirk and decide to ignore it.

Do all females call to him, to drive them home? It appears I am certainly in the majority, I summarise miserably, but now I understood why.

❦

The film lives up to the hype. It's the perfect mix of children's entertainment and adult humour. I can see it becoming a family treasure and mentally note to get it for Finn's Christmas stocking when it's released on DVD.

Once I'd begun to relax, I could enjoy the time with Finn, listening to him giggling in all the right places and watching him *open-mouthed* in concentration when Gru tries to rescue his minions. However, the fact that I am sitting in the dark, with Sebastian so close is killing me. I have to keep reminding myself to breathe - *there are children around for God's sake!*

The fact that we have Finn firmly wedged between us, assists greatly and the only real contact we have is the occasional and accidental finger touch, when grabbing popcorn, from the huge tub in the middle of Finn's lap. This causes delicious zaps of electric currents to travel up my arm, staying with me for most of the film.

I was just pleased that as far as Finn was concerned it was just his Mum and Godfather taking him out - in his eyes, *the norm.* He didn't pick up on the tension around us once, in fact seems to revel in our outing-of-three.

My phone vibrates on my lap and I lift it to see who it is. It's a text from him.

I can't stop thinking about you

I am a complete basket case at this about—turn, after this morning's cold send off, it was screwing with my head. He wasn't playing fair, showcasing nice Sebastian, the family man and sexy Sebastian the lover – it made me wonder if maybe this could be how it would be if we were in a romantic relationship? I choose to ignore his games; now I'm supposed to switch it back on?

Another text quickly follows.

OK, ignore my text but you can't ignore me forever.
God that mouth turns me on; so fucking kissable.

I can feel his eyes boring into me. Willing me to respond but I continue to watch the film with my profile to him at all times and when he's relaxed and appears focused on the screen again, I reply at my own pace, without duress. There was no point denying it anymore - he was right on all counts. I had to be honest with myself, and him.

I want you but… I'm scared - it was amazing but we are now so different together?

I'm so bloody nervous my eyes burrow deep into the film but something wills me to look in his direction and when I do our eyes lock, over Finn's head. The connection is so erotic and so full of pent up frustration, my entire body reacts, radiating shivers of lust, my core clenching. I know just looking at him he feels the same. I force myself to look away, swallowing to lubricate my now dehydrated mouth and gratefully before long the movie comes to an end.

I agree - but you can't deny the heat between us.
I ache for you.

Oh Jesus - seriously dry-mouth tasty.

In the cinema complex we decide to grab a couple of take away pizzas from Frankie & Benny's, as Finn is starving and take them back to the Range Rover. I cringe as I visualize Finn dropping tomato sauce on the plush new interior but Sebastian, reads my mind... again, and gets a blanket from the boot to place it around my messy piggy's car seat.

I'm not hungry at all – in fact I honestly think that if I ate, it would taste like cardboard so I pass on Sebastian's offered piece. Once the boys have worked their way through several slices each - the car filled with happy chewing noises - Sebastian dumps the boxes in the bin and casually climbs back into his new toy. I can tell that he is thrilled with it, the big kid, and I watch his hands grip the steering wheel. They are the epitome of manly. Big, strong and slightly roughened, with that developed muscle to the right of the top of the thumb joint, that I have always found so attractive on men. His hands ooze sex appeal and I'm immediately thinking about them on my breasts, working their magic on my waist, travelling over my tummy, dropping to cup my... *Right enough of that Ms. Myers, enough*!

I fold my own hands in my lap, almost primly in defiance but inside I am burning with sexual awareness. I vaguely hear the roar of the engine, as Seb puts it into drive mode and I peer into the backseat, to see that Finn has given in to his tiredness and his sweet face is deep in sleep already, his pouty cherubic mouth trembling with

201

each breath; little poppet. Sebastian immediately redirects the speakers ensuring that the music only sounds in the front, so as not to wake him.

Oh he is killing me with these kind and simple gestures!

Keane's *'Someone to rely on'* surrounds us and we make our way home. I love this song but it's as intense as we are right now and only adds to the pent-up frustration around us.

I watch the world whizz by outside, as the light is fading and dusk begins to roll in. The sky is a beautiful purple blue and the scenery should be calming and tranquil, yet inside me, inside this beautiful car, next to this beautiful sexy man, the music playing, my internal workings are in absolute turmoil.

We are silent for much of the journey. I can't bring myself to look at him but out of the corner of my eye I see he rests one hand on the wheel, the other on his knee. God he is fit! My heart leaps into my throat. I am still so on edge.

I almost jump when his deep voice cuts through my thoughts.

"Thanks for this weekend Lu. It's been really great. Just what I needed after being away for so long." He looks over to me briefly and smiles, his gorgeous face, even more sexy now that he is in charge of this powerful machine. He returns his gaze to the road, adjusting to check his rear view mirror.

"The boy is fast-on!" he comments shaking his head with the information. "Not a care in the world- lucky monkey!"

"I've enjoyed this weekend too Sebastian." I'm way too formal but am trying to mirror his own views without sounding like I'm too into him. It's still all too fresh and uncertain.

"Me too Lulu."

Looking across again at me, his eyes intense he grabs one of my hands and takes it to his lips, planting a soft kiss on my curled fingers. He puts our still lightly clasped hands back down onto the middle console and holds them there tightly.

I can feel both our pulses beating in the pressure of our palms. It feels so natural to be connected like this, but at the same time that connection is sending those now familiar, tiny electric currents up my arm and all over my body.

You are seriously losing it, Lucia Myers; he hardly has to have any contact with you for you to melt into a wanton puddle!

As we pull into Rose Avenue, I am torn with the feeling of

desperate relief to get away from him and the overwhelming disappointment that we won't be *together* tonight… in my bed. At the same time, Mum-mode has clocked-in and at 7.30pm I am fully aware that Finn needs his own bed; as do I – I am suddenly hit by a wall of exhaustion and I ache everywhere, especially in my most secret places.

Masterfully parking the monstrous penis extension in a very tight spot outside our house with ease, I marvel at the irony again of my analogy. I have to admit that now that I've seen the evidence first hand there was no need for any extension in Sebastian Silver's trouser department. *Stop with the dirty mind Myers – you're really not helping yourself here!*

Oh God, he's opened the door for me – really?

Er, yes - he did that before you slept together Lu - remember? He's always been a gentleman. Now you know he's a good guy AND bloody amazing in bed. Oh Bugger, I'm done for! He isn't relationship material, remember FBR no. 5 - just go back to being friends afterwards. Guard your heart girl or you're seriously going to get burned.

He assists me out of the 4x4, which is much higher than I had remembered, with my petite height, I am grateful for the helping outstretched hand.

"Come on Little One, I'll have to purchase a step specially for your entrance and exits. Or I could just carry you in?" My horrified glare says it all and I hear him chuckle.

"You get the door Lu and I'll grab Finn."

The control is back but I just go with the flow at this stage. I don't think I can take another *perfect family man* moment but I torture myself one last time and turn to watch him out the window. I'm undone as he folds my precious son into his body, protecting the back of his head with one of those big sexy hands, as he bends to miss the roof of the 4x4. Seriously the image should be used as a black and white poster. It's in that moment it hits me. Fuck! I'm a goner. One night together and I am a goner!

Placing him down on the sofa gently and covering him with a nearby throw, Seb offers to take Finn upstairs for me but I decline straight away. I need him to go – it's all just too much. I'm in a spin. I can smell him, almost taste him and I'm a complete mess.

"Right cheers Seb."

Frosty chick is back and I can tell he is unsure as to why. I am all over the place - poor guy. Making his way to the door he stops and looks back, first at Finn, then back to me, directly at me, boring his beautiful dark chocolate eyes into mine and with an arching an eyebrow he questions,

"I'll go then?"

"Yeah, I think that's best - I need to get him to bed."

"You and I need to talk Lu. You know it and I know it."

He looks pained and I get a sick feeling in my gut, this doesn't sound good.

"I'll be in touch Lady Lu," and he's gone.

The sharp click of the door hitting the frame makes me jump slightly, and staring at my son, I lift his warm, sleepy body into my arms, loving his special Finn scent and switch off the lights. I am shattered and the sooner I sleep the sooner I can reason with myself and decipher what the bloody hell has happened in the last 48hrs!

Chapter 21

Lucia

With Finn settled, I pad barefoot downstairs for a cool drink, and every intention of checking a few e-mails and my diary for the ensuing week before turning in. I'm just filling a glass from the filtered water-jug when I jump out of my skin, dropping the cup on the floor in the process. An angry male voice dominates the chaos.

"For fucks sake Lu you really need to start locking the door! I could have been anyone!"

"Bloody hell Sebastian — knock much?"

He promptly moves towards me taking quick strides which force me to head backwards in response until I hit the fridge and its open door, the only light in the darkened kitchen and taking the water jug from my hand he places it on the island and turns to face me again.

"I got home and realised I'd forgotten to do something," his handsome face watches me keenly, his eyes never leaving mine. My eyes are soaking up his mouth and the carnal look in his black eyes.

"What's that?"

I have an understanding, a hope, of what he is about to do as he lowers his head and I hold my breath in anticipation and excitement but when it happens it still takes me unawares as he moves that last step, so that we meet chest to chest, cocooned within the fridge; I grab the door for balance and placing a firm palm at the back of my neck, he draws me into him and swoops in connecting our mouths in a demanding, passionate kiss.

The chemistry is unmistakable, fireworks, flashing lights, dizziness. I forget everything and anything but what his lips are doing to mine, in that moment. Warm, wet, inviting and connected. Abruptly,

Sebastian ends the kiss, leaving me off balance and looks intently at me, whilst I struggle back to reality.

"That - I needed to do that. I've thought about your mouth all afternoon and couldn't leave without tasting you again." His voice cracks with emotion and heavily emphasises *tasting*. I lick my lips unknowingly and his eyes flicker to them as I melt. We connect once again, continuing to explore each other's mouths, and tongues and lips, leisurely the pace increasing and our breath getting hotter by the second.

"I can't get enough of you!" he pants through broken breaths, reaching down to slide my maxi dress slowly up my smooth legs, creating electric shockwaves all over my body, instantly making my nipples point to attention.

I instinctively try to move to try and stop the process, but using his free hand to restrain mine I'm trapped and I cave. Our tongues lock and tease madly as I pull him further into my body. I can feel his finger stroking small, figure eight movements on my now bare thigh and my skin burns hot at his touch, where my dress is still bunched in his grip. The chill from the open fridge is a welcome coolant as the temperature around us escalates to boiling point.

I feel his finger dip further towards my inner thigh, its direction obvious and I jerk as he hits that ticklish dip in my groin and with a hook of his finger my panties are pulled to one side and his fingertip traces my already moist opening. The act is purely hedonistic and possessive and I'm surprised how needy I am for the contact.

He deepens the kiss and I moan my pleasure into his mouth, as his fingers plunge inside me and begin to work their magic over my needy clit.

"You're so wet for me Lu - and incredibly hot."

I feel my sex throb against his fingers, at the sound of his words and hook a leg around his hips, allowing him better access.

"Think about my cock fucking your beautiful tight pussy."

His velvety tongue dips inside my mouth capturing mine, and thrusts in and out, mimicking what his cock would do. I feel the pressure of my impending orgasm building, my hips pushing back against his hand, desperate to grab what is just out of reach.

As my knees begin to buckle, I gasp, then moan aloud in utter ebullition, as he rams his fingers inside, pushing against my front wall and then swoops them back up, applying full, palpable pressure onto my erect clit. I explode around and over him, hot white lights flicker around me, and warm throbbing waves cascade all over my body, delightfully wrapping me in a delicious aura. I sense his warm breath at my ear and his deep growl of satisfaction as he kisses me gently there, calm as I catch my breath.

"That was the other thing on my *to do list* Baby. Make you come."

His voice is taut with sexual innuendo and I lean into him, too exhausted to talk but immediately in need of more. I feel his hand move away from me, and the release of the material of my dress - it immediately drops, to my ankles to cover my modesty. He kisses the tip of my nose and we gaze at each other longingly. I can feel the heat in my cheeks and glow of sex all over my body and press myself into him, keen to connect further.

His erection is fired up and positioned rock hard against my stomach, which makes me smile smugly - I did this to him. His hand cradles my cheek and I lean into it and kiss his palm. He is so passionate - I never expected him to be so passionate and it releases an overwhelming wave of emotion from deep within me.

I'm really falling for this man, my friend, my mate in both terms.

Sebastian smiles and releases me. "Go to bed and think of me."

I want to shout *"No! Come back here and fuck me. Let me do to you what you've done for me."* My pussy throbs with a void that needs to be filled and the desperation to feel him inside me, the joining of our bodies is all consuming. But I won't beg.

He moves away from me and I immediately crave the contact; I feel so empty. He then leans in kissing my forehead gently, our hands remaining linked until we are too far apart to maintain it and our arms drop, swinging by our sides. I smile, a little embarrassed at our carnal act, which was probably viewed avidly by the pervy neighbour in the terrace, which overlooks my kitchen.

"Night Lu."

I stare up at him longingly and will him to take me, right there on the island. Fuck the hygiene issues, there's always Dettol. Chewing hard on my lip to alleviate some of the pent-up frustration, I can see the same desire reflected in his now black glossy orbs. His body is taut and I can see his cock pushing against his jeans in its demand to be released. His eyes are fixated upon my mouth and I run my tongue temptingly along the bottom lip, and sensing I have his full attention, continue to rub both lips together, slowly moistening them.

"Fuck Lu I'm trying to be a gentleman here but if you keep looking at me like that...doing that with your mouth... "

I don't let him finish and immediately launch myself at him and in that second he is lifting me onto the kitchen counter, again reading my mind and pushing me down onto the cold hard granite, whilst at same time pushing my dress up around my waist and exposing me to his greedy eyes.

I feel his hands at my panties and a ripping sound as he tears them at the side-seam, peeling them off deliciously and tossing them in the direction of the bin.

"You don't need these. Next time your orders are to wear nothing."

I moan into his mouth and revel at the delicious freeing sensation that blows over my now naked and vulnerable pussy. We kiss deeply again and I feel him slip a finger, then another inside me, readying me but I'm already dripping from my recent orgasm and I hear him grunt in possessive approval at his achievement.

"You're like a drug."

I arch my back, turned on by his words and push my breasts up into his still fully clothed chest at the ripples of ecstasy he is creating inside me. Then groan as he leaves me feeling empty for a second.

"Put me inside you Lu."

I open my eyes and look down to see his huge erection throbbing between my thighs. Sitting up slightly, my hands tremble, as I grasp him, the girth alone, making me shiver as I guide his tip towards my entrance. He rocks backwards and deliberately slips his cock gently up against my clit, capturing the juice there to lubricate his length and exciting me further.

I lift my hips and in one forceful thrust, he is inside me.

"Just... fuck... me."

The words come from me and I stand by every one of them.

Our tongues duel with each other, collecting pace as I feel him plunge inside of both orifices in time. I wince slightly at the immense fullness and wait for my body to adapt to his invasion. I can feel him breathing heavily and know that he senses my body's hesitation, as he slows his pace.

"Baby?"

"Please...," my anguished moan is all he needs.

His growl of acceptance is so primitive it turns me on even more. He pumps into me, withdrawing only to drag me towards him to delve deeper and unite us even closer if that is possible. We kiss and suck our tongues, practically biting in our animalistic rush to connect.

I raise my pelvis to allow more access and feel his hand gripping my hip, to still me, and the slow rotation of his own hips, as he feeds himself in further. With each thrust I feel the build of the thing I need most, my release. My arms grab his shoulders for support, feeling the steely strength underneath his rigid muscles and as I run my nails down his back he groans in encouragement and his thrusting quickens. I can see from his face that he is nearly there; his look of almost pain is enough to drive me over the edge of my own orgasmic cliff top.

"Come on Baby; together!" his command is harsh and insistent but I can hear the slight crack in it showing his lack of control, at last.

Wrapping my legs even tighter around his waist, it pushes him deeper inside me and with a few long, strong strokes he delves so far within me, we are connected in both body and mind. As we stare into one another's eyes, he watches me as I shatter around his throbbing cock. My spasms are his undoing and I hear his cry, feeling him pouring himself into me and it's my turn to watch his face as an expression of shock, bliss and ecstasy cross over his features and he closes his eyes on a last sigh.

Sebastian carefully draws me up towards him, my hair tumbling down my back and onto his linked hands at my spine. He is still inside me as we slowly kiss. It feels raw and sexy and right. He gently moves a stray hair from my damp forehead and kisses my nose before removing himself and straightening his clothes. Reacting instinctively to his withdrawal, I wriggle my dress down modestly. That needle on the record moment is on the cards I'm sure.

The one where a sound sharply jolts us back into reality.

"I'm going to leave now…" He kisses one cheek then moves on to the other, " … so you can rest. I fear I've worn you out…" He reaches my mouth and looks into my eyes with a devilish smile.

God he was so cocky and sure of himself but I'm beginning to love that side of him.

"… I knew it would be like this between us Lu - raw and desperate and entirely addictive - you just had to be open to it." He rolls his lips in thought. "I'll let myself out *Little One*."

The term of endearment warms me and with one last lingering peck he's gone before I can comment. In the empty kitchen, the fridge door still wide open, the evidence of his release desperate to escape from within me, as I perch on the kitchen counter, I whisper, "Thank you!" and taking a huge breath head upstairs to shower.

Crawling into bed, I put my phone on charge and snuggle down, grateful for the cocoon of my meringue duvet. Replete, tender, fearful, annoyed at my own weakness and concerned at our lack of control in the contraception department for the third time this weekend. I turn as my phone's screen lights the darkened room and with just a glimpse of the words glowing brightly, I am filled with intense longing.

It never seems to be enough with you Baby. I always need more.

Amazing how he reads my mind like that. I'd just been thinking the exact same thing! The *need* is so great; it's never enough. It scares the crap out of me and rather than give any more of myself, than I'd already done, I revert to protective mode and type my reply.

I'm confused. Is it really possible to have great sex with a friend and go back to how it was before?

I bite my fingernail as I await his response. Why am I testing him here? - Because you *are* confused. Yes but surely now's the time to shout *It was bloody amazing?*

I look at the phone and sigh - serves me right. His response is nothing if not honest.

Me too. Honestly? I don't know.

Don't ever expect anything but the truth from a true friend. Now I've got total head-fuck.

Chapter 22

Sebastian

The reality of my feelings for Lu sting sharply, wounding so deeply, my chest aches with the force. Bitterness rises, like bile in my throat. Of course I'd fall for a woman more stubborn than myself. Bloody fate - that's what we are. What we've always been. But where do we take it from here?

I've one month of this blasted proposition to work through. One month to convince her that she could trust me. One month to convince myself that I can actually stick at a relationship. *Why did you send her FBR 5 then?*

I'm not sure why I haven't wanted to settle down before now. Business is great. I've achieved more than most in my 32 years. Women came easy to me but they also bored me quickly. One thing Lu had never done is bore me; one of the reasons we'd become fast friends. Maybe we should just have some fun and get it out of our systems but returning to what we do best? Mates!

I need to send her flowers, again - from that Fresh flower place, she loves in Lords. I make a mental note to ring through an order en-route to work. Women always love flowers and she deserved the best. This weekend I'd had the most incredible sex of my life - and I had sampled several delectable women over the years, from all over the world. The sheer need to possess her had crippled me, scared the hell out of me and consumed me all at once. I run a thumb along my bottom lip, envisaging her face as she shattered around my cock - my stomach somersaults.

I take a deep breath and try to focus on something other than the flickers of images running freely around my mind. Lucia, naked, and spread over the sheets- her gorgeous tits in my hands. Lucia, begging me to fuck her; Lucia, placing my cock at the entrance of her wet pussy; Lucia, in the shower. Lucia, handing me every blasted orange sweet from the fruit gum packet in the cinema - my mouth had been as dry as Ghandi's flip-flop; Lucia, making dinner. Hang-on these last two things weren't sexy!

Fuck me. I need to get a grip. I readjust myself, already hard again at just the thought of her.

It had been worth the wait.

Ten years had been too long but God it had been worth it. Her scent still fills my nose, clothing, is imprinted on my body. I'm not normally so bloody sentimental and I never procrastinate over sex.

"Seb - you still here?" I hear Chris' holler from the back suite of the house and watch as his nearing footsteps bring him to join me in the kitchen.

"Ahh coffee."

"Help yourself mate - new pot just on."

He pours himself a cup and ignores the milk I grab from the fridge.

"Black. Gotta be black today."

"Thick head?"

"Any noise is torture."

I chuckle at his pained look, reach into a cupboard and pop out two pink pills from my hangover saviour box. "Take these, lots more coffee and we'll grab a bacon sarnie at work. We've got to be in bright and early, heavy emphasis on the bright. I have a shareholder's meeting in London lunchtime and I'm probably going to have to stick around a few days.

Chris looks up in surprise. "So the sale is really happening then?"

"Looks like."

He refers to the Jannah Dubai Marina Hotel. It had been on and off for a few months now and finally, the paperwork was nearly ready to be signed. This was the project that I'd worked towards and would put me in the big league. I'd become a millionaire at 27 and at 32 I'd be in double-figures. It was too true what they said. Money talked. You needed it to make it and pretty soon I'd have enough to feel established; enough to feel like I'm worthy of a family - of Lucia?

"I need you to head on over to The Ashton today and keep on-top of the guys for me. Nathan will be there too." I drain the last remnants of my mug and place it in the sink. "Right, Ralph is waiting.

I'll see you in the office briefly before I head of to LBA airport."

"No probs Boss. Lucia will be fine with me. You and her seemed pretty cosy Saturday night? Anything serious going on there or is it just a drunk hook up now you've broken the seal with a mate?"

His sly wink should have softened the blow and normally would have but I'm on him in a flash. My blood boiling and teeth gritted, so tight I wince at the chalkboard crunch. I wish to God I'd never let it slip that we'd got in on, after the Champagne Bar.

"Don't talk about her like that Chris."

"Soz Bro. No harm no foul. Just messing."

"I mean it. Lu and I, we have history and its complicated."

Chris holds his hands up in defeat and with a nervous laugh adds, "So no chance for me then?" before looking at my stoney face.

"Alrighty then! Leave things with me today at the office, I'll sort don't worry."

"I'll call you for regular updates."

"No probs. Good luck with the meeting. You sure you don't want me there as back-up?"

"No. I'm all good, thanks Chris." Last thing I needed was Chris with his big gob, disrupting the applecart. He was great on site and a good manager but he was starting to have ideas above his station and had a mouth that ran away with him more often than not. He'd be more likely to do more damage than good.

"OK. See you in half-an-hour."

I head out to the hallway, before I say anything I'll regret. I can see he'd be keen to progress but I'll need to keep him on a leash here and I'm not sure that the whole *'Chris living here'* proposal was the best idea, even it was only short-term. We'd been mates for several years and worked well together in the construction industry but lately he'd been acting like a royal dick and if I'm completely honest his work had been more than a little sub-par. I'm starting to get the impression that he would like a piece of the Silver Con pie and that isn't going to happen, not before Nathan. Nathan would always come first.

Grabbing my suit carrier, case and briefcase I head for the door, nodding to Ralph as he enters the main door and takes the items from me. He leaves to place them in the car. I take a last look at the house before sliding into the comforts of the Limo. Hopefully by the time Chris gets into work, he'll have sobered up and stopped pissing me off. I'm not sure what grates me most, the fact that he'd talked about Lu so demeaningly, or that he'd made it clear he had intentions on bedding her himself. *She's mine and no other fucker is getting his hands on her this time.*

$$\begin{array}{c} \infty \end{array}$$

Lucia

After a restless night of tossing and turning in sheets that smell of Sebastian I decide to crawl out of bed and glancing at my phone I see its only 6am. Oh well at least I'd be organised this Monday. It'd give me more time to pack the mountainous necessities required for my boy's trip; toys and clothes for all seasons - it was the UK after all. Then rustle up a breakfast of porridge with cranberries and cherries for Finn and I to share together. I'm glad to have the time with him and we chatter away - Finn keen to reenact scenes from last night's movie. His laughter is a breath of fresh air and in that moment I know how blessed I am already - we were fine on our own. This weekend had been out of this world but Finn was my priority.

Packing up the car, I do a quick drop at my parents, leaving his small suitcase, toys, footballs, his *noo-noo* teddy, which had a silky label that he *had* to stroke against his face at bedtime, and a goody bag I'd done for him as a surprise; then nail it back, past ours and into Bodley to drop Finn at crèche. Kissing him goodbye I squeeze a little too hard as I won't see him until Friday.

"You be good for Ninni and Gramps poppet and have a fabulous time in Wales at the seaside. I'll miss you like crazy!" I plant umpteen kisses all over his soft face and head.

"Enough Mummy!" His giggles make me laugh too.

"Mummy's got a busy week with work but I'll call you and Ninni will face-time me, so we can say good night most nights, OK, my Darling."

He nods in answer and I wobble slightly. Five days is too long, but my parents had planned this short holiday with great gusto; got a little holiday cottage in Abersoch, North Wales, and Finn needed some adventure time. Plus it had worked out well with my workload. Feeling emotional I hand his backpack to the nursery nurse and with a last hug remind him, that Ninni was collecting him, before watching him run full pelt at his friends.

He was fine. It was me that was the problem.

It takes everything in me not to march in there and pick him up, but I know I'd make it worse. So I wave to a fellow Mum, and wince for her, as she struggles to release her daughter's monkey-like grip, from around her leg - we'd all been there - then I make a dash for it and head off to work. My phone rings and I smile as I see Suzie's name light up the screen – I wondered how long it would take her – she'd showed remarkable restraint, leaving it until Monday morning to pump me for info about my love life!

"Hiya Love!"

"Oh goodie I got you before you were in work. I knew if I rang at this time there was a good chance!" she stresses warmly knowing I'm a creature of habit.

"I'm all yours for another 10mins. Just dropped Finn off."

"Oh. You OK?"

"I'm fine - hate leaving him but he'd rather go on holiday with Mum and Dad. I'll be good, once I'm busy busy. What's up?" I reply vacantly as I try to reverse out onto a main road, whilst a woman in a people carrier rolls in, oblivious to my difficulties. I look at the amount of kids in her car and just think, *let it go* she has much bigger, more immediate issues.

Suzie is chattering away, as I return to concentrate on her spiel again. "I've just about recovered from Saturday night. It was wicked wasn't it? I think I really put my back out on the bronco." She chuckles and I feel for her, as I know her back gives her gip, after a nasty car crash a few years back.

"Fantastic night," I agree. "Another memorable party hosted by the D'Alisa's"

My attention is drawn back to the road ahead. Bollocks – huge amounts of traffic. I decide to risk it and take the back route.

"Am I making it up or do I remember someone riding the Bucking Bronco... naked?" I continue to chatter.

Suzie bursts out laughing. "Ha ha, I'd forgotten about that. Yes – he had a sock on the end of his willy; what a tosser! Anyway, enough delaying tactics. Come on - don't hold out. Did you have a good night... after you went home?" I can hear the unasked question in her voice.

I decide to ignore it. "Hey? I don't know what you mean?"

"Stop being coy Sis. Er durr! A certain male friend who seemed to stick to you throughout the night like glue and couldn't take his eyes off you and no I don't mean Theo the wanker!" she sputters obviously irritated by my unwillingness to spill the beans.

I smirk. I'd got the vibe that Suzie wasn't that impressed by Leo but she was normally more forgiving. "You weren't keen then?"

"Oh he was alright, I suppose. A bit boring! I don't know, I can't quite put my finger on it but I'm just not sure about him? Bit *too* nice? Him *and* Chris to be honest! I don't know - anyway again with the stalling tactics - spill!" My delightful sister holds no bars and commands. "I know it must have been pretty darned good; I could feel the heat between you, from miles away!"

She was right, on both counts so I comply, knowing that if I don't she'll turn up at work and demand a tell-all then and there and I didn't want Colin and Jackie knowing the intimate details.

"Nothing to say, really, Babe. We went home, he stayed and we had all-consuming, mind-blowing sex all… night… long; oh and the next morning too - in the shower!" I giggle like a schoolgirl and actually blush at the thought of how wonderful the night *and* replay had been. I swear my bits do a loop de loop in agreement; their awakening is evident with every naughty thought. I keep Sunday night to myself however - there was no need to divulge too much.

"Get the fuck out of here?" Her language is appalling today. "Why didn't you call me the minute he left? That's if he left? When did he leave?" she quickly takes a breath in excitement.

"Calm down Miss Red Bull, less of the questions," I snigger. "He left on Sunday morning. We later met for breakfast with Nathan and Abs and then Finn came home from his Dad's. I feel awful as that's two Saturday's on the trot I've not been with him but he seems OK; especially as Sebastian and I took him to see Despicable Me 2 yesterday afternoon."

"Seriously? I wanted to see that movie!"

I can practically hear her sulking. News of Sebastian and I have taken a backseat to a film – how did that work?

She corrects herself recognising her mistake. "Wow! You spent the whole weekend together? That's something Lu. It's about bloody time! As I've told you before, even *Single Mums* need sex. You're desperate, not dead!"

"Cheers Sis, that sounds like a slogan from a t-shirt!"

Smiling I slow down for someone to pull out in front of me and blare my horn in frustration and anger when they do so and continue at a pace of 10mph. *Oh come on!*

"Sorry. Car crash waiting to happen, just pulled out."

"Oh I hate that. Is it an old boy? Hey kudos to you Babe; check you out changing the subject. Nicely done," she graciously offers.

I laugh loudly but something within me decides its time to *'fess-up'*.

"I propositioned him Suze."

"Scuse me? You did *what*?" Her screech makes me regret opening my big mouth.

"I asked him for one night of pleasure. You know - to be my fuck buddy. He said yes but on the proviso it was more than one night. I'm good with that."

"I bet you are, you naughty girl."

"I'm not going to get down to the nitty-gritty yet… I'm still trying to process it all myself. I'm not sure how I feel. Anyway Hun, I've got to go; I'm pulling into work. I need to crack on with The Ashton project."

"OK, OK, I get it. I'm glad that one of you idiots made the first move at last but hurry up and *process it all* soon…," she mimics my own words with a patronising tone to them. "… and then you can blabber the juicy details soon. Just answer me this, how big was his co… ?"

I cut her off cheekily just at the right moment and end the call.

What I had said was the truth. It is all too fresh to be discussing anything I haven't come to terms with it yet myself. I'd much rather keep the *juicy details*, as she'd saucily called them, private for now, perhaps forever and enjoy reminiscing in my daydreams but I must admit I'd enjoyed relaying that we'd done the deed, at last. It felt cathartic somehow.

I lean over to change the track on my Ipod to my play list of the month and the track of the weekend, and feel a fizz of excitement as Sub Focus Endorphins blares out into the car, reminding me of the monumental sex cocktail I'd supped from all weekend and the irony of the title of the song; the endorphin rush I'd experienced had been exhilarating and dangerous, creating a delicious high. I'd definitely been holding on for some kind of miracle and this weekend it had been delivered to me. Now I had problems. I'm completely consumed by a certain sexy contractor and can't see how I could ever return to *just friends. You can - you just need to suck it up and enjoy the ride in the present. Remember this is about opening yourself up to new possibilities.*

Chapter 23

Lucia

As I sit at my desk, harshly biting down on my lip and chewing in concentration, I consider my sexual antics for the billionth time this morning. Lost in my thoughts I gasp in shock at the sound of a loud reverberating click in front of my eyes.

Bloody hell!

Shaking his fingers around in my personal space Colin is manically trying to get my attention.

"Sorry, Babe to make you jump, but I've been calling you loads – you were miles away! Anywhere nice?"

He rests his bum on the edge of my desk, slides long chino-clad legs out in front of him and rests his hand flat out underneath his baby smooth chin, in a cute little girl style. I shake my head at his pretty pose.

"Sorry poser. I was just thinking about the curtains for the master suite at The Ashton," I lie apologetically up at him, leaning back into my chair.

His eyes shrewd, he considers me, watching my face for hints, then hits my shoulder playfully, "Bollocks. You were thinking about a certain silver-tongued devil. Don't lie to me Lulu; you're a terrible liar."

Sucking in his mouth, his cheeks hollow and he dramatically places a palm on his pink designer polo shirt covered chest. "Unlike me, who can lie through the eye of a needle? Or... is that piss through the eye of a needle?"

I giggle at his confusion, bless him - he always got his clichés

218

mixed up.

"Well… either way I can do both." His eyes shine prettily, his long eyelashes fluttering precociously.

"You're in a particularly good mood today Col, I take it you and James are going good?"

"Oh Darling, you know me. We made it to date number three on Sunday and I'm not bored to death… yet, and I was dragged around a decidedly dull art show but I went and showed my line-free face, for his sake. It was one of his friend's exhibitions, and oh… my… God… it was bad. Finn could have put her crappy work to shame!" He claps his hand over his mouth dramatically and just as quickly throws it away. "But – the pièce de résistance was *me* covered in Nutella - later that night. James was overcome Darling I tell you. Well he came… all… over!" his tongue caresses his top lip saucily and I cringe at his blatant coarseness.

"Lady Boss, Damien Hirst is not a patch on all of… *this*!" his finger forms an invisible wiggly-line in the air, which travels down his body.

I laugh to myself at the gall of this over-confident man and wish I had half of his surety. "So yes… we'll see. It's *very* early days." His coy smile shows me that he likes his new beau more than he'd care to admit to anyone, including himself. He really is a poppet; a complete drama-queen but a star all the same. It appeared that the love and lust fairy had sprinkled her magic over everyone the past few weeks; Abby & Nathan, I tick off mentally - Colin and James, get added to the list - Sebastian and I? I screw up my nose in annoyance at the uncertainty of it all.

Lust 100%! But love? I shouldn't even torture myself this way.

"Come help me choose between sumptuous charcoal grey velvet or deep scarlet silk." I lead him over towards the large workstation we have in the midst of the studio. "I need to order some lunch. Do you fancy salad or sandwich?"

"I need carbs today doll, but don't tell anyone." His pats his lean washboard tummy, "I'm feeling hormonal and am after some stodge but I'm supposed to be juicing."

I laugh and agree. "Me too - in need of stodge that is. I'll ask Jackie to pick something up for us from *The Slug & Lettuce*."

I'm also sharply reminded that I need to pop out to the chemist ASAP and purchase the blasted morning after pill – shame I didn't have a raincoat, trilby and dark glasses to hand. The disguise would really help with the nosey buggers in my near vicinity. The whole drama was probably overkill; we'd only had unprotected sex once - no twice - make that three times, I correct myself, remembering the *kitchen* incident with crystal clarity.

No better to be safe, the way my luck has been of late I can't risk the additional problem of pregnancy.

Colin is stroking the samples of both fabrics along either side of his sun-bed enhanced face. "The silk, says luxury, sex, and is naughty but nice. The velvet is lush, thick and will look a... maz... ing in 9foot drop curtains - heavy though?" he looks up at me, arching his brow.

"I agree but I'm leaning towards the velvet as it will be so opulent." I pout my mouth. "Hmmm. What about if we combine the two and line the velvet with the red silk? That way when they are drawn back around those huge pewter finials we've chosen, you can see both fabrics. Hard and soft; perfect for the sensual theme of the suite?"

"Perfect Darling! Very erotic." Colin nods his head, licking his lips "Perhaps I can convince James to let us christen the room together, for its maiden voyage. Ahhh, now that's a thought."

I can literally see the cogs turning in his perfectly groomed head and knowing that I've lost his interest for the immediate time being I roll my eyes and head over to my assistant to order some much needed sustenance. My stomach is growling. As if she can hear my tummy rumbles, Jackie pops over, smiling fondly at us with her notepad and a huge round vase of white roses, studded with pearls in varying degrees of size.

"Here you go Lu. You really are popular at the moment!" Her face is genuinely gleeful and she delicately places the thick glass bowl in front of me and I melt at the beauty of the arrangement. It was so unusual and utterly me. I look in between the roses, dazzled at their quantity - there must have been two-dozen large roses tightly packed together, at least. There wasn't a card, but a silver foiled heart dangles from the grey velvet ribbon around the bowl and turning it over, I see the message I'm keen to locate.

It was our time.

Sebastian

The message is perfect and warms me to my toes. Even his bold confident scrawl was sexy.

"Right, enough about me." I shake myself out of my bubble.

"About bloody time!" Colin moans next me. "A man could die of starvation here - for food and love."

I ignore his petulance and thank Jackie, who is still ooh-ing and ahh-ing over the flowers. Both Colin and I give her our lunch orders and within minutes she's disappeared to the shops.

A few hours and soup and a sandwich later and I'm proud of my creative achievements today. I've caught up on some paperwork, and checked the calendars for the next few weeks, chased a few overdue accounts and am much further ahead with The Ashton business. I was annoyed with myself this morning, for not finalising some of my designs this weekend but I'd been otherwise occupied, by a certain delicious contractor and his tools, especially now I knew he was thinking of me too. We may be confused but he was showing he had no regrets.

There it is. Shit!

I'd done so well and he's back, fully imposed on my delicate mind, full frontal images of him and his magnificent physique, leaning against my bedroom door, climbing over my naked body, bending me over, soaping me up; the pictures are running carelessly around my head, taunting me, testing me and stressing me out entirely.

Enough! Taking a deep breath I decide to take a ride up to The Ashton and check up on the works there. Anything to get me out and en route I'd pop into the small independent chemist I'd noticed on the corner of the quaint village square, which sat just prior to the left turn up to the hotel. Hopefully I won't be recognised there. I feel so ashamed but I'd put it off long enough.

I force a fixed smile back onto my furrowed face. "I'll be back in tomorrow guys – I'm off to check on the Silver Construction lads and then going straight home. See you in the morning," I inform the team as I leave and thinking quickly on my feet add. "I'm actually not feeling that great, so I'm going to put my calls straight to voicemail

221

until tomorrow and try get an early night - got awful tummy ache."

Jackie nods her acknowledgement, whilst ending another call and as I near the exit, shouts, "Night Lucia. Take care."

Driving, I check in with Abby; I needed her advice big-time. Her bubbly voice answers on the third ring.

"Hola Honey!"

I smile despite my gloom and laugh. "Hey Abs. You OK?"

"All good my end Chickadee but I can sense all is not the same with you. What's the crack?"

That's what I love about Abby; she could read me like a book. I decide to get straight to the point.

"I need to get the bloody morning after pill? Which was the one you took when you were with Dave?" I can almost see her eye roll down the phone and I inwardly cringe at my stupidity. Dave had been her on off boyfriend for over 4years and she'd finally kicked him to the curb when she'd caught him balls deep in her cousin.

"Urggghh Dave the Dickless, don't remind me. Urmmm, let me think… it began with an 'L' - Simon Lebon something or other." She laughs to herself at her own joke. "Wait, did it split? You never said anything yesterday - unless it happened after? What did Sebastian say?"

I rub my temple in stress, the other hand still on the wheel. "He didn't say anything. He doesn't know and I don't want him too!" My horrified reply is clearly apparent.

"He must have known at the time though?" I can hear the disbelief in her voice. "Was he *that* big?"

I ignore her last comment but so does she, as she has realised how stupid I have been.

"Oh you didn't - Lulu what were you thinking?"

"Er - I wasn't and neither was Sebastian. We just got carried away in the moment. Abs it was *primitive*." My voice cracks with emotion and I sense her empathy returning

"I know, I know. We nearly messed up too. These Silver brothers are magnetic, I'll give them that but I still think Sebastian should know and go through it with you Babe. He's a good guy and I know it's a bit of an odd arrangement you two have going at the mo and you don't want the drama but I'd definitely be telling Nathan if it were happening to us."

I ponder her words, knowing deep down she was right but she was also right about the drama. I didn't want to be *that girl*. I'm strong enough to handle this alone; fuck, I've managed to set up my own business, run a home, bring up my son, as a single parent and get through a nasty break-up. If I can do all that, I can take a God damned pill to show some responsibility - albeit delayed responsibility.

"Really? Even when this is just sex?" I consider my own question and change my mind immediately. "No! I mean it Abby, Sebastian doesn't need to know. He tries to control everything and I need to feel like I'm the one in control here. Besides I want to just enjoy our time right now - not get too heavy - you know?"

"Perhaps if he'd been in control at the time of unprotected sex he'd have a leg to stand on but who am I to say?" Her dry judgmental hum is heartfelt but she is on a mission now and gaining momentum. "I mean, I love Sebastian, but why is it that men get to be all spontaneous, with their big cocks, amazingly buff guns and tight bums; turn-us-on to the point of losing all power over our minds and our sensibilities, and reduce us to melting pots of passion in seconds. We get amazing unforgettable sex and then *we're* the ones who have to cramp and puke in retribution."

I can tell that she is combining her own previous experience with *Dave the Dickless,* and her present situation with the delicious Nathan Silver. She has it sooo bad!

"Actually in my case, the sex was rubbish with Dave so I had shit sex, no orgasm and had to pop the pill anyway and thank God I did. Now Nathan on the other hand - I'm going to have to be careful with him. He wants to do it everywhere and on everything and fuck Lu he's hung like a freaking donk…"

"Abs, Abs, I get it." I laugh, happy for her and realising I've lost her full attention I try to change the subject. "I'll take it today but I mean it - don't tell Sebastian, Nathan… anyone!"

"Ok Lu. Pinky promise. I'll call you tonight to see how you've got on. If you need me I'm there with bells on and maybe some anti-sickness medication."

I smile and ring off just as I pull into the centre of Holdgate. It was time to pay for my sins!

⚬⚬⚬

Chapter 24

Lucia

Cringle's Chemist is open. That's a good start!

I breathe a sigh of relief as I park the Audi directly outside its doors. Perfect for a grab and dash. The Chemist itself is tucked away in a small courtyard, to the right of the Holdgate Village Square. It's Tudor styled exterior and chocolate box window merchandising is cosily inviting and away from the madding crowds and I am instantly put at ease. This Chemist is so unlike the local one in Bodley, where a neon red sign flashes DUREX, placed strategically next to the huge Pampers display in the window! No this place was the perfect foil for my faux pas.

A woman with rosy cheeks and Dame Edna red glasses welcomes me as I enter. The shop is empty. At least there wouldn't be the added embarrassment of others overhearing my intimate information. Gazing around, I'm in awe of the items of produce available. On the same shelf you could purchase a bottle of Head & Shoulders, hair clips, Tena Lady pads, nail polish remover, Vaseline, bum gloves (perfect for fake tanning) and a pair of socks? I try to focus on the reason that I am there. This was obviously what came with an independent village pharmacy. I've come to the right place if I need something to treat dandruff, incontinence issues, fix my manicure, moisten my dry lips, need lubrication for other areas, (oo err!) and need to cover my cold feet. Furrowing my brow in disbelief of the freakiness of the place I head to the counter. Vintage was too modern for this place!

With all this paraphernalia for sale, surely they could provide me with the '*I fucked up and got fucked without fucking protection* pill!'

"Good afternoon. How can I help?" her smile is comforting and I feel my shoulders relax their tightly arched position. I muster the courage, feeling like a naughty teenager and just go for it.

"Yes. I'd like to purchase the morning after pill?" My voice sounds calm but inside I feel sick and I haven't even taken the bloody thing yet. I wince in apology.

"Oh OK." The bubbly lady is perhaps a tad more judgmental? Or that could be my own insecurities. Sally, as her name badge advises me, disappears to the back of the shop and returns in seconds with two boxes.

"Right – we have two types of pill, Levonelle and Ella One." She holds each box up respectively, flashing one forward and giving it a quick shake, before switching it up and thrusting the second option in my face, so close the text blurs. I nod in all the right places; the first brand name, Levonelle, must have been the one Abby took; it definitely sounded like the guy from Duran Duran.

"Which one you take is dependant upon how long it has been since you had unprotected sex?" Her gaze is serious and questioning over her red comical readers but her matching pillar-box red lips relax in a close-mouthed smile, encouraging me to open-up to her. I mentally calculate the length of time since our kitchen sex session and outwardly feel myself blush.

"I'd say just over twelve hours? Give or take. (Boy did I give and take!) It was Sunday night," I add and want to kick myself at my honesty. Why not just tell her you were both too overcome with passion to consider slipping a condom on his enormous orgasm delivering cock?

Her face appears sympathetic however and she goes into great detail about the best option. "I think you'll be fine with the Levonelle tablet. This is to be taken within 72hours of the *accident*…" She whispers this in the same way that the famous Manchester born comedian Les Dawson used to say *Lesbian*, like it is a dirty word and gives me another *whoops* eyebrow raise. "… and you are well within that timeframe. The other pill can be taken up to 5days after *the event* but the sooner the better is my advice – Ella One is relatively new to the market so the decision is entirely yours but if it were me I'd go with the first choice."

I spend the next few minutes listening to the many horrendous sounding side effects and issues I could expect to come with this type of emergency contraception medication and inwardly die at the thought of my stupidity. One soapy wet embrace and a few neck nuzzles and I'm spread eagled around a certain God's hips and bouncing all over his cock.

"Scuse me Miss, are you OK?" Sally interrupts my daydream gently.

I shake my head in annoyance at my own ditzy attitude. "Sorry, yes, I'm fine. Take it tonight, with food. If I'm sick within 3hours I need a second dose from the Accident & Emergency department at the local hospital. Got it."

I hand over my debit card to pay £25.99 – the exorbitant price for unrestricted passion.

"Much cheaper than weekly nappies." Sally quips, reading my mind whilst punching in the necessary information on the PDQ machine. I nod weakly and enter my pin.

She discreetly wraps my item, in a Cringles branded paper bag and passes it to me. "Don't worry love. We all make mistakes. In a few days this will be a distant reminder."

I flinch at her words. The reality is whilst I need to take this pill - an unexpected pregnancy is not the way forward at present - I can't help but hope that it won't put a stop to all new beginnings. I don't want the weekends amazing sex to be seen as a mistake or become a distant reminder.

I jump as the sound of a bell chimes over the door and turn to see who's entered but there *isn't* anyone there. How odd?

Perplexed, I return to focus upon red glasses lady and frown as she says, "Young people today you are all in too much of a hurry. No patience anymore."

My confused face is evident and she hurriedly corrects herself.

"Oh not you Honey, sorry. No I meant the blonde girl with the black fur coat that was waiting in line behind you. More interested in her phone than anyone else."

Oh God I hadn't even noticed that someone had entered the shop. I had been so involved in my Scoobydoo strategy of obtaining the dreaded pill; I'd not turned around once.

"Thanks for all your help," I nod again.

I wish I'd gone to Lloyds now; they served you, hardly spoke and kept their personal opinions to themselves. Trust me to visit a Pharmacy with Yorkshire's equivalent of Claire Raynor & Ruby Wax rolled into one! Her comment about distant reminders has definitely touched a nerve. I remind myself as I leave that she was only trying to help, even if it wasn't really received.

⸏⸐⸑

At The Ashton I pull up next to a black Ford Ranger pick-up truck, emblazoned with the Silver Construction logo. That's a good start at least. I smile to myself; Sebastian and I had designed the corporate identity together for a degree typography project; that was so long ago. I am suddenly immensely proud of everything that he has achieved in such a short space of time. After Uni, we'd both graduated and gone our separate ways in business but remained a constant in one another's lives through friendship and work.

I much preferred to contract any building works I may require out to Silver Construction, and in the early days, when I was making my way up the corporate chain, grabbing every grain of experience I could, I'd put in a good word for him with my bosses and Sebastian would more than prove his worth. This reputation of quality and innovation, combined with his good head for marketing, had meant that the company had expanded fast and fiercely, and the smaller jobs tended to take a backseat. Now he was wheeling and dealing with the alphas, all over the world, with fingers in many of the high-end construction project pies he was involved with. His Dad had put into the business initially, helping him start out, which had been a real help but the rest was all Seb. Financially, he was set for life.

He'd fast become a real entrepreneur and I realise how fortunate I am that Sebastian has rearranged projects to ensure there was a slot in the diary for me on this brief. Everything had to be perfect at The Ashton, to ensure we get more business from James Marcell, and his many cultured contacts.

I head up to the honeymoon suite and am pleased to see that the construction-team have not wasted anytime in prepping for the ensuing weeks. All manner of protective materials shroud the room; from plastic sheeting to dust sheets and the customary site radio, flecked with paint and plaster, sits pride of place on an up-turned bucket. Work is already beginning on the bathroom and to the front of the room; a hole is being created to house the new fireplace.

I count two workmen; one cheeky apprentice who introduces himself to me, with a tip of his baseball cap as *Danny*, whilst he sips his coffee and another quiet soul, who is at present screeding the en-suite floor to level it, ready for the new surface covering. I feel for his knees, which are encased in pads for protection.

I need to re-measure the window spaces for the curtain fabric to supply the window dresser, one last time. As Sebastian always says, *"measure twice, cut once."* It appears that at every turn, I am reminded of him.

Jumping slightly, I feel a hand in the small of my back, my brain sends a signal of hope as to the owner of the hand but I instinctively sense that it is not *him*.

It is not his touch, there's no electric buzz shooting up my spine.

"Lucia, I didn't know you were popping in!" I hear Chris Booth's confident voice behind me, and slump. Today of all days I could do without his prying eyes and overzealous comments.

"Hi Chris - yes I thought I'd come see that all is as it should be."

I side step an abandoned toolbox and walk out of Chris' close proximity – the man really does give me the creeps.

"All is indeed in order! Sebastian asked me to come oversee things today onsite as he's away again."

My mind and body freeze at the words. He hadn't mentioned working away had he - he'd only just got back Friday night? I am filled with a huge sense of loss and disappointment and even though I had no intention of discussing the fact that I'd procured the morning after pill, to wash away the risk of any mistake from our passionate encounters - I realise that I am now truly alone.

"Oh – where's he gone?" I ask, hoping to appear casual.

"London for some big suits' meeting – bout the Jannah?" he supplies me, almost cocky with his knowledge.

"I fancied tagging along; we grafted on that job together you know, but he needed someone to *manage shop* whilst away and who else could he trust with his favourite female friend?" I'm niggled by the way he seems to be placing himself in Seb's shoes, in his absence.

"I wonder if he'll be meeting that Manchester lass Stacey whilst there – he doesn't like to travel empty-handed, if you know what I mean – or single for that matter and I know Toni isn't with him this time!" he winks, elbowing me a little roughly in the side. I swallow in distaste, nausea bubbling at the ready.

Chris ignores my now pale complexion and continues rambling.

"Yeah, think he's back in a week? Not sure really. Hey but you've got me and we'll be able to get down to it," he grins mischievously. In

228

that second I decide to snap out of things and take Chris for what I think deep down he probably is, a misunderstood guy who is probably lonely and likely harmless enough. I seriously hope that is the case anyhow. I actually think he is a little thick or maybe just thick-skinned?

Why would he mention Stacey though? She was the woman they apparently met in Manchester about the chain of restaurants Silver Con was tendering for. She wasn't anything to do with the Dubai hotel - was she?

I retract my black Prada frames from my briefcase and slide them on, pushing the glasses back with one finger to sit over my nose and cheeks comfortably. They were unfortunately a necessity since the birth of Finn, when my eyesight had altered from long to shortsightedness but the fact that they looked the part and made me feel business-like, was an added bonus.

"Right, so then let's get to it - 1) The bathroom floor; the tiles should be with you by Wednesday - 2) The tiles for the walls on Friday - 3) The plastering is to be done Wednesday also so that the decorator can begin next week…" I tick each item off with my fingers as I read through my detailed plan of action.

"Whoa, Whoa - slow down! Seb said you were organised to a fault but give a bloke a chance to keep up!" he blusters, raking a hand through his fashionably styled barber's quiff.

I laugh, relaxing a little. "Sorry. When I'm in the zone God help us. I've sent all the proposal times for work and deliveries to Toni via email, but I can 'cc' you in for future reference - if you'd prefer?"

He nods, his icy blue eyes concentrating in thought. "Yeah that works - or you and I could mull over some suggestions over drinks sometime?"

Oh no, I knew it. It's true what they say, an unhappy woman is not appealing but a woman with an aura of *'just been fucked'* and the men crawl out of the woodwork.

"Oh I'm not sure that's such a good idea Chris – mixing work and pleasure."

That's it. Well done, stop there.

"But you could always have a cuppa at mine sometime," I add feeling sorry for him.

Why oh why did I offer that? I'm too bloody soft. I really do hate to be rude.

He repeatedly taps his pen against his palm, but breaks off to click his ringing phone to silent, as he watches me. "That sounds like a plan."

Change the subject now! "OK, well I'm happy with the progress for the first day. If Danny can ensure that the fireplace is readied and the chimney swept and flue all in form for the fire to be fitted next week, that'd be great." *Well done chick, you've pulled it back to work.*

"Then the cornice in the corner, where it's worn away – who's sorting that?"

"What… hmm sorry, I was focused on your umm… glasses. Very sexy secretary."

Thank God he said glasses, but still this guy needed to get some new material. I prompt him. "Cornice?"

"Oh yeah, the cornice! We've tracked down a company that has taken a molding of the existing decoration and they are recreating it from scratch. You'll never know there was a glitch. All due to be completed by the end of the week."

"That's great news." I'm really satisfied with the remodelling so far. If things were moving along quickly at the beginning it left us more time to deal with the problems, which always arose at some point, close to the end of the project.

"Right, well I'll make a move. I've got to go collect my son." I sidestep a loose floorboard, feeling a little guilty at my white lie, as my parents were getting Finn - anything to get away sharpish. "See you lads!" I shout to the workers. Danny tips his head in a gentlemanly manner, and the loner can't hear me, due to his huge yellow ear defenders and continues head down in concentration.

"Come on - I'll walk you out."

I'm not given the chance to refuse as Chris returns his hand into the small of my back possessively and pushes me towards the corridor. I really am going to need to set some boundaries of personal space with him.

Once outside he sparks up a cigarette and appraises me in the same *clothes stripping* way he'd done at Suzie and Gino's party but I'm saved from feeling seedy when his phone rings again. I remove my glasses in retaliation of his preference for them and halt abruptly, as I hear Chris speak the one name, permanently imprinted on my mind.

"Sebastian – yeah, yeah mate I'm here now. Sorry I was busy with Lucia. Yeah, she's here with me now - we've been in the honeymoon suite, having fun!" Looking up he smiles at me suggestively. "Sorry mate - just kidding - how's things? Is all going swell?" he laughs at his own poor joke, continuing, "Really? You lucky devil you. Didn't expect anything less."

I watch him hold his hand out for me to wait.

"No worries mate. It's all under control. Lucia's going to make sure I'm not lonely whilst you're away. OK - I'll let her know. I will. I promise. I said I *will!* Right - bye now."

What the fuck?

He ends his call, smarmy smile back on and *the knob* is back. Yuk!

"Somebody's a little testy today me thinks," he offers but not particularly to me.

I'm probably giving the guy a harder time than he deserves, due to the wild thoughts now parading around inside my head. He really is away then. I feel a jolt of immense loss and instantly irritate myself.

And? Why does that affect you Lucia - no ties, remember?

"I need to get back to the office now Chris, so I'll see you this week no doubt."

It isn't really a question but he answers. "Oh you most certainly will Lulu. See you soon."

How is it that Sebastian and Chris were such good friends? They were such polar opposites - Sebastian the *chalk,* and Christopher the *cheese,* literally? I smirk to myself, and turn to walk to my Audi, as fast as my 4inch heels will allow on loose chip pebbles. I'm annoyed for feeling so petty that Chris has used my nickname and we're not that friendly. Sebastian is one of the few that I allow to call me Lulu - and he'd used it several times during sex, which made it even more personal to me.

It's only as I head down the expansive driveway that I begin to recollect in detail, the telephone conversation I'd overheard. My body is tightly strung at the thought that he is hundreds of miles away in another part of the Country and I didn't even know! At the same time, I conclude that just because we spent a wonderful weekend together, it doesn't give me the right to know his schedule and where he is at all hours. *You knew this was a bad idea from the start Lu - you don't do casual!*

My chest expands on a deep breath and I switch the radio on and instantly regret it as *Adele's Chasing Pavements* fills the Audi. I flinch; annoyed at my silly reaction to a song. How is it that all of a sudden every song and its words relate to Sebastian and I? I switch stations and am given a choice of *Coldplay's Green Eyes* and *You Got the love by*

The Source and shake my head in utter disbelief – I suppose its just like when you're on a diet and every advert on the television is about calorie laden puddings. Annoying though as I love all three of those songs and can't enjoy any of them right now. In disgust I stab the *off* button and drive home in silence, the only sound my ticking time bomb of thoughts, festering away uncontrollably.

Chris had suggested that Sebastian was not in London alone but I just hope that he was guessing or exaggerating the situation. I sense that he thinks that there may be something between Seb and I, and that he is not best pleased but I may be wrong. I'm not sure that he is *that intelligent*, although there's some serious jealousy there. Chris is most definitely inferior to his friend and knows it.

The thought of Sebastian with another woman now, doing to her what he'd done with me - I couldn't bear it. I have to resign myself to the fact that this was my fault and I was the one who instigated the arrangement. He may have added the rules but we never made any promises to each other and just because it was *us,* and we had a history of friendship - that did not guarantee a happy ending.

Besides, I'd never wanted that, had I? To be with Sebastian Silver in a long-term committed relationship? Why does that suddenly not sound so strange?

God, it was much easier when you didn't already know the guy – certainly less heavy so early on – I'd never had feelings for someone so fast before – never felt so utterly bereft at their unexpected disappearance. The emotion does not sit well with me – I don't do needy. I'm a strong independent single mother, who earns my own crust and is comfortable with my own company – this is a totally new experience for me.

I shake my head to myself, knowingly – no – this is the way it must be when it's real, unequivocally, and undeniably right. This conclusion only makes our situation more unbearable.

Do I want this to be a long-term thing? Surely I don't want to be with someone so controlling and with a sexual history that would make Dirk Diggler proud?

Following the winding roads home from Holdgate to Bodley, I glance across at my phone in its hands-free holder and notice a text message on the screen. It's from Jackie.

Leo called to talk to you about accounts.
I said you'd gone home ill with stomachache. See you tomorrow
hopefully Boss :)

Urgghh! I hadn't spoken to him since Saturday night and I still feel pretty bad about how I'd arrived with him and then dumped him. How bad was that? I'll ring him tomorrow and smooth things over. I'm sure he'd be fine. I had bigger problems than Leo to worry about.

Chapter 25

Lucia

6pm I crawl into bed for an early night and snuggle under the king-size meringue duvet in a tired heap. Soup and a crusty roll followed by a pudding of Levonelle, was not something I'd recommend off the menu. Half an hour in and there it is; the lovely nausea has popped in for a visit. Curling up with my cream, fluffy *Princess* hot water bottle I sigh in disgust.

You've no one to blame but yourself!

If I can just get through the next few hours, I'll be fine - grin and bear it, as deep down you know it was worth it; entirely irresponsible but worth it...

My thoughts are rudely interrupted by the bark of my phone and wearily turning to grab it from my bedside table I groan in discomfort. The text is boldly screaming at me in all its ultraviolet brightness and a quick glance tells me it's from Sebastian. My heart starts to pound.

I've been thinking about you; the smell of you - the feel of you - the taste of you. Sorry I had to leave on short notice - be in touch soon.x

I cradle the phone to my chest, the huge smile on my face threatening to crack open. Yay! He's thinking about me – he didn't forget... me. I re-read the text again, and a warm sensation blankets me. I settle down to fall into a deep slumber, happy that he is as restless as I am where *we* are concerned. Our texts have definitely gone to the next level, even if we haven't. Closing my eyes I succumb and feel myself relax for the first time all day.

The trouble with medication is it disturbs your sleep and I awake as a wave of nausea hits me again. Looking at my phone I can see its 10pm – I've slept for nearly 3hours solid, at least that means the pill is well and truly in my system now and its job will be complete.

I look down again and notice I've had 5 missed calls from my sister and 2 from Abby. I rub my hands wearily across my face in an attempt to focus properly, and enter the code for my phone, ringing Suzie immediately.

"Babe, is everything OK?"

I'm groggy but also acutely aware that I've not made enough time for my sister of late and we are well overdue a catch-up. I'm probably not on her *nice list* at the mo.

"How did it go?" she sounds a little snooty but concerned.

I wrack my brain for what she could mean. Surely she didn't mean…

"The Pill?" her voice goes up at the end of the sentence.

"Shit - did Abby tell you?"

"Yes she bloody did but only cos I dragged it out of her. I rang work first and they said you'd gone home with tummy ache. Then I rang Abs for some juicy goss about you and Seb and conned her into spilling."

Crap. Poor Abby, it wasn't her fault. I decide to go with the flow.

"It was OK. I spent a few hours feeling pretty horrid and went to bed early until my phone woke me."

"Sorry to wake you but it sounds like you got off lightly - in every way, Madam!" she says in her best *Teacher* voice.

I groan. "I know, I know, but it's done now. I just hope that this nausea goes away soon. Abs said it can last a few days."

"Well I'm warning you, Gino overheard me leaving a message for you earlier tonight – seeing as you weren't answering your phone!"

I freeze. "Does Gino know? Oh Suze, please ask him not to tell Sebastian?"

"Why the bloody hell not? He should have put something on the end of his dick! Why should you be the only one feeling like crap?"

I cringe; Abby and Suzie were cut from the same cloth. I'd hoped to deal with this on my own, to feel like I am in control still. The second Sebastian was involved it would become a huge drama and undo all the amazing part of our undeniable sexual chemistry.

"Well, all I'm saying is expect a call soon. Every cloud has a Silver lining, eh?"

"Right, OK Suze, thanks for the heads up. Better be off. I'll see you tomorrow at the shop - I need to get a dress for the party on Saturday."

"No worries my lovely. I'll put a few to one side. I need to talk to you anyway, as I have some juicy news but it can wait!" She always has juicy news but for some reason I sense that this news is important; she's being far too coy for it not to be.

We both hang up and I frown considering her last comment. Just like Suzie to feed me a little crumb and not the whole morsel; I'd be wondering what her *news* was all night. Well, anything to take the focus away from me for a while.

I'm dreaming that I can hear a tap tapping noise, which is persistently annoying. Tap. Tap. Tap - bang! It's not long before I come to the realisation that it's not a dream, but in fact a reality. I pause, holding my breath in the darkness and wait. There it is again. A pebble hits the window; this time the sound is unmistakable. Making my way to the window I notice that the clock on the chest of drawers next to it, glares a luminous green 11.43pm. Nervously, I peer out and see a now, familiar gunmetal Silver Range Rover Sport parked opposite my house. My heart leaps into my throat. *Oh no! I don't want him to see me like this!*

I'm a total mess, no make-up, and flannelette PJ's are so not a sexy look. He is the last person I want to see now and how I'm going to hide this from him I don't know.

What the hell is he doing here?

I make my way to the door, wishing I'd had the time to clean my teeth and release the bolt, then the lock before holding it slightly ajar; just enough to see him leaning irate against the frame. His sexy body encased in jeans and a quilted Barber jacket. He looks delicious and seriously pissed.

"Christ - you're a heavy sleeper. I thought I was going to have to replace that window, the amount of stones I've thrown at it."

"What are you doing here Seb? I thought you were in London?"

"I was - three and a half hours ago. Let me in Lu!" His face is tight and his brows furrowed.

"It's late, Sebastian. I was asleep and I'm not feeling great." I wrinkle my nose at my weakness but I'm hoping he'll be like most men and assume that means I'm on my period and run a mile. A wave of nausea hits me again and I recoil.

"That's why I'm here. Now let me in."

I'm tired and emotional and rather than fight him tonight, I cave and move aside for him to enter, moving to curl up on my favourite chair, as the dizziness overwhelms me.

"Whoa Baby. Steady there."

He grabs me before I collapse and ignores the chair, picking me up and holding me against his chest, he carries me up the stairs to my bedroom. I close my eyes, inhaling his clean male scent and link my hands around his neck, allowing myself to be supported for once. It felt so nice to relax against him and just be cared for.

"Right, Little One, let's get you settled."

I watch as he pulls back the cover and places me gently, into the bed, covering me completely. *Why was he here?*

Once he's refilled my water glass he kicks off his shoes and joins me on the bed, drawing me into his warm strength again.

"Why didn't you tell me Lu?"

I can feel his breath on my hair and his soft touch as he lightly caresses my wrist. Even feeling ill, his magnetism is so powerful I'm immensely turned on.

"Lu?" his gentle reminder brings me back to focus on the inevitable. I shouldn't hide this from him any longer.

"I didn't want to put pressure on you. We're just having fun and it's all a bit heavy." I'm embarrassed, upset and annoyed at my weakness all at once.

"For God's sake, Lu! Did you not think I'd want to know about this? Have a say?" I feel his body flinch and tense and the cold hits me as he slides out from beside me and off the bed. His hand rubs his head in frustration, as he comes to terms with things.

"What is there to say? We didn't use protection and I wanted to be safe." I sound blunt and bow my head, feeling severely ticked off and vaguely ashamed.

Maybe I should have told him? But seriously - what did he want me to do, risk it and get pregnant?

"Who told you Seb?"

"It doesn't matter."

"It bloody does to me. Was it Gino?"

At the shake of his head I continue "Abby"

"No."

"Nathan then?"

"No, none of them. Someone saw you buying it."

His eyes are so dark and intense, almost hypnotic as he stands at the foot of the bed, clearly agitated. "Look I don't like to ask - you didn't keep this from me because you've been with Leo did you?"

WTF?

My immediate reaction is to throw something at his head, anger tearing through my entire being. *Who the fuck did he think he was?*

Instead I snort in disgust. I can feel the tears threatening to spill over and I lift a hand to my brow to hide my distress, shaking my head - *don't let him see how much he just hurt you Lu. Be brave.*

The silence between us is deafening and I'm aware that my lack of answer is adding weight to his ridiculous notion but if I look up I'll break.

I hear his hiss before he fills the quiet. "Ah shit Lu - forget I said that - I'm sorry - bloody other people putting thoughts in my head - I know it's just been me. Just you and me Baby."

Don't be nice now... please. I can deal with bastards - I'm not used to nice.

"It has. You shouldn't even have to ask."

My voice sounds cold and withdrawn and I watch as he strides towards me, his eyes searching mine.

"I thought you were on the pill. I'm clean and I bloody know you are. But this is my fuck-up not yours. I should have been there for you!" his voice is lighter, more caring and I sigh in exasperation.

"I'm fine, honestly. I just feel a bit sick that's all. Seriously, you have no obligation here. I was just as caught up in the moment..."

"Moments," he interrupts.

"Moments," I repeat with a blush, remembering the additional shower and kitchen moments in equal clarity. "I was caught up in the *moments* and should have been more careful. *We* should have been more careful but *I've* taken care of it."

He ponders me for a while and I watch as his tongue flicks out to wash his sexy lips. "I should have bloody taken care of it at the time."

His jaw is stern. "I'm not sure what I was thinking? When you and I connect everything else goes out the window. I've never, *not* used protection with a woman. You are the first; another first shared between us." I watch his struggle, can see that he is uncomfortable with his statement. "You are not alone anymore Lu. Stop pushing me away!"

"I didn't realise I was? What did you expect me to do, make a drama of it and turn what *this was* into a total regret for you? It may surprise you but I'm not that type of woman. Besides, I know you are definitely not the *follow-up* type of guy!"

His look is lethal and the anger in his eyes, so black. I wince.

"What happened between us was *NOT* a mistake, Lucia! Don't *ever* call it that! You need to let me in and stop fighting *Me... This... Us!*"

He's pumped and ready to go but I can see the tightrope of control he's walking, forcing him to keep his head and allow me to answer as he heads towards the door. I can't help myself; I feel bullied, confused, awful. How could he think I'd been with someone else?

I don't ask him, instead I petulantly reply. "Stop trying to control me then! You can't control *everything* Sebastian!"

The icing on the proverbial overflowing cup-cake is enough to blow his steely demeanour and I watch as he struggles to wrestle with his inner strength, his teeth gritted and lips rolling tightly over them, near white in their tightness. My own chest rises and falls at breakneck speed with mounting anger, mirroring his body language.

God! When we disagree it's not pretty.

We'd not been in this position before and I am starting to see why Sebastian Silver was so ruthless in business. He always won.

Well not this bloody time!

"Look, you don't need to feel obliged here. I was the one who propositioned you. This was only ever going to be a one-night thing and then it became more and now I'm not sure what we are but seriously you're off the hook - we just got carried away.

"You may have offered yourself to me but I was the one who took you up on it and I was the one who fucked you."

God he was sexy - even experiencing roller-coaster waves, of nausea, I wanted to jump him.

"We fucked Seb and it was good - more than good but you don't owe me anything but our friendship afterwards - like we promised."

How had I managed to make what we had experienced this weekend, sound so inconsequential? In reality it had been all-consuming, defining, bloody monumental; a God damned epiphany!

I continue ignore my annoying inner voice. "FBR No.5, remember? What was it? Er... it went something like... no strings, no ties, no emotions, you're not boyfriend material, never will commit, you're happy to shag me but don't get heavy and we must always kiss and make up as mates afterwards. Sound familiar?"

I watch him flinch at my words - I may have exaggerated them hugely but said like that, the rule sounded pretty cold; at the time I hadn't cared. Now FBR Rule No.5 suddenly doesn't work for me.

How could I have agreed to this or been stupid enough to come up with the idea in the first place - we could never have sex and remain friends. Well I couldn't.

We stare at one another for a few seconds, both defiant and resounding in our viewpoints before he turns and opens the door, his jaw twitching.

"Rest and we'll talk again in the morning. I want regular updates as to your condition." *Arrogant bastard - obviously didn't take the hint not to control me then?*

With that severely patronising attempt at medical care and concern, I hear him head downstairs and a little while later the thud of the door slamming into the frame and the keys, as they are dropped through the letterbox.

I wish he'd never found out. Now for some reason it all felt so much worse and exactly how I'd feared things would play out. It had dirtied what had been such a monumental weekend. I felt like it had all become a big mistake.

I still can't believe he's driven 200miles to be with me and we argued like this.

Punching the pillow next to me in frustration, I fold it around my face and scream into it. Arghh - *that man!* I struggle as I feel the hot sensation of tears at my eyes and my throat tightening again, bloody hormones. *Who the Hell had told him and who had seen me buying it?*

Sighing deeply and settling down, I give in to the sleep I'd been fighting since he'd rudely awoken me. Hopefully tomorrow things would feel better but at this rate I sense it's unlikely.

∽⧉⌒

Sebastian

How could I be so irresponsible?

I berate myself for the second time since yesterday and indicate to make my way onto the motorway, bouncing across two lanes, foot hammered to the floor.

I'm not going to get much sleep tonight. My next meeting is in 6hours, back in Knightsbridge. Another 4hours and I'd be at the hotel, traffic dependent. I need coffee!

I should have fucking stayed - regardless of her anger and my stupidity.

I knew the minute Toni had rung to inform me of Lu's little visit to the chemist, it was my fault. I should never have allowed her to puts doubts of another guy in my mind. She'd seen her in Holdgate buying the morning after pill, purely coincidentally and after seeing Lu with Leo at the party on Saturday, put two and two together. I was more pissed that I was apparently the last to find out. What did I bloody expect though? I hadn't put a raincoat over my cock, twice - shit, no three times! Should I just have waited for her to inform me she was pregnant?

Now that's a question. Suddenly my mind is racing with all kinds of strange and unfamiliar thoughts I'd never considered. I shake my head. *Focus! You've got some serious work to do here to make this up to her - to convince her that you're more than just a player. That this was more than just a fucking amazing fuck!*

God she'd looked washed out. Her beautiful face, pale - huge lime eyes dulled. What a way to put a dampener on a fabulous night. Now I had immense bucket-loads of guilt. Now I had doubts about whether I was good enough for her.

She'd been so bloody angry. That stubborn streak flaring it's fiery head the second I brought my own to the fore. I'd been rock solid just watching her, all rumpled from sleep and firmly independent. I loved that about her that she wasn't a drip. I just wished she'd have told me - our friendship was wavering and I'm at a loss as to what I can do to reign it back in and maintain the pace of our blossoming sex life.

So I'm off the hook now am I?

We'll see about that – there's not a fucking chance! I'm all in, and this is far from over between us Ms. Myers.

Chapter 26

Lucia

I was wrong. A new day and a better night's sleep hadn't altered anything really; I still felt pretty shit about it all. Rushing around in the usual tizz that has become my habit on a morning, I grab a bite of my toast, and cringe as my delicate stomach flips in disgust; not quite there yet I agree with my body, as nausea waves engulf me again.

Thank goodness I'd not had to cater for Finn this morning. At least I'd been allowed the luxury of a lie in until 7.30am! I spy the designs collated yesterday, shrug into my suit jacket and locate my heels from the lego dump truck. The faint buzz of my phone alerts me but it is buried deep within my bag, amidst the escaped make-up, pens, spare change and MacDonald's toys; I just don't have the time to locate it right now.

Today was going to be just as manic as Monday, and I'd be firing on half cylinders, as I feel rather beaten up after last night's pill taking and impromptu visit from Seb. I really am going to need Colin's support over the next few days. With a last frantic look around the lounge, I mentally tick off what I have, whether I've forgotten anything and nodding to myself, shut the door – if it's not with me now, it was tough.

In the car I connect my phone to bluetooth and locate Suzie's work number. After a few rings she picks up.

"Good Morning. Dolly's Boutique," her happy voice filters through my handsfree system and I relax.

"It's me."

"About bloody time Missy. I've been worried sick! I was busting to call you first thing but Gino persuaded me to wait - well?"

"Thanks for the heads up, last night. Turns out I needed it, as Mr. Silver turned up all guns blazing at nearly midnight."

"Oh shit!"

"Yes. Oh shit exactly. He was lovely though. Really caring; carried me upstairs, and tucked me in."

"See! I told you he'd be nice about it."

"Stop interrupting me," she laughs at my bossiness. "It changed in seconds. I think I messed up - he was being all *controlly Sebastian* again. You know how independent I am." I can practically see the eye roll at the other end of the phone, and smile to myself. "Anyway we argued big-time; about whether the risk could be with Leo too? About why I didn't tell him, then got side tracked onto *us* and then he stormed out. I fell asleep. Pills stayed down. Feel a bit crap today but I'll be fine."

"Shut the front door - why would he think you'd slept with Leo?"

"Apparently someone put the thought in his mind. The same person who saw me buying the pill and kindly informed him."

"Sly fucker!"

"My sentiments exactly. I'd love to know who it was; I'd tear them a new arsehole."

"The anger hormone is raising its ugly head then Sis?"

I laugh at this. "Totally - my hormones are all over the place."

"Well, remember how you feel now, - the next time you're sliding down his Silver pole Madam."

"I know, I know! Lesson learned but I'm not sure there'll be a reoccurrence of that unfortunately - self-preservation me thinks. Anyway, enough about me, one of the reasons I couldn't sleep secret lady, is I've been too busy wondering about *your* drama? Come on, spill."

The phone is silent at the other end.

"Suze - you're starting to worry me."

"We....lllll! Maybe now's not the right time to say anything after you taking the morning after pill... but... oh sod it! I'm pregnant!" her excited voice is full of joy, and I'm immediately over the moon for her.

"Oh. My. God. That's amazing news sweetie - you daft thing. When did you find out?"

"Yesterday but you were indisposed. Normally you'd have been in the loo with me, whilst I pee'd on that stick and you know it!"

We laugh together as she's totally on the money.

"I'm already 14 weeks gone!"

"What?"

"I Know! I thought I was just getting fat and you know how dicey the Myers' female cycles are!"

She's right. My mum, Suzie and I, all had dodgy periods but she'd never seen fat! But I suppose on a tiny size 8, a fourteen-week pregnancy belly would show.

"So you'd be due in what… January sometime?"

"Ahem - a few weeks after New Year. I'll be the turkey this year, Auntie Lulu."

A baby. I'm suddenly surprised at how emotional I feel.

I'm so, so happy for her and Gino - it was definitely the right time for them and they were both fabulous with Finn.

"Finn, will be made up to have a cousin. Can I tell him?"

"Of course. I'm over three months now, so the scary time is over. I'm telling Mum and Dad tonight."

"Great. They'll be so excited too. Ah, you've really cheered me up, Hun. I can enjoy today now, as nothing is going get me down after this news. I'm going to be an Auntie!"

"Go. Bugger off and let me do some work… and ring Sebastian - you two need to sort things before they go on too long. You're good together - he's put the glow back into you."

He's put much more in me I think naughtily, aching for his touch. I miss him badly.

"I'm not calling him. Anyway he's away now on business until his party. I'll catch up with you this week. My congrats to G."

"Oh don't! He's strutting around like he's God's gift to women! Obviously, *I* had nothing to do with it."

I know she's joking, but I also know the Italian in him can make him rather less, modest, shall we say than us British, so I empathise.

"Seriously, I'm not sure I can take another 6months of Gino the baby maker. Its been one day and he's feeding me pre-natal vitamins, checking the temperature of my bath, so it's not too hot, won't let me lift anything! The man's gone mad - gorgeous - yes - heart in the right place - yes, but utterly bonkers! We are *not* calling the baby Sonny, Tommy, Frankie, Fat Larry, Vinnie, or anything remotely related to The Godfather or Goodfellas, if it's a boy. He's just going to have get over it."

I burst into laughter. She was on a rant. Funny! Good luck Gino trying to convince Suze of any of those names; *although, surely she's exaggerating with Fat Larry?*

"Bye my Lovely. Best news ever. Speak soon."

We hang up and I continue on my way to work, in complete awe of my recent findings. It's true what they say; behind every cloud is most definitely a silver lining.

⚜

Cracking on with the positive news, I achieve plenty. As a team we work tirelessly and I thank heavens for Colin and Jackie. The only thing that reminds me of Sebastian, and is enough to send me off track is the hand delivered Rose from FWC, which I sign for as I'm about to lock-up at the end of the day. I'd already sent J & C home. They'd worked through lunch and been great so what was 30 minutes, if it meant they'd do it all again for me, willingly, tomorrow?

Happily, this meant I could open my delivery in private and the monogrammed cream card that accompanied it. Lifting the lid with a warm feeling, I note that the rose is as usual, stunning and mentally I clock in my head, it's the fourth I'd received. He really is *very* romantic and I hope that this is an olive branch of sorts. I pick up the bud from its tissue-bolstered bed and smile at the now familiar jewelled middle. Each time I'd receive one of these special roses, I've added it to the large lustre vase in my lounge. It's a nice feeling to watch it blossoming, as our sexual relationship progresses.

FWC

Alka Seltzer settles the stomach, I hear.

Hope you're feeling better with <u>no</u> regrets?

The note is a caring but more friendly than romantic. *With no regrets? Regrets, about what?*

Taking the morning after pill or making the decision to sleep with him? At least he'd sent me said olive branch; last night had not ended well between us, mainly due to my own stubbornness and I hate the bad feeling between us, I wasn't used to it at all. This meant he was still in the game.

Locking up with my goodies, I head for the lift. As I exit on the ground floor, I throw my bright coral handbag over my shoulder, nod to the security porter and head towards the huge revolving glass doors. Its only as I'm about to enter, I glance over my shoulder, with the prickle of someone walking over your grave, running over me, and I sense that I am being watched. I look both ways and back towards the lift, but no one is there and, shaking it off, I head out.

I'm seriously getting paranoid here.

I need some sleep and pasta carbs tonight; the early onslaught of hyperglycemia was making me feel overly anxious.

Later, as I curl up on the sofa with an indulgent hot chocolate with marshmallows, back-to-back The Good Wife and my trusty laptop, my Facebook page bleeps at me. Glancing briefly at it, mid deliberation between bedspread or bed throw, for The Ashton, I scrunch up my nose in annoyance. I had a private message from Seb.

Lu,
The other night did not go well. Probably our first proper argument - not so pretty eh?
Either way, I know you are independent but I wish you had spoken to me about the MAP, so I could have helped. Maybe driving 200miles was not the best thing to do without calling you first. Hope you're not feeling too rubbish now. I'll sort out protection from here on out. I'm here if you need me. Always.
Like I said I'm all in for this proposition. We've only just begun having some fun. I know your mind, let me get to know your body better. You really are more than I could have ever hoped for Lu. We have a sexual connection, a heat, which I've not experienced before and you've so much more to give.
Rules still apply. No.3: to be explored further.
Yours,
Seb x
P.S When I get home, you won't sleep for a week.
P.P.S Look out for a delivery tomorrow & keep the night free - no excuses, as I know Finn is away.

I feel my smile reach my ears and I flush with overwhelming happiness. I couldn't wait for the lack of sleep either. How wanton was I? *I wonder what flowers he'd send this time?*

Crossing my foot underneath my knee, and settling back onto the cushions, I sigh in contentment - this message and the rose I'd received earlier today were all working wonders to appease my ongoing doubts - he certainly knew how to romance a girl. Not sure that was a good or bad thing? I'd placed the rose inside the vase on the mirrored console, alongside its predecessors and it shone, full of life against the three others, now losing their vibrancy, the diamante crystal pin, twinkling for attention within their centre's.

My eyes flick over his message again and revert continuously back to the end, '*Yours, Seb x*'. *I'm beginning to wish he were truly mine, in mind, body and soul.*

Chapter 27

Lucia

By Wednesday, after a much better night's sleep, and feeling more organised, I'm much more Lulu-like. Its as I'm about to leave to meet Chris at The Ashton, I receive the promised *delivery or rather deliveries* to the office. I know they're from him, the minute Jackie hands them over to me, her excitement hardly contained. In truth I'd been watching and waiting since his message last night. Opening the first discreet brown parcel, I'm surprised when I ease out the palest iconic pink box emblazoned with the Agent Provocateur logo. Sensing that this is the type of gift to review in private I grab the other two boxes and remove myself from the office, disappearing to the ladies. I'm just glad that my co-workers appear to be deeply in talks about Colin's love life.

Taking a second to indulge, I run my hand over the beautiful packaging, then anxious to see the goodies, slip off the black satin ribbon. It drops from the corner as I lift the lid, surrounding me with the scent of luxury, sensuality and naughtiness. Inside, wrapped in tissue, sits a black satin and lace bra. At least I think it is. There's not much to it! I hold it up to my chest, admiring the under-wired demi cups, sheer mesh, pretty lace, matt satin and bows - but they only go about a quarter of the way up? Each cup has a strip of satin, which reaches around the top of the breast and joined the strap with a bow - giving the look, a bondage feel. While the open top cups are barely there, just a whisper of French lace, scattered with the odd black sequin, which sparkles in the light. Finally my eyes are drawn to a huge drop cameo pearl, dangling from the plunged neckline -

absolutely stunning.

Wow - my nipples would be completely on show!

Oh My.

My belly flip-flops in excitement.

I select the next item; panties made from the same matching scraps of glittering and matt black satin - the back a thong made from a strand of creamy white pearls. I'd seen these before but never purchased any and as I turn the fabric around I realise that the front is missing too.

They're *crotchless*!

I feel my cheeks flame and lick my lips. He'd chosen these for me. He'd thought about me in them. A suspender belt with the same bondage strap detailing and lace topped stockings complete the evocative look. Beneath the erotic lingerie, winks a black satin mask, trimmed with lace and pearls and attached wide sashes; I presume, these tie behind the head.

Ok this was really getting kinky.

He did say I had to be open to anything. Hell, *I'd* said I'd be open to anything.

Sebastian had also said that the next time we were together I was to wear no panties. *I suppose crotchless comes close.*

I open the smallest of the three parcels next - a white jiffy-bag, which houses a plastic business card, and a hand-scrawled note. *Eh?*

Looking inside I discover a beautifully designed red keycard holder, with a monogram design to the front; the letters SH entwined in Gold. I can practically hear my heart pounding as I turn it in my fingers. I moisten my lips again and scan the letter.

LU,

YOUR PRESENCE IS REQUIRED @ 8pm TONIGHT -
WEAR THE ITEMS PROVIDED.
ADDRESS: SCARLET HOUSE; LORDS - ROOM 22
HAVE A DRINK IN THE HOTEL BAR.
AFTER 15 MINUTES GO UP TO THE ROOM &
LET YOURSELF IN WITH THE KEYCARD PROVIDED.
BRING THE MASK & REMEMBER TO BE BOLD
FORGET YOUR FEARS.
GIVE IN TO YOUR DESIRES.
UNTOLD PLEASURES AWAIT.

SEB X

He must be home?

Again my heart beats erratically, my palms are clammy and my sex clenches in anticipation. Fuck me, this man is good. I re-read his message. My eyes are drawn back continuously to the last three lines.

Forget your fears. Give in to your desires. Untold pleasures await.

I open the last box tentatively, almost afraid of what would be next but all nerves go out the window when I see the red soles, glossy and brazenly winking at me. Oh. My. God! He's bought me a pair of Christian Louboutins. He's bloody bought me some Luby Lu's!

I've wanted a pair of these shoes forever to add to my collection of do-me-shoes. Like an excited little girl I shriek in silence, careful not to alert my design team to my glee, and delicately remove each shoe from their tissued bed, marvelling at their remarkable design. They were black suede pointed toe stilettos, with at least a four-inch narrow heel and at the part where the heel met the shoe; three large chunky pearls were embedded and encrusted with diamonds. *They are bloody gorgeous and totally me!*

Even if Niall had been drunk enough to relax his hold on his credit card, he'd never have chosen the right style to suit me, or the right size. Sebastian had managed both.

Pondering on that consideration I carefully place all the extravagance back into their respective packages and carry them with me to the office, before locating a huge carrier from my drawer.

Was I actually going to go through with this?

I hadn't seen him since the other night and did feel fine after Monday night's pill episode. But was continuing this proposition such a good idea? I loved being the object of desire but at what cost and for how long? His controlling ways were increasing and I was falling deeper. I fear my heart won't take the hit from a Silver break-up.

On a worried sigh I mutter something about The Ashton to J & C and head off with my new gifts - the drive to Holdgate would give me chance to clear my fuzzy mind. The little voice inside there, reminds me that I should be thinking with my bits and not my brain right now and for the first time ever, I tend to agree.

Half an hour later, I've managed to reduce Chris from an Octopus to a crab for the time being. I'm not sure which is worse but we get through the fireplace plans and the suite is beginning to look busy as more helpers have arrived, one of them being Nathan. The plaster is being refreshed and under floor heating added to the bathroom. The result is a big dusty chaotic mess and I smile as that means something shiny and new will emerge in time. It was exciting!

"Hey Lulu – looking far too lovely for this grubby worksite," a genuine smile lights up his already college boy handsome face and he blows me a kiss, pointing apologetically to his dust covered body and protective goggles, now sitting on his forehead.

"Don't think that under this suit and heels, there isn't a hard headed business woman Nathan Silver – I'm a feisty little thing when I want things done!"

"Bloody not wrong there." Chris agrees sulkily. "I've never worked so hard – although I do like em feisty!" He winks and laces the last word with extra zest running his appreciative eyes up and down my body. "Didn't think you'd be in today Lady Boss - got the painters in I hear?"

My questioning frown encourages him to continue, as I grapple with what he's talking about? *'Painters'* and *'Having them in'* - the decorating team I use aren't due in for a week at least, I think to myself dimly, looking around the room, that still resembles a building site. As I focus on Chris again and hear the words fall from his lips, the penny suddenly drops and I wish I'd just ignored him. What a complete prat!

"Ya know, time of the month - your assistant and Seb said you were off with tummy ache."

Bless Jackie meant well but maybe Chris wasn't the best guy to offload my health issues onto. As for Seb what had *he* told him?

"No, no, I'm fine thanks Chris, all good now - that was a few days ago. There's these amazing products now called Tampax and Codeine, so we can still get the job done and not rely so heavily on you macho men," my voice drips with sarcasm.

I don't wait around for another crude retaliation and instead head over to Nathan, who is looking perplexed. "You OK Lu?"

I shrug off the comment, probably with too much gusto. "What me? Tough old thing - you know that," I laugh his concern away.

"Seriously though, does Seb know you've been ill?"

"I've not been ill - just a bit of tummy ache and yes, your punctilious and totally over-the-top protective brother knows all about it." I add pointedly.

His nod of approval both annoys and warms me. "Right, let's see what you've been up to."

Back to business Na proceeds to show me his work on the window seats; the beautiful rococo style woodwork is exactly what I'd envisaged, in my original designs and I pat his shoulder in thanks. For the next few minutes we buzz off each other's creativity, sketching concepts for the bed, panelling and ornate frame that will house the 50inch LED TV.

"Looks like you've got an admirer there!" he thrusts his head in the direction of Chris, who is chatting to the plumber.

I screw my face up in disagreement. "Nah, he's harmless really – I hope. Just a bit of a cheese ball."

"Better not let Sebastian see him pawing you like that. I've a feeling that wouldn't go down so well," Nathan smiles.

I assess Nathan's face and let the words sink in, pleased with the knowledge that Seb's own brother can see that he would possibly be jealous – but conscious that Seb and Chris are friends and I don't want to come between that – it was a recipe for disaster, in any relationship.

Changing the subject, we return to peruse his highly skilled joinery.

"Good eh? If I say so myself," he adds modestly.

"Not just good – bloody gorgeous. I'm so pleased Nath."

We spend a minute or two going over the plans for the huge queen size bed and somehow the topic leads to Abby and Seb.

"Seen much of Abs lately?"

"I saw her at the weekend with you but not since. We've been in touch though."

He nods, pondering something, which is obviously bothering him, and I remain quiet, aware that he might clam up and I'd not get the knowledge I know I need to obtain for Abby.

"I think I like her Lu." His face is pained and I can tell it's not something he really wants to admit to anyone, let alone himself.

I empathise. *Hell I'm in exactly the same predicament.*

"I think the feeling is mutual Nathan. Just take it easy and let it happen. You two are perfect for one another."

He smiles, white teeth flashing at me brightly, amongst the dust. "Yeah - she's a keeper. I knew it that Saturday night when I saw her dancing in the Champ bar." He shakes his head to remove some of the remnants of wood in his hair. "What about you and my bro?"

I sigh and roll my eyes to the ceiling. "It's always a game with Seb - you know how he is – the chase - going in for the kill. Once he has it and it's maimed for life, there's nothing left to pursue." We both laugh in unison at my dramatic analogy.

"Woah, heavy stuff – just wondered if you two were seriously hooking up?" We continue to giggle like kids.

"Bit much?"

"Just a bit," he agrees. "He's a goner Lu. I've not seen him like this before but to be honest he's always adored you. What changed?"

My lips curl in a cheeky grin. "I propositioned him."

Nathan practically chokes in response. "You what?"

"I asked him to take me to bed. Get me back into things, you know sex-wise." My casualness does not go unnoticed by Nathan but I smile at his shocked frown.

"Niall treated me badly Na and I'm good now but Abs was right… she said to me a few months back I'd lost my zest and I needed to start dating again. Sex was an issue. So in Seb I saw a solution. He's my best friend, a major player and apparently fabulous in the sack and I trust him." *Bloody amazing - I can attest to that now.*

"Jeez. No wonder he looks like the cat that's got the cream but like it went sour too! I haven't been able to figure him out. Talk about happy one minute and crazy the next. Are you sure you two aren't making a mistake here - I mean fucking up your friendship?"

I assess his expression and worried eyes and if it weren't for the work clothes I'd have grabbed him in a hug then and there.

"I'm fine. Honestly. Seb isn't a commitment kind of guy, so it's a win-win."

I can tell from Nathan's face he's not convinced. "Really?" Maybe Seb is ready to try something real?"

I wrinkle my nose. "I don't think so but we're having fun - plenty of fun. Just keep it shtum - I don't think he'd want everyone knowing."

"Good luck with that - we're all aware that something is going on!"

I'm about to answer, when *The Crab* interrupts, slinging a loose arm around my shoulders. I instantly tense.

"Right, better get back to it Boss!" Nathan raises his eyebrows at me and winks.

I grin affectionately at our shared in-house joke. "See you soon. If not this week, Saturday at Sebastian's house party."

Already in full work-mode again, sandpaper going ten to the dozen, he nods and mumbles through the protective mask, "See you there."

Chris still hovers around me like a bad smell. "I'll most definitely see you there Honey, after all, I live there now."

Lucky me!

I placate him with a wave over my shoulder as I make a hasty exit. I've too much to do to put up with Creepy Chris another second. *Like dress for a sexy illicit tete a tete.*

Chapter 28

Lucia

I fidget nervously with the pearls at my wrist, as my eyes scan the impressive interior of the Limousine that has collected me for the evening - its leather seats filling my nostrils. The knock at the door had been a shocking but welcome surprise; I'd been about to call a cab but upon seeing the sleek glossy black vehicle parked outside, just sitting there at my beck and call, courtesy of Mr. Silver, I'd happily informed the fair-haired, thick set driver I'd be out promptly.

Let's hope Meg hadn't seen the flashy arrival - she'd be itching to check it out.

Now happily ensconced within, I'm wondering whether it had been such a good idea. The smart young driver with a Polish accent had presented me with a glass of chilled bubbling champagne, before setting off in the direction of Scarlet House and with a quick buzz through the intercom, he had now informed me we were only two minutes from my destination.

My heart is beating ridiculously fast and mouth so dry I'm glad of the champagne and guzzle it down greedily. I'd spent two hours preparing for tonight and changed my mind a zillion times in that 120minutes. The one thing that had spurred me on, was the thought of his mouth on mine, his fingers splayed across my body, parting me, delving inside me, opening me and taking me over the edge. I'd had a taste of him; and now I craved so much more.

I certainly looked the part; Sophie, my amazing hairdresser had worked wonders with my hair, curling and pinning it loosely high up on my crown, the odd tendril escaping. The result elongated my neck and showed off my smokey eyes and full red mouth. I knew he liked me in bold matt red lipstick.

I'd bathed in oils, buffed, trimmed, shaved and moisturised. My skin felt delicious and the whole process of getting ready for him had me turned on, before I'd even slipped the lingerie in place. My skin felt alive and expectant.

The bra fit me perfectly, perhaps a little snug but only assisted in pushing my breasts up and in - allowing them to be shown to their best advantage; my areolas, rosy and flushed from my bath, balanced perkily upon the cups, winking delicately behind the carefully placed lace. My nipples however, were entirely free and erect. The panties came next and I slid them over my hips, adjusting the pearl stringed thong to rest neatly between my cheeks - the little balls running from the top of my bottom, underneath my perineum and stopping at the tip of my opening. I'd squirmed initially at the odd cool sensation they created before sliding each lace topped stocking up one leg, then the other, careful not to ladder them. A hook and eye fastened the suspender belt in place and a quick snap shut on the sexy bondage straps connected everything together safely, finished with a pearl adorned black satin bow. The entire outfit was pure sex - designed by a man for a man's pleasure. Old style Dita Von Teese with that erotic edge. Adding the to-die-for Louboutins, I'd stood for an age, assessing my body in the full-length rococo mirror.

Holy Shit! My laugh had been immediate, holding a hand up to my mouth to touch my lips in awe. I was amazed how sexy I looked. *Could I dare to part my thighs - see how open I looked too?*

The sexy lace and satin glittered in the light temptingly, giving the look a magical aura but the bondage strapping around my breasts, waist, and thighs kept things dirty. 10 denier stockings, showed my shapely legs off nicely and the shoes were pure genius, elongating and curving my legs in all the right places. Holding the mask up to my amethyst smoked eyes, I'd appraised myself from every angle; the lace panel lying across my eyes, creating a veil; not completely blind but cloaking me in mystique.

I hadn't wanted to ruin the beautiful outfit Sebastian had selected for me, besides, what clothing would work over it? So I chose to be bold - my motto for the night, and wear a black high collared satin coat, nipped in at the waist, which spun out into a full skirt ending at the knee, tied with a black Swarovski studded satin sash. At the last second, I grabbed a long rope of creamy white pearls and wound them around my wrist. Perfect.

I now played with the end of that sash, panicked at my decision. There were no buttons to fasten my coat; just this makeshift belt and we were going to a hotel. I'm practically naked under here - what had I been thinking?

You'd been imagining him taking it off you and revealing yourself to his beautiful black eyes.

"We're here Ms. Myers."

I jump at the interruption to my lascivious thoughts and hear gravel crunching under the car tyres and the handbrake activated. *I'm here.*

Polish-guy assists me out of the car and at the last second, I remember my bag, and reach back for the large red clutch. It houses the mask, the card key, my phone, my purse, make-up essentials and that's it - I'd not come with an overnight bag. The door opens and I swing both feet neatly together and place them on the ground, and smile coyly as I follow the driver's focus, transfixed on my lace stocking topped thigh. Rather than feel embarrassed I feel empowered as I elegantly pull the coat to cover my modesty, but not all the way, leaving the slightest hint of lace peeking through. I take his outstretched hand and stand.

"Thank you for driving me?" I assess his pale grey eyes, and realise I don't know his name.

"Ralph."

I nod. "Ralph. Well good night then."

It is time to go inside Scarlet House and be one hell of a Scarlet Lady.

❧

Looking up at the impressive townhouse I make for the entrance, situated between two large bay trees covered in white fairy lights. I throw one last glance over my shoulder at the limousine waiting behind me, that feeling of being watched is compelling - *now or never* - then turn and twist the door knob.

The moment I enter Scarlet House I know I'm about to experience a night like no other - the interior is dark, gothic almost in its design; like a luxurious gentleman's club, with dimmed wall lights and the intoxicating scent of the large display of black orchids on the main desk. Black velvet damask wallpaper drapes the walls, with glossy black and gold Louis XIV replica chairs and a thick black

257

carpet that my Louboutin's sink into. Deep blues and golds, add warmth to the predominantly noir facade but the ultimate vibe is sensuality, opulence and sex - not unlike what I am trying to create at The Ashton.

An older, smartly attired grey haired gentleman takes my name at reception before escorting me through large indigo velvet upholstered double doors, into the drawing room and subsequent guest bar. Music fills this space - seductive and intoxicating.

"Table or the Bar Ms. Myers?" His expression is friendly but I'm too on edge to engage.

I choose the bar, easing myself onto a high stool and placing my clutch in front of me. I take a moment to check for Sebastian. He isn't here… yet.

Surveying my surroundings, the boudoir decor continues with the general ambience, rich and glamorous. The watered silk wallpaper to my right subtly depicts erotic illustrations of Marie Antoinette's era, in Karma Sutra positions, some of which I have to crook my head to fathom. The exotic music fills my ears, intense and throbbing and sensual. Behind me, there are several couples at tables, transfixed with each other - *tactile* is the name of the game here.

The whole place was decadent and purely indulgent, with just enough rakishness to be a fabulously louche atmosphere. I absolutely loved it!

How had I never heard of it before? *Because Mrs. you've never had a sexy man send you a saucy invitation to meet him here - you've never been with a man who'd asked you to be bold!*

Fiddling with the pearl drop at my lobe, I moisten my lips and cross my leg over the other, feeling the satin fabric of my coat slide open - I choose to leave it and watch as a young, immaculately dressed barman, heads my way with a tumbler, its rim encrusted with sugar. He places it front of me before smiling appreciatively, "From the gentleman in Room 22."

My heart begins to pound again. *He was here already - upstairs perhaps?*

"What is it?"

"Dark and Stormy."

How appropriate. I take a tentative sip, my mouth immediately filled with flavours of warm rum, ginger and zesty lime - the sugar on the edge a welcome sweetener and chunks of ice, soothing the burn of the alcohol.

I look up into expectant eyes, "It's good - really good."

His nod of approval is quick before I'm left to my thoughts. A quick look at my watch tells me I have ten minutes before I need to be in the bedroom - as per his bloody instructions. I have to admit though; I'm enjoying being told what to do for once. Abs was right, there were some parts to submission, which I think I'd be open to.

I wiggle on the seat, the pearl thong was playing havoc in my nether regions - not because it was uncomfortable, entirely the opposite, it was creating delicious pressure around my bottom and vulva and made me want to grind down on that stool to get myself off.

The drink goes down smoothly, in large, quickening gulps, the burn travelling down my throat and warming my chest, where just under my coat, my nipples beg to be touched. It relaxes me, numbing my mind and setting my skin on fire - I'm sure that had been Sebastian's goal. The 15minutes gives me time to think about what is waiting for me upstairs and makes me wet in anticipation, every minute passing by empowers and steadies me.

Time to nip to the ladies, before making my way up to him, at last. Slipping off my perch, I notice the couple behind me. The man's hand rests high on her thigh; her hand openly caresses his face. They look enraptured with one another, teasing and kissing audaciously. My core clenches just thinking of Sebastian upstairs, waiting at my disposal.

What was this place? Sex was the main thing on everyone's mind here- sex and sensuality - mine included.

The door to Room 22 is an imposing glossy black panelled creation, with a huge crystal handle. It looks like all the others on the corridor but it was unique in that it housed Sebastian, on the other side. Card key in hand, trembling visibly, my stomach in knots I pause - *could I really do this? Be this bold?*

My eyes drop to my hand before scrunching it tightly around the card, flexing and tightening once again. I take a deep calming breath and sliding that key in and out, sharply - *no going back now,* I think for the fiftieth time since I'd arrived. The light flashes green on the lock and composing myself, I enter.

Inside the room is dimly lit, candles flaring sporadically scattered at corners, casting an alluring glow amongst the shadows and my eyes take a second to adjust to the light. The room is huge and as opulent as the rest of the town house and at its centre, an ornate four-poster bed takes pride of place.

"Sebastian?"

Was that my voice; all-sultry? God I'm shaking - where is he?

"Put your mask on."

His voice reverberates right through me, hitting every nerve ending. I shudder, before retracting the satin and lace accessory and tying it behind my up-do, obediently.

His distinctive scent engulfs me - musk and caramel and masculine, before strong arms fasten loosely at my waist and I lean back into him, letting him take my weight. I feel his hands working the knot free and the sash as it falls to the ground, air hitting my chest and stomach, as the coat gapes. I hear his breath hitch and he lets out a low groan at the revelation of my lack of clothing and smiling, pleased at the reaction, I arch and assist him, shrugging out of my coat, desperate to feel his sexy hands on my body.

"Let me awaken you."

My chest expands, nipples ruching in the cold, my whole body screaming out in answer to his words - *yes please*! Then I feel the wet of his lips on my neck, tickling the soft tendrils there, the swirls of his tongue delicately laving my shoulder and it's my undoing.

I spin and force myself into his solid male frame, cocooned in the heat emanating from his rock-solid, muscled body. He is dressed in a black shirt; sleeves rolled back and suit pants and looks mouth-wateringly sexy.

"You look so fuckable," he breathes, stepping from the shadows.

"I was thinking exactly the same thing." The words fall from my lips without a thought.

He's practically on me, in me, my senses are on high alert and finally I'm given the chance to see his gorgeous face in all its glory. In that moment I do not see Sebastian my friend, but the stunning and suggestive man who's lured me to this hotel; a man who makes me feel things I've never felt before. Someone I trust to show me pleasure I've only ever achieved with him.

I feel my clit throb in reaction to our words and the impact of this delicious man.

Through the lace I can make out his liquorice eyes, glittering with fire in the dark. They travel up and down my body, assessing the seductive lingerie he'd purchased for me.

"I knew these would be perfect for your shape - show how sexy you are."

His hands cover both breasts in unison; his moan of passion released as he cups them, before elongating my nipples and rolling them leisurely. I cry out, shaking at the sensations flowing through me, triggering shockwaves to all my feel-good zones.

"Beautiful." Placing a kiss softly onto my nose he whispers. "Tonight is the next step towards showing you how sexy you are. Now, no more talking."

Dropping to his knees I feel his hot mouth at my stomach and my breath quickens and I wrap my hand onto his head, "You smell so good."

I inhale as his tongue trails along the top of the suspender belt, his hand reaching to brush softly against my inner thigh, following the line of the bondage strap there, tickling the edge of the lace stocking, and stretching my legs further apart. His palm flattens over my V, cupping me, before slipping his fingers down, in search of access. The purposely-designed hole between my legs is gaping, now I'm pushed wide, open to his eyes. *Touch me please.*
His fingers dip, deliberately avoiding my pussy and knuckles graze against the pearls. He traces one tip across the rope, in a sweeping motion, causing small vibrations to ricochet up towards my clit and I moan at the contact - *at last.*

"Did this feel good Lucia - rubbing between your legs?"

I bite my lip, at the exquisite sensations he is creating with the friction over the pearls. "Yes."

"I can't hear you."

"Yes." It comes out on a sigh.

"You're so wet for me already Baby."
I squirm under his touch and throw my head back - his words are dirty and forbidden; they turn me on. I plead for him to bring me off, I'm nearly there and sense the coolness of a pearl being rubbed into my clit, the strand now pulled to one side, more malleable.

"Ahh, Seb!" My hands run over his head, his own cupping my behind, forcing me into his face. His mouth is inches away from my clit, whilst his fingers work their magic - *reach out with your tongue and lick me, I beg silently.*

His finger dips from my cheek further around, underneath, temptingly tracing my anus, placing pressure there, circling gently and I flinch just before his wet moist tongue swoops in and suckles over my erect nub, washing over it- my knees buckle, I'm soaring. His

261

finger presses further and I reach my climax - the pearls rubbing every sensitive nerve. My pussy aches to be filled as I pant with desire - I'm out of breath.

"Oh God!"

I reach back, running my hands over my hair, the mask still in place - I'm trembling. Sebastian slips the panties down and over my shoes, leaving the fabulous footwear in place, and leads me towards the huge four-poster, laying me gently within its centre. I hear his clothes, being discarded, and the weight of him as he joins me on the bed. Immediately I'm lifted to a sitting position, where I can see he is entirely naked and extremely hard, his cock jutting engorged and huge in its erection. I raise my hand to touch him and am immediately ceased by his.

"Not yet Baby." *Control is there at the forefront again but this time I like it.*

Reaching to the silver table beside the bed, he alerts me to a tray, complete with ice bucket, champagne, cherries, strawberries, cream and red coulee. My mouth waters at the thought of such pleasure - I love all of these delicious things but to consume them with Sebastian, in this setting, naked - serious food-play. With anyone else it would have been cliché but not with him. *Not in this setting.*

I can see through the lace but not as much as I'd like and before I can remove it, Seb dips a dark ruby red cherry into the cream, feeding it to me, caressing my lips with the yumminess, and plopping it in my mouth. I moan in ecstasy, which is immediately stifled by his kiss, his tongue swooping inside to collect some of the sweet and tart combination and the pip, which he places back onto the plate.

"Delicious."

I roll my lips together, savouring the sweetened juices on the edges of my mouth and lie back onto my arm, watching as he repeats the process, this time swirling the cherry from the stalk, around my areole, and dragging the cream upwards onto my erect nipple - then lapping it like an ice-cream - the sensation is bliss - I squeeze my eyes shut, as my clit springs to life again - it's only been a few minutes but I'm needy already.

I delight in Seb leisurely licking fruit and the fluffy whipped cream mixture off my body, my mouth and the hot and cold thrills created send my nerves into overdrive again. Each time I reach for him, he grabs my wrists and places them above my head, forcing them to refrain from touching him. I watch as he bites gently into a succulent strawberry, his beautiful mouth seductive, teeth white and teasing whilst he holds my gaze throughout. God he's hot as hell!

Reaching for my wrists, he unravels the pearl necklace twisted there, until it loosens. Leaving it looped in two strands around my left wrist, he rubs a thumb over the soft flesh at my pulse, placing the lightest of kisses there. My heart hammers in my chest, the moment so simple but so erotic, as I watch his eyes darken.

"As you can't seem to do as you are told, I need your other wrist."

At my shocked look, his expression softens. "Please."

I lift my right wrist and present it to him without further question, my trust in him fathomless. Shivering faintly as he slips my hand through the middle of the rope of pearls, winds it around my wrist again, and pulls. Tight. Finally wrapping the excess around his finger and pulling through the loophole, creating a loose knot. He'd definitely done this before.

I test the strength of the bonds. Instinct really, and I'm surprised how strong the pearl rope hold is and how sexy it makes me feel to be trapped by him.

Sebastian assesses my reaction, smiles seductively, placing my bound hands above my head and moves his attention to my chest, tracing the strawberry delicately over my breast, down onto the curve of my quivering belly and along the edge of each suspender strap. As the bed dips, I feel him at my pussy, blowing gently there, encouraging me to open for him - instinctively I do, I feel his fingertip flex over me, slide up my slit, I'm so wet after my orgasm. He settles between my thighs and my toes curl involuntarily - *Jesus - again?*

I'm not ready - I can't take anymore. *Can I?*

His tongue tentatively licks across my lips, and I buck. *Yes I want more.* Again, I feel something wet on me, cooling but foreign, and then I realise it's the strawberry. He gently strokes it back and forth, across my needy clit and I jump at the sensations, rotating my hips in encouragement - it feels amazing.

"You always smell like cherries to me; now you'll taste of strawberries, Baby."

I arch my back, pushing myself into his face and he collects the ripened fruit with his tongue, forcefully pressing down on my clit at every point - then swirls around it, before taking it in his mouth and licking his lips. I'm so turned on I could explode but I need to reciprocate.

"Gives a whole new meaning to the fruit of your loins." I chuckle at his corny joke and love that we can still make each other laugh, whilst experiencing such raw energy.

Sensing my need for physical contact, one hand hot and firm clasps my straining breasts, before he kisses me, and then reaches for the champagne. I close my eyes in anticipation of what is to come, his lips on my throat and something cold grazing my nipple. It burns, and tingles. My eyes fly open in shock.

"Easy Baby - its just ice, frosting over your amazing tits."

I quiver as he drops his mouth to suckle the ice-cold tip, his hot wet mouth a welcome sensation, before repeating the process on the other breast. I kiss the top of his head; lick the side of his face, needing contact at all times -desperate to touch him.

His trail continues, ice cold and wet, down, around my belly button and over my thigh, up and inwards and I tense, before he swirls the now dripping chip of ice all over my pussy, cupping me, the wet dribbling down, and over my thighs onto the sheet. His mouth teases mine. Duelling our tongues, he deepens the intensity of the kiss, as I feel his cock straining against my stomach and I open my legs instinctively to entice him.

"You've no idea what you do to me. I need to be inside you now – I've got to be buried to the hilt; to feel you take all of me."

I shudder at his words, their meaning so much more than sex - this was so much more than just sex. It was trust, passion, pushing the boundaries of everything I'd ever known sexually. *Fuck - was it love?*

I'm lost in my thoughts as I feel his fingers untie the knot at my wrists and with finesse unwind the pearls, until my hands are free. Gently he rubs them both, bringing life back into them, and I flex all digits simultaneously; a little numb but worth it.

"OK?"

"All good." My sultry voice is still unrecognisable.

"Good because something else needs those hands on them."

With a wicked grin, he clasps my hand and draws it downwards, placing it around his thick cock. *He is on fire.* His body twists and I move to retain my grip, when he reaches over and locates a condom. He was as good as his word but the feeling of despair that I won't have him inside bareback, is all consuming.

"You put this on me Baby - let me watch you."

My startled expression, must be obvious through the mask, as he searches my eyes, smiling,

"Have you not done this before?"

Shaking my head he nods.

"A first? It'll be a gift to me then. Something we can share together."

Easing off the side of the bed and drawing me to him to nestle between his legs, my breasts heavy and aching over his balls, I take the condom, tear the wrapper, and place the rubber over the head of his protruding cock. I'd seen condoms put on before, so knew to pinch the end and after a slight fumble, do so, leisurely rolling it down his shaft. Firm strokes in a downward direction seem to do the trick, as I feel him grow bigger and more rigid by the second; the heat emanating from him there a complete turn-on. When I'm done I look up for approval, into blackened eyes, so filled with lust I feel myself grow wet.

"Knew these things could be sexy if placed in the right hands!"

He lowers his head to mine, takes my hands encouraging me to stand, before turning me 180 degrees. We are back where we started.

His hand reaches around to play with my breasts, gentle in this fondling, whilst his cock juts at the entrance to my behind. I feel his hand at my suspender strap and a push as he bends me over the bed, dragging a languid wet lick up my spine, from waist to neck. I shiver.

"What a pretty sight."

Blushing in the dark as I think about the view he has, my bare behind, and wet pussy, glistening, decorated with bondage straps and lace topped stockings - all wrapped up for him, ready to open and delve into.

"Look up Baby."

His voice is deep and husky and I do as he asks and I'm rewarded with a huge 7foot gold gilt mirror, glimmering directly opposite us. I hardly recognise the wanton woman staring back at me, flushed and brazen. Normally I'd have looked away but I'm immediately seduced by the fact that I can watch him fuck me; in all my agent provocateur finery - lace mask in place, curls tousled, some tumbling down onto my neck and shoulders. My tits, protruding like perfect globes on my demi cups and nipples erect and proud. Even I could see that I looked sexy. We looked sexy together - his hot muscled body, against my silky olive skin - our goals the same.

"Keep watching."

He orders me on a growl and I do.

I stare transfixed as he places his cock at my entrance. My eyes grow hooded as he slides easily within me, his hands dropping to my hips and his deep breath of pleasure as he is clouded in tight silk. I watch as my mouth forms an 'o' shape when he plunges fully into me to the root - and I stop to catch my breath, before moaning again, when he removes himself to the tip, then delves in and rotates, gaining momentum as my tits swing with the vibration. I watch his face grow tense, the veins in his neck proud, as he nears his climax. He reaches a hand around my body, and with the pad of his index and middle finger, I watch him pinch my clit, opening me, and lifting me slightly so I can see his wide cock swallowed by my pussy, my folds surrounding him and shiny with desire. My nub is swollen and throbbing and I push back onto him, desperate to create some form of friction. He answers my plea and leaves his palm there to add pressure where I want it most, as he thrusts into me.

"Darling, tonight you are mine." His voice is thick with emotion.

Darling? His love words soften the coarseness of the position we are in and I position my arm behind me, on his taut behind, forcing him into me further. I needed him to fill me completely, and tip me over the edge.

My low moan is all the encouragement he needs to finish the deed. He withdraws then, almost fully and I moan again at the loss of his scorching heat and in answer he thrusts into me so hard, his balls bang against my behind. Our passionate mating is animalistic in the mirror - both driven by the hot demands of our bodies and as his cock continually hits my g-spot, I shatter around him, his fingertips rotating in lazy swivels across my clit, deepening my orgasm. He looks wild and beautiful as he pounds into me. Everything an Alpha male should be. A predator.

My hands grip the sheets, my body dips lower as I sink, nipples scraping pleasurably along the bed, every nerve ending frayed - at that moment, I look up into his blackened pools knowing he is about to come. I can feel his cock spasming and watch as he throws his head back on a roar of ecstasy, my name on his lips, as he wraps his arms around me. Entwined.

We lie like that for several minutes, our breathing laboured and bodies slick, until I feel his cock slip from me. The sensation of loss is worrying but I'm quickly preoccupied, by the scorching warmth of his mouth; the contact of his body against mine, once again. Skin on skin.

I sigh. Raining kisses all over my back and neck, he slides us both up onto the bed, spooning his muscled body around mine.

"That was incredible Lulu."

"I agree. You were right, strangers make better lovers - there had to be no friendship here."

"Initially yes, but this is you and me Baby. We'll always be friends."

His lips caress my shoulder and I moan, curling into his warmth. Will we always be friends? I'm not sure I can go back to friendship, without the sex, after what we've just shared? Maybe I like the fact that I can submit for once; let him take control. Finally, someone else can take care of *me?*

Let's face it, Sebastian is your soul mate and you know it. You want love, sex, friendship; the whole fucking works!

Exhausted, but entirely replete, I shift positions and turn to stand. Seb pecks me on the mouth gently and excuses himself, heading for the bathroom to dispose of the protection. I hear water running and listen to the soothing sounds as I relax on the resplendent four-poster bed. Staring up at the black painted ceiling, I stretch my thoroughly worshipped body - talk about the girl that got the strawberries and cream. That had been nothing short of exquisite. My naughty smile is wistful at the memory of the night.

Hmmm. Where has Seb got to?

I glance at the door to the en-suite, slightly ajar and allowing the drum of heavy water to filter through, and swing my legs over the edge of the bed, before stepping towards the bathroom. As I open the door fully, I'm hit by a wall of steam, which rises sensually from a huge black circular bath, nestled majestically in the centre of the room. Looking at the decor, I see that the black and gold theme continues in here, and rather than appear ostentatious is perfect for the atmosphere Scarlet House is trying to offer its guests.

Black glittering marbled tiles, wash the floors and scale the high walls; the noir façade is then broken up by a gold panel, more bronze in its tone, that fills one wall behind the sink, where the lighting cleverly creates a warm metallic glow. I can still hear water and entering deeper into the room, I notice that the right-hand corner is entirely blackened and L-shaped; it's a wet room.

I follow the sound of the water and find Seb, eyes closed, legs spread, and palms flat against the wall in front of him. The water is lashing down from the immense watering can shower-head in the ceiling, all over his body, brutal in its force. *Oh to have had this shower when we had our morning nookie at mine.*

I can't help but stare at his body with awe as water cascades over his muscles, dampening the hair on his body and tightening his skin with goosebumps. He was cold?

"Seb?" My question is tentative.

His head flicks up, water covering me, from his lightning reaction, his eyes bore into mine. Intense and sexy but troubled. *What was up with him?*

"You OK?"

"I'm fine Lu. Sorry, I fancied a shower."

He looks apologetic but switches the tap off, steps out of the enclosure and walks towards me. Dripping wet and cock swinging. He was semi-hard, his balls tight as a drum. His eight-pack clearly defined with the glistening drops. I can't help but stare at his magnificent physique and suddenly feel conscious in my underwear attire, where my boobs are still clearly on show, with no knickers to cover my modesty.

"I ran you a bath. Here let me help you undress."

I'm touched at his thoughtfulness and turn my back to him, as he unhooks my bra, suspender belt and unpins my hair, leaving me in just my stockings.

"Sit."

Directing me to a nearby Louis chair, like the replica one in the reception foyer, I sit. He kneels in front of me, slipping one hold-up off slowly, before rolling down the second and placing them both with my other items. As I'm sitting, naked, watching him at my feet his eyes grow hooded and I feel my nipples ruche. I'd never sat before a man naked. I feel so exposed, yet as he kneels in front of me, his own body on show for me. I relax in the moment. It feels right. We are strangers remember Lu. Not friends. Lovers.

"Come. Let's get you in the bath before it gets cold."

He holds a hand out for me to rest my weight on, whilst I manoeuvre myself into the bath, before stepping in behind me and sinking down into the foamy bubbles. Bliss! I lay back against his chest, feeling his heartbeat thudding against my back and my own gallops to mimic it. The heat from the bath, warming all my secret places and tired, never-used muscles, is cocooning and I close my eyes, inhaling the scent of the bath creams, magnolia and vanilla and musk - all wonderfully fragrant and soothing.

How lovely to have a bath big enough for two. I bet Sebastian's is just as abundant at home.

"Feel good?" His whisper at my ear sends shivers across my flushed skin.

"Ahh yes. It's heaven."

"How are you feeling after taking the morning after pill? We haven't spoken properly since I tore up the M25 and nearly put your window through."

I watch his hands move in front of me, collecting the soap before lathering his hands and gently brushing the tips of both nipples, as they protrude through the bubbles. I arch against him, instinctively and automatically am met with his erection at my bottom. Already? This man was insatiable.

I push my breasts upwards, desperate to feel more, have him touch every part of them and he subconsciously answers my demands. His hands work my tits, stroking up and down my arms, massaging my shoulders and neck and generally relaxing me, until I'm almost sleepy with desire and comfort. I only open my eyes as I feel his fingers delicately washing between my legs. Such an intimate invasion of privacy and he is my first. I part my bent knees for him to gain further access and roll my hips as he circles my folds.

I revel in the feel of his firm long legs, alongside my smooth petite ones. Everything about him was large. Hands, muscles, cock - mmmm. He turns me on to the point of insanity. I quite literally ache for his touch and after he's removed it; I'm craving it again.

I hear the squirt of a bottle and then I'm ordered to dip my head back into the water. As I do so I look up into his eyes, crinkled at the corners and glinting with mirth.

"I've never washed a woman's hair before." He says matter-of-factly.

"Another first for us. Condoms and hair-washing - we really know how to live dangerously."

I'm rewarded with a playful tap before groaning in pleasure, as his magic fingertips massage shampoo into my scalp and through my hair, creating a foaming lather. Tension leaves every part of me, sending shockwaves all over my body. I'm floating as he rinses and repeats, with conditioner and moan at the loss when he whispers in my ear.

"All done Baby. Let's get you out and dry. The Chinese will be here by now."

My tummy growls in happiness. I'd not eaten since this morning and that had been a light breakfast of toast and banana - oh apart from the strawberries and cream but you could hardly call that sustenance. Since the pill-popping episode, I'd not managed to get back to normal eating habits; actually, since Sebastian and I had started fooling around, really but the past couple of days more so and I'm suddenly ravenous.

I allow Seb to pat me down with fluffy white towels and fashion a turban for my hair. It was nice to be pampered and after all the sexy paraphernalia, lovely to be naked and back to basics. I grab my bag from the bedroom and comb through my wet hair, scrunching it as I go - its times like these I'm glad of naturally wavy hair. I'll be leaving it to dry au naturale - the tousled look would have to do in the morning. *I take it we must be staying over then?*

We head off to the lounge area of the suite, where a bevy of Chinese dishes await, all under silver domes, which I lift consecutively - all my favourites, I squeal in delight, much to Seb's pleasure.

"Thank you for organising all of this - so thoughtful."

"All part of my cunning plan Lady..."

My questioning look makes him smile. "... I need to keep you hydrated and well fed so I can enjoy your body for longer. There's method in my madness!"

I laugh with him before snuggling down on the sofa in front of the coffee table to indulge. Seb and I had a history of having a *'grab-out'* together and our usual choice was Chinese or pizza; it stemmed from our Uni days and we'd trawled pretty much every take away joint in our quest to savour the best on offer - we'd finally found it in our third year - Peking Palace; nothing beat it, until now.

"Ahh - this is amazing." I moan happily, as I feast on chicken in black bean sauce with stir-fried noodles and prawn toast.

"Mmmm - good isn't it."

"I hate to say it, but I think it's as good as Pek Pal." My face is shocked; it was a bold statement.

"Really? Well it should be." His wide smile, reaches his eyes as he feeds me a part of his won ton."

My mouth full, I realise what he's suggesting and chewing, make lots of facial expression as it dawns on me entirely. "You didn't? Did you order it in specially? How did you get it here? We're nowhere near them."

He taps the side of his nose cheekily and winks. "What my Lady

Lu wants, she gets. Plus it helps to have money and a Limo driver named Ralph."

I make a mental note to thank him at some point - my stomach was in love.

I'm really touched - he'd gone to so much trouble but also really thought about tonight. I reach out and stroke the side of his face and he places his own hand over mine, holding it there, before allowing it to drop. For a while we just munch in silence, enjoying the food, atmosphere, champagne and good company. My stomach has unfortunately shrunk over the past few days and I sit back replete after only a small amount.

Seb takes my plate from me and places it on the table. "Don't worry - we can have more later. Time to get back to business Lady Lu. You and I have a date in that Princess and the pea monstrosity in there."

I'm not given the chance to answer as he lifts me over his shoulder, fireman style and strides into the bedroom. I'm given the delectable view of his arse, clenching, cheek by cheek as he walks and itch to smack him but I'm not allowed the chance; as we reach the bed, he lifts me by the waist, sliding me down his naked body, untying my towel, at my breasts and dropping it to puddle at our feet. His hand finds my nape, pulling me towards his mouth, the other palm cradling my face, drawing me into him and I melt into his warmth, reaching my arms up around his shoulders, sighing at the pleasurable sensation when my nipples graze his chest hair. Beads of water still linger lovingly on his body, and I reach out and lick one, sighing with pleasure at his clean masculine scent.

I feel emboldened by his approval of my body and lick his chest, in upwards strokes, tickling along his collarbone. His hands grab my bottom, squeezing it softly, as our mouths meet once again, more leisurely this time. The kiss is soul-wrenchingly good; wet and deep and full of meaning. This means so much more than sex. I know it does. *Does he feel this?*

His arms reach up to feed through my hair, caressing my temples, scalp, and back down my spine. I can feel the molten lava bubbling between my thighs again.

"Seb - I want you in me."

"I know baby."

Feeling brave I part my lips and moan. "I want you to fuck me."

"I think that could be arranged Lady. In fact I insist upon it."

271

I'm encouraged to climb onto the bed and try to do it in an elegant fashion, before lying back onto the thick cotton bed sheets. His sexy body looms above me, arms stretched taut on either side of my waist.

"Spread your legs wide."

My eyes flicker to his - his command is firm and I bit my lip in hesitation. My clit throbs, core tightening deep within and I just go with it; slowly opening my legs like scissors, under his watchful gaze. His growl of success is muffled when his lips drop to press hot wet kisses along my inner thigh, left then right, teasingly ignoring the pulsing erect nub at their apex.

"You're so fucking beautiful Lu."

I reach out to touch him, running my fingers across his head, cradling in my hands, as his lascivious mouth rains little drops of heaven across my hipbones and stomach and licks a trail down my bikini line. "So smooth."

His mouth searches for mine and I kiss him with every ounce of passion in me, savouring the now recognisable electric current, which never fails to flare between us. The kiss is deep and breath taking and within minutes, we're both panting with lust.

"I can't get enough of your tits. They're fucking incredible."

I smile in the dark. I've been told this before but I'm pleased he thinks so. I only want Sebastian's approval and his touch. His mouth answers my plea, and I wonder if I asked him out loud, as his tongue flicks over a nipple, then the other and then I arch as he feasts upon me, sucking and rimming and blowing until my pussy aches to be finished off. I apply a little pressure to his head and push him down past my breasts and stomach until his mouth meets another set of warm wet and accepting lips. His tongue darts and flicks firmly and directly across my clit, the pleasure is almost painful in its intensity. I moan and thrust my head back, closing my eyes in bliss, then look up towards the ceiling to enjoy the ride to heaven!

My hands clutch at the bed sheets, gripping so tightly as I push myself into his face. "You taste amazing baby."

Ripples begin to form, as my sex clenches in reaction to his words. I swear he must be able to see my clit jumping for attention, beating ten to the dozen. "I'm nearly there, don't stop. Please don't stop."

His fingertips quicken their swirling pattern, swooping in to collect more juice to slide across my nub, increasing the pressure each time. I ache to have him inside me.

"Tell me when you're going to come Baby." His finger plunges inside me, and I gasp at the delicious invasion and again when his mouth laves my clit, working in tandem with his fingers, plunging and licking. "God I can feel you tightening for me."

"I'm going to come, Baby."

"That's it - let go."

My scream echoes throughout the room, as I judder beneath his expert touch, jerking uncontrollably at the force of the orgasm ripping through me. I lie back, listening to my breathing returning to a more sedate pace, as I hear him rustle and don a condom. He has something else in his hand, shaped like a squished letter 'U', with a thicker and thinner end. It looks a bit like a purple vibrator. *Sex toys now?*

Leaning forward with his forearms taking his weight, he settles between my quivering legs. I feel his hand reach between us and gasp as he slips the wider arm of the smooth silicone inside me.

"Relax. It's a toy that's going to hit your g-spot just right; it will heighten the intensity - trust me."

"But I want *you*."

"Don't worry baby I'll be inside you at the same time - enjoying the buzz." His hand clasps the controls in his palm. Always the one in control but right now I don't care.

Not sure about how he'll fit in as well as the wider end of the vibrator I'd just seen, but I decide to go with it. His cock nudges into my opening, lying alongside the machine.

"Christ you're tight."

I wriggle to accommodate him further and then I feel it, the low buzz of the vibrations, from the narrow end, delicately zapping at my clit. Wow! I didn't think I was ready for more pleasure across my most sensitive part but I begin to rock to meet the intensity, pushing the wider end, inside me, onto my g-spot. Seb was right. This was amazing.

He begins to rotate his hips, delving deeper with each movement and rocks us upwards, creating further friction across my clit. His mouth finds mine, as I wrap my arms around him, holding him close to me. I hear a click and the mode swaps to flutters, lightly bouncing off my swollen nub - hmmm, *nice* but not persistent enough, Finally he answers my silent plea for more, with a second click and a deeper intense version of the first vibration. *That's it.* The shockwaves must be filtering over his cock at the same time as the muscles in his back grow taut and I feel his balls banging rhythmically against me. One last thrust into me, and he grows even harder.

"I'm going to come Lu - hard."

At his words, I shatter around him - my climax, ricocheting deep within me and across my nub simultaneously. I'd never experienced anything like it.

Sebastian lowers his head to my chest and lies there, listening to my heartbeat and I kiss his head with such fierce emotion, I know I need to breathe deeply before those feelings overflow.

"You were so worth the wait Darling." He kisses me languidly and I revel under his husky tone. I created that sex voice.

"Hold me."

"Gladly Baby - I'm not letting go."

<hr/>

We must have fallen asleep. When I open my eyes, it's still dark in the room but twisting as much I can, the clock tells me its 6am. Sebastian is curled around my body, fast asleep, his arm across my waist. I need a wee, desperately.

I prise his forearm away from me, careful not to wake him and slip out of the luxurious black bed, grabbing a white fluffy robe from the hook on the back of the bathroom door. After the longest pee ever, I sigh in relief at the disappearance of bladder strain and go to the sink. The mirrors there, reflect a woman I hardly recognise. A woman who's been well and truly catered to. My eyes are huge and luminous in their emerald tone, and look back at me with their newfound secrets. My cheeks are flushed and lips swollen from his kisses.

What a night. Magical. Life-changing.

I flick the shower to hot and discarding my robe, slip underneath the water. Ahh bliss! I wash quickly - careful to avoid wetting my hair, as there wouldn't be time to dry it later- and after a few minutes, step out to swaddle myself in the fluffy towels we'd enjoyed last night.

Two minutes later and I'm in my robe once again and cleansing my face at the sink. There were all kinds of products lined up to assist me. Cleansers, toners, moisturisers, hair products, perfumes, and make-ups - it was like a Harvey Nichols' beauty department and I take full advantage of them all. I'm about to clean my teeth, after finally locating the toothpaste, when I am rewarded with a very sexy sleepy Sebastian, wandering in, butt naked in all his morning glory.

"Morning Gorgeous."

He disappears around the corner, to have his own waking wee and I run the tap to drown out any sounds. I'm not ready to hear him peeing yet, although I have to say I do like the intimacy of us getting ready for our day together.

Returning to shower he dives in, spends a couple of minutes thoroughly blitzing his body. I tease myself with hooded glances in his direction, licking my lips at his physique. He really is magnificent and even sexier when dusted with that sexy morning twinkle.

Seb wanders out, wrapping a towel around his lean hips, his amazing eight pack on show and my mouth-waters - literally. I ogle him in the ornate mirror above the dual black sinks, as we begin to clean our teeth - the intimate everyday moment, another new thing to share between us. We are both intent on freshening up but both reluctant to leave our sex-filled cocoon.

"Right, now that we're all clean and fresh again - give me a kiss Lady."

I place the toothbrush down, cheekily lick a stray bit of mint from my lips and his are on mine, his tongue squeaking along my teeth.

"You're my best friend and now we've seen each other naked. I'm honestly not sure which side of you I prefer - the friend, or the lover? I'm lucky to have sampled both, but I think it'll work best for *us* if we find a way to amalgamate the two - you're kind of perfect you know that? And so worth waiting a decade for."

Oh God - my stomach is doing somersaults at his words; my skin covered in goosebumps. *Please don't say things like this. Change the subject.*

"I'm starving!

His chocolate eyes, watch mine, his brow furrowing in question but he decides against pushing me further. "Me too. It should be here any minute. I've already ordered. Hope that's alright?"

I nod, happy that he's distanced himself a little. The protective blanket needs to be wrapped around me here - I'm in way too deep.

The knock at the bedroom door is the saviour I need and slipping his own robe on he heads out to answer it. I continue with my make-up, adding foundation, mascara, blush and a light eyeshadow from the gorgeous products available to me; lippy would come later.

"Lu, foods up!"

We eat in congenial silence, with lots of munching and yummy noises and the daily news playing in the background. I wish we could stay another night. I didn't need to get back for Finn but I did need to work today. *No rest for the wicked!*

I tuck into my Scrambled eggs and smoked salmon with nutty brown toast and sigh in ecstasy when it melts in my mouth. This is seriously good. It's not long before I've eaten the lot and I settle back in the comfy chair and watch my lover in contemplative silence. Sebastian finished ages ago, after inhaling his breakfast in one mouthful and is glancing at the morning paper, sipping his coffee and I reach out to touch his hand and retract mine instantly - still surprised at the electric current I feel sizzling between us when we touch. He feels it too. Our eyes lock and I fill the silence.

"Thank you Seb for last night - it was…"

"Meant to be," he finishes for me and I look up in question. His eyes have taken on an intense look…

He places a hand out for me to clasp, tentatively I do as I'm asked, then squeal as he makes a grab for me tumbling me to the mattress, behind us and we kiss, all sign of friendliness and laughter quickly dissipating.

"Seriously Lu. This is just the start."

"I know but now I must get dressed Mr. Silver."

"I'd rather you didn't."

"I have too! Plus, I have to be at work in a couple of hours and I need to get a taxi home to get changed…"

"Ralph will take you home."

"In the limo?"

"Yes."

"Oh!"

"That stopped you talking – finally." A smile plays across his sexy lips. "Now where were we Lady - let me start your day off with a bang."

Chapter 29

Lucia

Last night's illicit encounter is like a dream to me. *Did it really happen? Had I really let myself go like that? Been so uninhibited?*

Oh to be able to go back in time and relive each delicious morsel over and over again. My lips curve in a knowing smile - it had been out of this world and utterly filthy. Sebastian had shown me a different world of pleasure and awakened a part of me I hadn't known existed.

After a hot shower and a quick change of clothes I head into the office. I had a meeting with the upholsterer at 11am and then at some point Colin and I would need to head over to Silver Construction. I'd taken him with me on the last few occasions, when dropping in deliveries for the re-fit. Not the best use of his time I'll admit but I wasn't prepared to risk bumping into Chris again - alone. Today I am alive and sexually charged and not in the right frame of mind for him - I was giving off way to many pheromones that would attract his tentacles from miles away.

It's several hours later, and I'm rather less chilled out than I had been earlier that morning, when Colin and I roll into the Silver Construction headquarters for the third time that week. Jumping out, Col goes to collect the samples and decorative to-die-for glittery pewter tiles for the border of the bathroom, from the boot of my car. No Sooner, are we in the reception area to SC, when I'm met with a frosty stare from an extremely and now unfortunately familiar, well-put together female - her pouty, over glossed lips showing her utter disdain for me. I take a minute to peruse her as discreetly as possible, whilst Colin informs her of our deliveries.

She was still very attractive. *Shit.*

Today her hair shines in an artistic bun and her wasp-like waist is cleverly accentuated with a wide elastic belt, over her bright pink dress. She doesn't shake my hand but reluctantly asks us to sit, showcasing the plush seating area, to our right with a graceful arm. Animosity coils in the pit of my stomach like barbed wire but I rise above it and return my focus to the reception area she is guiding us towards. It has a cool vibe, plenty of silver, gunmetal, black and white. The result is professional but masculine. It suited the Construction

Industry, perfectly and I could see Sebastian's design stamp in every direction; it represented him to a tee. I take a seat.

"Toni."

"Lu..chee..ahh," she whines, her voice slicing right through me.

"This is Colin Duttine – he is part of my design team and working with me on The Ashton project."

"Hmmmm. What seems to be the problem?"

God, this lady is annoying and sooo condescending. Isn't she supposed to welcome clients and customers with a warm reception – First rule of PA duty?

"We've brought a portion of the required tiles and the fireplace brochure, that Chris required?" I supply smiling through my gritted teeth. "I've narrowed it down to three options, but Chris is going to analyse them and advise which one will suit the existing chimney and flue. He knows my preferred option."

"Good, good – yes I do believe that he mentioned that you had not provided him with the information required yet." She looks down her rather pointy nose at me. "We do need these tiles now, as the bathroom is taking shape very nicely but will *not* be finished if we are *not* supplied the fixtures and fittings *on time.*" She clasps her binder closely to her chest, with her mouth pursed and her eyes shrewd in their concentration on belittling me.

Bitch! This woman was a total be... atch! Definitely someone you wouldn't want to get on the wrong side of; someone who spoke over you to vent her power, and did not allow you the same privilege. She treated others like they were the hired help - *well missy you're in for a*

shock.

"Well – that's it for now. If you could let Chris have them today, and ask that he gives me a bell if there are any probs? I do need to know with regard to the fireplace by the end of today, however - you know - to ensure *we meet deliveries on time,*" I add mirroring her own patronizing tone.

Colin chooses that inopportune moment to excuse himself to *spend a penny* – I could kill him for leaving me with her. The atmosphere is strangled – or maybe I just wanted to strangle her there and then!

"Sebastian has been keeping me involved at every level Lucia and all is good at *our* end. *If* The Ashton is not ready on time, it will *not* be down to Silver Construction," she smiles matter-of-factly. Urrgghhhh!

I nod placating her. It really isn't worth adding fuel to her fire - she'd probably relish the burn.

"I'm sure things will be just fine Toni."

"Are you feeling better now Lucia? You look a little peaky."

I pause and watch her shrewd navy blue eyes crinkle in pleasure. *How did she know I'd been ill?*

"Yes, I'm fine thank you." My tone is wary.

"Sebastian mentioned your little dash to the backstreet pharmacy."

My nostrils flare in anger. This woman was such a bitch! *Why would he tell her that information?*

But then it hits me. He wouldn't. Sebastian was the ultimate professional. He'd never gossip about personal things like this with his PA. The only reason she would be aware of my morning-after-pill debacle was if she'd seen it for herself. *She* had been the blonde in the black fur coat behind me that day; the one who'd left in a hurry and the one who'd taken great pleasure in informing Sebastian. Total bitch! The term backstreet made it sound dirty and a mistake!

"No, he didn't but thank you for your concern."

I move to stand and place my hand out to shake her own but she chooses to ignore it, looking me up and down with feigned boredom, instead focusing her attention on Colin's return.

"Sebastian and I go way back you know?" Her gold hoop earrings swing as she shakes her head, glossy bun wobbling slightly.

Don't rise to it girl. Like you have already realized, it is not worth it!

"Oh?" Colin places a loose arm at my back and dives right in - both he and I already know that Seb's only known her a few months.

"Yes. We met a few years back, when he was working on a new-build for my brother and we've been together since," she supplies smugly.

All of six months; God this woman was obsessed.

Colin looks sheepishly in my direction. "At work you mean?"

Trust Col to jump right in there.

She screws her face up as if she has a bad smell under her nose. "Well yes, but Sebastian and I are a good fit and are *so* much more than just colleagues."

Colin rolls his eyes, indiscreetly at me and pats Toni's arm. "I think you'll have to get in line Love – think Sebastian may have realised that *the one* is staring him right in *the face.*"

He cricks his neck and hitchhikes his thumb in my direction. I could kill him for his indiscretion but at the same time appreciate his show of support. We are not even a couple. Fuck buddies, yes, but not an item and I didn't want to appear too desperate in front of this cow!

She puckers up her face, so full of air I fear she'll pop and blow across the room. "Well *my* Sebastian does like to play, and he just *loves* the chase but he always goes back to his roots," her voice drips with spite.

"Speaking about roots," Colin mutters under his breath, discreetly air patting a fake hairdo and I giggle rudely. *God, get me out of here – it's unheard of for me to be so bitchy!*

"Nice to see you again Toni – I'm sure we'll be in touch soon."

That's as nice as I can muster. It's not often I dislike a woman so abundantly but this one is a frigging nightmare. This is my friend's business, not hers!

"Hmmm. Well let's hope that this little job is done and dusted soon and we can get back to working on the high-fee paying projects - I keep telling Sebastian that he's outgrown your little business!"

I can see what she just tried to do and I'm annoyed at my own instinctive pathetic reaction to it. I hate the thought of the two of them discussing me, hate that he has anything to do with this silly blonde. My teeth are so tightly ground, I wince as my jaw crunches. I want to scream at her that this *little job* was the beginning of 40+ further *little jobs* on a similar level, at The Ashton and that meant great business and great profit, but I don't give her the satisfaction. She is not important enough to know company information and just not worth it. *Rise above - it'll annoy her much more than if you'd retaliated and you know it - kill her with kindness.*

"I'll be sure to tell Sebastian you've been, when I see him at home tonight – you should pop round - he's been away all week and we've lots to catch up on but I'm sure he'd love to see you - maybe surprise him!" She plays her trump card well and smiling, disappears back towards the office at the rear, her petite figure wiggling, with an exaggeration that would make Marilyn Monroe proud.

"That girl is a bloody psy...chohhh!" Colin twirls his finger next to his head in a spiral movement, spelling the last word out in slow, dragged-out syllables. I have to agree he's not far off the mark on this occasion. Serious single-white-female tendencies here; Sebastian will need to watch out with this one.

"She's obviously got it into her head that she is going to be THE Mrs. Silver and they will run their construction empire in unison." I laugh at his dramatic analogy.

"Poor girl – I think she's just another of Sebastian's conquests and believe me I can see why she is so hooked. That man makes all men look like students in the bedroom," I begrudgingly allow her.

"What's all that about *talking to him back at home tonight*? Are they living together?"

"Not that I'm aware of, but who am I to know. Seb and I don't keep tabs on one another. I am starting to wonder if he and Toni ever had *a thing* or if it's all in her extremely deluded head?" My stomach coils again with waves of nausea, a habitual process, recently developed.

"Well he's back home tonight apparently, so get every scrap of that lovely body of yours ready and be sure to have make-up and mints at hand."

"I suppose I could go around as Finn isn't back from Wales until tomorrow." *And I really want to see him.*

I smile at his exceedingly expert advice. Bless him he really was very sweet and I didn't have the heart to tell him I already knew he was home - had received my welcome home fuck last night in fact, and again this morning in Room 22. I can feel myself blush at the memory and it crosses my mind that that could be the reason for the chosen name of Scarlet House - how very appropriate.

With that thought, we head out to the car park and I half-listen to Colin waffle about how he and James are trying out sex toys tonight for the first time together and shake my head in mock-surprise. With Colin, there were no boundaries – it was full throttle, full disclosure

281

or nothing at all; there was no middle ground with him. I just hoped that he wasn't running before he could walk, where James was concerned. The little bunny was certainly more rampant than usual.

I use the drive home to tame the mounting nervous bubbles threatening to pop in my stomach – it's been less than 8hours since I last saw Sebastian. I cannot begin to describe the sheer craving I have to catch the slightest glimpse of him. To think that only two weeks ago, I hadn't seen him for months and I'd missed him but not in this way. Now it was a deep-rooted *need* that ripped through me 24hours a day. Now, I was in way over my head. *I am bordering on desperate I think, disgusted with myself. I really need to get a grip.*

He fills my every waking moment - so much for treating this like a mutually beneficial fuck buddy arrangement. I had to start being honest with myself. After only a brief affair, I wanted more - more than friends? We weren't even that right now - something we'd always managed. Tonight, I'd resolve that. Tonight, we'd finally talk about a possible future. If he couldn't offer me any, I'd walk away now, before he smashed my heart into Silver pieces. *Like it would be that easy.*

❦

My phone vibrates noisily on my laptop, and glancing across at its position on the passenger seat, I cringe. Niall. The last person I want to speak to - but it could be about Finn. I hit accept and his voice streams through the hands-free.

"Lucia. Are you free tonight for a drink?"

Of all the things, I never thought it would be that.

"Not tonight I'm afraid. Why what's wrong - do you want to discuss Finn?" *Where the F was Karen?*

"No everything's fine. I know he's away at the moment with your parents so I figured you'd be lonely - thought we might go have a carvery at The Ring O Bells, for old times sake."

WTF? Oh fuck it - I'm fed up of this guy. We have history and Finn but this isn't about Finn and I'm tired of him making me feel beholden to him. Besides I do have a life!

"Sorry Niall I'm at Sebastian's tonight."

The Silence lasts so long, I figure he's hung up and glance back at the screen - nope still there.

"So you and him…?"

"What Niall?"

"… are you… fucking now?"

"Don't be so crude. We are friends - as *you* well know. I am dating though - not that it's any of your business. Look - I'm going to hang up now Niall. Let's keep it civil for Finn's sake but not get personal."

"Well I'm sure Karen will join me. She's one who likes to please me."

I bite my tongue; can practically see his cheesy wink down the phone. Oh yeah, she's bloody perfect.

"Yes - whilst we are on the subject of Karen - would you ask her not to talk about me to my son. Calling me a stupid bitch, around him, isn't something I want him to hear happening and if it continues, he will not be staying over with you, when Karen is around."

I'm proud of the finality and calmness of my voice.

"Sorry Lu - I didn't know." I can hear the sarcastic tone lacing through his voice and breathe deeply through my nose to refrain from losing it. "…I'll have a word with her. She shouldn't be saying things like that I agree, after all, one thing you've never been is stupid, after all you chose me. The other word…well?"

Dick!

I end the call before I get any more wound up. This was my huge concern about falling any deeper under the spell of Sebastian Silver. If things didn't work out I'd lose everything; his friendship, his sexual prowess, our connection and we'd just end up like Niall and I - two people who weren't meant to be.

Chapter 30

Lucia

Quickly checking my appearance in the rearview mirror I remove a smudge of stray red lipstick, flick my tongue over my teeth and take a deep calming breath. Both knees are literally knocking together due to such frayed nerves. Shaking myself to get a grip I smooth down the chosen fitted Cream peplum dress and head towards the door of *Silver Birches*, deluxe home to the most delicious and devilish man – Sebastian Silver himself.

After hearing that Seb was to be in tonight, courtesy of the queen bitch herself, I knew that it was now or never - a chance to hash out the whole situation, move forward as more, or end things as friends; both put the fear of God into me.

Maybe it was the hormonal cocktail I'd downed at the beginning of the week but I've been a wreck - all over the place really and I needed to know if we are potentially going to continue as friends (and if so, fix our friendship) or become... *well*... more! The lovely way he'd supported me on Monday night at first, was a distant reminder after the atmosphere had quickly burned with stubborn arrogance. Then he'd given me the night of my life, as promised, at Scarlet House - my mind is filled with images of sexy Sebastian naked, strawberries, champagne and that sizzling hot mirror sex. I still can't control my breathing at just the thought. We'd become distant to achieve great sexual peaks but now I'm not sure where we sit - we're totally unbalanced; great together - awful apart.

The problem is, that if this had happened with any other man, we'd be taking it slow; I'd be going with the flow - certainly not being

284

so overwhelmed by thoughts of the man in question at every bloody waking moment. I feel totally and utterly consumed by Sebastian.

I haven't yet decided if this is down to our history, our friendship and that is why my feelings have escalated so fast or if it's just because the chemistry is so powerful with this one individual man. The latter scares me the most.

Could he be The One? I think bloody so and it frightens the hell out of me!

At the front door, I pause for a moment and taking the plunge ring the doorbell. My heart is beating so fast as butterflies dance around my tummy. The light above the porch comes on, and I can hear someone scrabbling around inside when a voice hollers.

"Just a minute!" *Wait… didn't that voice sound female and rather familiar? Toni? She must be here, after all.*

My fears are confirmed as the door is yanked open and the shell shock on my face, must have been a picture, as I am now face to face with the navy blue doe eyes of Toni, the bitchy PA – but the biggest issue by far is that she is wrapped in nothing but a large fluffy graphite coloured towel.

Appearing blasé, she drinks in my discomfort and smiling slyly blurts. "Yes?"

"Oh hello, Toni. Is Sebastian in?" I try to look past her scantily clad body, as she leans her wet head, against the frame, holding the door ajar - just enough to let the light from the hallway protrude.

Noticing my attempts to see inside, she opens the door further and sweeping her arm out in a gracious welcome, she steps aside.

"Do come in Lucia."

God this woman was hardwork. She was acting like it was her bloody home and why had she just showered?

I already know the answer to my question, but I'm desperately trying to find another reasonable reason for this scenario - something, anything!

Walking into the foyer I follow her semi-covered form, until we reach the luxurious hall; I can hear *Adele's Set fire to the rain*, playing on the Bose surround system and my fears deepen. Very romantic!

"You wish to see Sebastian? I saw you earlier today I could have passed on any message on your behalf?" Her arms are crossed over her towel-clad body.

Hang on didn't she gaily tell me to pop in?

Through gritted teeth, I maintain my resolve to kill her with kindness but ignore her nosey questions.

"Is he in?" I say a little more forcefully this time, making it more than apparent that she is not the reason that I'm here.

Why hadn't I just text him? Saved myself this hassle. I should never have listened to her.

She watches me, carefully dragging out the uncomfortable atmosphere, over several seconds and grinning with her invisible raised knife, she delivers the first blow.

"He's in the shower – I left him, to get the door. We thought you were the delivery guy with *our* pizza."

I can tell from her evil glare, she is proud of her archery skills. Her words have pierced my heart and splintered it into a million pieces.

"Sebastian does get hungry after sex."

Seriously? What a cow – like the first blow wasn't enough!

I clench my jaw, lift my head and force a weak smile and through gritted teeth manage the words.

"Sorry to have disturbed you. Would you tell Sebastian that I'll speak to him later." I can hear my voice tremble slightly.

"I've told him no more work today Lucia, just pleasure. We've got a lot of catching up to do, as he's been away a few days." She raises her brows. "If you know what I mean. But I'll pass the message on."

I take in her stance, a look of deep satisfaction embedded upon her face.

My feet are rooted to the spot, as though stuck in concrete and I look around briefly and take in the Jo Malone candles burning on all surfaces, the two glasses of red wine on the table and the scattered clothing on the floor. Bringing my eyes, which threaten to spill over at any second with hot tears that would be likened to Niagara falls, back to smug bitch Toni with an *'i'*, I watch as she attempts to re-fasten her towel, letting it purposely slip and in the process almost completely drop to the floor. I am allowed an entirely deliberate and carefully planned exposure of her extremely fake breasts and completely shaven haven. I'm annoyed that I even give her the reward of briskly assessing her naked body but I begrudgingly admit to myself that she is *very* toned.

Her look is one of pure feline confidence in her own physique and her eyes literally glitter with the burn of success.

"Whoopsies!" she pretends to appear bashful. "Sebastian likes me stripped bare -everywhere!"

Copious amounts of false eyelash fluttering, add drama to her outlandish statement and pouting, she provides me with a bored sigh.

"Well, if that's all Lucia?"

I can't even look at her, let alone respond. It's taking all my resolve not to grab her by the hair and throw her naked arse out on the doorstep. However, I breathe in through my nose, and exhale, mentally poised. Then woodenly manage to move my leaden feet, making my way back towards the doorway and on a heavy heart open the door – I honestly don't know what to say *or* think. I just need to get out of there, fast before I see Sebastian.

She pushes the final nail in the coffin gleefully. "Thanks Lucia – have a good night. *I* most certainly will."

The door slams behind me, it's finality echoing and bouncing against my bruised and battered emotions. I think I stand on the porch for a few minutes in shock, mouth open, before I force my legs to put one step in front of the other and cocoon myself inside my car.

Oh. My. Word. Colin and I were completely off the mark with this one. Toni and Sebastian know each other exceedingly well, I conclude miserably. How could I have been so stupid? How many fuck buddies did this guy have?

<hr />

I take a second to compose myself and jumping, do a quick about turn in the direction of the large conifer tree at the bottom of the drive. I could have sworn that I saw something there; someone maybe, watching – there was definitely a noise? But upon thoroughly perusing the surrounding area, in the dusk lighting there is no one – nothing. I shiver with that *someone's just walked over your grave,* sensation that always gives me the creeps and turn the key. I've had this feeling often of late. I'm seriously acting ridiculously paranoid – for all I know, it was Toni getting her kicks from the window, at my misery!

The minute the engine starts and music filters through the speakers I break. *Clubbed to death by Rob D*, blasts through me, every beat hitting me over and over again, only adding to my crushing anxiety. I turn the volume up full whack and let the emotion of the song, wash over me and drive away from Hugh Hefner's mansion in a rage of hurt, tears, and utter devastation.

The one thing that was at the centre of *all* my thoughts, at that exact moment was *the shower.* The fact that he'd been getting down and not so dirty, with his playboy bunny, after our own monumental soapy sexual encounter, less than a week before. That was our *thing.*

How could he?

I drive so fast I'm in danger of losing control and take a moment to wipe away the uncontrollable flurry of wet tears from my face, with my forearm. I need to clear the fog away and focus on the road.

"I can't fucking believe it!" I scream into an empty car, hitting the steering wheel with the heel of my palm and wince as pain instantly reverberates throughout my arm.

Oh why not there too - everywhere else hurts right this minute!

Why would he do this to me? I know we weren't a couple but surely I deserve better than this?

At the same time, my inner voice reminds me that this is what Sebastian *is* - what he does, and has always done - he's a player.

I knew this when I propositioned him. I knew this when I had sex with him the first time and I know this now, whilst we dance around this sexual affair. My own ego allowed me to expect that I'd be special enough to him, to be unique enough to be treated differently than his plethora of sexual partners. I hang my head in shame at my own stupidity.

You want more Lu - that's the problem - he's only given what you agreed. Fuck, he's given a hundred percent more than that - yet still you want more - you want his heart, his soul; his everything. You want him to love you.

Well not anymore! Not after he'd been with that skank Toni; they were welcome to one another.

If only it were that simple.

Chapter 31

Lucia

"I'm telling you Suzie this bitch was so in love with herself she didn't have room left in her to put another person before her own needs – I bet she's shit in bed!" I add cattily and instantly regret it, filling up with hot expectant droplets… again.

Suzie shakes her head in sympathy. "Oh my lovely, I'm so sorry. I can't believe that Sebastian would do this to you. It's so out of character for him?"

"Do what?" Gino shouts from the corner of the lounge, whilst keeping one eye firmly fixed on his play station thrashing.

"Bloody Seb has gone and cheated on Lucia – caught red-handed the bugger!" I can see Suzie is fuming for me, her protective sisterhood loyalty kicking in big-time.

It's only when he speaks I realise that Gino has come to join us on their cream L-shaped sofa. Hmmm, he must care, giving up the games console for me. I'm touched!

He rakes a hand through his jet-black slightly wavy hair. "Seb and you? When did that happen?"

I smile up at him, with big liquid green eyes. "Its OK G. I know Suze told you. Right Suze?"

Looking in her direction she shrugs, innocently in a *'Sorry I had to'* way and I shake my head. "It's fine, *really* - you're man and wife."

"Thank F for that - I'm no actor." The relief on Gino's face is heartwarming.

"Anyway - no way Seb cheated - he's a player but even he's not that stupid to get caught!"

Suzie belts her husband across the arm in anger. "G! What the fuck? Did you know anything about this?"

Bless, he looks a little torn. I'm his sister-in-law and Seb is his best friend - tough call. Lifting his hands and shoulders towards the sky, in an, *'I know nothing'* pose, he frowns apologetically.

"I honestly don't know Lu – I know he is really into you, even though he won't admit it to the lads – but men never do. We're dicks really. He's never mentioned putting it to the PA though. He always said never to mix business with pleasure."

I can see he is mentally working this one out. But it immediately reminds me that that is precisely what he has done with me, so he obviously doesn't abide by his own rules, and therefore may bend the rules for other soapy enhanced females.

Gino continues. "Look, if it makes you feel any better, he never told us boys about the proposition. Nathan and I knew something was going on between you - I mean, who didn't? Shit - sparks fly around you two these days, but if you want my opinion, you may have started this, but Seb has wanted to finish it for a *long* time - it was the perfect chance for him. Si?"

"Thanks G I don't know what to think. It's all pretty screwed up. When we are together, it's..." I stop and blush, composing myself before continuing, "... animalistic but when we're apart we just... *don't work*! What was I was thinking? How could we ever dabble with our friendship like this?" I feel a sharp pain stab through my chest, a reminder of his recent escapades.

"If you could have seen her – she dropped her towel in front of me – showed me everything God and the cosmetic surgeon gave her!" My face crumples.

"Slut!" Suzie shouts bluntly and at the exact same time Gino says, "Cool!" Thus rewarding him with another whack from his wife.

Justly reprimanded he continues unconvincingly. "Sorry Lu – definitely a very slutty thing to do. Sounds like she has made her stake for him though. She's playing the game like a dude."

I nod, agreeing wholly. Toni had most certainly gone at this full-throttle. She'd thought things out and planned to the nth degree.

"She's completely waxed down below," I add petulantly. "Nothing there. Nada. Zip."

Gino's ears prick up again; he's such a perv. "Really? I prefer a bit of a runway strip myself - to you know - land the jumbo!" he winks cheekily at Suzie, who just gives him a withering glare and shakes her head. I can tell he's trying to lighten the mood.

"Not so keen on a jungle bush though, just somewhere in between – Suze gets it just right - don't ya baby?"

"Did you see Sebastian then?" Suzie ignores her sexually frustrated husband and sips her tea, gently encouraging me to continue and bring the conversation back to me.

"No, I never saw him - he was in the shower apparently?"

"Whoa! Whoa, hang on a minute – you didn't see him?" Gino suggests keenly, folding his arms like he has just solved the crime of the century. "Well there you go – maybe it wasn't him? Or maybe she was just bullshitting?"

"Hold on there Miss Marple, just because he's your mate doesn't mean he isn't capable of doing this!" Suzie spits out to Gino before chewing on her lip. "Although you do raise a valid point. It doesn't account for her being in Sebastian's house at night though, naked - I might add?"

I rub my now raw eyes, as they sting with the humiliation of it all.

"Lets not beat about the bush - no pun intended..." his eyes glint with mischief, trying to lighten the mood but his words fall on deaf ears and result in a third smack from his obviously rather hormonally aggressive wife. "Easy Babe... I was going to say, before you rudely interrupted me, 'lets not beat about the bush... unless you saw it with your own eyes, you can't be 100% certain it happened."

I understand his reasoning but he hadn't been there. Seen the floozy in question and the house all lit up in seductive ambience.

"Thanks guys for your support, I guess I need to just put all this down to a lucky escape but it doesn't hurt any less. He showed me a good time, we had some fun and but I guess he missed sipping from several cups. We were only ever meant to have some fun - that's what he provided. I just fancied more..."

Those words hit me hard. He was going to sleep with other women again - already was!

"I know we've been mates for years but I think I was falling in love with him, which doesn't follow the FBR rule no.5."

The words are out before I can stop myself and at them I feel myself collapse from within, even further. *It's true, I am more than halfway in love with him, probably always have been. Why today of all days, has my brain finally caught up with my heart?*

"Oh Sis - come here!"

She uncrosses her baby blue velour designer tracksuit covered legs and draws me to her in a loving cuddle shooing Gino away at the same time. Taking his cue he leaves us to it. I snuggle against her, comforted by the scent of Topaz Lenor fabric conditioner.

"I think you and I need to focus on having some much needed fun this bank holiday weekend, don't you?" I nod mutely, drained and overcome by numbness. She was going to make a great mum, I consider, my mind drifting, as I sink into her cocoon-like grip.

She ignores my unwillingness to talk and chatters away despite it. "I know that Saturday night it's *the party* and it's at Mr. Sex-addict's house, but you *are* going to go, whether you like it or not and at least show him what he is missing. Do *not* give that *C U Next Tuesday Toni* the upper hand!"

I cringe inwardly for both her vulgar language. I hate the 'C' word but right now, she can use it to her heart's content, where that cow is concerned - she deserved far worse. Crap - I'd forgotten about his house warming. He'd planned it ages ago – there is no way in hell I'm going and humiliating myself, no bloody way!

Let's just hope that this has put an end to it now - *better safe than sorry* was my motto, no matter how much I missed out, in life with it. Sebastian Silver had finally tupped the Yorkshire lass he'd been mates with for years; probably the only girl within a 100-mile radius he hadn't already slept with. Now he could tick it off his bucket list and scratch another notch on his already battered bedpost and move on - leaving me the hell alone!

Whilst I feel like I'm wearing my heart on my sleeve at work the next day, I must be better at acting than I realise, as no-one seems to notice my despair - not even Colin, and he picked up on every mood swing usually. I'm glad for the gruelling gym workout I'd pummelled out first thing this morning. My fitness routine had changed since all this commotion with Seb and it was time I got back in the swing of things. The incessant treadmill run and cross trainer workout had been brutal and both drained and pumped me - my music blasting from my earphones; Tinie Tempah's 'Heroes' on repeat, sweat dripping from my body. I'd pushed myself beyond my usual limits - desperate to punish my body for its weakness and drown my thoughts out with angry dance music. It wasn't often I could get into my gym so early, as I usually had Finn.

Speaking of my superstar - the one little ray of sunshine, keeping me going, was due to be dropped off this afternoon. I'd missed Finn so much and my mum had text me earlier to say that they were making good headway in the traffic, despite hitting roadwork's. Apparently they'd had a ball in Wales and I'm so pleased he'd not only had fun but been well behaved for them.

My phone interrupts my thoughts. It's him again. He seriously needs to get the message now. *Do one!* I decline the call and slip the ringer to silent. That must be the tenth call since last night. Soon he'd get the message. I don't want to talk to him!

I get my head down and choose to ignore the empty ache I have clawing at my insides, a constant reminder of Sebastian's unfaithfulness. The Ashton was beginning to take shape but also getting to that stage, where little mistakes could easily be made, if I wasn't on the ball and let's face it my head is all over the place!

Jackie interrupts my thoughts. "It's Seb, again Lu - I told him you're out. Shouldn't you just talk to him though? Save all the calls. He sounds pissed."

I shake my head, reluctant to discuss the situation; I'm not ready to do that yet.

She smiles knowingly. "No probs. I've told him that you are out for a meeting now, so that should give you some breathing space; although why you'd want it with that man. He sounds delish!"

He is delish too.

My phone buzzes with texts from Suzie and Abby, both questioning how I am and wanting updates. I don't have the strength to respond in detail so just post each of them a quick 'x' and go back to my designs.

Twenty minutes later, doing a little vibrating dance on the desk, a text comes through from *him*. My heart pounds, mouth dry – I can't look; can't believe I even want to see what he has to say for himself.

Incredible. Worth the wait. Ache for u.
Not sure why you've gone AWOL but I'm thinking of
u Lady Lu xxx

I can't take any more of this. I reel off a quick text to my mum to say I'll meet them back at theirs and gather up my paraphernalia. Laptop, bag, and swatches - right, I have everything. I say my goodbyes to Jackie and Colin and head out to meet my favourite man. One of the perks of being your own boss was making your own hours and today I am taking full advantage and leaving early.

Sebastian

Why wasn't she answering her phone?

I'd called her sixteen times since Thursday night. Now I looked like a fucking stalker!

I'd had Ralph drive me home in rush hour traffic on a Friday to get back in time to meet her at work only to find she'd left early for Finn. I hadn't heard from her, spoken to her, since we kissed one another goodbye yesterday morning.

Was that only yesterday? God it felt like weeks ago.

For fucks sake, she occupies my thoughts all day, every day. This was bordering on obsessive.

You're losing it mate.

Sleep with them, treat them well and move them on, without ties - it had always worked for me in the past. I'd not really wanted to go back for more. Well maybe a few times and with my first love, who I'd dated for two turbulent teenage years. At 17 I had ended things, when I caught her getting off with one of my best mates at the time. Needless to say, trust didn't come easy to me with women. I loved women - I just didn't love any one woman - apart from Bitzi; my Mum was a tough act to follow.

My parents had the epitome of a great everlasting marriage; it sometimes made it harder, as a relationship would have to be bloody good to compete on a similar level to theirs. Lu had the same with her own Mum and Dad. Walking into Nina and Mac Myers' house was like being in the twilight zone. Everywhere I looked, I saw my parents. From the Laura Ashley cushions in the lounge, to the Marks and Spencer's food in the fridge - the similarities were uncanny. Our parents had the same taste and the same likes and dislikes. Even the Julio Iglesias crooning loudly that welcomed me the last time I arrived for a party at the Myers' Senior, was the same god awful CD, my Dad used to play on a loop in his car when Nathan and I were young.

I smile with fond memories. Our families had made no bones about informing us they thought we were perfect for each other; this had done nothing more than force both our stubborn arses in opposite directions. Then Lu had become pregnant with Finn. I lick my bottom lip in thought.

In Dubai I'd realised how much I missed her - missed being home and near her. I've always travelled with my work but never been away for a period of time so long, without visits home. I'd entertained myself out there with the odd tall blonde beauty, my usual type but that's all it had been - entertainment. I'd craved meaningful, witty conversation with a petite, feisty, green eyed, brunette beauty. I'd craved intimacy and family.

God I miss her.

My cock springs to life at just the memory of what we shared in Room 22. She was magnificent. Open and uninhibited and bold! I couldn't have asked for more. My hands twitch, desperate to knead her perfect tits and stroke her velvety skin, so soft against my own. Her confidence was definitely growing sexually and wasn't that what this had all been about - this blasted proposition? Getting her back in the saddle with someone she trusted. I'd just encouraged her to delve deeper and bring out the wanton horny little devil that had lain dormant within her beautiful curvaceous body for some time - perhaps ever. The thought of her with Niall, giving herself openly, the way she had at Scarlet House made my blood boil.

She is mine now.

Fuck - the minute I feel like we're connecting and it's moving past the proposition part of our agreement - I sense her withdrawal and mine. We only work when we are together - once we part everything just gets murky.

Isn't that down to me though? Are you playing the game like always?

I need to kiss the tip of her stubborn nose, watch her eyes deepen from lime, to forest to teal green and flicker with fire, whilst inhaling her perfume scent; Gucci - she'd worn it since Uni and I could still smell it on my shirt from the other night. I'd been reluctant to wash it.

That's how sad I've become!

I swallow hard. Something wasn't right. I felt it - but what? When we'd parted yesterday morning, everything had been great - more than great - we couldn't keep our hands off each other. I hadn't wanted to leave her. I shouldn't have left her.

I'd sort things this weekend. This was her first night back with the Finnster and I wasn't about to come between the lioness and her cub.

Why had I decided to have a bloody housewarming, now of all times?

I wanted her all to myself - the house free to fuck her in every room, in every position possible. *You'll have to get rid of Chris first.* Yeah, think Mr. Booth might need to find somewhere else to live and sharpish!

I grab my phone and text her. Then get on to my jeweller mate - time to try a different tactic; time to get creative and buy her something special.

Chapter 32

Lucia

"Hey Mum where are you?" I shout up the open staircase in the direction of her bedroom.

"Hi Darling – I didn't hear you arrive. Where's my favourite little bundle of joy?"

"He's out with Dad, feeding the swans on the pond – think they'll have sunk by the morning. He just gave Ken, the male one, a full heel of bread!" I laugh alongside my lovely Mum, who looks fresh and happy in a long floaty, Per Una M&S skirt, matching camisole and flowery cardigan, with chunky pearls adorning her neck. I give her a big hug and hold onto her Chanel No.5 scented frame, a little longer than normal.

"What's up my lovely girl? I sense a sadness about you." Her face is enquiring, perfectly threaded brows raised but she shows genuine concern.

"I'm good Mum, just having a few issues with men – that's all!"

"Honey if I knew how to handle the opposite sex I'd have whipped your father into shape years ago – never did figure out how the male mind worked so I just took to whipping him! He rather liked it!" She lifts her dainty shoulder in a saucy shrug and I roll my eyes.

"Mum! Too much information!"

The thought of my Mum and Dad deep in the act of S&M is a confusing one to say the least but I suppose I am happy that after 35years of marriage they actually still want to give it to one another and keep it interesting.

"I better go I really need to go get ready for Sebastian's

housewarming." I take a quick check through Finn's overnight bag, to check I've packed everything he'll need.

"You go – have fun Darling. Anything you haven't packed, I'll no doubt have it upstairs. Just try and relax - you look tired."

Crap, always the truth with parents but she was right, I looked worn out and felt totally drained but it was nothing that some serious foundation and bronzer sculpting wouldn't fix. My phone buzzes in my pocket for the umpteenth time and flicking a quick glimpse at the screen my frown deepens.

I've missed seven calls from him!

Angrily I shove the phone back into hiding and return to my Mum's concerned gaze.

"What are you wearing? Do you want to borrow anything of mine? Maybe some shoes – I have plenty of do-me-shoes!"

The saucy look is back in her eyes and I smile, as my Mum's wardrobe would put Carrie Bradshaw's shoe addiction to shame - she had it worse than me - I'd definitely inherited my fetish from her. Everything from Jimmy Choos, to Kurt Geiger, filled the racks in a small extension off the main en-suite. It was a room that made me *Ahhh* upon entering and was pure indulgence.

"No, I'm good."

I'm going to wear the sexy new shoes Seb bought me; the ones I wore the other night when he took me from behind, as a 'fuck you' to him.

"But thanks Mum – you know me, once I'm in there, I'm done for and I need to go. Are you sure you're OK with Finn…again? I've only had him back a night and now I'm shipping him off again." I truly do feel like a terrible mother.

"Darling – don't be silly. He's had a lovely little holiday in windy Wales with your Dad & I and Madam Tina of course and that useless biological father of his, seems to be making an effort at least. There was always going to come a time when you were ready to get out in the dating world again. It's important that Finn isn't the only male constant in your life. It's a busy time for you with work but that's what Grandparents are for."

She hugs me again and practically shoves me out into the drive. "Now get in that car, straight home, tittify and go wow them – Sebastian, I presume?" she adds dryly and I wave her answer away, not ready to answer questions about him.

"Thanks Mum. Love you."

I dash over to Finn who is aiming more bread at the Swan's heads than mouths, and giggling madly as they contort their long necks to duck and catch. I wince at my Dad and he shrugs his shoulders, unconcerned.

"Boys will be boys."

I kiss his salt and pepper hair and he squishes me to him, and awkwardly orders me to go have fun. Finn puckers up for a sloppy plant on my cheek and squishing his adorable bottom I leave and guiltily slide into the car. Finn's not bothered I know, but I do feel bad. Maybe this is the bone of contention with all parents, the constant guilt that you're not doing enough - being there enough, for your child. My Mum is right though, I've spent the past year trying to be the model mother and it probably *is* time to enjoy some much needed *me time*, even if it's just to tell Sebastian Silver where to stick it!

I do the customary six-beep salute and head off to beautify. The deeply embedded nerves instinctively awaken and fly around like butterflies inside my tummy again.

Why am I putting myself through this?

Because, Lucia, you are not a pushover and you will go and make him see what he is missing! Remind him that you are the best he'll ever know and he'll never have you again. I can't help but think that this is going to backfire on me and I'll be the one seeing what I'm missing, in return. For fuck's sake, just the thought of him is turning me on; the sight of him will no doubt reduce me to a wet puddle of lust and drool - I haven't seen him since Scarlet House!

My phone bleeps, interrupting my nervous thoughts and alerts me to a text. Looking down, my face flushes in annoyance. He'd been calling and texting me since Thursday night and I'd not answered any of them. Even the one last night sent *To Finn, from Sub* - I just couldn't. I'd been tempted - believe me I'd been desperate to pick up last night - just to hear his voice. But I knew that the second I did I'd be done for. The constant harassment must be because he knew he'd been caught. I'm presuming that by now Toni has informed him of my visit in glorified detail. *I thought* I'd deserved at least a face-to-facer, to explain his two timing crappy behaviour.

Why won't you answer your phone Lu?
Call me... NOW!!!

I immediately delete the text in anger.

Who the hell does he think he is, ordering me around like that? Fucking control freak. He can bloody do one! I'm not here to do as he wishes, - to be there at his beck and call and bend over backwards – well maybe once, thinking back to the lusty mirror sex… that once had been worth it but never again. The guy was seriously pissing me off - get the picture I. Don't. Want. To. Talk. To. You. I shout into the empty car.

I've too much shit going on to deal with a moody gorgeously handsome contractor on a rampage - he's worse than Finn, when he doesn't get his own way! He couldn't even last one week with the same woman, let alone one month!

As I pull-up outside home, I zap the doors, and head up the path; blocking the top step is a now familiar looking, luxurious black box.

That Shit!

He actually thought after what had occurred last night, he could just send me flowers - beautiful flowers, but flowers none-the-less and I'd be fine with it all. Forget the *Ho* in the towel and her childlike lady-garden - or rather lady-beach.

I'm tempted to kick the box to the curb and head inside and for a second can't believe my own weakness at questioning such a decision. Annoyed at myself, I push the box aside with my foot, shove the door open and escape from all temptation, leaning back against the door for added measure. I last a couple of minutes - give or take, before I crumble.

Yanking the handle inwards I sneak a glance each way up and down the street - no one there - and grab the black box to my chest. Just because I was pissed doesn't mean to say I wasn't keen to see what he could possibly think would be enough of a message… this time.

Wading through oodles of tissue paper, I sigh at the scent of roses. I'm actually more of a fan of the tulips, lilies and peonies bouquet I'd received the week before, but I have to admit that the smell of these black roses is intoxicating. This would be the fifth single bud that I'd had in two weeks and like the others, it held a large diamante crystal in its centre to mark this. I lift the flower and inhale deeply, stroking the velvety petal against my cheek. What I really want to do is smash it hard on the coffee table to my left, causing every petal to fall. I wanted to break it, the beauty of it - the way we were now broken.

Taking a deep breath, I screw my eyes shut and wrestle with my inward voice as I pick up the thick cream envelope. Shaking my head,

I bite down hard on my lip and hurriedly slip a finger underneath the seal. My eyes scan the bold script font...

FWC

Tonight you'll be cherished.
In the morning you'll
be watched over!

... and then I launch the card in the direction of the bin, missing by a country mile. What planet was this guy on that he thought I'd be staying over at his tonight?

Seriously?

Chapter 33

Lucia

"You look divine! Stop fussing." I hear Suzie command under her breath.

I nod my head at her and take a small sip of my Kir Royale. If I didn't feel so apprehensive, I'd agree wholeheartedly. Even I had to admit that the full-length black Body-con dress I'd selected earlier did my curves justice. The front was simply designed, with thicker satin straps that housed shoulder pads, a round necked corset which nipped in at the waist, allowing the dress to curve softly at the hips and fall slim line to the ankle; not forgetting the discreet split, baring a flash of thigh when walking.

I loved the look but knew that the back would be what grabbed Seb's attention. It dipped in an extremely low scoop, from the straps to the top of the crack of my arse - it was deliciously obscene really! But what was the pièce de résistance were, the eight ropes of pearls that hung, stitched from each strap, and following the curve of my sides and waist, in the shape of a cello. They rested, descending in size, as strings of necklaces, creating a kind of pearl cowl, at the top of my bottom, where the fabric hugged lovingly to enhance my hourglass figure.

I'd accessorised with an emerald green cocktail ring and my shoes were the black suede Luby Lou's from Sebastian. I'd drawn my hair back into a messy chignon and fastened small diamond earrings at my lobes. The effect was simple yet seductive. I felt dangerously naughty.

I was not wearing any underwear, due to the constraints of the dress - thank God it had a built-in corset bra - a good job as nothing would have worked with this get-up. The thought of my nakedness

302

sent fizzles of excitement all over my body - with one slide, Sebastian could be inside me. Not that that would happen! I was dressed this way purely to get a rise out of him and make him regret his actions with Toni.

That's right, you keep telling yourself that love if it helps protect your heart; shame you've forgotten to mention it to your overly-sensitized body.

We'd entered the party a few minutes ago and selected a drink from the large, crisp white linen covered table to the right of the door. The house looked stunning; Sebastian's Mum, Bitzi Silver had worked her green-fingered magic, sprinkling flower creations, more likened to pure works of art, across every surface. Candles glimmered from secluded nooks, only reminding me of the other night and I swallow my distaste - the remembrance of his indiscretion shrouds me. *You can do this.*

The style of the house was very much like Sebastian himself, both traditional and modern, with a cool edge to it, a *money, can't buy* polish. The immense hallway opened out into another large living area, perfect for the overflow of partygoers. It wrapped around towards the kitchen and had doors leading to three further reception rooms. There was a study to the left as you entered and a huge guest-suite to the back of the house on the lower level with bathroom. The house was light, airy, vast and exuded luxury at every level.

The stairs, however, were the objet d'art in my opinion. I remember years ago Sebastian saying that he'd found the staircase he wanted to replicate in his house one day, on a Harry Potter movie and he'd redesigned it, with an additional modern twist to a tee. The steps were nestled towards the back of the hall and curled up majestically, before opening up and arriving on the opposite side of the room, directly above the entrance below. The effect was breathtaking. The balustrade was a deep pewter tone, with black spindles and the steps - they were made from white marble, topped with a luxury thick soft grey runner, hemmed with black. Chunky silver stair rods nestled in the crook of each step, tipped with a glass ball, which gleamed brightly underneath the immense bubble chandelier above. The result was luxurious, modern and homely; a difficult feat in interior design.

I'm pleased he'd taken some of my advice though; I could see little creative touches of Lucia here and there. I smile sadly, as I recognise a huge abstract canvas I'd painted and given to Sebastian as a birthday gift some years ago, it was sitting pride of place above the open fireplace in the hallway, its colours working fantastically with the decor, like it had been commissioned for the space - blacks, pewters, grays and white, washed determinedly across the painting. I remember creating this and the exhaustion I'd felt upon completion. My eyes are drawn to where the light from the Chandelier is catching the metallic silver and Latin words inscribed across the oils.

ipsa scientia potestas est

This was a phrase that we had lived by throughout our studying days and continued to this day.

Knowledge itself is power!

For a split second I am touched by the sentimentality that he has chosen to adorn his walls with my work and not another expensive, more recognised artist, but the fleeting memory of Toni in her towel, and the meaning of the words, which relate unquestionably to the sham of our current situation, sharply diminish any nostalgia I may have.

Shaking myself out of it I plaster a fake smile upon my face and try to appear interested in what Suzie is chattering about with Gino and a few others. However that smile becomes genuine as I spot Abby making her way to join us, alongside a very dapper looking Nathan.

"I've had my feelers out and no sign of the queen of all bitches... yet!" she whispers into my ear loyally.

"Thanks Hun – what about Seb?"

"He's chatting with some friends in the lounge, said he'll join us in a bit. Don't think he's realised you were here yet," she adds protectively.

I'd caught up with her last night about the Toni nightmare and I know she has my rather bare back tonight. I blow my mouth out in a huge calming yoga breath and shake my shoulders, like a boxer getting ready for a fight

"All I need to do is show my face, let them both see it doesn't bother me and then I'm off."

"Aren't you going to talk to him? Get his side of the story?" Abby sips her drink but nods her approval of the question. "I really think you should."

"Why? I'm not sure what he could say that would make this any better Abs – I was just in a different place to him about monogamy whilst we dallied – obviously!"

My tone is entirely sarcastic and I'm aware that I'm being a little too harsh on her and shrug apologetically and smile lightly at Nathan, who appears to have lost his tongue.

"Sorry Na. Ignore me."

"Not sure I can in that dress Lu - you look hot. Oh we are in for one interesting night - wait till my bro sees you. I almost feel sorry for him."

"Na's right Babe - you look fabby - lurve that dress." I grin at Abby over the rim of my glass, raising my brows at her.

"Likewise Abs - we owe Dolly's boutique big time!"

She preens under Nathan's and my obvious approval, smoothing her hands over her scarlet gown and I wink and add.

"Very Julia Roberts in Pretty Woman."

"So long as it's the Opera dress you're referring to, and not the *pick Richard Gere up on Rodeo drive dress.*"

My deep laugh is instinctive and much-needed and I squeeze her arm in silent thanks before chuckling again, as we clink glasses and Nathan toasts us with," I'm happy with either Abs - I'm all for a working girl - thigh boots and peaked cap - bring it on."

She wrinkles her nose at him feigning displeasure, which earns her a seductive whisper in her ear, causing her to beam instantly. At her sympathetic wince at their playfulness, I assure her it's fine, with a wave of my hand and excuse myself from Suzie, Gino, Abby and Nathan, feeling rather the gooseberry and make my way towards the lounge. My heart is beating so fast, I'm certain that its going to combust, as I manoeuvre my way through the guests, stopping and chatting amiably with them, here and there. I recognise a couple of them as family, and a few work colleagues. It's as I enter the high ceilinged lounge that I hear the shrill-pitch of my nemesis.

Don't worry girl you look hot! Nathan's recent words ring clearly in my head.

"Sebastian Darling, there you are! We must go and mingle with our guests!"

Toni hasn't seen me yet, so I am allowed the opportunity to weigh up the competition. Her spectacular body is poured into an electric blue strapless dress, so short I fear for her modesty, if she curved her body anymore there'd be a flash of the hairless bits. *Then again, who am I to talk - the breeze is most definitely liberating!*

She towers in silver Gina Sandals and plays subconsciously with a diamond tennis bracelet on her wrist. Toni instinctively sends a glance in my direction and her eyes automatically narrow at the sight of me. Openly appraising me from head to foot, she continues to rest her arm on Sebastian's forearm and leans in deliberately showing me the slight crease of her arse! Bitch!

"Get your bloody arm off him!" I want to scream.

She's obviously decided to play hostess-with-the-mostess, at the party and she and Sebastian definitely appear to be together. I ignore her and head towards a waiter to take a second Kir Royale, the sweet liquid was hitting the right spot and going down way too easily. I was going to have to be careful to keep a clear head.

I sense him before he speaks - the air fizzles around me, lifting all the hairs on my arms and sending shivers down my spine. *How did he have this effect on me after only a few nights of passion?* The man was irritating beyond words!

I watch the hunger reflected and burning hotly within his eyes and I revel in it. The dress had been worth every penny. *Wait until he sees the rest of it.* I'm glad that I still have the ability to stir his interest - who didn't want to be *wanted?*

"Lu, I didn't know you were here?"

His voice loosens every part of my conflicted body in longing, and I feel my disloyal nipples tighten in response. My body is frighteningly in tune with him. Turning to face him I put on my heavily practiced fake smile and soak him up.

Oh crap!

He looks devastating wearing a sharp Navy Suit and expensive black shirt and tie - his two-day stubble, giving his polished look, a lethal edge. I could seriously jump him right this second and subconsciously rub my legs together to ease the throbbing between my legs. Annoyed with my desperate wantonness, by my body's disloyalty, I revert to safe and frosty Lu.

Treat him as a friend. It's what works for you both. It's what you know. This is Sebastian the playmate, not the soul mate.

God I wish I could look at him as a friend still. It's as though the minute we slept together, the seal was broken and we can't go back; the sexual tension between us has been released and needed attention. Now all I could think about was his handsome face when he was positioned between my legs, his dark liquorice eyes assessing my reaction as his tongue dips in and out and flicks my swollen, needy clit. His manly hands gripping my thighs keeping me wide open to his mouth and seductive gaze. I can feel the heated flush begin across my skin.

For goodness sake woman, get a grip - he's probably done the exact same thing to his bloody brazen PA- it's what he was doing to her the other night!

'Sebastian." I raise my glass to him, snapping out of it. "The house looks super."

I can tell that he is weighing me up, assessing my mood and haughty manner. He looks a little surprised.

How is that possible? Arrogant bastard!

"You look beautiful, Lu."

He licks his lips in an obvious response to me and I jump deeper into my confusion. Inside I'm doing a victory dance; *look what you could have won Mr. Silver.*

"Did you not get my calls?"

"Yeah I did." I reply bluntly, making him work for it.

"Texts?"

"Yep. Got those too."

His brow furrows in anger and through gritted teeth he lower his voice. "Why didn't you answer then?"

"It may surprise you Sebastian but you are not my be all and end all. I've been busy!"

I think I see a sweep of hurt cross his features but I may be wrong. However, I dial it down a notch. I'm hurt but not a total bitch - it's not in my nature to be unkind.

"I'd hoped to see you last night. I went to the Elysium office but you'd left for the night."

"Oh." I am aware I couldn't be less involved but I'm having a tough time not launching myself at him and taking my anger out on his sexy mouth and that fact pisses me off even more. He didn't deserve to look so hot.

He'd come to the office looking for me? Why? To put his side of the story across?

He leans in towards me; one hand casually in his pocket, the other lightly resting on my arm. I focus on his Omega watch and try not to stare at his hands - such sexy, manly hands. *What he could do with those hands.*

"You could have left a message about The Ashton with Jackie, Seb. I'd have got right on it first thing Monday - no need to deliver it in person. In fact I'd rather you didn't."

"It wasn't about the fucking Ashton - what's got into you Lu?"

"Nice party." I change the subject and raise my glass to clink. "Anyway you need to go and mingle with Toni. It's *your* party. I'll do my thing and you go do yours."

The harsh line of his jaw shows me he's struggling to maintain his anger. His dark brown eyes have a turbulent storm brewing within them and his frown is quickly replaced with that lethal Sebastian smile.

I turn my back on him, with one graceful movement, every intention of heading back to my friends, when I hear his breath hitch and then complete silence behind me. My cocky smirk cannot be seen by him, but it warms me, as I realise he's been hit with the full effect of my daring pearl gown - it had been worth every penny!

Forcing myself to take another step and continue on my path away from his divine body, I straighten my back and wiggle my arse, especially for him. The pearls rub silkily against my skin, their weight causing the ropes to swing. I'm nearly in the hallway before I feel his hand at my back, steadfast and determined to still me.

Through his teeth he spits. "There is no way you are being left alone in *that bloody dress.*"

My belly flip flops and I repeat the victory dance in my head and make a mental note to buy Suzie some flowers for her fab advice.

"I need to fuck you so hard."

I turn to face him, wide-eyed and innocent, I hope.

His face appears almost pained and so outside of his comfort zone, that like Nathan has mentioned earlier, I almost feel sorry for him.

Almost.

In reality I need to focus on myself, and my own weaknesses here. His words are reducing me to that puddle of weakness again; hot and sexy and dirty and I'm almost willing to do anything for a quick tumble with Mr. Silver - but no longer. I want more and he couldn't give me that - had already proven it.

"You're a tease Lady."

My nipples are alert and I feel them pushing through the soft fabric of my dress, Seb's eyes are immediately drawn to them and his own breathing quickens. My skin is on fire and every fibre of my being is itching to reach out and touch him, hold him and kiss him for the last time. For a few seconds we ravish each other with our

308

eyes alone; deep emerald zest, meeting dark chocolate pools; watching, caressing, approving.

Even though I hate this man for his disloyalty, my God damned best friend - I am not blind. He oozes sex appeal and I haven't seen him in three days. My body has gone into starvation overdrive, desperate to feast on such delicious meat.

I can see Toni over Seb's shoulder focusing on us; her shrewd eyes gauging the situation and I watch her begin to make her way towards him -snake like in her path.

"Sebastian Darling - I *need* you?"

I hear her snooty voice and the anger returns low in the pit of my stomach. Sebastian ignores her whiney demands and instead roughly grabs my hand and drags me in the direction of the stairs - ignoring the stares from guests happily chattering and alerted to the minor commotion. He halts as we reach the top of them, rapidly decision making as to where we go from here and I look down from the mezzanine landing, to the crowd below and catch Abby mouthing,

"WTF?"

I meet the narrowed eyes of Toni, at the bottom of the steps where we left her, hands claw-like in annoyance and a face likened to a person spitting glass. Her silver sandal smashes into the floor in annoyance and a petulant huff reverberates up the hall stairs. It had been worth it just for that although now I'm here, alone with the devil, I am not sure if she got off lightly. He is sorely pissed!

I'm pulled through a nearby door and slamming it behind us, we are surrounded by inky darkness – the only light that filters in, is from the huge arched window in the centre of what now appears to be the master-suite.

His room. His domain. His terms.

I immediately feel on the back foot and freeze - all the facade of my confidence is stripped away here.

Placing both palms on the door behind me, they rest on either side of my head and with his foot wedged between my legs; I am trapped there for his perusal. He looks deep into my eyes and his own glint in their challenge for me to look away and without another word, he angrily takes my mouth, and I am a goner. I don't for one second think about pulling away. I should, but I can't. There would be no point.

Our tongues instinctively wrestle and we pant heavily as we

devour one another, not able to get enough from mere kissing. The term eating each other would be underplaying our assault on our lips. He sucks and licks, imprinting his scent and taste inside me until I'm quivering - stroke after stroke, melting my icy veneer. Stony faced he moves towards my corset, tugging until my nipple pops free and I hear his guttural groan as he takes it firmly in his fingers, tweaking and rolling, happy in the knowledge that I'm unrestricted and available to him. I sigh in sheer bliss at the sensation of our skin on skin.

"God I've missed these."

His erection is hard and pressing against my stomach; my aching breasts straining against the beautiful dress. It was becoming too tight. I needed to be naked, to feel him against me.

Just one more time and then I'd end this.

"You chose this dress for me after our night at Scarlet House Baby?"

His eyes search mine, as he fondles my left breast and suckles the free nipple, watching me for my answer. I lock eyes with him and nod.

"Every time I see a rope of pearls now I'll think of you; of them rubbing you between your pussy, tied around your wrists - makes my cock twitch at the thought, and when you turned your back on me, little minx - that indecent glimpse of your crack, I could have fucked you then and there!"

His breath is ragged, as he works his way back to my mouth, my loins on fire at his words. I can see the desire in his eyes, and kiss him back with every ounce of my being; my hands on his hips encouraging him to bury himself into me.

I feel his hand lift my gown, and a finger tracing a path up the split of the dress, sensually but firmly grasping my stocking-clad hold ups, and massaging my thigh. Quivering I lift my leg around his body, encouraging him to explore further and stroke a hand down my calf. I wrap it fully around him, opening me up to him, and shiver with pleasure as his hand travels down to clasp my shoe.

"Ah Lu you're killing me here. Worth every penny." *I smile to myself - my sentiments exactly.*

I'm enfolded into his warmth, desperate to feel him inside me, whilst he licks back and forth over my erect nipple, when all of a sudden I freeze.

"You're bare here for me Baby! Are you bare here?"

His other hand drops to the high split, inching inwards, and in that second I'm brought back to reality with a huge bang. I push at his hard chest in panic, desperate to get away from him and retain composure. I cannot bear to be near him, I feel dizzy, sick and am close to the embarrassment of tears. Clasping at his vice like grip, in a last ditch attempt to free myself from his close vicinity, the pent up anger and desolation threaten to explode from within me.

Are you bare here? What was I thinking? What am I doing?

He likes me stripped bare! Toni's words play over and over in my head.

"You fucking bastard - you have balls I'll give you that – balls of stainless silver."

I spit the words out, fighting again against his strong grip to remove myself. His look of total shock and confusion is disconcerting. I can tell from his eyes that he fears I've completely lost it but his firm hold on my arm doesn't waver.

I hate this nasty version of myself, it isn't me and I'm pissed that he has turned me into this weak willed bitch. I maliciously clamp my teeth around his arm and bite down, hard. His yelp of pain stills me but it slackens his reign and he releases me.

"What the fuck Lu? What's got into you?" He instinctively rubs his arm with the discomfort.

I give him a filthy look. It serves him right. As if he didn't know.

"I came to see you on Thursday night, so we could have *that talk* that *you* so desperately wanted?" I prod him harshly in the chest.

He rubs his head in the way he always does when he is stressed about something and shouts an angry groan of frustration into the room. I can tell he still doesn't get it!

Taking a deep breath I exhale slowly and smooth down my dress. Every particle of me wants to grab his face in my hands and kiss him again until we pass out from our obsession, but sensible Suzie's voice echoes in my head.

Tell him Lu. There are two sides to every story!

"Toni told me you weren't available Sebastian – that you were otherwise engaged."

The adrenalin is flowing and encouraging me along my path- sexy sultry Lulu has been replaced with stony-faced prudish Lucia. He looks completely perplexed and somehow this only endears him to me more. *How does that work?*

What is this hold he has over me?

311

"Toni? – What the bloody hell's she got to do with anything?" he demands flippantly.

Rage embodies every part of my anatomy.

"Toni with an *'i'* – you know your PA? She answered *your* door in a towel - all wet from *your* soapy sexual escapades."

Hopefully that would trigger something in his ridiculous loss of short-term memory – were there that many women that he couldn't remember this one occasion? I can imagine my eyes are glowing green with jealousy and passion. I can feel my body come alive with the emotions and don't remember ever feeling so angry. I'm on fire and his words cut into my reverie with a cold heartless rush.

"It wasn't me Lucia," his voice is firm and crystal clear.

"But..."

He places a hand up to silence me and shakes his head and I close my mouth instantly, ticked off like a naughty child. "No. No more! You will listen to *me* now!" His voice is threatening and I know I've tipped him over the edge. "Is this why you haven't been answering my calls?"

I nod mutely.

"Jesus Lu. I don't know why Toni was here Thursday night, or why she said she was with me but I'm telling you, *she wasn't.*" I study his face, his blackened pools for any glitch of distrust, there is none. His eyes burrow into my own with a force so great I find it hard to blink and impossible to look away.

"I didn't get back until Friday night - *last night*. I came back from London on Wednesday - as you well know."

I blush under his reprimanding glare. "Then spent Thursday until Friday night, back in Manchester. It wasn't fucking me - nor would I do that to you. I told Chris to tell you where I was - didn't he?" He moves and raises a hand to his brow, strutting in small steps to control his increasing fury.

"No."

"Well I did. Do you really think after what we shared in Room 22 I'd just come home and tumble the company PA?"

"Honestly? I don't know Seb." I'm embarrassed by how bad it sounds now, when aired aloud.

"Well I wouldn't. This is you and me. You and I started something a few weeks ago - an agreement, a proposition, whatever the hell it was - it's become... more. We've become more - more than just fuck buddies."

We stare at one another, chests heaving, both passionate about our viewpoint. I take a good long hard look at his beautiful face, the face I know so well as a friend and now as my lover and in that moment, I am certain that he speaks the truth.

"That is the last time I'll say it and you *will* believe me Lucia. I didn't fuck Toni - I never have and I never will. She is not for me."

I take a few quick steps and throw myself at his mercy. Our mouths bang together, teeth clashing, in our urgency to unite. I feel his hand work its way around the small of my back, roughness hitting smooth, where my back is naked and his sigh at the contact with silky smooth skin. His other hand reaches into my hair almost roughly and draws me closer to the heat of his body - his grip is intense and commanding.

Possessive.

I'd tried to resist him, tried to keep away but my self-control has packed up and left for the night. My mind is still bombarded with the vision of him fucking Toni, plunging his cock into her; the rage is unquenchable. But as he moves in, pressing his heat into my body, stroking my back, whispering words of encouragement and making me quiver – I feel myself relax. He didn't do it. His satisfied groan is beyond irritating but I don't care. All I want is *him!*

"You are not off the hook here."

"Look at me Lu. Look what you do to me. You're driving me crazy but it makes me rock hard!" His hand draws mine over the bulge in his trousers - solid.

I can see the emotion in his gorgeous face, even if he doesn't realise it himself and it warms me. My heart pumps madly, as I feel the tension in his arms.

"You don't get it do you?"

My confused frown is enough for him to continue.

"I've never been like this before – with anyone! I've never needed another woman to surrender to me so badly. I've never wanted to bed only one woman and go back for seconds, thirds - *fuck;* until I can't get it up anymore!"

My sex clenches in victory and I moan as he works his lips along my neck, sucks my earlobe and I sigh in thanks when I hear the zipper of my dress. I break free and slip out of it, one strap dropped at a time, slinking and sashaying seductively until it drops to the floor, where I step free sexily, in my hold-ups and suede heels. I smile brazenly at him, as I delicately place the fashion masterpiece on the chair, near the door and walk towards him - offering myself, naked on a silver platter. I revel as the air hits my throbbing pussy; the breeze flickers across my clit, as light as a feather but I'm so wet already I shiver at the chill.

"God, Lucia you can't believe that I would want another woman? Not when I have you. When we have this…"

His tongue delves deep inside my mouth again, dancing with my own. I feel his fingers part my lips and ready me for his pleasure.

"You're so wet for me– always wet for me Baby!"

He pushes me towards the bed and I'm flipped so that I bend over the edge, my face on the mattress. I am entirely bare to him now; am open to his hungry eyes and eager cock and my pussy glistens with arousal and expectation. I realise that he is choosing this primitive position as a reminder of our amazing night - to ensure he is entirely in control.

Licking my lips, I turn to watch him unzip his suit trousers and release his fabulous weapon; its size never ceases to amaze me but he is so hard, so rigid for me, it just turns me on more. This man is solid everywhere.

Hearing him fumble with a condom, I feel a sense of loss that I won't be able to feel him completely within me but this quickly passes and I gasp, as he positions the head at my moist entrance. With one hand on my hip he reaches around to pull harshly on my nipple, the erotic gesture sending shockwaves directly to my nub. I groan in angst. I need him to touch me now! I hear myself scream out in frustration and his laugh at my torture. This is my punishment for not believing in him and I deserve it. He is entirely in control again - I am weak and desperate.

Rubbing my eager nipple repeatedly as he moves leisurely into me, in delicious rotating movements I arch my back in bliss, stretching like a cat and try to grab him to push deeper within me. Instinctively he complies and I hear him suck in his breath.

"I'm going to fuck the truth into you Lu." He slams deeper into me. "There can be no distrust between us from now on. Ok?"

I listen to him, biting my hand as delicious sensations begin to quicken around my g-spot. His cock is hitting it, bang… on… each… time. I know that this is his plan but I am still in awe at his expertise.

"Lucia – Ok?"

I feel him stop and twist to see why. He looks seriously hot, fully dressed, just his pubic hair and the base of his wide cock showing but

314

his face is deadly serious.

"Ok. I trust you." *Just fuck me you gorgeous control freak.*

I groan, desperate for him to continue with the ripples of pleasure overwhelming me. I know that he is trying to fuck some sense into me, to prove that he wants me and only me. To show that he was right and I was wrong. *What all this means, will have to be dealt with later.*

I sigh in relief, as he begins to move, rhythmically, this time for seconds before he thrusts so hard inside me, I fear he'll hit my womb.

"I've wanted to do this to you all day, everyday since the last time – you feel so fucking good."

I nod my head in encouragement and pant as he withdraws and thrusts, getting quicker with each push; withdrawing and thrusting, thrusting and withdrawing, torturous in his strokes. I push back onto his length to assist him, allowing him even deeper into my body and I feel my pelvic floor tighten around his girth as I begin the spiralling helter-skelter ride to my release. He crashes into me and I feel him lean forward and brush the pad of his finger firmly across my swollen and needy clit. I cry out in ecstasy, as that final pressure is my undoing; whilst he fucks me harder and harder I shatter around his cock, my dripping entrance making it easier for him to manoeuvre in and out. My climax is so great that I hear his name on my lips and don't recognise the deep, sexy and broken voice as my own.

"Sebastian - please!"

"Ssh - I know baby – I'll meet you there."

His own release is seconds later, and even through the rubber, I feel him empty himself into me, his twitching body delivering every last scrap of himself inside, proving 100% that I am his and he is mine.

"Fuck! Only you and me now," he whispers hoarsely into my neck.

I am hit by a huge rush of feelings for him and know that it is futile to deny it any longer my feeling for Sebastian Silver go way beyond any one month proposition - I wanted him for keeps. I brush it to one side, in need of private time to process this realisation and hug it to myself a little longer. After some adjusting of clothes and dispensing with the protection, I am drawn back to his body and we hug like that for some time, standing in silence - many words unspoken. I turn to face him; our mouths meet lovingly and slowly, the intensity satisfied for a short while.

"I suppose we should go rejoin the party?"

I murmur into his chest, inhaling his fresh vanilla and musk scent and blush as I wonder if any guests had heard our passion.

I hear his deep scoff. "I'd rather get you completely naked and into my bed."

"Give me a few minutes to freshen up and I'll meet you back downstairs."

"Ok, Lady Lu. I'll give you your few minutes but after that, you are not leaving my side. Like I said that dress is lethal - ever wear it again, without me and I'll arrange for Ralph to accompany you."

"Ralph? Your driver?" I refer to the handsome Polish chauffeur who'd escorted me to and from Scarlet House.

"Ralph is not just a driver Darling. He's security."

"Oh." *Not sure I'm so pleased about having some guy following me around on Seb's orders but I'll deal with that later.*

"Let me give you my gift now Lady, before I forget - I wanted to give it to you Friday night but you weren't answering my calls." His brows furrow in fleeing annoyance but the expression is gone in a second.

Looking down, I watch, as he extracts a silver bracelet from his pocket with a thick chain. A large silver heart, swings from the clasp. It's from Tiffany's - I know because I'd told him I wanted one, years ago, when we were at Uni.

"Oh Sebastian it's beautiful. Will you put it on me?"

"Its no way near as beautiful a you, Lulu but I saw it in London and it made me think of you; of us."

I'm deeply touched by the present - proof that he's been thinking about me on his business trips. The thought sends pools of liquid heat to my core. I clasp the heart in my fingers, feeling the weight of the Silver.

"I'll buy you charms for the rest of it Baby. The heart is to remind you of us, and our proposition. I liked the message, so I added my own..."

I scan the script clearly. "Please return to Tiffany's New York..." *He knows I lurve New York and was the reason I'd wanted the item of jewellery all those years ago.*

"Now turn it over."

I look up at his expectant face and smile. The other side of the heart has a similar style of engraved writing and reads, "Please return Lucia Myers to Sebastian Silver - she's mine!"

"What are you like? You controlling bugger - I love it!"

"I'm glad you do." His eyes shine with pleasure and he bends to kiss my nose, slipping the bracelet onto my outstretched wrist and fastening it with a soft click. The weight of it sits, as a reminder of him and his feelings for me, securely around my arm and I shake my hand happily.

He watches me fixedly, with that gold-flecked twinkle in his eyes, before dropping a slow peck on my lips. The moment is so unlike anything we've shared together to date… another first. I'm almost at a loss for words. The gift was nothing flashy but so much more than I could have ever asked for. The sentimentality of it spoke volumes.

Reaching up on tiptoes, I kiss Sebastian one last time and push him jokily towards the door. "Right go! We can't go back down together – it'll be obvious what we've been doing!" I smile back at him.

He nods at me in understanding although seems reluctant to leave. "I think *everyone* will know what we we've been doing anyway - and be jealous as hell."

His naughty bedroom eyes are enough for me to figure *who* he means by *everyone; Toni*. I'm glad he realises how important it is that she is dealt with.

I smile contentedly. Who could have foreseen that this would be the outcome, after the events of Thursday night? I truly believed him though and now that I wasn't clouded by sexual emotions I could see that Toni was even more evil and manipulative than I'd first thought. This girl meant business and really needed to be taught a lesson - I'd certainly made an enemy of this bitch!

I look up as he's about to slip through the door. "Don't be long! Oh and Lu one of these days you and I really *are* going to talk about us."

"We *do* need to talk." I bite my lip worried that yet again our passions have overcome our sensibilities. More importantly I need to know that he is feeling the same way as me. I need to know that he agrees that this is much more than we could have ever imagined. I know he wants more than fucking but a relationship; maybe love? I'm not sure.

"Lucia be sure in the knowledge that whilst you and I are having sex, I won't sleep with anyone else. Just you. You have my word, I promise. I would have thought that a given with our proposition, but after *this*, you obviously needed to hear it."

His face is gentle whilst he delivers this unintentional blow - full on nail-driven-into-coffin-moment. My own blissful split-second shattered, my shoulders slump in sadness. I have some serious decisions to make. Enjoy the time we have left together and prepare for the inevitable devastation or get out now before I lose everything, including our friendship and my self-respect.

I clenched my fists at my sides, trying desperately to restrain myself and remain calm but invisible steam is erupting from every orifice. *Ooh he makes me so mad.* My Grandma had always said to me that the best relationship was one built like a seesaw, where love and hate rocked back and forth over the years, toying with one another's weaknesses. Love reigned the majority of the time, as the heaviest and most grounded party, whilst hate tipped the balance every once in a while, to mix things up, managing to add weight in order to bring passion and communication to the forefront of a long-term relationship. Hate was the reminder needed in every relationship that you loved this person in the first place. One did not work without the other. A relationship without hate was a relationship without depth. They were both necessary to ensure both parties still felt deeply enough about one another. I'd never truly understood her analogy until this very moment, with this man. At this very moment, I both hated him, and loved him, at the exact same time.

Oh crap! I knew it would happen - was helpless to stop it.

I'm desperately in love with Sebastian Silver. The one man who doesn't do commitment!

Chapter 34

Lucia

"Where have you been Lulu?" I hear Abby's questioning tone, as soon as my foot hits the bottom step into the hallway. The throng is so busy I am pleased that my arrival goes unnoticed to all but my caring friend.

"Don't ask. I kinda got waylaid." I blush; annoyed at my body's ultimate betrayal of my mind.

"Seems to me you just got laid. Full stop! You dirty bitch! Speaking of bitches - did you talk about that cow-bag Toni?"

I take a gulp of the much — needed drink she places in my hand and pat my hair to check it's still holding up.

"You won't believe it Abs - she bloody made it up! Totally bullshitted about being in the shower with Seb; he wasn't even here until the day after!"

"No. Fucking. Way! Do you believe that? Him?" She bites her lip, and concentrates wholly on my answer, encouraging me to take my time - I don't need to.

"He didn't sleep with her Abs. I know it *here*!" I place my palm across my heart, completely sure of my instinct and in my trust of Sebastian.

"Well that's enough for me - problem is, that means that this girl is a whole shed-load worse than we thought — crazy MF!"

"I know. Then one thing led to another and before you knew it we were having make-up sex."

"Dirty bitch!" Abs repeats and grinning clinks her wine glass with

319

mine. "Might just take your lead and ask Nathan to show me the spare room myself! May as well put these gorgeous undies to use," she cheekily pushes her breasts together and pouts prettily.

"You do that girl. I need to go find Suzie and tell her the news before I speak to the blonde assassin in person. That woman is going down!" I snap my fingers in a Z shape and we giggle together at my reinvigorated attitude.

Abby waves me off, wishing me luck and I head in the direction of the lounge once again. It is there that I see Chris and Toni head to head, deep in what appears to be a fairly nasty confrontation. He is trying to engage her in some form of physical display but she is definitely having none of it and pushes his tentacles away angrily. Looking around, Chris checks to see if anyone has seen them, obviously embarrassed at her dismissal and laughs it off but she continues to give him a severe ticking off, in an albeit lowered voice.

To the right of them, standing near the grey velvet sofas and the roaring open fire are Suzie, Gino and Sebastian. One look at his face and I melt.

"Lucia. *Come! Come* join us!" his voice drawls with heavy emphasis put on the word, *come*. He is impossible.

Suzie looks from me to Seb and back again, her eyes nearly popping out in her desperation to know what is going on. We chatter about work and Gino's new dick of a boss and I feel Sebastian's warm hand at the base of my spine, tracing delicate circles over and over again across the sensitive skin there, his fingers playing with the ropes of pearls. His hand shows ownership and I go with it but for how long would this be the case?

The second that Seb and Gino leave us, to get more drinks Suzie pounces on me. "Well?"

I sip my drink and ponder on how to play this one. Suzie could hold a grudge and I needed her to see that whilst Sebastian and I are yet to be a couple, he did *not* cheat on me.

Her beautiful face scrunches in annoyance. "Lulu did you have it out with him or what?"

"Yes Sis – it's sorted. It wasn't him! Toni delivered bucket loads of shit from the bull!"

I can tell that she is not entirely sure what to believe but gives me the benefit of the doubt. Her eyes fluttering as she mulls the information over.

"If it wasn't Sebastian then who was it?"

"I think its more along the lines of *Miss Toni with an 'i'*, set me up!"

"What a cow!"

"Complete and nutter!" I agree and we clink our glasses affirmably, laughing at my play on words.

"I did say to you that it wasn't like Seb didn't I?" she enfolds me in a sisterly hug

"Oh I'm so pleased, Gino and I were so happy you two were finally getting it on and after Thursday night – we panicked that we'd have to choose between the two of you!"

I flinch at her words, surely there wouldn't be a choice, seeing as we were siblings but I choose to ignore the comment and blame it on her pregnancy hormones.

"Yeah, now all I need to do is make sure it's long-term."

"Honey, in that dress you'll have him eating out of your hand – anything else you wish – the man hasn't taken his eyes off you all evening."

I glance over to Seb's direction and we connect, sharing a knowing sexual smile that's full of promise and satiated satisfaction.

"I remember when Gino used to look at me like that."

"He still does Darling – God he's proud as punch about your news."

She looks across at him adoringly, lightly placing her hand on her still flat abdomen. "I know, bless him – you'd think no one had ever got a woman up the duff! He's strutting about like a peacock!"

"I still can't believe I'm going to be Auntie Lulu – I'm so excited."

We laugh together but again I am drawn to Sebastian.

"Just go you hussy! The way the two of you are looking at each other, its practically live porn. I'm getting turned on and that's just sooo not right!"

"No Sis. I'm taking your earlier advice and I'm going to let him chase me. Play hard to get; or harder to get at least."

"Ooh, play him at his own previous game."

"Maybe? – Maybe just make him come to the notion that he can't live without me."

"He already knows that Honey – one look at the way he has an eye on you at all times and everyone can see it, but men take longer to come to terms with it. They fight it! You want him to need you as well as want you. He knows it, he just doesn't *know* it!"

We laugh at her cryptic quote. "At least you know what you're talking about Suze!" I grin and contemplate her happy glow.

"God help us when the hormones go on their rampage!" Rolling her eyes she sips her fresh orange juice in distaste. I feel for her, the champagne is plentiful tonight and delicious as ever. I kiss her soft cheek and shove her in the direction of her Hubbie and looking about, head off to circulate.

After chatting comfortably with a couple of freelance builders I'd met when Seb was building the house, I move on to catch Abby and Nathan, both looking suitably flustered, with that just fucked aura. They'd definitely had some fun time and Abby and I share our mutual secret with a synced eyebrow raise. Dirty mares that we are! The Silver brothers are too irresistible and annoying as it is, my body thanks my mind for just going with it for once. I'm about to find Sebastian and make my excuses when I hear someone call my name.

I see Meg before I notice the person who's accompanied her. We air kiss and dish out compliments on our respective apparel. She looks lovely in a black evening jumpsuit and gold sandals, very chic.

"Sorry Meg, I didn't know you were coming, I'd have shared a lift with you." I feel bad I've not really seen much of her the past few weeks.

It's only as I wait for her response that I divert my gaze to the silent male figure at her side, nervously fiddling with his glasses and shiftily looking everywhere but me.

I raise my brows as I see that she has arrived with *Leo* of all people.

"We've just been out for a meal at that little Italian in Bodley – gorgeous scallops with garlic and parsley – anyway Sebastian asked me when we were out in Lords, if I wanted to come along tonight and I thought we'd pop in for a nosey. It's not a problem is it?"

She rambles on and appears embarrassed by the fact that she is with Leo; immediately I put her mind at rest, and smile graciously – she's my friend after all, although I would have preferred not to have an ex, albeit minor one encompassed with my friends. Besides Leo and I still worked together, kind of, so we would be mixing in some future circles.

"That's great Meg – I'm so glad you came and you too, Leo."

With his hands in his pockets, he nods mutely. I cannot help but notice the Napolitana house sauce on his tie and inwardly cringe at my poor original judgment; he had seemed a nice man though and I'm genuinely pleased for Meg, if he treats her well. He did say that he liked kids.

"How's things Leo? Work good? I'm so sorry I've not returned your call - think you called the office when I was ill didn't you?" His eyes light up at the mention of the banking world and my own immediately glaze over and he nods at the mention of his call.

"Yes Lucia. Feeling better now?"

"Much thanks."

"And work for you - how's that going? Weren't you decorating some big Hotel in Holdgate?" he enquires politely.

"Yes, The Ashton. It's really coming along nicely, thanks. Hopefully will be the boost we need for the business."

"That's great, Lucia. I'll have to meet you for lunch to go over the last quarter for your accounts soon."

"Oh we don't need to do that Leo - we can just meet in the office." *With Jackie and Colin around for back up.*

"No, no. I insist. I'll call next week."

Meg slings her arm around Leo, in an attempt to return the focus to her — she appears to have over-indulged and is relaxed enough for the both of them; I presume with a helping hand from Mr. Chablis.

"Leo has been telling me that he has a new hobby bird watching, he's been buying all sorts of new equip...." Meg waffles on brightly and is rudely interrupted by Leo's brush off.

"Meg we don't need to bore Lucia with my life." *Why stop now, Leo I wonder to myself? I can't believe that it was only a week ago that I was at another party with this guy. Things have happened so fast between Sebastian and I; I've hardly had time to catch my breath.*

I am saved from further discomfort as Sebastian joins us placing a possessive palm on my bare back, enclosing the pearls draped at the base of my spine. He kisses Meg's cheek and welcomes them both warmly. A firm handshake between the men seals the situation nicely and Seb, ever the gentleman saves the day.

"Nice to see you both."

I can hear the surprise in his voice but to anyone else he is natural. Leo appears aloof, thoroughly absorbed in weighing up our relationship, trying to ascertain if we are now *a couple*. I feel his eyes watching our physical contact, the way our bodies link unknowingly, joined by the invisible thread which binds us and shows all spectators that we belong to each other. It must be undeniable and I have the good grace to feel sorry for him but at the same time, I remind myself we had only ever had few dates, never slept together and were never going to work. It was best we just kept things work related.

And he isn't Sebastian, my inner voice screams out.

The men chatter about the latest Rugby game as Meg turns her back slightly, flicking her chic hair over one exposed shoulder sexily. I feel for her as the obvious flirtation goes unnoticed by her beau. She tries so hard that it can come across as desperate and I remind myself to talk to her one of these days, as a friend; tough call though - how do you start that conversation?

"You don't mind do you Lu Bu?" Her face is sincere.

"Mind what? *You and Leo?* Don't be silly, Meg I'm pleased for you." Although I'm not sure that they are the best fit but they do say opposites attract.

"I wanted to tell you this week but you've been so busy with work and Leo only asked me out on Monday night, when we bumped into each other near my house. I know you two didn't work out. Then he's pretty much holed up there on and off ever since." Her shy shoulder lift has me smiling.

"It's fine, honestly. Leo and I were not best suited and I said as much at Suzie and Gino's party last weekend."

"Oh good. I just felt a bit bad that Leo had ended things and now he's seeing your neighbour." She has the good grace to wince in apology.

Leo ended things did he? Well maybe that will make him feel more of a man. *Just leave it Lu.*

"I'm pleased for you Meg. Seriously." *Not so happy about the idea that Leo is potentially so nearby to my home though.*

I'm awash with physical attraction as I watch Sebastian's interaction with Leo, politely listening to the lesser man droning on about facts and figures. Leo wasn't a patch on him, poor guy – Sebastian's raw masculinity was so addictive, that all men aspired to replicate him and all women desired to fornicate with him. I could see that Leo continued to watch our close contact and I genuinely feel bad, after all he had been very civil when I had ended things between us.

"How did it go - the date that is?" I ask Meg politely, making conversation. What I really want to say is that the guy needs to get new material, as he took me to '*Damario's*' on *our* first date but I'll speak to her later about it. He was new to the dating malarkey again after all.

"Yeah - I'm not sure if he's too straight for me but you never know – underneath that financial suit and glasses there could be an animal in bed?" she shrugs hopefully.

I think it highly unlikely; the only kiss we had ever shared had been exceedingly chaste but then again with the right person and all that. He was very kind looking and Meg needed a kind man in her life – certainly a calmer person, to tone down her dizziness.

"I suppose straight is better than him turning out to be gay!" Meg tosses out and then blurts, with a scrunched up expression, "I've been there too!"

I laugh at her candidness and give her a quick hug saying we'll meet up at mine for a cuppa next week and then make a grab for Sebastian.

They move on in search of more alcohol and I'm reprimanded jokily. "Thank fuck for that Lu! Take your time much?"

I belly laugh at his genuinely pained face.

"Poor Leo – he's a good bloke really. Harmless enough. Must admit I didn't think I'd be seeing him anytime soon, however but we do live in a small world."

"Enough about *Theo*," he grins and winks his mistake entirely on purpose and I giggle.

"You and I have to get rid of all these merry drunks so we can carry on our own party upstairs."

He whispers into my ear, his breath softly caressing my lobe, sending shivers down my spine. "Seriously - I ache for you. Now I've had a taste, I need to feast some more, which appears to always be the case with you and me, Ms. Myers. Terrible apart - fireworks together."

He purposely runs his tongue along his bottom lip and I'm undone and feel the excited buzz of pure sexuality begin to take hold of me again, just at the sound of his *need*. I don't know where I find the strength but I do and stand firm.

"Seb, I'm going home tonight. I don't want to, but I need to."

His look of anger could slice through a victim with a clean cut – ooh this man wasn't used to not getting his own way – full on teddy out of the cot moment!

"No."

His word is final; a command that irritates the shit out of me.

He leans in kissing me tenderly on the tip of my nose, ignoring my frown. "I love your cute little snub nose."

"Sebastian I'm going home tonight. Stop changing the subject - flattery will get you nowhere."

Who am I trying to kid? Flattery will get him everywhere, especially in between my legs and then deep inside me.

I inhale to regain some form of control and can see that he wants to drag me upstairs again and fuck some sense into me and the reality is it would probably work; I'm so weak where he is concerned.

"I've had a great night but I'm shattered and I've got the boy back tomorrow lunchtime."

At the mention of Finn he relaxes and his face lights up. "How is he?"

"He's great but it's been a tough week and I've hardly seen him. He went to Wales with my parents for a few days, as you know..."

I feel his fingers gently stroking the inside of my wrist, our hands linked. The connection is palpable.

"I only got him back yesterday and then he's back at Mum and Dad's - I feel like a shitty Mum."

"You're an amazing Mother Lulu. Just trying to give him the best life you can, that's all."

I look up into his inky liquid eyes and smirk. "Well done Silver – good diversion tactics."

He grins "What me? Besides *The Finnster* is a great diversion; I've missed the little lad."

I watch this gorgeous man's animated face, as he talks about my son and I'm happy that he can see how amazing Finn is. It's hard for people without kids to relate but being part of his life since birth, has meant that Sebastian has had the luxury of watching this lovely little man, develop into the funny bundle of joy and energy he now exerts at every opportunity. Still I am fully aware of how unique our situation is and I intend to take full advantage of it. You didn't often get chances like this in a lifetime and I am being given a do-over!

"Seriously I've had a lovely night – your house is amazing! I much prefer it to the old one. Although we have many fond memories in that one." My voice is wistful.

I just wish I'd seen more of Silver Birches and we'd been alone.

As is reading my mind he responds. "We'll make many more in this home - especially naked."

I smile up at his arrogant expectant face. God he is delicious.

"It's not a home to me yet – it's missing something – someone," his voice lowers and is full of promise.

Oh. My. You Silver tongued devil.

"Will you call me a cab?"

"I've no landline."

"Really? Could you call from your mobile?"

"Flat battery."

"Could you charge it? Wait… let me answer this - broken?" I smile wickedly at him.

"Nope. Lost it." His big grin makes me melt. There he is, Sebastian my friend of old. *Where've you been hiding?*

"I'll just grab my phone from my bag then…" I make to leave.

"I'm not going to convince you to stay and sleep with me, share my bed, let me watch you whilst I take you over the edge over and over again - am I Baby?"

I shiver at his words. "You don't play fair Monsieur Silver. I have to retain some control. You dominate every situation."

His look of pure arrogance exasperates me yet also makes me want to jump his bones right then and there. Saved at that opportune moment we are interrupted by guests and as he shakes hands and air kisses a group of work colleagues who are leaving. His hold on my hand at all times is strong and I take a moment to study his handsome face and the way his body moves, his broad back muscular and defined through his tailored suit jacket. I lick my lips in arousal. He really is *all* man and I could enjoy him tonight.

Why am I refusing a night of passion with this beautiful man?

I shiver as I feel someone watching me and turning to look across to the base of the stairs, where I see Meg and Leo, chatting with some of our friends. Leo appears to be deeply involved in a discussion and I feel for Meg who seems to be wearing her hoochy on her sleeve, her eyelashes fluttering like she has an uncontrollable twitch. Leo is oblivious to all the flirtatious cries for attention. Jumping, I sense warm breath against my earlobe before a deep sensual voice follows.

"Just give me ten minutes and I'll have everyone rounded up quicker than a cattle herder. Please don't leave."

I study his face with big moss green eyes full of lust, already resigned to the knowledge that he has won. I am not going anywhere.

Bringing both hands up on either side of my face he cups me gently and leans in to plant a long smooth kiss on my mouth. The moment is so simple, yet incredibly poignant and stepping back to look into my eyes, he repeats his words.

"Ten minutes I promise, and then I'm all yours."

I watch him disappear into the lounge, stopping to chat to his catty PA en route. Amazingly I remain calm, after that kiss and the way Sebastian has not left my side tonight, Toni should be fuming and I smile at the warm feeling that gives me. Revenge is sweet; although it certainly wasn't enough payback for the way she'd deceived me and lead me to believe that she and Sebastian were together. *What a complete madam!* I am well aware that this girl has a screw loose, and the sooner Sebastian removed her from his business and his life the better for all concerned.

After a quick visit to the loo and a freshen-up I open the door and crash straight into the queen of evil herself, in full electric blue glory. She appears as stunned as I, but promptly composes herself and flicks disapproving eyes deliberately up and down my physique. I can tell she is nervous, underneath the war mask of Urban Decay and realise that my revenge has not only been the fact that Sebastian and I have been stuck to each other like glue all night, but that she didn't know *when* I would *call her out*. It was now time.

"Lucia." Her precocious sneer is evident and the nerves a distant memory. "You are obviously more forgiving than most. Didn't think you were the type to play second fiddle?" Her laugh is light but brittle. What an unhappy woman she was.

Then again if Sebastian didn't reciprocate my attraction for him, I'd probably be just as bitter.

Her eyebrows raise and smirking lips purse. "Either that or happy to share. Sloppy seconds can be fun with the right man."

I consider her heavily made up face and almost feel sorry for her. She had it bad, maybe as bad as I did. The only reason a woman would stoop so low would be for some mixed up profession of love.

"I had *nothing* to forgive Toni, as well you know." She controls her surprise at my realisation of her manipulation but I see the brief startle in her eyes. "You staged the whole thing and Sebastian wasn't even home."

"Is that what he told you?" Her voice is less calm and lilts in desperation.

"Yes it is. He told me the truth then spent the rest of our time in his bedroom showing me the truth, no words were needed for that - just good old-fashioned body-language." I state definitely. "Unlike you, *I know* when Sebastian is lying and he isn't lying now. I believe him unequivocally."

I am pleased from the look of her rather red face that she fully understands *how* he showed me that it was all lies.

To give her some credit, she maintains her smile and continues laughing fakely. "Sebastian gets bored very easily - *I know that about him*. You'll not be around for long, so don't become too comfortable. In fact don't think you're the only one he's got on the go - he was in Dubai for a *long* time - times flies when you're having fun." Her nasty little mouth purses in pleasure at her dig before adding, "You're not Mrs. Silver... yet."

I choose to ignore her desperate attempts at knocking me off guard, and instead sigh politely, showing my disdain for her.

"Toni. You opened the door in a towel, showed me everything God and the plastic surgeon gave you, and faked a sex fest with your boss. I think you need to take your own advice and *not get too comfortable*. You are an employee nothing more and I'll give you a little tip - most *real* men, like their women to look like *real* women down below. Not little pubescent girls; Sebastian being one of them. Landing strip - yes; plucked chicken - not such a good look."

Her eyes screw up in anger and I know that I've finally hit a nerve. She continues to rant at me in her highly pitched catty voice.

"For your information Lucia — I didn't fake a sex fest. I was having sex, very dirty shower sex, with..."

I interrupt her with a voice so laden with contempt I hardly recognise myself. "Enough Toni; stop! You're making a fool of yourself. Regardless of what Sebastian and I are to one another, above all he is my friend and I won't have you spread vicious lies about him to anyone."

I take a breath to compose my now boiling temper. She ignores me and continues her babbling. "As I was saying... I had amazing, dirty shower sex with the resident of this house - whether *you* want to believe it or not."

I take one last look at her. Her eyes are glistening with hatred, her mouth smug, large breasts heaving. I'm annoyed that the last of her cuts, actually stings and hits me where she intended.

No — It wasn't Sebastian, Lu. You know that, don't let her spiteful fabrications work her way in again - she really isn't worth it.

But if it hadn't been Sebastian who was it?

Suddenly my brain seems to catch up and the clink, clink of cogs can practically be heard, rotating back and forth within my head. *Oh my word how could I be so stupid?*

The resident of the house... it must have been Chris; smooth smarmy Christopher Booth. *He* is the *other* resident in the house and the other resident man-whore. I just hope that he had not been aware of her plan that would be too cruel to Sebastian, his supposed mate.

I glance up in her direction and move to pass her and make my way down the staircase, where I can now see a concerned Sebastian, riled and ready to pounce.

"It was Chris wasn't it? You and Chris hooked up and you made out it was Sebastian?"

She bows her head, and has the decency to appear *caught out* but only for a second.

"Well you'll never know will you - you'll always wonder because Sebastian *will always b*e a player!"

Her petulant pout is fleeting as she storms past me, strops down the steps, stopping to annoyingly reach out to Sebastian and run her fingertip enticingly along his forearm, as she reaches the bottom, whilst bitchily assessing me, for my response.

His hand flies up with lightening reaction to catch hers, mid movement and stems the gesture, with a look that shows nothing but contempt. I'm too far away to catch what he whispers to her, but from the look of her childlike strop, it can't have been good. Thank God he has finally seen her for what she truly is. Heading tentatively downstairs, towards Sebastian's outstretched hand, I gratefully slip my own into it and am enveloped by his warm radiating strength. I watch as Toni heads full-steam in the direction of the door, black fur coat in hand, only stopping to talk Leo, which I find odd but everything about this woman is strange. Then I glance over at Chris, who looks in our direction and shrugs at Sebastian, with a '*What can you do?*' face and whilst grabbing his mobile to presumably call a cab he guides his lover outside.

I slump against Seb's warmth.

Two weeks in and we are already experiencing some serious drama. Maybe this is how fast things happened when the person you are sleeping with is *The One*? Or, perhaps this kind of thing was the norm when you are seeing Sebastian Silver?

"Wow – tonight's been more exciting than an episode of Coronation Street." Meg slurs and hiccups, against my shoulder. I wince at her bluntness and Abby saves me from retaliating; she's just pissed.

"Come on Meg, I think its time you and Leo made a move, we're all on our way out now."

Nodding at Leo, she snuggles into Nathan, and Leo reluctantly leaves us to attend to his date, throwing out. "Good to see you again Lucia. Sebastian." I wave at them both and have pity for Meg's head in the morning.

Leo leans in close to me on his way out, still holding an exceedingly drunk Meg at his side. "Remember Lucia, the tale of the tortoise and the hare; slowly, slowly wins the race."

He doesn't stop to see my open mouthed shock. For a moment I stand there, completely freaked out by his very odd behaviour and strange comments. But I'm not allowed the luxury of dwelling on it, before Sebastian returns to my side and draws me into his warmth. The slowly, slowly catchy monkey freaky moment is forgotten and I smile into his darkened sexy eyes and rest my head onto his chest.

Over the next half an hour, the guests trickle out and before long the Silver Birches house is finally empty apart from a select few; ready to stay and have a lock-in. Sebastian disappears to chat to a family member who is in need of a taxi and the extraction of his keys; he's not too happy but reluctantly agrees, amidst a lot of slurring and wobbling. It gives me a moment to take in my surroundings and calm my thoughts, before I join my friends in the lounge but I jump as I feel a hand on my shoulder.

"Oh I'm so sorry Lucia. It's only me." I turn to be faced with Bitzi Silver's pretty face.

"I've been meaning to grab you tonight but my son has monopolised your time," her eyes roll in a knowing way. "He's so like his father."

Her tinkly laugh is infectious and I follow her glance in Bob Silver's direction, whilst he is collecting their coats. He is very like Sebastian in height, looks and has that same magnetic air about him.

"Handsome isn't he?" she raises her brows playfully with a twinkle in her chocolate brown eyes, so similar to Sebastian's. "One look and I was a goner."

"They are very dynamic." I smile back at her warmly and watch Sebastian from afar.

"Darling I've known you for years and prayed that you and Sebastian would pull the wool from your eyes one of these days. I'm telling you now, the cashmere is down and you need to just sit back and enjoy the bumpy ride. Once a Silver man finds his woman there's no stopping him. Honey - it's tough but it's also delicious. Hang in there. Fast. Furious. Scary. Exhilarating - every emotion all at once." she rubs my arm again in sympathy.

"I never knew it could be like this. Why didn't I ever see Seb in this light?"

It must be obvious to Bitzi how confused I am, as she sighs. "Lucia. Sebastian has always adored you but the Silver men, like to do things on their terms. It's all about the control."

"Boy you're right there," I interrupt in agreement.

"I'm proud of you, for how you handled that blonde hussy earlier - never did like her myself."

It clicks as I realise that Bitzi must have been upstairs when it all kicked off. *Oh Crap, she'll know about the sex.*

"I'm afraid I was eavesdropping but you gave it some welly girl!" She rummages in her bag for her YSL lippy and reapplies it in two well-practiced sweeps. "Always knew she had designs on Sebastian and I hate the way she swans around acting like she owns my son's business." I smile. Her look of distaste speaks volumes and mirrors my own views on the matter.

"You and Sebastian are made for each other Darling. I'm the only Mrs. Silver at the mo but hopefully not for long." With a sparkly wink and happy smile, she kisses my cheek and adds, 'Enjoy this time – oh to go back forty years, it was divine and so very, very naughty."

We hug briefly and I shake my head and hope that I'm as cheeky at her age – the love of a good man does that to a woman; I've been fortunate to see that with my own parents. I watch as Bob and Bitzi make their way out. Bob nods at me over his wife's head, his blue silver hair, eye-catching against tanned skin and blackened eyes - Sebastian in 30 years time. I wave back; the seal of approval from the in-laws, that's something I suppose.

Does everyone know about us though? Is it that obvious that we are being intimate? Who am I trying to kid, it's written all over my face and my heart and from what people are saying, Seb's too.

I just wish I could hear it from him. I'm still not convinced. My heart wants to *believe* and my head is saying *get out now* before he crushes your trusting heart in a million tiny pieces and starts on the next victim, leaving our friendship in tatters.

Chapter 35

Lucia

We are lolling around on luxurious plumfy sofa's, picking at leftovers around the real fire and listening to the hisses and crackles of the logs, whilst we chat amiably with one another when I take the opportunity to peruse the scene. Sebastian is sitting to my right, lazily stroking my ankle and leg, kneading in all the right places, through my stockinged feet. Nathan massages Abby's sore and severely reddened toes from her new *do me shoes* (they had done the trick though so I'm sure the pain was worth it!); her beaming smile lights the room.

Suzie, from her perch on the floor, is ensconced between Gino's legs; her own curled beneath her, whilst he works the knots at her shoulders. All three women, have a knowing look on our faces - talk about hitting the jackpot with these guys - very attentive, very sexy, very male.

The moment is so natural and unforced. The men are discussing the latest super-bikes, and Suzie smacks Gino jokily across his knee in mock horror at the thought of yet another bike in their overcrowded garage.

The atmosphere is perfect. The people, the perfect mix, the man next to me - *perfect*.

All in all, I'm really content, apart from that nagging itch, which reminds me that he said *'whilst you and I are having sex, I won't sleep with anyone else'*. What did that really mean?

My fearful thoughts are interrupted when I realise that the conversation has altered and Toni has become the hot subject matter.

"Crazy bee...atch! I can't believe she would pretend *Chris* was

333

you!" Abby pronounces to Seb, whilst moaning in ecstasy at the taste of the beef and horseradish morsel she's just popped in her mouth. "Mmm, these are goood! Why didn't I get more of these tonight?"

"I know - right on both counts," Suzie agrees, helping herself to a canapé and holding it up to *Cheers* it with Abby, she continues. "That's one serious stalker Seb – you'd better watch out. And you too, Lulu – you are definitely on her hit list; more than ever now."

Looking in his direction I can tell he is as shocked as we all are, at the turn of events and he squeezes my leg in comfort. "Shame, as she was pretty good at her job. Guess I'm going to have to find another P.A…"

I experience a bittersweet moment low in my belly, knowing that he cares enough to eradicate any distrust between us but the good person in me, still feels bad for her. I didn't want her to lose her job. Sensing my doubt Sebastian clasps my hand and rubs his thumb gently over the knuckle of my index finger. I smile distractedly at him in confirmation.

"Where *is* Chris anyway? What's he got to say about all this crap?" Nathan enquires casually, topping up his drink whilst his arm curls Abby inwards to his body.

"I told him to make sure Toni got home OK and stay out tonight. We'll talk later."
Seb responds offhandedly but nonetheless ever the gentleman – *annoyingly so.* His tone is clipped and I can understand he is pissed.

I better not tell him that Chris has been trying it on with me at every turn then, that wouldn't be wise.

"Seems like our Christopher likes to dip it in every wick, never mind the consequences." Gino drawls and adds quickly. "Don't think he was in on the deception though."

"Me neither – he's just a walking hard-on that guy. Likes you too much Lulu, me thinks. I've seen it on site." Nathan nods, raising his brows and flinching at his last comment. He shrugs his shoulder in Sebastian's direction, "Sorry Bro, but to be fair, you haven't said you're exclusive, so he wasn't breaking any rules. Don't think he even knows about your proposition."

My eyes flick across to Seb, trying to gauge his reaction to Nathan's words. We'd never openly talked about our arrangement together, in front of others. They all knew but still, it felt a little off kilter.

"Lu is off limits and Chris should know that - he does know that.

I've fucking warned him."

"Sorry Bro. Don't shoot the messenger. Weren't you the one who always said *any game is a fair game?*"

Bloody men – Now women are *game?*

I'm tempted to launch a cushion at Nathan's handsome head but I can see he's goading his brother intentionally and I silently thank him for it. Watching Seb's profile, his jaw clenching and cheekbones jutting, the tension in his face is clear to all; he really doesn't like the thought of me with another man. *That's a good sign isn't it?* Or maybe he's simply pissed off at his slip on the leash.

On a scowl he replies. "Hmmm. Well we've always had a tendency to be attracted to the same women."

I'm reminded of the comment Chris made in The Champagne Bar, two weeks earlier and instantly am annoyed by the fact. If that *were* the case, then Sebastian would also be attracted to Toni wouldn't he? Stop woman! You're here now, you're the one he is with and has made it clear he wants to be with, for tonight at least anyway. The fact that he has chosen to ignore his brother's comment about exclusivity, I can't dwell on it. No, for tonight I just need to treat this fresh relationship like any other brand new *two-week*, dalliance, as though our history doesn't equate and it's far too early to be feeling so-needy so-soon. The gut voice *screaming to be heard* inside my head reminds me that it is nigh impossible to treat this like any normal relationship; it was Sebastian.

My jealousy has always been my weakness in relationships but with him it appears to know no bounds and I fear it'll destroy me, and any chance I have with this man, if I allow myself to fall too deeply for him.

The crackle of the fire is so soothing I feel my body succumb and relax, enjoying the soothing noises of my mates cheering and laughing and turn to lock eyes with a pair of dark, stormy pools. The passion is evident and prickles of sensuality fizz up my arms; his fingers stroke gently at my nape and I roll my head into the electric currents flickering there, addicted to his touch and the sensations he creates with the lightest of brushes.

I close my eyes and sigh.

After several minutes of such sweet and tender torment, whilst his fingers expertly knead my shoulder, neck and the base of my skull, I'm drowsy with desire. I fear my whimpers of need will be heard by all and shiver excitedly, as I feel his lips on the back of my nape, his teeth lightly nipping at the skin there. I control my breathing but it goes out the window as he growls against the tendrils of hair that have escaped and now frame my neck.

"I need you naked. Now!"

Deep breaths. I can't respond to that verbally, my mind and body are not working in sync. I'm aware that we have company but my nipples don't care as they ping to attention, tightly pushing against the material of my dress, desperate to be freed.

All I can do is raise my wanting eyes to his commanding gaze, which softens as I smile coyly at him, and nod my acceptance. His seductive spell is too strong over me and I am desperate to fulfill the promise of what is yet to come.

With my submissive gesture, Sebastian clears his throat, stands up, and holding out his hand encourages me to join him.

"Right Guys. Help yourselves to whatever you want, find a room - crash here if you like - but Lucia and I have some important and unfinished business to take care of."

He slowly draws me to my feet and places a possessive hand on my bottom, sending me sideway glances of pure sexual heat. My heart does flip-flops in expectation.

"Sounds good to me!" Gino laughs from his spot opposite us, and bending forward scoops Suzie up, his arms cradling her, under her knees and back, and rushes in front of us to find a bed. Her squeals make everyone giggle and can be heard as they retire to one of the luxury upstairs guest suites at the back of the house.

I extract myself from Seb's hold for a second and bend to kiss Abby on the cheek, as Nathan squeezes her hand. "Enjoy each other."

She smiles knowingly back at me, and mouths, "Ditto!"

We leave them to their own possibilities and Sebastian and I, with clasped hands, make our way to his bedroom in silence. A very different walk up that fabulous staircase to earlier that night - the promise of what is to come, lying heavy in the air.

The second the door shuts behind us the friendly relaxed mood changes to one of pure unadulterated hunger and I feel myself melt into his arms. I'm tangled in his glittering web, aware of the potential danger, as I struggle to control my pounding heart; drawn to his body with such a shocking longing that it scares me but doesn't stop me. I *can't* stop this.

We fall in to each other and kiss desperately, the lines between need and desire becoming blurred. I'm vaguely aware of my dress being unzipped, and its soft swish as it hits the floor at my feet. I step out of the puddle of fabric and it is dispensed with, with a deft flick of Seb's wrist.

A soft bite nips at me, as the air hits my skin and I'm naked but rather than hiding from it, I take full advantage of his obvious approval. I reach behind me to remove the hairpins from my chignon and shake my hair loose; it falls in waves over my shoulders and onto my breasts. Seb parts my locks, slowly, one side at a time, allowing my hair to caress each breast on its path, whispering over my nipples with the lightness of a feather. They automatically stand proud, needy for attention, achey and heavy and now with my hair framing them, they protrude; framed and completely on show - I'm open and naked to him.

Strange, how I feel both vulnerable and empowered, all at once.

"You were made to be devoured; slowly."

His seductive groan flows over me as he brushes the pad of his thumb across one erect tip, sending shockwaves directly to my vulva.

"You were made for *me!*"

Our eyes lock in combined sexual tension and I move to unbutton his shirt and slip it slowly off his shoulders. My hands lightly caress his skin and I hear his breath hitch as I lean in to soak up his familiar spicy vanilla male scent, planting a soft feathery kiss on his shoulder, collar bone and onto his chest but it's not enough. I need so much more. I need it all now, again and again. He's right. It's never enough with us. I'm completely consumed.

I feel him twist slightly and realise why, as the first beats of Portishead's Glory Box, surround us in the dark; he must have discreetly activated the in-house Bose system. I've never had sex to music and the beat throbs in time with my own pulsating demands. It's pure erotica. His hands clasp my face, drawing me towards his mouth, his breath hot against me.

"I can't breathe when you're near. You drive me crazy."

We lose ourselves in a kiss of such intensity I fear I'll fall. Reading my mind his hands move to support my back and move me further into his body. The moment is extreme, intense, loving, tender, raw all rolled into one and I've never experienced anything like it, in my life.

I don't know what it means but this kiss means more.

I change tactics and pushing Sebastian backwards harshly, he lands on the bed and I straddle his still covered legs. His arms instinctively encircle me at my waist, their heat warming me and they settle for a second before dropping to cup my bare bottom. The need to connect undoes me and I'm in utter shock at the driving force to have him inside me, on me, around me. The heat flowing through my veins flushes my body from each nipple and along my lightly curved stomach to the throbbing apex at my thighs. I feel empowered and glancing down at his beautiful face I move to kiss him again and teasingly stop just short of his lips, trailing soft languid licks along his jaw line, his neck and down towards his lightly feathered muscular chest. I can feel his cock nestled urgently at my most sensitive area and I wriggle to enhance the pressure there but forgetting my own pleasure continue my trail along his chest, ribs and down to his waistband. I deftly unzip his pants, move whilst he shuffles out of them and sigh when I see that he too has chosen not to wear underwear, since our earlier dalliance.

"Do you approve Lady?"

His confident smirk beckons me, as his magnificent cock springs free and I choose to answer with actions and immediately close my mouth down on to its head, licking the pre-cum droplets away and grinning at the pleasure it brings me to know that I can draw this from him. His gasp and sharp intake of breath is enough to know he is mine; at this moment *I* am in control.

I use my other hand to position him better, slowly squeezing the head and stroking up and down lazily with particular pressure just underneath the ridge. With my other hand I cup his straining balls and hear him curse.

"Fuck Lu, that feels good. Oh yeah."

I feel his hands in my hair, twisting it almost painfully, before throwing his head back on a moan. I continue to lave him with my tongue, licking lower until I suckle gently on each of his balls, ensuring dutiful and equal attention is given to each. His hiss is such a turn on; I love to be in such control and like the feeling that although I can feel his hips rocking forward desperate to embed his swollen cock inside my mouth, with my hand I can secure him, leisurely stroking and wanking up and down his length and feel his legs twitch. His hands fist in my hair again.

"That's it Lu, let me fuck your beautiful mouth." I can feel myself wet, and throbbing, at his reactions and the groans coming from within him and stop a moment to place his engorged cock between my breasts. Looking directly at him, I leisurely push them together and stroke him up and down with my cleavage.

"Fuck you look amazing."

I drop to continue my exploration of his velvety head. The slightly salty taste of his arousal is not unpleasant and encourages me to take him deeper, as deep as I can before he hits my gag reflex. Lifting his legs with a groan he buries his hands on my neck, carnally encouraging me to go further, to take him completely within me. I wish that he could be both in my mouth and inside me from behind as my rocking motion creates a breeze at my aching vulva. I relax my mouth, increase the pressure on his cock and with two fingers drop my other hand to press firmly at the base of his sac, almost near his arse. His gasp of pleasure tells me that he likes that.

"Oh fuck I'm going to come."

I continue to pump him passionately, not willing to break the rhythm, even though my wrist aches with the repetition. His semen explodes within me, the hot liquid fills my mouth until I cannot breathe I'm so full and I swallow deeply and remove my hand from his balls. I can feel him twitching the last remnants of his lust into me and I move up over his body and roll to lie beside him.

After a few minutes his arms enclose me and pull me towards him. "Your mouth was made for my cock."

I glance up at him foxily, and pout, licking my lip, but I pause at the seriously intense look plastered across his face. The fire in his eyes burns right through me, rushing through my veins on a direct path to my pulsing clit; the lighter moment passes to intensity once again.

Would there ever be a time again when we could just look at each other without the burn? I hope not.

Cupping my breast and lowering his head to suckle on a nipple, pulling and licking at the same time he continues. "And these were made for my mouth and my cock!"

I throw my head back and smile in the dimly lit master-suite and close my eyes in happiness, as I feel his hand travel downwards towards my eager and needy sex.

"Do you want me to touch you Lu?"

I groan and arch my hips in answer to meet his touch.

"Tell me you want me to finger you and swirl my finger around your clit until you pass out with pleasure!"

I sigh, blushing in the dark at the way his words send me further over the edge, his fingers slowly replicating his intentions. My voice breaks as I ask him to do want I want most.

"Touch me. Make me come Sebastian."

He groans in agreement and I thrash about as his magic fingers press down and over my clit, stopping only to swoop inside me collecting my arousal to lubricate me further. My orgasm begins for the second time that night and I rotate my hips to assist him when I cry out in pleasure pain as the delicious ebbs stop abruptly. I open my eyes to see why and catch him looking down sexily at me, his gorgeous eyes watching me intensely. He shifts position and lying backwards on the bed pulls me with him.

"I want to watch you whilst you come and see you let go."

Instinctively I raise a leg and straddle him, settling both legs on either side of his hips. He reaches over to the bedside table and after a quick fumble I watch in awe and extreme lust as he slides a condom over his straining arousal. The simple task excites me and reminds me of my own naive attempts in Room 22.

His hands support my bottom and I feel his fingers kneading my cheeks gently, softly caressing the soft sensitive skin around my private place, then trailing leisurely up my back and I'm pushed forward to meet his mouth. That moment when I see his hot gaze; his dark eyes showcasing his abandon - is the moment I sense that this means so much more than just getting down and dirty with it.

"I need you to make-love to me." My voice sounds tentative and husky. "Show me how you really feel about me."

My hair falls over my shoulder and I place a hand on his chest to balance myself. Our lips meet and we unhurriedly savour the moment. I pour every part of myself into that kiss as I'm engulfed by emotion and yes… total adoration. His big sexy hands fondle my aching breasts and I sigh at the contact and reaching between us I grip his completely revitalised and awakened erection and place its tip at my entrance.

With a slight wriggle I sit backwards and am impaled upon him. The now familiar need to adjust to his size passes quickly as I'm so wet and ready. His roughened hands cradle me as I begin to move, undulating my hips and rocking back and forth. I reach behind me, thrusting my nipples out for his attention and cup his straining balls, massaging them lightly in rhythm to our movement.

"Oh Baby … you and me - it was always you!"

Seb groans and pushes upwards, bucking underneath me to speed up the process but I'm enjoying the power too much and continue at my own pace, sitting back down and strengthening my grip with my knees and feet on the covers. His words embolden me, and my hands fly around to grasp his shoulders, pulling him closer.

I can feel his length hitting my g-spot, as before and my now erect clit is rubbing against him with each friction movement; screaming to be allowed the chance to erupt once more. I throw back my head again and push my breasts out to be captured by his awaiting hands. My nipples are immediately pulled and elongated, rolled between his fingers, almost painfully and I moan with the exquisite sensation; the triangle of pleasure being activated - my nipples and my clit being attended to at the same time. I can feel him tightening, nearing orgasm as we speed up to meet our end goal, both trembling with the ferocity of our emotions.

"I'm going to come."

"That's it Baby - let go. I'm nearly there." Seb's voice is in the distance.

Our bodies glisten with sweat and his hands are now gripping my bottom and hips and forcing me to rock faster back and forth; that is my undoing, as I shatter from within, vibrating in wracking spirals around his cock and whilst the condom creates a barrier, I'm warmed by his spurt, as he spills himself inside me.

"Kiss me!"

Biting hard on my bottom lip, and ravishing my mouth we crash into one another. This time it feels different somehow, we are more united, more invested - even more than at Scarlet House. He has invaded my body, mind and soul - I adore him.

I kiss him back, letting everything go and just focusing on the now. We look into one another's eyes, as Seb rocks me faster over him and I hope that he feels the same bond that I do between us. We groan in unison as our releases slow to hollow twitches.

Everything I had to give I'd given. That moment was so emotional and unlike any other I've known. I am filled with a breathtaking unfamiliar affection for this man and feel the hot burn of emotion in the back of my throat.

I love him so much it hurts. I'm completely, undeniably head over Christian Louboutin heels for this wicked, magnificent, controlling, beautiful specimen of a man. But I can't tell him... it's too soon.

We hold each other as we still and the darkness enfolds us; the music fills my ears again - odd how I hadn't noticed it much during our mating. U2's One ebbs around us - how perfect. My skin is covered by a light sheen of goose bumps and I shiver.

"Here, let me warm you up Baby."

We move to reposition ourselves underneath the covers and he draws me close to his body. *I'm so mixed up. Surely after what we just shared together he must feel as heavily invested in us as I am?*

"Hey you? You OK?" His throaty question makes me jump and I nod against his gorgeous ripped arm.

My throat burns with welling emotion. "Yeah." *Just desperate to spill my heart out, for you to trample on it, that's all. I'm fucking madly in love with you; that's all.*

I feel his finger at my chin forcing me to look up at him. "You're very quiet Baby. I didn't hurt you did I?" his beautiful black and flecked gold eyes full of concern and I sigh.

Please don't be nice to me; it's only going to make this harder. You didn't hurt me but I've a feeling you will.

"No. No just the opposite. It was…"

"I know Baby. I know."

Don't cry Lu.

I feel his lips brush against my forehead and snuggle into his warmth - his musky, vanilla lemony scent, all fresh and sexy. As he drifts off to sleep, his body relaxes, within minutes; sex has the opposite effect on me. I can feel my heart pulsating; I'm desperate to tell him how I feel; bursting to shout it from the rooftops.

I now know unequivocally that he is my soul mate.

I itch to caress his chest, just run a finger from the top of his breastbone, all the way down the eight-pack, snake down one side of that sexy *v*, kiss his neck and press my lips to his skin until I can't hold my breath any longer. Just linger there, inhaling him.

My eyes grow hot with expectant tears and I snuggle in the crook of his arm. We've missed out on so many years of possibilities. I could have been in his arms, received a decade of worshipping - but then I wouldn't have had Finn. We had found each other now and I have to be content with the notion that for now, this is right.

Our time is now.

"I love you," I sigh into the darkness.

Chapter 36

Sebastian

I wake to the delicious sounds of a well-spent woman, lightly breathing next to me. Her glorious, glossy ebony hair tumbles over my pillows, long lashes fanning her cheeks. She really is stunning. Thank fuck I'd been able to sort things last night. When I think what Toni had tried to do to us - my blood boils? The girl had worked with me for about a year now, on and off and I'd never expected this degree of manipulation.

No wonder Lu had ignored all my calls - she must have been devastated.

I sneak from the bed and check my phone. It's early still, for a Sunday morning but I've already had a missed call from the psycho PA and I don't want Lu worrying unnecessarily. I lean over to give the sexy piece of ass, sprawled across my sheets, a soft kiss on her snub nose and my heart tightens. I liked the sight of her here in my bed and not just for sex and it surprises me.

Last night we'd made love. No doubt about it. The feelings I have for her - I can't put into words but I don't want to address them... yet.

She'd said she *loved me*. I'd nearly been asleep but I'd heard the words, whispered from her sexy mouth. No more sleep for me after that. I'd lain awake most of the night, wandering what to do with those three monumental words.

How did I feel about it? She was mine and I loved her back, always had but was I in love with her? The thought of *'forever'* with another human being was so foreign to me; I'd not considered it before but I do know I don't want to lose her.

My phone blings, again.

Ignoring it, I jump in the shower, - quick freshen up, throw on some jeans and t-shirt and slide on my flops and then head downstairs to grab some much needed coffee and see what Miss Toni with an 'i' was calling about.

Half an hour later and I'm wearing holes in the garden as I discuss the reasons behind her mock-sex-feast.

"I'm sorry Seb."

"Why did you do it Toni?" Her voice irritates me beyond belief - *had she always been so whiney?*

"You must have known how I felt about you…?"

I hadn't. Shit. Now I felt like a prize dick.

"I'm sorry Toni. No, I didn't. It was always professional between you and I - that was the reason I employed you. It's no excuse for what you did to Lu though."

"I know. I feel sooo bad. Honest. I don't know what came over me."

I'm not sure her statement is that heartfelt but I go with it. I'm wracking my brain for any possibilities that I ever encouraged her? I'm a bit of a flirt but I'm pretty sure I've never gone beyond work friends with Toni. She wasn't my type.

"Sebastian? You still there?"

"Yep? I'm here. Look, Toni - you've put me in an awkward position. What you did was a sackable offence."

"Oh please Sebastian. Come on - it was only a bit of fun."

"At whose expense Toni - my girlfriend's and mine - *your* boss."

So she's your girlfriend now? Hmmm OK - well at least you're recognising its more than fuck buddies.

"Look, I can't have you working at Silver Con anymore, but I can give you a good reference, in light of my history with your brother and the fact that you were actually bloody good at your job. I've made a few calls and I've a mate who has an Architect firm in Lords - he's looking for a PA pronto." *Let her be his issue.* "You'll have to interview for it but the job's pretty much yours if you want it."

"Thank you, Sebastian."

"OK Toni. Good luck but I don't want you near me or Lucia again, understood."

"Understood. I know I don't deserve it… the help with a new job, that is." She has the decency to sound genuine and remorseful. "In fact, as a way of an apology, I've arranged for a present to be delivered for you and Lucia today to the house. Chris will bring it over for me when he comes home. I really am sorry."

"There's no need Toni." *WTF? The last thing Lu will want is a gift from Toni; no matter how heartfelt.*

"I insist. Really."

"Ok. Well thanks."

"Goodbye Sebastian Silver - enjoy the gift - shame I won't be there to see the look on both your faces when it arrives. It came from the heart."

The line clicks dead before I can respond. For the second time that morning I consider, why I hadn't realised before how unstable a character Toni was.

I need to call Chris ASAP, and find out if he knows anything more about this mystery parcel - for some reason I have a bad feeling about it.

Lucia

The morning sun filters through the small split at the corner of the black out blind, casting a spray of twinkly rays across my face, enough to raise me from a deep and luxurious slumber. Testing my aversion to the light my eyes go from blurred to focused with rapid amounts of blinking and rubbing, I remember my surroundings and smile and stretch contentedly.

My body feels nothing short of worshipped and as I move to check the time, I'm pleased that I'm actually not that sore. I've adapted to his big body and the regular sexual workouts of late have enabled me to go the distance without the immense muscular aches afterwards. Last night had been a whirlwind of emotions and drama, but most importantly I had concluded that I am irrefutably and undoubtedly in love.

Boy, am I in love!

Part of me wishes I wasn't, which is ridiculous, as I feel like for the first time in my relationship history, I can be utterly honest, open

345

and free. The other part of me is happy to just enjoy the luxury of knowing that I am the one that makes Sebastian Silver laugh like a naughty schoolboy and groan like a naughty Silver-tongued devil. I have never loved a man like I do Sebastian. If I'm honest, I knew it the first time we had sex; *fuck* - probably the first time that we met, all those years ago in The Cave Bar.

Padding downstairs in one of Sebastian's shirts and nothing else but a pair of thick cashmere socks I'd located in his bottom drawer; I head for the kitchen in search of serious sustenance. All is pretty quiet and I figure that most of our friends are enjoying a lazy Sunday lie in - shame Sebastian hadn't wanted to do the same. The bed had been empty when I'd awoken and I'm ashamed to say I'd been disappointed not to enjoy some relaxed morning nookie with my lover.

My lover. *My love...er!*

I like the way that sounds. The way it rolls off my tongue. It feels right and sexy and forbidden and I feel very fortunate. It feels like we've moved into a new part of our relationship, one I'd not ever expected the day I'd propositioned him with that text.

As I make my way into the kitchen I can hear his voice and my steps quicken. But reaching the door I slow; he sounds angry. Unsure whether to tiptoe back out the way I'd come or act like I couldn't hear him I decide to do what I always do when I need distracting, start cooking and with a quick glance around the room I nod and head for the immense triple mirrored fridge for ingredients, my catering plan taking action in my hungry mind.

From my position at the stove I can see Sebastian pacing outside on the patio, in faded grey jeans, a worn All Saints v-neck T-shirt, and leather flops. The man oozes sex appeal, whatever he chooses to wear - yet always manages to look effortlessly stylish.

He re-defines fine!

Unfortunately, his shades cover his eyes, so I can't read his expression clearly but from the distinct amount of arm gesturing and head stroking, he is passionately pissed off about something or someone. I wonder what or whom?

The house is still hushed, as I locate two plates and matching mugs and set about serving up my futile attempts at Nigella style cooking - well the sexy man's shirt helped a little.

"Something smells good."

I smile at the sound of his voice, noticing that all traces of annoyance appear to have disappeared and jump as he playfully taps me on the bottom.

"Oi! Hands off the Chef and get tucked into this!" I laugh, placing the mushrooms, scrambled eggs, tomato and grilled bacon in front of his greedy eyes. "I'm not just good for one thing you know." Winking saucily, I pour freshly brewed coffee from the cafetière into his mug and tea into mine.

The absence of any clever comeback makes me stop pouring milk and look up, at the serious expression on his very handsome sexy face.

Oh my! Who needs food in the morning when you're with Sebastian Silver? He was more than enough to feast upon.

"You look beautiful."

I swallow and lick my drying lips. Don't ruin this moment Lu with a silly joke - enjoy the compliment; enjoy the moment.

He instead comes to my rescue and speaks for me, recognising my surprise at the sudden change in mood.

"Let's eat before it gets cold or the scavengers arrive to feast."

I study his face as we sit opposite one another at the sparkling granite island and ignore the steaming plate of delicious food in front of me, instead reaching for my tea. I'm suddenly not hungry, well not for food. My pleasure is taken from seeing and hearing his obvious approval at my thrown-together fry-up. He truly was a pleasure to cook for - very easy to please.

For the next few minutes the meal is given his full attention, lavished and fixated upon and entirely gobbled-up. As he wipes his mouth with a nearby napkin, I realise that I share a kinship with his Breakfast. I feel much the same as his food every time he decides that I'm on the menu.

"Aren't you hungry Lu?" His face shows concern nodding at my still laden plate. I push it towards him with a gracious hand offering him, what's there.

"I was but now I'm..." I stutter over my words and shake my head smiling up at him through tilted coy eyes. God he is sexy.

I press my thighs together to quash the heat building there.

"What? What are you now Lu?"

He's now at my side, and I'm spun on the stool to face him, his warm rough hands on my bare thighs, the shirt rising higher; my legs part. His eyes drop to spot on the stool where my thighs join and shadow begins. I can feel the breeze on my naked pussy, peeking out beneath the hem of the shirt.

From the look of pure need on Seb's face it hadn't gone unnoticed.

"I'm horny," I whisper.

Oh shit did I actually say that out loud?

I must have, as I immediately feel the whip of air as I'm lifted, fireman style and thrown over his shoulder, his hand cheekily patting my behind, as he heads into the utility.

"I think, Baby, that you and I need to attend to some much overdue laundry."

Eh? Are we not on the same wavelength here?

Sebastian's utility is probably the size of a family kitchen and could be accessed from both inside and outside the house. As we enter, he turns and locks the door behind him, continuing to the outer door to check it too is securely ensconced.

Ahh! Now I get it. Privacy.

I feel myself lowered to the oak floor beneath us, my feet instantly soothed by warmth from the heated flooring. Several washers fill the left corner of the room, followed by two tumble dryers, one already spinning and then all sorts of ironing and steaming equipment. The man was seriously indulgent. I bet he didn't do any of it himself; probably didn't even know how to use the technology.

My mind goes blank again as I feel him move behind me and push me in the direction of the working dryer. As we reach it Sebastian turns me and bends to kiss me lightly; the first kiss of the morning. He tastes salty and of bacon and fresh coffee and Sebastian. He tastes delicious.

His wandering hands grasp the collar of the shirt and yank tightly, forcing me into him further. I melt as his nose brushes my neck, nuzzling there, inhaling my scent. His voice breaks the spell, deep and seductive.

"You look good in my clothes. You'll look better out of them."

I shiver as he undoes three top buttons, allowing him to release a shoulder and push the shirt aside, planting a soft wet kiss there. I shiver and thrust my breasts out begging him to free them too.

Working his way in a trail of tormenting licks he travels teasingly up my neck and finally back to my mouth, where the mood changes in that moment. Jolts of electricity feed along every nerve in my body as our kiss intensifies.

He locks his eyes on mine. I lean back onto the machine behind me and supporting me with one hand, he uses his other to expertly flick each remaining button open. I hold my breath as I feel his huge warm hand, at my neck, and using firm pressure with his palm, he grazes a path down my body, between my breasts, over my stomach, dipping lightly over my navel and curved tummy and smoothing over my pussy. I move to instinctively squeeze my legs together but his foot wedges them apart. His shirt now drapes either side of my body, open wide to allow his visible access to my main assets and his socks, which ruche like leg warmers at my ankles.

As if he can read my mind he orders. "The shirt …and socks stay!"

Fisting his hands in my hair, which tumbles over my shoulders, I melt into his body and tug roughly at the hem of his t-shirt. He is wearing way too much clothing. It lands in a heap on the floor and turning back to me, his face intense and sexy I lick my lips in expectation. The bulge in his jeans was enough promise to excite me.

"Jump!"

The command is a growl and without a word I trust him and using his arms for leverage do just that, sliding carefully backwards onto the juddering dryer at my back. The heat is an unexpected shock and I gasp as my bare behind adapts to the slight scald. I instinctively open my legs to support myself better, and his eyes are immediately drawn to the dark apex at their peak. I watch as his dark brown eyes, deepen to black and gold-flecked pools of fire and fill with desire and need and something else?

"Just you and me now."

He softly scrapes his nails down each thigh and pulls me roughly towards him. The dryer is thankfully designed to be waist height and is perfect for us and as he pulls me nearer the edge, he hits the spin button and I feel the delicious vibrations expand and filter through my already pulsing core. Sebastian clamps onto my hips in a vice-like grip, keeping me immobile against the movement of the machine beneath and then with one rotational grind, he encourages me to continue circling my pelvis to appease the building pressure and reach my goal. I lose myself in the moment but know that his focus is on me at all times and it turns me on.

"That's it Baby - come for me."

As I collapse onto him and rotate on the dryer my body racked with tiny pulses of ebbing need, his hand cups my breast and tweaks a nipple, flicking it hard, almost painfully; his mouth finds the other, circling it and lavishing it with attention. I arch my back, throwing my head back.

My body is on fire. I want to touch him, kiss him. I want him inside me. I want all of him. In that instant I feel his hand cup the back of my neck and his hand fiddling in his pocket, before slipping between my legs. The rustling of packaging, causes me to look down and I sigh in pleasure at the sight on show, as he slides protection over his arousal.

"Now!"

Could this man read minds?

I'm thrust towards him, and impaled on his cock. The fullness of him, makes me groan aloud in both pleasure and pain but the uncomfortable sensation doesn't last and I throw my arms around him, whilst his hands move to hold my ass, sexily massaging it in time to the bounce of the dryer.

His tongue delves deep and searches for mine. We suck and lick and plunge into one another's mouths and bodies until we are one - climbing the ladder of desire to meet our mounting climax. I hear my moan, our pants become quicker and his grip on my behind as he pounds into me, tightens. The spin on the dryer buzzes uncontrollably, and just like getting off with a vibrator, I feel myself exploding but with Sebastian inside me the sensation is amplified - my emotions are magnified.

As he kisses me over and over, I moan into his mouth. "I love… how you know my body so well." I'm rewarded with his final plunge and as I sense him lose himself in me and brush my hand over his inky hair - cradling him to me to inhale his masculine scent.

We stay like that for a while, holding one another, with my legs wrapped around his waist and his cock still deep within me. I can't help it. I have to say it again. The words are building within me, desperate to burst out and I know that now that I've spoken them aloud, the seal was broken and there was no going back. I'm putting myself out there and entirely vulnerable. I don't care. I kiss the top of his head and give in to the temptation, desperate to burst free.

"I love you, Seb."

The spin cycle ends and all is still. I lift my head from his chest and we lock eyes and moving a strand of hair from my forehead, he kisses me passionately. In that moment, I know he feels the same, I can sense it in his touch, even if he's not come to that realisation himself yet.

I ache, to hear the words fall from his sexy mouth. It's almost painful. Sometimes unspoken words are more sincere - I remind myself in hope.

Chapter 37

Lucia

After a quick shower and freshen up, I throw-on the dress, worn to tempt last night - bloody hell that had been an understatement! Thank goodness I carry around all my make-up essentials, including foundation, and in five minutes, I've added compact, blush, mascara and nude lips to my tired but happy face. I'm about to spray some of Seb's D&G on my wrist, when there's a knock at the door.

"Come in!" I holler, whilst throwing my hair back and scrunching it, in an attempt to smooth the *sexy bed hair* frizz.

"Well don't you look all refreshed? Foundation please?" Abby dives for my make-up and shoves me off the seat.

"I look like a dog and brought nothing with me - men have it soo easy!" She moans, attacking her face with baby wipes.

"You look gorgeous - very radiant." I smile, taking a seat on the edge of the bed. "I take it all went well last night between you and Nathan."

"Didn't you hear us?" She gigged uncontrollably. "I thought we were going to wake the neighbours."

"There aren't any, Hun - well not for 200 yards or so.

"Exactly!"

We laugh together and I rummage under the bed for my shoes.

"Fucking awesome - gorgeous man; gorgeous room - and that bed! It's honestly better than any hotel bed I've ever stayed in - I had a hard time getting out of it this morning. The only reason we did was because Na and his hunter gatherer nose, could smell bacon."

"That was me I'm afraid. I awoke to an empty bed, found the man of the house downstairs having an irate phone call and decided to cook."

"Hmmm Nigella always works." She turns and smiles at me. "Well providing there's no baking soda in the recipe." She laughs twitching her nose like an addict.

"Are you two OK now, after last night? Did you sort everything out?"

"Kind of; sort of. I told him I loved him."

"Shut the fuck up – OMG! What did he say?"

"Nothing?"

"You're kidding me."

"Stop frowning, Abs. He couldn't say anything - he was sound asleep!"

"Oh Lu."

"I know. I wanted to say it so badly. It was the right time, you know, it felt perfect; like he felt what I was feeling and then I just bottled it. By the time I'd plucked up the courage to just *get it out*, he was snoring.

"I'm not far off myself Lu - Nathan is the real deal, so I know how you feel. The way he reacted last night, there is no way that that man doesn't love you back."

"Well I'm not sure about that yet but he's never tried to fuck me in the behind, so as far as I'm concerned, he's a keeper!"

We burst into uncontrollable giggles, before Abby calms down and adds. "Well... he hasn't yet anyway!"

"Seriously though, I think you're right - if Seb *could love* anyone I'd like to think it could be me, but I also know how he is. Controlling, arrogant and he doesn't do the long haul Abby - not in relationships anyway. I really hope I've not jumped out of the fire and into the bloody incinerator!"

She stops mid lip-liner. "Look don't worry - you two are at least dating now. Toni is out the way. You're monogamous. There's nothing standing in your way. Go downstairs, let's have a cuppa and catch up with G & Suze before you have to leave to meet Finn. Sound good?"

I smile at her through worried eyes. "That sounds like a great idea, Hun. Tea always makes us feel better."

Making our way downstairs, we bump into Gino, who informs us that poor Suzie will join us shortly, once the morning sickness has passed. I offer to go see to her but he shakes his head vehemently, adding that she had booted him out with strict orders not to allow anyone else in.

Bless her. I'd give it a short while and check on her no matter what he said.

I'm still not hungry, possibly due to the permanent dancing butterflies in my tummy, but someone has placed trays of hot croissants, pecan danish, muffins and a huge glass bowl consisting of all types of fresh fruit topped with muesli and greek yoghurt, and it all looked delicious. Coffees and teas are brewed as we land and handed to us, by Nathan as we curl up on the grey velvet sofas and I share a knowing look with Abby, whilst she theatrically sends up a prayer of thanks to the man or woman in the clouds, for sending her Nathan Silver; promptly dropping her closed palms as he turns to face her.

"Tea for the ladies walking the walk of shame." He grins at us saucily and pecks me on my check, then leans into Abby for a lingering soft morning kiss.

"Wow. This all looks scrummy, and just what I fancied. Did you sort it all Mr. Silver?" she thanks him playfully.

"I did." Nodding like a proud child. "With the help of Seb. I've already downed a bacon butty and Seb said he'd eaten earlier and done laundry - find the latter bloody hard to believe?"

I practically choke on my tea and smile inwardly. *Boy did we do laundry.*

"If I'd known you were so domesticated Na, I'd have had you serving me grapes by the fire, wearing nothing but a loin cloth, ages ago." Abby tempts him twisting a wavy lock of hair around her finger, not dissimilar to what she's doing to him.

"All in good time, my cheeky Abigail," he plays back. "Get tucked in Chicks. Seb is on the phone… again. It hasn't stopped since I've come down and I'm just going to get Gino a butty."

With that and a kiss to Abby's forehead he's off in the direction of the kitchen, leaving us to snuggle up and indulge.

"Dreamy!" Abby throws her head back and sighs happily

"What the man or the house?" I smirk taking a bit of my croissant, laden with apricot jam.

"Both - but seriously this house is fabulous Lu isn't it? Last night was a great party. I can definitely see you here, hosting more of the same. Lady Lu of Silver Birches."

I flick her opinions away with my free hand, and fidget in my ridiculously over-the-top dress, for a Sunday morning. I'm about to reply when I see Sebastian walking towards me. His face is serious, but it relaxes slightly as it drops to mine.

"Feel better?"

"Much. The shower was goood."

He watches me. His eyes entirely focused on mine, and leaning in, whispers his reply.

"Next time I'll join you Baby." Taking a seat next to me, he crosses his foot up to rest upon his knee and rubs his head anxiously. He seemed very preoccupied.

"Morning Abs. You look very pleased with yourself this morning. Have something to do with my little bro me thinks?" he winks at her slyly.

Abby blushes. "That bloody charm oozes out of you two. Do you have it on tap? We had fun. Yes. Thanks for letting us stay over Seb. I had a great time."

"You are always welcome here Abs - always."

I hear the patter of feet; weakly tapping along the oak floor in the hall and looking up see Suzie enter. "Hey Sis. How are you feeling?" She looked rather washed out but still lovely.

"Urgghh. Don't ask! Roll on 16weeks." She settles next to me in a large high backed black velvet chair.

My questioning look and raised eyebrows alert her and she shakes her head. "Sorry. That's when sickness is supposed to get better." We all nod our heads in succession.

Seb hands her a tray with a tall glass of sparkling water, 4 crackers, and 4 ginger biscuits. She looks shell-shocked at his thoughtfulness.

"Gino said this is your menu of choice at the moment in the morning. I hope I got it right?"

"Yes, absolutely. Oh you're a star Sebastian. The sparkling water has been a Godsend - it really does help. The cracker/ginger biscuit combo is odd but doing the trick to get me up and running and at least some food in me."

She looks like she could get emotional so I pat her knee and she shrugs in a cute Suzie-way, and lifting a cracker bites into it delicately, holding a flat palm up at Gino as a no-no, to come near her, after his piggy-bacon sarnie. Poor G, the hormones were rife and he was just going to have put up with the moods for the sake of their offspring. Pregnancy must give you serious sensory overload, as he had been practically in the kitchen.

Seb's slips an arm along the back of the cushion, behind my back, just as Nathan comes to join us and he and Gino chatter away about the Rugby game that's on that afternoon; Gino is safely at the other side of the room. I look up at his sexy-stubbled face and pout.

"Well, much as I've had a great time I really need to go. I must pick Finn up from my Mum and Dad's before lunch and I need to change first." I say looking at my phone. It was already 11am and that didn't leave me much time.

His own phone bleats at the same time. I can see a blurred text come through. But he ignores it. Who has he been on the phone with all morning and why don't I feel comfortable asking him that simple question?

Making a move to stand up I place my mug on the large glass coffee table and straighten my evening gown, when I turn at the sound of footsteps.

"Morning All!" Chris Booth's booming voice carries as he enters the lounge, all smiles and cheeky-chappiness about him.

I feel Sebastian plant a hasty kiss on my cheek, slide from behind me and head his way, in a hurry.

"Chris. You're back. How'd you get on last night - I've been ringing you?"

"All good. All good. Toni escorted home. Party end well? Look's like nothing was ruined?" He looks directly at me.

Seb answers for me. "Party went great. Thanks mate. Anyway, help yourself to food - there's plenty but I'm about to get Lucia home now."

"Ah mate, think you might want to think twice about that. Maybe someone else could give her a lift?" He looks around at the rest of our friends, wincing.

Seb looks pissed. "Why would that be then Chris?" Seb didn't like to be told what to do by anyone, friend or foe.

"Because I bumped into another lady friend of yours, delivered outside in the drive and was kind enough to let her in. She's come all the way from Dubai, Seb."

Seb looks behind Chris in horror, shocked to see what he's taking about but there's no one there. "Chris, what *are* you talking about?"

"She's just nipped to the toilet, said she's been calling you all morning?" He holds his hands up relinquishing all responsibility as per. "Anyway, I'm beat so I'm going to crash. Didn't get much sleep last night." Winking at Seb. "Thanks for that set up mate - girls are always up for it when they're on a downer with another guy."

God, could this guy get any viler? He really didn't get it, did he? Talk about thick-skinned. I didn't like Toni but she didn't deserve to be used; no one did.

Abby's eyes meet my own over the table and we roll them consecutively to the ceiling. I don't know why, but I had a bad feeling low down in my belly and suddenly everything that was good about this morning was beginning to feel like it was about to take a huge nose-dive.

It gets worse as I hear a seductive, honeyed female voice cooing from the hallway.

"Hello Sebastian. Did you miss me?"

The *lady friend's* slim sleek body is spilled into a navy and pale blue stewardess' uniform - her blonde glossy hair in an elegant low bun. She looked like an Estee Lauder counter girl. Make-up perfect, legs endless and lip-gloss in bucket loads. I shrink, feeling uncomfortable, in last night's dress, messy hair and bare feet.

"Ray. What are you doing here?"

To give Sebastian his due, he looks as perplexed as the rest of us but I'm not hanging around to find out the answer to his question. Its pretty obvious that she is more than a friend, and here to stay, going by the Louis Vuitton vanity case on her arm and three large suitcases at her feet.

Suzie warily looks at me, her eyes nearly popping out in their desperation to silently communicate. "We are going now, so we can give you a lift, as I drove. Remember?"

"Get me out of here now!" I gulp, muttering it low to her and Abby, who now has her arm around me and is looking as worried as I am. The general vibe has gone sour. My initial feeling is to panic and go but something makes me halt.

Ray makes her way over to Sebastian and places a long, well manicured hand on his chest, leaning into his body. "Darling, what do you mean, what am I doing here? You invited me. I missed you."

She kisses him on his cheek, just at the corner of his mouth and I hear my own gasp and release the breath that I'd unknowingly been holding. I run my eyes around the room and can see that every other person is watching her actions with the same look of horror and then their eyes travel to me to see my reaction.

What and who the fuck was this? How could he do this to me?

My eyes fill with hot expectant tears, my lungs are tight - I feel so stupid and to do it in front of all our friends. The *total bastard!*

"Right." I hear my voice thankfully clear and calm, and air stewardess Ray, turns to focus upon me, for the first time, as if to say *and who are you?*

"I'll make a move then. Thanks for a great night Sebastian. It's been… informative."

His face is taut, angry, annoyed, and despondent. I almost feel for him. He'd been caught out big time; this time it appeared for real. I was here to see him with my own eyes.

"Lu, don't go. Let me deal with this and then we'll talk…" Rachel continues on, reaching behind Sebastian and helping herself to a pecan danish, daintily taking a bite.

"Darling? Which one is our room? I'm totally shattered after the night flight." Her overly bubbly voice flows throughout the now extremely quiet house. You could seriously hear a pin drop.

"Rachel. Just. A. Moment!" Seb rubs his hand over his hair, in angst. I can tell he's trying to weigh up the situation and figure out how to deal with things. Unfortunately, *Ray* has other ideas and she whines at him in a *babyish* voice.

"But S - your friends can see to one another now. You haven't seen your girlfriend in three weeks. We've some serious making up to do." I feel nauseous, bile rising.

Ray or Rachel or whatever her bloody name is, is oblivious to the total carnage she has just caused but she is not willing to relinquish any of Sebastian's time and I don't want to spend another minute in his vicinity. The man has just proven what I'd always feared he was, an utter player. He'd never change.

His girlfriend? He had a bloody girlfriend! How could I be so stupid?

My mouth is dry, I can't get my breath; I feel sick. Deep breaths, deep breaths.

Nathan and Abby are great. One look at my ghostly pallor and they sidebar Sebastian, and Suzie and I head straight for the door - Gino quickly tagging along behind. Nathan would be in big trouble later with Seb but I don't care and remind myself to thank Na later. I just had to get out.

I turn as I remember I'd left my bag on the lounge sofa and dart back into grab it.

"Start the engine Suze. I'll grab my bag and be out in a tic.

"You sure?" Suzie queries warily, but heads out at my nod, and scuttles outside, and Gino quickly follows her lead.

Taking a deep breath, I pelt back inside. Sebastian is hand gesturing and gesticulating with Rachel whilst she is coyly looking all, innocent. All I hear as I run past them is…

"Rachel why now? You said no when I asked you to come *visit* last month."

"Sebastian Darling, Dubai or Dull Yorkshire? Seriously. How was I expected to keep up this tan? But pretty soon I realised I should have come home with you - The Middle-East was no fun without the Silver Con team."

I'm definitely going to be sick. Get out without him seeing you now! Oh Crap. He's seen me.

Sebastian continues pumping her for information

"Why didn't you call? Some notice would have been good?"

"I did!" Her voice squeaks. "I spoke to your PA and she said she'd let you know. Then late last night she confirmed my flight and sent me your address info. She's awfully efficient."

More head-rubbing.

I take back everything I'd said earlier about Toni, she deserved everything she got!

"I've been on the phone most of the morning with Toni and she never mentioned you. In fact she is no longer an employee of mine."

I locate my bag on the couch and jump, as I hear Abby hiss from her hidden stance at the corner of the wall, behind the area where Seb & Ray are talking. Bless her, she is majorly eavesdropping and I know it's for my benefit.

"Pssst."

She waves me over with the crook of her arm and I see Nathan, to our left, frantically tidying up in the kitchen. Obviously trying to occupy himself, with something. Seeing me he makes his way over. My shoulders slump; I don't want pity. I just want to go.

"Are you OK Lu? I thought you'd gone. All was a bit manic."

Abby sshhh's him with her finger and using the hitchhiker sign points to the wall behind her. "They'll hear you and I'm ear wigging!"

"I'm leaving now Na. Thanks for earlier. I can't deal with this now.

"Stay and speak to Seb, let him explain. Rachel and he, well… she's not you."

I look up at that. "You knew about her?" To give him his due he bows his head like a naughty schoolboy.

I don't wait to hear his answer, feeling betrayed by him too.

I walk out into the hall, visible to both parties but keep my head focused on my exit. Unfortunately the sound of my heels on the wooden flooring alerts him to company and looking over his shoulder he sees me, frowns when he acknowledges it's me, and then rushes forward arms outstretched.

"Lu? Wait. Thank God you're still here. Please hear me out." His voice is pleading.

Great! He hadn't even noticed I'd left.

"No Sebastian." My voice could cut glass. It's lethal and threatening and off enough to raise the neatly arched brows, of Ray.

"But you're not allowing me to explain."

"For once in your playboy life, you are not going to get what you want. I'm leaving.

"Who *is* she Seb?"

"Yes Sebastian who *am* I?" I mimic her cutesy tone and look at him directly, willing him to use this chance to put this right but he isn't given the opportunity.

"Lu. Lu?" Rachel is racking her brain for where she knows my name. "You're not Lucia are you his mate from Uni - Ah I've heard about you from Seb and Chris?"

I bite my lip and nod my head through gritted teeth.

"Yep. That's me - Sebastian's mate, from University. That's all, just a friend. We've never been more than friends." I look right at Seb at this point, willing him to fight for us.

Why is he just letting this happen?

"Oh Hi - I'm Ray - his girlfriend."

I purse my lips tightly together and nod, giving a sarcastic *you don't say* expression.

"Lu - this isn't what you thin..." He finally grows a pair and intervenes but I don't allow him the courtesy of finishing.

"*Pretty much* got that one too." I ignore him and direct my reply solely at her.

Shame I didn't know that a few weeks ago before I bared my fucking soul.

Sebastian actually buries his head in his hands. *What the fuck?*

"Well, that's nice for you, Rachel but you'll excuse me if I don't stick around for the niceties and introductions. As I said, I'm late to collect my son."

"No problem. I'm sure we'll meet up soon."

I wouldn't say she was nice, but she wasn't a bitch either. Just straight to the point.

"I don't think that likely."

If she is surprised at my distinct lack of warmth, she doesn't show it. Instead, she shrugs her shoulder, in a whatever kind of way and wanders off around the hallway, commenting to no one in particular about the decor and how lovely everything is. My shoulders raise a degree if that is even possible. Any higher they'd hit the ceiling.

Seriously - she's like the female version of Chris.

Sebastian and I lock eyes.

The pain in mine is reflected in his. But he does nothing. *Nothing!* Doesn't move. Says nothing!

I *will* him to speak - rush forward and claim me as his; to thrust Ray to one side and drag me back to his bed. Please let me go back to sleep and have this all be a horrific nightmare.

Breathing through my nostrils, my jaw tense and cheeks hollowed; I break into a million pieces for the second time in a week but find the ounce of resolve I need to make it out of the doors in one piece. This man has taken my heart, ripped it to shreds and handed it back on a silver platter and I had no one to blame but myself. He had only ever been what I had feared.

He'd never promised me anything but monogamy *whilst we were together.*

More fool me.

The pain is physical, slashing through me, knifing through my heart for both my loss of him as a lover and my best friend. We couldn't ever be friends like we were, after this. He was no better than Niall.

My chest is burning; it feels like I have a tight band of steel wrapped around it, making it hard to breathe. I look at his beautiful face once more; his own chest is rising and falling in desperate waves.

Why had I told him I loved him? Why had I given myself to him so freely; so completely? Why had I risked fucking everything?

Fuelled with all types of emotions, I angrily yank open the door and pause, I needed to give him this last chance to explain - I owe it to him as my friend; deep down I should but I can't be here anymore. The pain is sheer agony. I feel broken.

I watch his face, a montage of the past two weeks' sexy moments flickering in front of me, and grit my teeth, as a hot tear, makes its descent down my cheek, plopping onto my shoulder. I knew all this was too good to be true.

"You knew the type of woman I was Seb – I'm *not* a one-night kind of girl. That's your thing. You're the bloody whore. Sorry, man-whore!" I correct myself, the contempt in my voice evident. "It took everything I had to ask you to spend these past few weeks with me. It was amazing - everything I'd hoped it would be. But there are too many secrets and I simply don't trust you. First Toni, now... her!" I lift my arm out in Ray's direction.

"I never thought that *you* of all people would make me feel so used, so worthless... so cheap! You don't seem to have taken my feelings into consideration nor had any kind of respect for our friendship. I can't see how we can ever be friends after this.

I stare long and hard at him, trembling with anger, despair and loss - the pearls at my back, swinging and holding me prisoner to memories of that monumental night at Scarlet House. Biting my lip I take a deep breath.

"I love you, Sebastian but this is goodbye."

I rush out, desperate to escape him, the silver heart at my wrist jangling alerting me to its presence. I yank hard on the chain, wincing as the links catch the fine skin there. The break reverberates close to my ears with a forceful snap and I feel the heavy heart drop and raise my palm to catch it. The warmth and smoothness comforts me for a split-second, and I allow myself to remember when he gave it to me; allow myself that one memory. With a last glance I throw the treasured heart backwards, over my shoulder and don't look back to see where it lands - then climb into the waiting getaway car.

Chapter 38

Lucia

I'd jumped into this far too quickly. Messed up the one true friendship I'd ever had with a member of the opposite sex. Seb had never pretended to be anything other than a lover of women. He was the ultimate player.

Bugger - isn't that why I'd gone to him in the first place?

This had to have ended at some point and whilst I'm utterly distraught, it was better now than in another couple of weeks, when I'd fallen deeper.

I love him. I need him. I ache for him. *I fucking hate him.*

This beautiful sexy man, had done *what it said on the tin* - showed me a great time, got me back in the saddle, with no ties and no commitments. The only rule we hadn't managed was to retain our friendship. My heart clenches painfully; that wasn't possible, not when I feel like this.

He was it. *He is The One.*

The one who I'd been waiting my entire life for but I hadn't been enough for him - not enough for him to commit to one person. Not enough to fight for.

I flick on the TV, in the hope that it will drown out my tears - the last thing I need is Finn hearing me - then pick up my work pad and pen. I've so much to sort for tomorrow's big week at The Ashton and I half-heartedly, draft out a to-do list. I feel raw - vulnerable - used but at the same time back in my comfort zone - here I was safe and in control.

A bright light glints outside the window, interrupting my tears and I glance up, rubbing my eyes spontaneously. It's hard to see out into the blackness and I presume it's a neighbour and settle down under my martyr duvet. Just another hour and I'd head off to bed. Tomorrow, I'd start my week without Sebastian - just that thought rips at my heart.

He'd been watching her for 30minutes now, more or less and he was hard, his cock straining against his jeans, palms sweaty. Moving to alleviate his numb behind in the driver's seat, he puts down the handheld scanner and slips out his earpiece. She must have put the boy to bed, he thought as he licked his lips watching her, nestled on the sofa – her long dark hair curling over her shoulders and fuckable mouth nibbling on a pen. *I know what those lips should be wrapped around and it doesn't spill ink.*

She looked like she'd been crying! *Don't cry my Lucia - not unless I make you.*

He takes a bite of his chocolate bar and settles in for the next few hours. She'd probably be sitting there on her laptop for a while... working on some project or another.

Hmmm. She is a busy little bee, full of creative ideas - wish she'd turn that bloody TV off, can't hear anything though.

From here he had a great view of her fantastic tits in a tight vest top, nipples peeking through just enough to darken the fabric. He licks his lips in concentration, and breathes deeply. He continues to appraise her body as she wriggles her tanned, toned legs underneath her, encased in shorty PJ bottoms. *I wonder if she's wearing anything underneath them - why bother, they were barely there now? Slut.*

Whether she liked it or not he was going to show her that *he* was the one. Sebastian Silver could come and go for all he pleased but he was going to be there for the long haul. The little lad was OK and would be with the grandparents mainly anyway. He clasped his phone in his hand, the glass front warm to the touch, from being inside his jeans pocket.

Should he call her? Was it time… finally? He'd been more than patient.

He was itching to connect with her properly. Touch her. Smell her. Be inside her. Let her know how he felt and how right they were for each other.

364

He shook his head vehemently, as though fighting against his own viewpoint. *No… not yet, but soon.*

Soon the games would start. Soon the fun would begin. Soon he'd be in there with her, surprising her in the dark, slipping into her bed, whilst she slept and fucking her hard from behind. He'd be the one showing her who is boss; wiping that *'sorry I'm not interested'* smile off her face. She'd thank him eventually.

His jaw twitches, teeth grinding down hard in his focus but his wildest dreams are interrupted and narrowing his eyes, he grunts in anger, as he spots the bright lights of an oncoming car, in his rearview mirror.

Fuck. It was that bitch of a sister of hers. She wasn't keen on him and he sensed it.

Ducking down, to ensure he wasn't seen from his prime viewing position, he puts the car into gear and takes a last lingering look at Lucia's front window, thoroughly annoyed his time with her had been cut-short.

Until next time then my love.

365

Coming soon

Watch out for Book 2 in **The One Trilogy**

THE ONE
Addicted

THE SECOND EROTIC NOVEL IN **THE ONE TRILOGY**

Message from **Alexandra North**

I hope you enjoyed the start to Sebastian and Lucia's love story.

Please take a short while to leave a review on Amazon for me.

These reviews make a huge difference to getting the books moved up onto the bestseller's list and therefore getting them populated. So, if you enjoyed this look out for the next in the series, The One Addicted and continue Sebastian and Lucia's journey with me.

Thanks so much for all your support.

Contact Alexandra North at the following social media sites:

www.facebook.com/alexandranorthauthor

Twitter: @alexnorthbooks

www.goodreads.com/alexnorthbooks

40141137R00226